REVOLUTIONARIES

REVOLUTIONARIES

JOSHUA FURST

ALFRED A. KNOPF   NEW YORK   2019

THIS IS A BORZOI BOOK
PUBLISHED BY ALFRED A. KNOPF

Copyright © 2019 by Joshua Furst

Published in the United States by Alfred A. Knopf, a division
of Penguin Random House LLC, New York,
and distributed in Canada by Random House of Canada,
a division of Penguin Random House Canada Limited, Toronto.

www.aaknopf.com

Knopf, Borzoi Books and the colophon
are registered trademarks of Penguin Random House LLC.

Library of Congress Cataloging-in-Publication Data

Names: Furst, Joshua, [date] author.
Title: Revolutionaries / by Joshua Furst.
Description: First Edition. | New York : Alfred A. Knopf, 2019.
Identifiers: LCCN 2018044984 (print) | LCCN 2018047614 (ebook) |
ISBN 9780525655343 (ebook) | ISBN 9780307271143 (hardcover)
Classification: LCC PS3606.U78 (ebook) | LCC PS3606.U78 R48 2019 (print) |
DDC 813/.6—dc23
LC record available at https://lccn.loc.gov/2018044984

This is a work of fiction. All incidents and dialogue, and all characters with the
exception of some well-known historical and public figures, are products of the author's
imagination and are not to be construed as real. Where real-life historical figures and
public figures appear, the situations, incidents and dialogues concerning those persons
are entirely fictional and are not intended to depict actual events or to change
the entirely fictional nature of the work. In all other respects, any resemblance
to persons living or dead is entirely coincidental.

Jacket photograph by Jekaterina Niktina / Getty Images
Jacket design by Tyler Comrie

Manufactured in the United States of America
First Edition

For Ernie

and

Vince

The true revolutionary is guided by a great feeling of love.

—ERNESTO CHE GUEVARA

[I]

VOLUNTEERS

Call me Fred. I hate Freedom. That's some crap Lenny dreamed up to keep people like you talking about him.

And it worked. Right? I mean, you didn't drive all the way up here with your tape recorder and backpack full of good intentions to learn about me. I'm just the kid. What you want is more of him. More of the '60s hoopla. All that rebel music. The tie-dyes and free love and taking it to the streets. Even now, twenty-eight years after he died, you can't get enough.

So, fine. It's been like that my whole life. Who am I to judge?

By the time Lenny was the age I am now, he'd changed the world—or, anyway, that's what he would have claimed. And me? I'm just some dude who's done some carpentry. Some bathtub restoration. Sustained myself by staying out of sight. I've worn ironic T-shirts and thought ironic thoughts about the commodification of revolution, worked at coffee shops and bookstores. Whatever it took. I've run some scams. I've had scams run on me. I've deflected and I've survived. If there's one thing you learn when you're Lenny Snyder's son it's how to bullshit your way on through to the next day.

But really, I don't know anything about anything.

Except Lenny, I guess. I know a lot about him.

I know I let him down.

But he let me down too.

Why? How?

Well, where to start? I guess, with him. Lenny Snyder. Alpha. Omega.

This might take some time. You want coffee? I've got instant.

If Lenny were here, he'd say he cut his teeth as a Freedom Rider. Did that for years. Learned how to organize from John Lewis himself. Eventually he found himself hanging around Liberty House, the storefront on Bleecker where the SNCC sold its tchotchkes. He spent his days unpacking handwoven rugs and wooden earrings, burlap dolls with button eyes. Stocking displays with pickled green tomatoes and peach jam. Doing his part for the poor black folk of Mississippi by hawking their product to the guilt ridden, socially conscious engagé in New York. Feeling restless. Wasted. No longer in the action. Just a good-intentioned shopkeeper shilling for Snick.

He'd say things were happening there in the city. A new energy gusting through the streets, blowing the youth of America, kids nobody wanted, kids who'd lost faith in their parents' gods, over the bridges, through the tunnels and into the city. They'd wander around the shop a bit dazed, a bit hungry. Not exactly sure why they were there. They'd go for the candy—peppermint, caramel. They'd weigh it, shyly, in their hands. Ask how much and, when he told them, they'd say "groovy" and pretend to browse for another minute before placing it all back on the shelf. Without a word, they'd shuffle out of the store and hump it back to the Lower East Side, where they'd shiver and starve and wonder what they'd been thinking by coming to this town. He'd stare out the window, watching them go, and think, Why am I in here when I should be out there? Snick would be just fine without a Jewboy like him ringing up sales and balancing the books.

Lenny would say, These kids, they weren't hippies. What was a hippie? A hippie was something he hadn't invented yet. These kids were just runaways attuned to the cosmic vibes in the air. They had draft cards to burn and were looking for something new, whatever that might be, an alternative to the Southeast Asian quicksand rising invisibly around their ankles. Well, he knew what it was. That something new was him. He stopped cutting his hair. He put away the oxford shirt and the dress slacks, threw on a T-shirt and a pair of jeans, and headed across town to join the youth culture.

He'd say, The revolution needed its heroes. He just happened to hear the call.

He set himself up as a trickster, a satyr, the great god of Pan dancing on goat's feet through the wilderness of the Lower East Side. He set about using his organizing skills to create a new society. Saying, Never trust anyone over thirty. Saying, Today is the first day of the rest of your life. Saying, Flower power is people power. Free your mind and your world will follow. Reality is what you make it. The revolution is in your mind. Tune in, turn on and drop out. Everything should be free.

And drawn by his message, the kids just kept pouring in.

When he saw they were hungry he wheedled a deal with the old-timers who ran the local greasy spoons, Poles and Puerto Ricans and Jews who spoke his language. You set a percentage of your produce aside, maybe some of that meat too, and I'll keep these longhairs from looting your shop. He made stews every Thursday and ladled them out to whoever happened to be loitering in Tompkins Square.

When he saw they had no place to sleep he told them, Come to me. I'll point you toward the closest crash pad. I know where they all are. We're taking this hood over one building at a time.

When he saw they had no clothes, no shoes, nothing of their own, he broke into an empty storefront and flung its doors open wide. He carted inside whatever he found on the street—couches and dressers and stacks of old books—and supplemented this with more luxurious items, suede jackets, miniskirts, the latest fashions that he liberated from the backs of trucks. He'd go to Macy's—the service entrance, late at night—and load up the chipped, discarded floor models of last year's furniture, haul them downtown, loose them into the world. Kids would stroll in. "What's this cost?"

they'd ask about some broken umbrella, some battered frying pan with a melted handle; if they were daring, a Formica table. And Lenny would tell them, "You want it? It's yours. Just leave something in its place. Or don't. It's free. This is a free store." One day he showed up with a state-of-the-art color TV, a massive thing built into its own cabinet with a hi-fi record player tucked in the lid. Top of the line. Straight from S. Klein's department store. It even had a remote, that's how fancy. He'd driven his van up and given the manager some story about the warehouse wanting it back. Walked right out with it. Put it in the window, a sign taped to the screen: EVERYTHING FREE. Kids came and went taking what they wanted—loose buttons, comic books, moccasins and boots—but for some reason they never touched the TV. Never even asked about it. They couldn't make the leap to total freedom, not yet. Lenny had a shitload of work to do if he was going to change their frame of reference.

When he saw they had no dope he'd roll them a joint. You couldn't put a price on the new consciousness.

When he saw they wanted music he stormed the Fillmore East and demanded that the shows be put on for free.

When he saw they had the clap he stole them penicillin.

When he saw that they were often suicidal he set up a hotline for them to call. A handful of bleeding hearts he sometimes fucked who were willing to stay up late talking the kids down.

When he saw they were getting arrested for loitering, littering, pissing on a tree, spurious charges, like most crimes in this country, he strong-armed the head shops and record stores that had built their fortunes off the kids' desires into floating a bail fund. No interest. No payback. You dig it? We're free.

He held town meetings and formed committees. Gem Spa's raised the price of its egg creams? Let's boycott. Leshko's won't serve you if you've got long hair? We'll sit in. The cops down at the 6th Precinct are harassing the Puerto Ricans again? Let's go show those motherfuckers what it feels like.

He got himself a mimeograph machine and printed up leaflets by the hundreds. Out on the streets all day and all night, he handed one to anybody who walked past. A crudely stapled pamphlet full of subversive survival tactics. Neighborhood announcements. Locations of ad hoc health clinics and community gardens. There's gonna be a block party on 12th Street this Sunday. Watch out for the blond guy in the red felt hat—he's been groping women on St. Marks Place. The Icelandic five Aurar coin is worth an eighth of one American cent. It's the exact same size and weight as a quarter. Score yourself a handful, head to the Automat, slip these slugs into the machines and feast away.

When the streets needed cleaning, the city having allocated its limited resources to neighborhoods with boulevards and home-owners who actually paid taxes, he and his cohort dressed themselves up as clowns, complete with greasepaint and size 26 shoes. They procured a bevy of janitor's brooms and swept the streets themselves, amassing mounds of trash and public nuisance summonses at the end of every block.

He nudged and prodded. Said, Let this melt on your tongue. I'll be your spirit guide. Let's meet on Saturday at the Great Lawn. We'll float up there on papier-mâché wings. We'll strip off our clothes and dance and be happy, and unlike this fucking country of ours, we'll know no sin. Ten thousand people made the trip with him, and when they arrived, he pointed to the sky and ten thousand flowers rained down around them. And for a while, a few Technicolor hours, they all forgot they were going to die and who it was who was trying to kill them. Next time they'd remember. He'd make sure of that.

Love was in the water, in the lead-laced soil, winking through the cracks in the pavement. You couldn't walk out the door without stumbling over it. Girls were acting like men, giving it away for free. He partook, how could he not, in the beauty of creation. He met my mother one day at the Free Store when she backed a delivery truck up to the door, flung open the back and released a hundred chickens onto the sidewalk. A storm of feathers. A squawking and clamoring over each other as they raced off to coop out all up and down the street. And then there she was with the body of a vixen and the body language of an urban guerrilla. Ironed hair hanging straight down to her ass. She could have wandered in from the hills of Cuba.

"What's this?" he asked.

"Animal husbandry," was her answer. "Come on. The next load is goats."

In the cab of the truck, heading out of town, he asked, "What gives? What's the big idea?" She reminded him of the girls he'd known in Brooklyn, so much tougher than the boys, striving to get their ya-ya's out before they took the frum. Those girls who'd shown him how to swear and taught him the meaning of swagger.

"Give a man a fish, you feed him for a day," she said. "Teach him to fish, you feed him forever. Not so long ago New York was clogged with livestock. People might've been poor, but they didn't go hungry. They harvested their own eggs, milked their own cows. What we're doing now is repopulation."

"You're blowing my mind," he said. "Lady, what's your name?"

"Suzy Morgenstern. What's it to you?"

She had a brown spot in the white of her left eye, a liquid beauty mark. The sexiest thing he ever did see.

Two weeks later—they were already fucking by then—they repeated the stunt, this time with saplings liberated from Van Cortlandt Park. A neighborhood beautification project. Plop a tree in the middle of the street. Surround it with dirt until it stands upright. Bring the jungle back to the concrete jungle. The hippies—they were hippies now, no doubt about it, but what did that mean? It meant people without limits, no need for authority, different from bikers only in that they were scrambling toward God, not the devil. They thought Lenny's reforestation project was far out. Each time a new tree materialized on Avenue A or 4th Street or Delancey, they'd rise from the muck to wrap it in ribbons, flower children dancing around a maypole. It had the added benefit of stopping traffic.

Lenny would say this was more than fun and games. He'd say he had a plan all along. Power to the people.

He'd remind you there was a war on. People lived in terror of getting drafted. We had to show them the garden before they could ask who owned it. Who *should* own it. Who would care for it best.

We had to give them hope, gain their trust and educate them. That's why the puppet shows and mimes and clowns. That's why the massive yellow submarines. That's why the body paint and dandelion necklaces. That's why the Be-ins and Love-ins and Smoke-ins. Tell them, Hey, take a look, all the old folk are gawking. Stare into their souls. Your mother? Your father? What do you think of them? That man in the suit reading *The Wall Street Journal*? Those guys gathered in the situation room, dreaming up new strategies to get you killed? What do you think they think of you? He'd say the gambit all along had been to inject an activist spirit into the youth culture. He was thirty, not a kid at all, and for him getting stoned and playing bongos in the park was a job, not a spaced-out way to kill an afternoon. Public relations. An act he put on to build community among those he considered his constituency. It was serious work, galvanizing them and setting them loose on the nation. When he wasn't on the street, he was in a meeting in any of a hundred flash points scattered through the city—a stalwart old leftist's apartment or a church basement or the AFL-CIO offices or a classroom filled with those untrustworthy cocksuckers in SDS—crouched on a folding chair, ready to spring.

The people in these meetings, they annoyed him like hell. The sanctimony. The condescension. The unending ideological debate. It all made him angry. The old Left—and the new Left too—were a bunch of pompous asses. Maccabees, he called them. No sense of humor. They wouldn't know joy if it kicked them in the head. And worse, they were boring. A total snooze. Things that could be said in three words required a two-and-a-half-hour speech. He longed to leap up and hang from the ceiling fan, hoot like a howler monkey and shut them the fuck up. He longed to throw his chair at their leaders' heads. To say, You keep droning on about revolution but really all you want is more of the same. A cadre of saps and earnest pacifists patting themselves on the back. Talking about empathy and the tears of the world. Wake me when you're done singing "Kumbaya."

He'd show them. He and his army of freaks would turn their revolution upside down.

And they did.

But first, one more celebration of love. Another Be-in in the Sheep's Meadow. This time, a marriage. My mother and Lenny, two wandering Jews dressed in their sharpest native garb. Old-timey robes hemmed with thread of blue and gold, cinched at the waist with ropes made of hemp. The straps of their sandals snaking up their calves. The rabbi came courtesy of city hall. There's no best man, no maid of honor. Just four thousand witnesses tripping on acid and a photographer from the Associated Press. It's Easter. Lenny tells the assembled crowd, "We're living right now in a culture of death. We need a new life. A new covenant. We need to reassert the possible. We need to court transfiguration. What I'm saying is, let's make love, not war." He and my mother untied their robes. They let it all hang out, every inch of their skin. They embraced and lowered themselves to the grass and committed a transgressive act of sexual love right then and there for everyone to see. Conceiving the new vision of humanity that, ten months later, would become me. Freedom. Fred for short. To Lenny, just the kid.

In the meantime, he had a generation's consciousness to change.

Lenny would say, We presented the timid with a vision of the future and told them, "This could be your present. All that's stopping you is you." He'd say, We told them, "Don't be a slave to the death cult of money. Come outside and breathe the fresh air. You wanna see what's in the hearts of the money changers? Come on. I'll show you." He led a ragged band of hippies downtown to the Stock Exchange. "Let's take a tour. Observe the animals in their natural habitat. They filed in like tourists and assembled on the visitors' deck overlooking the trading floor. See how they're crammed into that overcrowded pen? Note the leashes Windsor-knotted around their necks. The cacophony of growls and barks as they barter over paper chits. Can you smell their fear? They sure as fuck smell yours. Pity them, for they know not what they do. But wait!" He fished a crumpled dollar bill from his pocket, held it over the railing and let go. The bill fluttered and twirled like a butterfly. It floated over the herd of traders. First, one guy noticed it. Then another. Then a third snatched it out of the air. Lenny dropped a second bill. He gave my mother a signal and she dropped one too. A handful of traders had caught on by now. With each new bill, more of them hooted at the deck. Lenny's eyes bugged in mock surprise. He threw his head back and shook his mighty mane, cackling with his signature glee. "Free money," he called, letting loose another handful and watching the traders scamper. They were like children at a parade, arms outstretched, faces contorted with the effort to contain their excitement, screaming hoarsely at the man on the float who might or might not aim his candy at them. Each falling dollar instigated a scrum. Lenny cackled and cackled. "You see what we're dealing with?" His friends all got in on it. They'd stuffed their pockets too. Hundreds of one-dollar bills. And eventually so many fell at such a rate that the traders erupted in an all-out battle, mano a mano, every man for himself. No one was watching the boards anymore. All trading halted. The market shut down. 'Cause why flip numbers and bid on abstractions when cold hard cash is pissing from the sky. "Score one for freedom," Lenny told the press assembled on Wall Street. "All for one lousy buck. Those people are animals. I feared for my life." Then he pulled the last dollar bill from his pocket, held it up to the cameras and set it ablaze.

It's all about disruption, he'd say. We pissed in their corner and claimed it as ours.

He was no longer a *he*. Now he was a *them*. An *us*. A tribe. All those kids who'd flooded the Lower East Side now decked out in feathers and headdresses. No chiefs, only warriors. No central-ized power. An *us* against the *them* that used its money and its institutional force, its tactical police and educational endowments and media and corporate structures and branches of government to send us to the slaughter in Vietnam, to throw us in the slam-mer for two measly joints, to build bombs and plasmatic chemical compounds capable of wiping out half the Third World, all the while enslaving our brothers and sisters here, especially those who happened to be black, shoving them into ghettos, standing by and watching as those ghettos burned.

He'd say, We rounded up the trash on the Lower East Side and carted it uptown to Lincoln Center, where the elite went to be told how special they were. Garbage for garbage, we said as we filled their precious fountain with the refuse of the poor.

He'd say, We dressed ourselves in combat fatigues and headed to Midtown to play capture the flag. Using the streets of the city—its skyscrapers and plazas and double-parked trucks—as their battleground, they hid behind phone booths and under public benches. Toy guns in hand, they brought the war home. Some of them fought for the red, white and blue. Others for the Viet Cong. Someone had mounted speakers on the corner of Park and 57th. At the designated time, the music began, first softly—*Appalachian Spring* floating through the canyon—then louder, more militant, with the soaring chords of imperial power, Wagner and Dvořák and *Carmina Burana,* and suddenly, when Lenny—their non-leader—gave the signal, they surged into traffic, pretending to get hit by yellow cabs, reviving the slap-and-fall scams they'd perfected in junior high. They shot at each other. They trampled passersby. They leapt onto the hoods of cars stopped at red lights and fired balloons filled with cow's blood at limousines. These balloons, when they exploded, man, blood splattered everywhere. Shellacking the streets. Running in the gutters. When the cops arrived and started cracking heads, the avenue became a genuine war zone. They got their asses kicked, but like true guerrillas they gloried in the conviction that they'd won by losing.

That was the first battle. There would be more.

They painted a maple leaf on the army recruitment center in Times Square and scrawled *Canada wants you . . . to be happy and free!* across it.

They procured a brick of the sweetest Thai stick and stayed up all night rolling perfect joints. Using the white pages and a dart—so they claimed—they chose a thousand of their fellow citizens to receive these gifts in the mail. They were magnanimous, their portions generous, and they saved just a small ration of weed for themselves. It so happened that among the random names selected were Peter Ingstrom, Mayor Lindsay's chief of staff; the Honorable Judge Benedict Fieldston of the 9th District; Aaron Lemoux, the fallen son of Oliver Lemoux, the president of Standard Oil (addressed to the family home on Fifth and 81st); and, since the message meant nothing if no one heard it, Chet Huntley, news anchor for NBC. To make sure these people understood the full implications of opening their mail, Lenny included a small typed message in each package: "Congratulations, friend. You are now in possession of a marijuana cigarette. Enjoy it! Keep it for yourself or pass it around at your next dinner party. It's yours to do with as you please. We suggest, though, that you bear in mind the following fact: Simply carrying this cigarette on your person or having it in your home is a felony offense in this country. If Officer Friendly finds out you have it, he'll be forced to do his duty and put you away on a five-year sentence. Welcome to the other side of the law, friend. We're sure you'll like it here as much as we do."

They imagined themselves to be outlaws now. To prove it, they made mischief for the cops. They called them pigs and exercised their free speech by oinking whenever they saw one. They tossed marbles in the street as the horse brigade trotted past. They released rats they'd trapped in their tenement apartments into the conference rooms of the Hyatt and the Plaza, a nuisance that on some days tied up half the force. Set off M-8os and smoke bombs on strategic rooftops across the Lower East Side and watched as the pigs—oink, oink—swarmed around, confused, thinking that the whole neighborhood had exploded. Which it had, just not physically. The real bombs had gone off in the minds of the young—not only here, but all over this great nation of ours. There were thousands of them now, millions. Though Lenny didn't lead them, they followed him wherever he went.

To DC, for example, to exorcise the evil spirits lurking there. Dressed in the garb of druids, shamans, witches and monks, 200,000 strong, they waggled their fingers above their heads and spoke incantations, chanting and spinning to the music blaring at their backs. When the National Guard raised its rifles at them, they stuck flowers in the barrels and passed by unharmed. They made love on the National Mall and roused the stone effigies of the great leaders; you could see the smile curl at the edge of Lincoln's mouth, you could hear his blessing float over the crowd. They pried off the lid of the Capitol building, and with the mighty force of their love, set the demons lodged inside loose to twirl toward the heavens, a maelstrom of peace, an anti-Armageddon. They raised the Pentagon off its foundation, levitated it twenty-four feet above the Earth. The way it glowed. The rancid gunk that oozed from its plumbing. The smell. A heavy scene, Lenny would say. But man, it really happened. I saw it with my own eyes.

A few weeks later they trailed him uptown to make peace with the enemy and conjure the end of the war into existence. Playing it straight, their hair combed and shirts ironed, they hooted and laughed and danced in the streets, rejoicing. They pressed copies of *The New York Times* into the hands of ad men, insurance execs, delivery boys and secretaries, all those squares speed-walking through the pneumatic tubes of commerce—their own edition, identical in every way to the real thing except for the words on the front page and the two-inch headline above the fold: JOHNSON UNCONDITIONALLY WITHDRAWS FROM VIETNAM. Hey man, didn't you hear? The war's over. And for an afternoon, it seemed like it was true. The joy in the air. The relief, even among buttoned-up types who would never dare to criticize the president.

Then on to Grand Central Station, the place from which the life of the city flowed, with its train schedules dictating the rhythms of industry, funneling the commuting *machers* from their homes in Westchester into its clogged chambers and spitting them out into the metropolis, where their time no longer belonged to them. Grand Central was the cinch in the hourglass. Break it and you'd unleash who knew what—ancient winds blowing a million grains of sand over this vast, seething, overpopulated land. First in small, then larger groups, in platoons, in battalions, his freak army slouched into the great art deco church of time. They carried presents bound by string, and at precisely five o'clock, they pulled the cords and out soared festive balloons, each one streaming a banner imprinted with a word: PEACE and LOVE and LAUGH and FUCK, but also WAR and KILL and DEATH. Pick your poison. Take one home.

There was another balloon, much larger than the rest. This one dangled a canvas sack, $$$ stamped right on it, like a *Krazy Kat* gag come to life. Reach for it, as many people tried to do, and you'd release real money. Shades of the Stock Exchange, but this time the bills rained down on decent, average Americans. People picked them up, studied them. And they noticed a message stamped minutely on each one: "Enjoy this free money. Go buy yourself an ice cream. While you eat it, consider how lucky you are that this isn't napalm. If it were, you'd be dead."

More freaks tumbled into the chamber, overrunning the commuters. Gobbling up all available space. They sang songs. They chanted. They strummed acoustic guitars and ate pastrami sandwiches. They toked up or took acid and watched the constellations on the ceiling dance. They whispered sweet nothings into a corner and someone on the other side of the room heard them and whispered sweet nothings back. They sat on the railings of the great stairwells. They perched on the counters of the cashiers' windows. They scaled the information booth and from this roost sent messages ricocheting around the room: Time is an illusion. Poetry is in the street. Commodities are the opium of the people. Boredom is counterrevolutionary. Concrete breeds apathy. We're all undesirables. Time is an illusion. We'll say it again: Time is an illusion. Kill time. Kill time. Kill time. And then someone reached out and snapped the hands off the landmark clock atop the booth and the pigs swept in. They'd been watching and waiting for their chance. Truncheons out and swinging, they squeezed in from all sides, four new walls of bristly, engorged pink flesh constricting around Lenny and his tribe. There was nowhere to run. Bones were broken. Heads cracked. Another ass-kicking, this one more intense and dramatic than the last.

It was beautiful, Lenny would say. The cops went ahead and made our point for us.

He marched them up to Morningside Heights, to invade the citadel on the hill where Columbia University shielded its students from the brute repercussions of their entitlement. He took the hippest undergrads on a campus tour. "Here's the building where the science labs are housed. PhD candidates. Tenured professors. They submit proposals. The school approves them, or it doesn't. Some of them are given budgets to fund their experiments. The money comes from grants, and that's where things get interesting. Who provides the grants? You wanna guess?" He's chewing gum. Blowing bubbles. Fucking around with a translucent yellow yo-yo he bought from some subway hawker on his way uptown. There's a charger inside that revs when he flicks the string, and the yo-yo lights up like a carnival game. "Oil companies. Pharmaceuticals. The US Department of Defense. Since the school wants the money and the scientists want the labs, the proposals are tailored to appeal to these benefactors. That building right there, that's where napalm was invented. Agent Orange, too. The hounds of hell. Use your imagination. Whatever you dream up will be much less terrifying than the reality they're concocting in there. Is this right? Is this just? Does this surprise you at all?" He's flicking that yo-yo up and down. Windmilling it. "Come on. Let's take a stroll down Amsterdam. See where your tuition money really goes. While we're walking, I'm gonna give you a pop quiz. You kids are good at tests. You must be. You're driven. Ambitious. I see it in your eyes. Your entire lives have been dedicated to casing the system so you come out on top. And now here you are at an elite institution of higher learning. I'm curious about what they're teaching you. So, tell me: Who's the largest landholder in New York City? No. No-no-no. It's the Catholic Church. Who's number two? That's right. Columbia. A nonprofit dedicated to the public good, by the way, at least according to the school's charter." The gum has been wedged in his cheek this whole time to free his tongue for speechifying. Now he molds it into a ball with his teeth and then—*thwat*—spit it with expert aim at a pig cruiser double-parked in front of a bodega. He's still at it with the yo-yo too. "You see that building there?" he asks, jutting his chin at a five-story brick façade in desperate need of repointing. "That's one of their properties. The one next to it too. The whole block belongs to them. Everything from here to 132nd and on over to Frederick Douglass. They don't look so bad from here, but step inside and see what you find. Wouldn't be hard to do—the locks are all broken. Some of those apartments haven't had running water for two years. Families living twelve to a room—aunts and uncles, granny, great-granny, everyone shoved into six hundred square feet—they have to beg Ernesto at the Cuban-Chinese every time they want to take a shit. Your august institution of higher learning doesn't give two fucks about people like them, not like it does about you. They're collateral. Property. Pawns it can use to subsidize the verdant lawns of your campus, the passionate conversations in your classrooms, the catered meet and greets with your faculty and, of course, the sulfurous experiments taking place in the bowels of Pupin Hall. You want to know how much Columbia loves you? Let's cut through these projects, over toward Columbus. There's a park over there. Basketball courts. A playground. Some grass where the locals can spread out blankets and have picnics. In summer, that fountain there is clogged with little black and brown kids, shrieking as they charge through the water, cherishing this brief respite from the sweltering claustrophobia of their apartments. A nice park. Not the prettiest you've ever seen, but it does the job. My question for you is, do you want these kids to keep playing in the park? To experience fresh air? To know what it feels like to run for a better reason than because the pigs are chasing them? I thought so. But listen. Columbia University doesn't. Columbia University believes these people don't deserve their shitty little park. Columbia University believes it has a responsibility to build *you* a new multimillion-dollar gym on this park. A swimming pool. A weight room. Handball courts. Anything your little hearts desire. It wants to please you. To make you comfortable. It wants you to know how special you are. And once the gym's built, you better believe Columbia University's not gonna let anybody but you use it. Is that fair? They're taking these people's park away and giving it to you who have so much already. Is that just? I don't think so either. Aren't you sick of the lies and hypocrisy?" He flipped the yo-yo into a cat's cradle. Held it there for a dramatic second—spinning futilely with nowhere to go. "Columbia University belongs to you. What do you think would happen if you told President Kirk that you refuse to learn the lies they've been teaching you?" Ever so slightly, he tugged the string and the yo-yo bounced and spun incrementally faster. "That you refuse to take part in bullying the people who live under the university's heel?" Another pull. Another bounce. "That you know what freedom is and this ain't it?" Another pull, this time with such force that the yo-yo flew up out of its cradle and swung around the finger to which it was tied. "Let's liberate this school from its shackles." Pinwheeling the yo-yo faster and faster until, finally, he fell to a knee, slammed his palm to the ground and shattered the fucking thing against the sidewalk. "I've got a hundred friends right over there just waiting for the word to help you do it." And lo, his freak army rose up behind a chain-link fence. They pressed forward, fists raised in revolutionary salute, thrusting their weight into the grid of metal, pushing and churning and knocking the fence down. They marched on, the students and Lenny with them, up the hill, onto the campus, taking on more students at every turn, and when they reached Low Library, where Kirk kept his offices, they invaded and pushed everyone else out, anyone who challenged what they were doing, anyone who maybe just didn't care. They barricaded doors. They encamped and proclaimed the university free. They liberated it and then occupied the premises for six days until the pigs goose-stepped in and again showed the good people of this nation the brute force their government and moneyed interests were willing to bring down on anyone, even their own children, if they dared ask what the fuck was going on.

He'd say, With each loss, our army grew. The whole country on our side, against the war. Against the pigs and their vicious pig-like ways. When the press asked him, "Okay, but what are you fighting *for*," he said, "Fighting? Who's fighting? Not us. We're peacing." And since I'd been born by then, he raised my squirming body to the camera and said, "We're peacing for Freedom."

And what freedom looked like was kids everywhere peeling off their clothes and painting their skin day-glow blue, green, pink and yellow. Red and black. Dropping acid. Getting stoned. Wandering out in the light to let their true allegiances shine.

He'd remind you, This was when those who did lead were being killed. Martin Luther King. Malcolm X. Bobby Kennedy. Murdered, all.

He'd say again, I never led. I listened. Sometimes I made suggestions. Mostly I just followed the vibe in the air.

It's not my fault, he'd say, that I had all the best ideas.

He sent the word out. Days are dark. Death hovers over us everywhere. So, let's celebrate! We're gonna throw a festival of life. Free music. Free drugs. Free love. Free life. Yippie! See you in Chicago. There would be another, competing festival in town that week— a political convention held by the Democrats, the party that unleashed this death across the nation, and Vietnam too, that bequeathed us all with this fear and loathing. The party that would take your size and fit you for a uniform, send you off to see the world, knowing you'd never return. "They'll be there," Lenny said, "and we'll be there—which party would you rather attend? Can't decide? I promise, by the time the week is over, you'll have made up your mind."

The dawn had almost come. He could feel it in his blood, in his spleen and his balls. This one battle would be the last. He knew it, his friends knew it, the whole country knew it. And he was confident they'd already won. He'd seen it in a dream: His troops lined up, hands to shoulders, gyrating like Chinese dragons. They'd form circles and beat drums and spin like Sufi mystics. Burn so much incense that the scent would carry the thousand miles to Mount Rushmore. That was the start. They'd slip acid into the water and get everybody high. They'd fill their squirt guns with LACE, a secret substance that glistened on the skin, entered through the pores and turned on everything it touched. Visions of the whole city stripping down and joining the orgy; the sagging skin of ancient women pressed up against the sweet flesh of youth; men with liver spots bouncing joyous birds on their wrinkled knees, laughing and canoodling, setting their loins free; even the pigs embracing one another, stroking each other's cocks like they'd secretly fantasized of doing for so long. They'd choose their own candidate for US president, run a cow, or a chicken, or maybe a pig, and their candidate would win against any asshole either party put forward.

These were the tactics, he would say: Be free. Have fun. Say no to fear. The strategy required a police response. The pigs would see the love we shared, and our peace would surpass their understanding, short-circuiting their brains. They'd surge. They'd riot. We'd be slaughtered. Some of us might really die.

The saps and pacifists planned to be there too, shuttling back and forth with their quaint signs, trying to be reasonable, dignified in their dissent. They'll see, he'd say. They'll realize the limits of their good intentions. They might wish it wasn't so, but when Mayor Daley set loose his pigs, when the batons started swinging like they had in Washington, on Park Avenue, in Grand Central, at Columbia and so many other places, they'd see the absurdity of their cherished rationality. Their heads would be caked in blood just like his.

And they did. And they were. It all came to pass.

As the youth of the nation watched their brothers and sisters get clobbered by the pigs night after night, as they saw the politicians grimace in distaste when we kept kicking back, these kids knew they were us and we were them, and the only way they could possibly survive was to join us at the barricades. That's what Lenny would say.

Chicago made him famous, notorious, from sea to shining sea. He was always there—wherever the cameras were—with his nonstop zingers, his somersaults, his contraband shirts sewn from American flags. The Sid Caesar of the counterculture, said the oldtimers. You can take the Jew out of the Borscht Belt, but you can't take the Borscht Belt out of the Jew.

One night the pigs ripped the flag right off his back. Beat him to a pulp. Three cracked ribs. A lost tooth. "I regret I have but one shirt to give for my country," he said, the blood trickling down his chin. He grinned at the cameras and flashed two fingers, a sign of glorious victory at war that when flipped meant fuck you in some parts of the world and that in a savvy act of appropriation he and his cohort had turned into a universal symbol of resistance to the martial spirit it was meant to celebrate.

The only thing left was to throw one last Be-in. They invaded some poor schmuck's farm in the foothills of the Catskills. Set it free. Five hundred thousand people came from every corner of the battered nation. A three-day celebration of music and love. Children were conceived. Water turned to wine. New visions of the future fluttered in the breeze. And the pigs, outnumbered, stayed away this time. And nobody ate the brown acid. And this would be called

Woodstock and forever after, those who attended—or wished they had—this transcendent incarnation of lawless harmony and effervescent love would be known as Woodstock Nation.

He'd say, You know why they chased me underground? Just look at everything I accomplished. He'd dreamed a new society into being. No way could they let him live free after that.

For what it's worth, that's what he'd tell you. And some of it was true but a lot of it wasn't. Most of it was just wishful thinking. His own private craziness thrust onto the public stage.

Or here's one about me. A kind of family joke.

May 1970. Everyone wanted a piece of Lenny, if not to join the movement, to bask in his fame—or bust him in his honking kike nose. He'd been flying all over the country—the lecture circuit, the leftist circuit—going anywhere he could get away with, sometimes sneaking into states where he'd been banned, where he'd caused so much trouble and gotten himself arrested so flamboyantly in the past that the terms of his probation stipulated he could never set foot there again. Sometimes, thinking he was clean and legal, he discovered that the state legislature had convened a special session and worked through the night to preemptively outlaw his presence.

This time he was in a place called Hidalgo Springs, just outside Boulder, Colorado. He'd been invited by a confederacy of back-to-the-landers, nature enthusiasts who'd camped out there in hopes of being left alone to climb mountains and pick berries and gape, stoned out of their minds, at the sunset. They lived in a crevasse where two mountains met. A little forgotten nook that had been allowed to return to its natural state and inspired them to do the same. Sheer cliffs on either side. A cold-water spring that fed an overgrown creek. Raw jagged beauty surrounding a curative pool that had once, briefly, served as a fashionable weekend destination for the region's landed gentry but was now overgrown and slick with algae. There was one rutted road, more potholes than pavement.

Turned out the state, which for decades had negligently owned the land, had entered discussions with a corporation called Vitality, which wanted to build a bottling plant on the site. The plan, if it went through, was to clear-cut the forest straight to the spring, replacing the breathtaking splendor of the place with a strip of highway, a parking lot, a series of steel towers slung with high voltage cables, all feeding into a shiny new assembly line.

For this to happen, the hippies had to move. They'd been unwittingly squatting on government property—just showed up one day, thought it was pretty and stayed. They had no right to their patch of paradise. But they *felt* like it was theirs because they loved it so much. Panicked to discover there were actual rules binding people to the world in which they lived, one of them spent three days in the Boulder library, giving himself a crash course in the uses of public land. Pouring through the transcripts of city council meetings, he realized there'd been no civilian input on the issue, which seemed ethically untenable, though he didn't know if it was technically illegal.

Clinging to this nugget and its opaque implications, they petitioned the county and managed to collect a hundred or so signatures from the stoners who threw Frisbees on the University of Colorado campus. They pled their case at a Boulder city council meeting, where the officials indulged them with surprising courtesy before passing the buck to Denver. They wrote their congressmen and senators. They attempted to lobby the governor's office, but their messages went unreturned.

For the public good, said the *Rocky Mountain News,* the spring that allowed the canyon to bloom begged to be let loose. Its mineral-rich water extracted and captured and carried away to the parched regions of the country whose inhabitants would happily pay for quality hydration. Also, the county had been assured x number of jobs and y amount of increases in tax revenue if Vitality got its road and the lease to the land. It was a done deal. The papers had been signed. Now that the spring thaw had come and the mountain passes were accessible again, the creative destruction would commence in a matter of days.

That's when they'd called in Lenny.

He heard them out. He smoked up and let his mind wander. He figured, hell, why not throw these fools a bone. He liked them, liked how soft they were, how bumbling and sun-blind. He liked that they were, however ineptly, living out the notions he'd thrown like confetti into the air—tuning in, turning on, dropping out. I'll give him credit where he earned it. He was generous with his attention, always ready to run off and hang with whatever space cowboy crossed his path. Even in '70, at the height of his drawing power, when he was commanding thousands a pop from student groups around the country—money he needed, money that flew, *shoop*, right into the pockets of the lawyers he paid to keep him on the street—he was drawn more to the fuckups and vagrants, the half-crazy dreamers shouting at phantoms, than to the shuck and jive of imitating himself for the amusement of two thousand coeds.

"Dig," he said, "I'll man the barricades with you."

He'd been scheduled to speak that week in Boulder anyway and had a couple days to kill.

My mother must've begged him to let us tag along 'cause he carted us out to Colorado with him. The concerned citizens of Hidalgo Springs set us up in a yurt at the end of the grassy path they called a road, and from there he went about doing what he did: an exhausting day slouched in a folding chair, feet up on the card table they'd provided for him, hands clasped behind his head, eyes closed; the only sign that he was awake, the wriggling of his lips as he heard their grievances.

Once they'd talked themselves dry, he hopped to his feet. "Winning the argument, being right," he said, "that's the easy part. What I want to know is, you ready to go to war? Dig. The name of the game is obstruct and shame." He invoked Gandhi and MLK. He taught them how to snake dance. How to turtle under the pigs' bludgeons. How to wrap a wet bandanna over the nose and mouth, and wash the tear gas out of the eyes. "You better believe there's gonna be press. Press like you've never seen. A storm of locusts. They're gonna paint you as dirty fucking hippies. They'll say you aren't Christian. That you hang around, not working, plucking your guitars and fucking each other's wives. I dig it. Why shouldn't you sing and dance and fuck all day? Who *doesn't* want to live like that? Free love, right? Back to the garden. But that's not the trip the press is on. Their gig is to tell a story. And our job's to make sure they tell the right one."

He was like a messiah to them. His presence alone made them feel like they'd been saved.

Using the huckster's gifts he'd developed as a kid on the corners of East Flatbush, he led them toward conclusions they'd already drawn. They cold-called their friends and allies, the students who'd signed their failed petition, cajoling them to come out and show support, whispering, "Hey, I don't know if this is true, but I heard Lenny Snyder might make an appearance." They drew posters—*Save the Trees, What's Good for the Planet Is Good for the Children, Tell Vitality Our Water's Not for Sale*—and stapled them to cardboard tubes. The men trimmed their facial hair. The women wriggled back into the modest dresses they'd worn to the city council meeting. They readied themselves for the picket line they'd force the bulldozers to cross. But to Lenny it was all disappointingly earnest and naïve and boring. These people weren't about to go out trashing. They weren't the uncompromising wildcats who followed him around the Lower East Side. He was going to have to make his own fun.

Of course, being Lenny, he had a trick up his sleeve. From the moment we rolled into town, he'd been fixated on a particular ponderosa pine near the entrance to the canyon. A beast of a tree. An elephant. Hundreds of years old. When he first saw it, he cackled and elbowed my mother. "Check that fucker out," he said. "It's hung like a horse."

My mother used to describe the tree like this: A beautiful specimen of native fauna with so many knots and turns in its limbs that you could imagine the hardships and threats it had run up against over the long, lonely seasons of its life: the search for the sun, the water from stone, the wildfires twisting all around it. You could imagine it almost thinking, breathing, striving for its sliver of a chance at survival. It happened to have made its stand smack in the center of the new highway's footprint. The existing road actually veered around it. A surveyor would mark it as the first tree to go.

Both of them saw its potential.

"Freedom," he said to me, "you wanna be a big boy and help your daddy?"

I was two years old. According to my mother my major passions in life were garbage trucks and Daddy. So, yes. I did want to be a big boy. Whatever he asked of me, I'd toddle off and do it.

On the morning of May 2nd, so the story goes, when the bulldozers rolled into the canyon with the sunrise, they were greeted by the residents of Hidalgo Springs, along with a disappointing turnout of supporters, maybe fifty people in all, including children, trudging in a fitful loop, clogging the road.

A standoff ensued, but as Lenny knew would happen, as soon as the cuffs came out the picket line melted.

Behind it: Lenny and my mother, stoned like they often were on a big day, putting the final touches on the statement they'd prepared. He's dancing, all boxy knees and jangly fingers, like he's a leprechaun all of a sudden. Susan, my mother, is talking at something, pleading with it, shoving an orange slice into its mouth. They step away for the big reveal and there I am, snotty nosed, dirty faced, anointed in glitter, suspended four feet up the trunk of the pine like one of those gnomes people carve into the bark.

"Behold, the first child," Lenny shouts, camping it up, searching for the cameras that aren't even there, "returned to the garden, greeting the dawn—naked, natural, clothed in nothing but the sweet milk of his innocence. A senseless, small creature who maybe, just maybe, will inherit a simpler, kinder world than our own, one without tyranny, one without fear, a world that knows no injustice, only love and peace and love. Behold, the majestic spirit that lives in this tree presents the child to the rising sun, an offering, a promise, a new covenant." He cackles, a machine gun shooting off rounds. "Let's see you try and pave paradise now."

There's a loop of heavy chain padlocked around my waist. Ropes bind my wrists, pulling my arms out behind me. That's how they kept me up there—how they kept the cops from just cutting me down. My heels push against a scrap of two-by-four that Lenny hammered into the trunk to give me a footrest. On my forehead, a peace sign has been drawn in body paint. On my belly, the Earth radiates—what? Sunlight? Thunder bolts? Squiggly yellow lines.

The way my mother tells it, I was a perfect angel. Eager to do my part for the cause. I didn't cry once, just grinned and babbled and grabbed at the paint, and that might have been true as long as she was shoving those orange slices into my mouth, but . . .

Look, there's a photo. I've got it here somewhere. Documentary evidence. It's not the napalm girl. It's not Super Joel placing his carnation in a quaking rifle or any of the other iconic shots from that era, but, it's all right there: me hanging from the tree like Christ crucified, wailing like I've just been shown Armageddon.

Is that abuse? I don't know. You tell me. When Lenny told the story, he played it for laughs.

In any case, the bulldozers retreated. We packed ourselves up and took ourselves home.

One lonely reporter had made the scene—an intern, really—from *Rolling Stone,* who was in Colorado not to cover Lenny but to bring Hunter Thompson a suitcase full of speed. It would have made the cover, but two days later Kent State went down and bumped my tree and me to the back pages.

And then of course, three weeks after we left, the pine was chopped down and the hippies were booted to make way for the highway. So there you go.

[II]
WHAT'S GOING DOWN

What I remember is . . . well, I was very young.

Mostly it's his voice. That cracked-whip cackle. Ragged and spiky. Jittering like a sack of broken glass with the rhythms of Brooklyn, the Yiddish jangling against Italian and Polish and German and whatever else.

Even whispering, his voice cut the air like a siren. "Kid," he'd say, squatting, holding me between his knees, and he'd tell me a secret.

I'd laugh, thrilled to be the focus of his attention, which made him laugh too, a different laugh, a silent undulation of his abdomen, a laugh that for once, and because of me, wasn't a performance.

He'd fall back, taking me onto his chest, and he'd hold me there. "Atta boy," he'd say. And to my mother, "Kid can't tie his shoes but he knows the score." And I'd feel like I'd accomplished some hugely important thing.

That voice . . .

And the hair, obviously. That nest of black curls like a Chia Pet gone wild. I used to poke it. Get my fingers caught in it. He never combed it. I'd stand on his bony thighs and dig my hands in and he'd say, "Knock it off," but I knew he didn't mean it. "Knock it off, knock it off." Him thrusting his lip out for me to twist, smirking at me with that flirtatious I-dare-you expression of his. It was a thing we did.

"Fucking knock it off."

I'd dig in again and tug my hands through the knots, over and over, thinking one of these times I'd find a prize in there but also testing, waiting for him to enact part two of the game. The funner part. Thrilled by the anticipation, the not-knowing when it was going to come.

"Knock it off or I'll fucking knock your block off," he'd say.

And he'd open the trapdoor of his legs and send me falling hilariously to the floor.

Our special little game.

I remember people coming and going. Some I knew, some I didn't.

Phil Ochs with his guitar like a rifle strapped to his back and that innocent, happy-to-be-here way about him.

Sy Neuman, Lenny's real and metaphorical partner in crime. Shrimpy, hairy, like a human Tribble. He always wanted things Lenny couldn't or wouldn't give him. It wasn't until years later that I understood how the two of them had invented each other. I'd been too young to remember them in action, Sy dressed like a guerrilla, hectoring crowds of thousands with hard facts and statistics and Marxist theory while Lenny incited them and made them laugh. I'd missed the years during which they spent every waking hour spurring each other toward greater outrageousness, binding their imaginations together, absorbing American culture as a team and projecting it back as the grotesque Technicolor absurdity it was.

There were others. So many people tromped through our apartment. Allen Ginsberg, Marcus Kirsh. Rip Torn and Geraldine Page—they were all fire. Ray Garrett, vibrating equal parts joy and rage in his fogged-up Lennon glasses and his gauzy loose linens— Lenny affectionately called him the Fag. More. They're mostly faces, postures, body odors.

The chance occasions of their arrivals and departures. The total lack of structure they brought to our lives. Like our apartment was less the place where we lived than the place where, on any given day, ten or twenty people might be hanging around, raiding the fridge, filling the rooms with smoke, pissing in the sink, blissing out on the Mexican rug by the plastered-over fireplace. Like it belonged more to them than to us.

The soapy, musty smell of the vegetable curries they and their friends were always making. All that cumin. As though cumin alone could transform the country.

Fragments of conversations. The intensity of them. The way they filled the whole apartment with frenetic, molecular motion, made it seem like the molten core of the world. At the white-hot center, Lenny, radiating and glowing. His energy like an atomic wind incinerating everybody where they stood.

And the crazy shit that spewed from his mouth:

"You got to give it to Charlie Manson. Dig. He put his money where his mouth was. The spirit of the thing, it was beautiful, man. It's the execution that was the problem." Leering at his audience, the scruffy magpies chugging beer in the kitchen, daring them to bust him on his bad taste. "Too much psychic mumbo jumbo. The politics weren't legible."

His friends chuckling. Shaking their heads and staring at their boots. Never sure how much of what he said was a joke.

Lenny talking tough. All transgressive bravado. Trying out one-liners.

"Ask not what your country can do to you. Ask what you can do to your country."

"We're all niggers now, brother. Some of us just won't admit it."

"The beautiful thing about liberals is you can spit in their faces and they'll thank you for it."

He said to me once, "Hey, kid, you wanna make your papa proud? Learn how to shoot a gun. Live the revolution. I'll tell you who you should assassinate first: Ronald Reagan. Dig. He'll bury this country if he gets the chance. He's already doing it to California. Somebody needs to stop that motherfucker. Might as well be you."

Crouching to meet me man to man. Staring me down like he thought I might cry or piss my pants. But I didn't. I raised my fist in a black-power salute.

For weeks afterward, he and my mother fell over each other imitating me, taking turns saluting and shouting "Right on!"

Sy, dressed like an American Indian, stripped to a loincloth, his hairy legs and chest smeared with greasepaint. Red, green and black streaks smeared onto each cheek, wedged into the tiny swatch of skin that wasn't buried beneath his massive beard.

We were in DC. I remember that clearly. Lenny, Mom, me and Sy. Standing in the sun outside the Capitol. There was a chill in the wind. We'd been out there forever.

"They better let us in soon," Sy said. "Look." He flipped up the front of his loincloth and showed us his underwear. "I'm freezing my fucking balls off."

I remember one time, I was maybe four, sitting on the floor surrounded by a bunch of smelly dudes, all leaning as one toward the TV, their chairs tipped on two legs, poised there, watching, waiting for Lenny to appear on the screen. I could feel their excitement infiltrate my body and send my heart racing.

Something was about to happen. A talk show. The theme music. The host making funny.

And somewhere behind us, watching us watch for him, the real Lenny slouched against the doorway like he could give a shit.

After the first commercial break, the guy holding me in his lap—he had a humongous head, perfectly round, and his hair and beard frizzed out around his face in a way that made him look like a bloated sunflower—he pointed at the screen and said, "You see that? That's your dad." I could hear Lenny's voice crackling from the speaker. But he—his image—wasn't there. Just the host sneering in his skinny tie, hunched over his desk like a dyspeptic baboon, and next to him, where the guest should have been, floated a pixelated blue box. Then the second commercial came and Lenny—the one there in the room—clapped a single clap and let loose his cackle. "Fucking perfect," he said. "Those cocksuckers censored me. Dig it. They just told the whole country, be afraid of this man, brother, be very afraid. It doesn't get much better than that."

And the sunflower dude and the rest of them puffed up, smug and fat, like they were the ones who'd pulled off this great feat.

They lived off his vapors. He was like their king. And since he was important, I was important too.

Seeing myself in the cracked mirror propped against their bedroom wall. A guayabera shirt. A bandanna around my neck. Jeans—dungarees, Lenny called them. We argued. Jeans. Dungarees. No, they're jeans. Listen to me: They're dungarees. The uniform of the hardworking man. Mine were faded blue, baby-soft, with patches sewn onto odd, useless places. A peace sign on my ass. A dancing bear on my hip. Bell-bottoms. Under them, a pair of child-sized cowboy boots made out of shiny black pleather. A costume, but it wasn't Halloween.

Oh, and I was wearing a black beret. A fresh-faced Che Guevara. My unruly hair jutted out like wings over my ears.

We were going somewhere special. I have no memory of where or why. Just the costume itself. Me, the tyke revolutionary.

And Lenny, hovering. Bouncing around the room. Hammering slogans into my head. "*Huelga! Viva la resistance! Hasta la victoria siempre!* No justice, no peace! We'll make a fighter out of you yet, kid."

A sense of pride as I walked around with him. Of specialness and celebrity. Even the cops stopped to say hello.

A sense of holiness—from both of my parents—like in their profanity and filth and chaotic refusal they were holding up an ideal only they could achieve. Daring the whole world to be as free as they were. They really, truly believed they were molding a new human out of the rubble. The question was whether that human would be me.

Things I knew without having learned them. Ideas and attitudes.

That right was wrong and wrong was right. That the people the TV said to fear—the dangerous elements with their rude behavior, the revolutionaries robbing banks and stealing Brinks trucks and writing manifestos, dudes arrested at the border with their seaplanes packed with weed, the balaclava-shrouded men engaged in armed struggle all over the world, taking hostages in the Olympic Village in Munich—they were our heroes. Brave freedom fighters. Our people. Compadres. Lenny was one of them. My mother, too.

And the truth was always the opposite of whatever you were told it was supposed to be.

But also, dread. A sense that the city, maybe the whole country, might explode. Currents crackled in the air, an electric buzz, flowing through each and every person in each and every restaurant, saloon and market, that was amped, unstable. The folks crouched on fire escapes, packed on subway platforms—their internal energy was running way too hot. You sensed that one or ten of them might be live wires, that a fire might ignite at any second.

Bombs were going off, not every day, not even every week, but often enough to impress a kid, to teach him not to grow too attached. Shit blows up. Angry people fight back. Not where we lived on the Lower East Side, maybe, but elsewhere. We were safe in our ghetto. Safe because here the battle had already been waged. And we controlled the wreckage. I knew this was true 'cause my mother told me so.

But, elsewhere? Watch out. It's a war out there.

.　　.　　.

I remember running. The momentum of forward movement. It's more a sensation than a specific event. I don't know the location. I can't place it in time. We were in a city—I couldn't tell you which one—and there was a disorienting onslaught of sound. Of crowds. We were running with a mob, pressed in on all sides. Or my mother was. I bounced against her chest, bound to her by some sort of makeshift sling, holding on with all my strength, but my hands kept slipping and I was sure I was going to slide off and be trampled by the horde of protesters behind her. Especially when she stutter-stepped, which she did frequently to avoid tripping on the obstacles scattered everywhere. She shouted herself hoarse. Her breath and the strident force of her bleating percussed against my temple. The rage in her. The kinetic disturbance. It propelled us forward. Kept us running. Set our pace. It felt like we'd be running forever, clang-ing garbage can lids together. Stomping our boots and beating our drums. We ran. When a siren yelped, we ran faster.

I glimpsed something burning up ahead. A car was on fire. Tipped on its side. Flames licking out of the passenger window, twirling in the wheel wells and searing the steel of the undercarriage. A cop car.

We ran right past.

There were times when my mother had a bat in her hands. She'd swing it and I'd reel with the momentum of her body. Trashing, she called it. Destroying the Satan who went by the name of Property.

I remember, sometimes, when Lenny was away, listening for bombs in the night, waiting for our building's foundations to shake, won-dering what it would feel like to die. Thankful that he wasn't there to see my fear.

Panthers, Weatherpeople, freaks killed and captured, all added to the growing roll call of martyrs. How the gravity plunged in our house on those days. I was confused about a lot of things. The spe-cifics, the whys and hows, were beyond me. But I knew not to ask. These weren't things I was supposed to understand.

News of shootings, standoffs, lone individuals frothing at the mouth, nailing list after list of demands on the doors of power. In our house, we strained for the details of each arrest, listening for word—was this one of ours? Sometimes it was and sometimes it wasn't and often you couldn't really tell the difference.

Bombs in Philly. A bank. Its marble columns collapsing like ancient ruins.

A man and a woman at our front door. The steam rising off them. The way their hats sat oddly on their heads. The way, even after they stepped inside, they refused to take their sunglasses off. The sense I had that they were different, spookier, more threatening, than the usual flotsam passing through the place.

And the furtive discussions that went on above my head, everyone mumbling, swallowing their words. My mother guiding me to another room. "Come on, Freddy. Let's go find you a toy."

Lenny's voice—I could just make it out—"Hold on," and then the screech of Hendrix's guitar shredding the space like a chain saw.

Later, Lenny, serious, grave, crouched next to my mother in the back room with us, whispering. Her nodding, reaching for his elbow. "Go. Do what you have to do."

The thud of the door pounding shut behind him. The way the record skipped in that moment.

Then, my mother lifting the needle from the groove. Silence rushed in. I knew not to break it.

Another time when I sensed Lenny was proud of me.

Wandering the streets. Walking up the avenue. He pointed people out.

"That guy?"

"No."

"Him?"

"No."

We were identifying undercover agents.

"That one there with the rainbow belt?"

"Yes."

"How'd you know?"

"The shoes." It was always the shoes.

I cracked Lenny up. He cackled like the world itself had pleased him.

Bombs in LA, Atlanta, Dallas, Boston, Cleveland. Federal buildings. State government offices. The way Lenny's eyes flashed with life at the news.

They didn't bother with babysitters. India was in the air—the incense, the pajamas, the sitars and jangly anklets. They'd cue a raga up on the hi-fi and take off for the night, leaving me alone with Ravi Shankar and the great spinning circle of creation.

No bedtimes, no discipline, no supervision.

They let me play in traffic.

They let me run around the block half-naked, my circumcised little penis exposed to all the neighbors.

Sometimes they dragged me along to parties.

Up a hundred stairs, through hallways crammed with boxes, bricks of twine-wrapped newspapers, power tools and broken plains of sheetrock. Down into basements, death traps, all exposed beams and unfinished floors and ceilings, extension cords strung like trip wires, plugged into work lamps, moss and creeping weeds leaking through the cracked cement, Tic Tac–shaped pebbles strewn everywhere—the black ones were rat shit, the brown ones poison. Industrial spaces. Abandoned warehouses. Semi-converted lofts. Liberated or forgotten places. Falling down. Unreconstructed. The rotting bits and pieces of the city that Lenny and his friends had scavenged and claimed. We'd squeeze into freight elevators with twenty other freaks all dressed up like refugees from another time, legs squeezing me from every side, corduroy and denim squishing against my face as the platform groaned and the chain clicked, and up we went until with a thud, we'd come to a stop.

Wherever we were, whatever night of the week, the same tea-stained scene, the same cheap prisms bending light, distorting it, taking it apart.

I was a party trick Lenny pulled from his sleeve. Something to be passed around and poked and prodded, the dog you got drunk so you could watch it flail. People would be lined up all the way out the door waiting for their turn to blow smoke in my face, giggling about the bizarre thrill of shotgunning a three-and-a-half, four-year-old child.

Then the horror would kick in. Heavy. Dark. Glassy. Smeared with Vaseline. Beaded curtains rattling in my ears. Silly putty faces floating close and laughing. People spoke to me at the wrong rpm, droning and distorted, telling me things like "John is dead." Lenny didn't care. My mother didn't care. If the party went till dawn, they'd keep me there all night, crashed out and shivering on a bean-bag in the corner.

Bombs going off in Washington outside the Pentagon. The scorched façade on the TV screen. Cops in hard hats, circling, studying the debris.

That couple—the one that had shown up so furtively at our door—on the nightly news, stripped of their sunglasses, hands cuffed in front of them. The speed with which my mother stepped to the TV and turned it off. The sense that even in my freewheeling home, there were things I wasn't supposed to know.

And always Lenny's voice, his manic patter, running me over at great velocity, trampling me under a stampede of words. He was so enthralled, sometimes, by his own performance that he didn't notice if I was listening or not.

Him boasting at parties: "I told them, don't lay that on me. That's your trip, not mine. I didn't ask you to manufacture a hundred thousand Lenny Snyder dolls. It wasn't my idea to give them pull-strings so they could yelp 'Power to the people' and 'Groovy!' You're trying to turn me into a fucking hula-hoop. That's what I told them. And the American flag shirts for twenty-seven bucks a pop with the patch on the shoulder of me flashing a peace sign. The empty boxes that, you open them up and they shout 'Dig it!' and laugh—ah, ha-ha-ha-ha. The posters and trading cards—a whole set, me and Sy, Leary, Hayden. Eldridge Cleaver. Smelling like sugar from the stale gum inside. I said, that's cool. I still have my mint-condition Yogi Berra rookie card. But listen, chewing gum's a snooze. And bad for the environment. Let's swap out the gum for a tab of acid. You do that, you've got a deal. If not, I'll tell you what I've told every other cocksucker who's ever tried to commodify me. Go fuck yourself. Lenny Snyder ain't for sale.

"The record deals. I told them, Go fuck yourself.

"The film crew—they had a vision. An antic Lenny Snyder racing from one national landmark to another, the Statue of Liberty, the Lincoln Memorial, Mount Rushmore, everywhere, the whole enchilada. High-stepping up the steps, peeking around marble columns, doing cartwheels and periodically leaping and shouting 'Yippie!' as a paddy wagon full of Keystone Cops chases me—*sexy* ones with big tits and miniskirts. I said: What? You think I'm a long-haired Benny Hill? Go fuck yourself.

"The publishing house—it wanted to put together a book of letters from the hundreds of women who've fallen in love with me. Come-ons and fantasies. Daydreams about my hair. I asked them, where you gonna get those letters? I'd like to vet them. I want names and addresses. They said we'll write them ourselves. The contents don't matter. It's the packaging that counts. Right, I said. Of course. Go fuck yourself.

"I said to all of them, I'm not your product. I don't want your money. I operate in a different economy. Tell you what I'll do, though. I'll consider your offer if you let me decide what happens with *your* profits. We'll give them to the Panthers, the PLO, the IRA. Every cent. Publicly. We'll hold a press conference.

"That's what I told them. Join me where I stand. I ain't coming to you.

"And you know what they said to that? They told *me* to go fuck myself!

"So I remain free. Ha-fucking-ha!"

But also, the silence during those stretches when he disappeared. Like the apartment itself was yearning for his presence.

He had women everywhere, girlfriends, groupies, chicks he picked up on the street. My mother knew about them. They had an open marriage—the kind that only went one way—so, she pretended not to care, but sometimes, on especially bad days when he'd been gone for a week or more and she'd heard rumors that he was maybe shacked up in the Chelsea Hotel with some fuck-me poetess or carting an eighteen-year-old runaway with him on his trek through the college campuses of Ohio, she'd work herself up to such a hyperventilating pitch that when he finally did come home, you could see her deciding—making a conscious choice—to indulge her elemental rage. Stamping her feet, bringing all of the power in her petite frame down like bang snaps on the scratched and distressed hardwood floor. Whipping her arms like buzz saws at his head. Sobbing. Tearing at her hair, her clothes—*actually rending her clothes*—like some wailing woman from the old country. The accumulated sorrows of the generations—the long line of women of her tribe who, going back to the City of David, had all silently endured their philandering men—channeling through her onto Lenny's head.

What he would do was watch her. Just watch her. Hands dug to the wrists in the pockets of his jeans. Ducking once in a while when she came clawing toward him but mostly just standing there, a witness, alive with admiration, stinking of pussy, proud of himself.

"My very own *balabusta*," he called her. "My lunatic love."

He taunted her. "Right on, babe, let it out. You can do better than that."

My mother crashed again and again against him. Exhausted herself. Fell back to rev up and crash into him again. The endorphins flushing through her brain. The adrenaline crackling. A kind of euphoria.

Never mind that they always chose three in the morning to act out this Punch and Judy show. Never mind that I was still awake, tucked into myself, doing everything I could to make myself smaller.

Eventually, inevitably, Lenny would hold up one long finger, like, Wait, I have an idea, and my mother, having spent every ounce of herself by then, would pause for him to justify his existence. He'd raise a leg and cut a fat, juicy, distended, orgiastic fart. A slow, tricksy smile lighting up his face. It took me my whole life to understand that he had his reasons for behaving like this and that he wasn't the only one getting something vital from the transaction. He'd cackle and, just like that, she'd cackle too. You could see it all over her, the total, relentless joy she found in him. And then they'd be in each other's arms, jitterbugging through the room like there'd never been anything but love between them.

Riding on his shoulders, hands tangled in his hair like I was holding reins. We were at yet another massive demonstration. From way up there, I could see the scope of the crowd surrounding us. Thousands upon thousands upon thousands of people. An undulating sheet of humanity sprawled out in every direction, restless, waiting for something, anything, to happen, to be told to march, to be lit on fire.

Off in the distance, the Washington Monument. It meant something but I was too young to know what. I was more interested in how it looked not real—like it had been put there by Lenny and his friends as a backdrop for the pageant about to commence. I was more interested in how the breeze slapped my face and made my eyes tear up. The beach balls soaring over people's heads. The various clusters of folk who, having grown sick of standing, nestled in the grass and sang along with that one guy in each group who'd brought a guitar. I knew all the songs. "We Shall Overcome." "Blowin' in the Wind." "Give Peace a Chance." "This Land Is Your Land." They were my lullabies.

Lenny wandered through this pastoral scene, bouncing me, his hands clasped around my feet. Everyone wanted a piece of his attention. A crumb. To touch the hem of his shirt. To slap me high-five. It was fun for me. I felt like a superstar. But he couldn't stop grumbling.

"They think they're at a fucking party," he said—to who? Sy was there, and Phil Ochs, and Ray Garrett, the guy Lenny called the Fag, and a slew of other players in their scene. The sunflower dude. Everybody. It was a family reunion.

Lenny complained to all of them. "This scene is a drag, man. It's bumming me out."

He was sped up, angry at the very people who adored him, mostly *because* they adored him.

We ended up in a holding pen of some sort. There was a stage and a banner and a tower of speakers and a parade of folks waiting their turn at the mic. "Give 'em what they want," Lenny sneered. "Flatter them. Fucking liberals ruin it every time. Just look at them. They think being here is accomplishing something."

"It *is* accomplishing something, Lenny," someone said. "It means we're winning." I think it was Phil. You know what? I'm positive. Fingering his guitar. Tuning it up. Going over the set list taped to the barrel.

And Lenny lashed out at him. "Oh? Is this what winning looks like?" Talking with his hands. Bucking me around on his shoulders. "I'm telling you, the first sight of blood and these motherfuckers will scurry back to their fallout shelters. But, hey, it's cool," he said. "You go ahead, Ochs. Climb up on that stage and lead your sing-along. Shower the people with nostalgia. I'm telling you, though. This scene is over."

Phil looked like he might cry. But he always looked like that. "Oh," he said, absorbing, considering. "Then w-what's next?"

Lenny darkened. "What's next? You wanna know w-what's next? *Le déluge,* motherfucker! That's what's next!" He just wouldn't stop. "Go on, man. It's your turn. They're waiting for you. I'll tell you what, though. I'm done tap dancing."

Certain things you just know. Immutable truths. Some kids were scared of you, others scared you. You knew which were which just from the look of them. Something in their stances. The way their clothes hung on their bodies. The size of their voices. The farther east you went, the more you had to pay attention to the messages your skin was sending you.

We lived on 7th Street between First and Second. Kids from SoHo, the Village, they didn't impress me. They wore their backpacks high on their shoulders. Kids from the east side, south of the park, where the language of the street was Puerto Rican, they were tougher. You might find yourself regretting having answered back as you stepped out of one of their botanicas. But the most terrifying kids lived in the squats north of Tompkins Square. They squirmed on the stoops in hungry packs. Watched you with cold, dispassionate eyes, flinging butterfly knives between their own feet as their naked little brothers and sisters played chicken with traffic. I don't remember any one thing about them. Just the sense, any time I was over there, that they were waiting for their chance to fuck me up. The problem was they didn't believe in anything. The problem was they had no code; or if they did, it was so erratic that any random cruelty could be justified. The problem was I belonged to Lenny and they knew it and I knew it and they didn't like it. Something to do with him taking credit for having liberated the shitholes they lived in. His posing as the leader of their mangy clan.

I remember him dragging me over there one time. Me asking, "Why do they always stare at me like that?"

"Like what?" he said.

"Like *that*. So mean."

And I remember him thinking about this for a second, sizing me up and then saying, "They think you're a pussy." And me not knowing if they were right or wrong, but sensing that he did and that he didn't like the answer.

The more desperate you were—the more emotionally unstable and materially endangered—the more he respected you. We'd be walking along and he'd have one eye out for people in a jam, gaunt, distressed drunks sobbing in the gutters, guys who'd been on the street so long they'd fallen out of time, grown ageless, so worn and leathered they no longer begged for change, just wandered around in a daze, scavenging, hiding in the subways where the rat economy allowed them to survive, surfacing every once in a while to expose their sores to the bracing fresh air, their thin hair blowing wild and beards down to their bellies, like Hasids banished from the tribe, lost and searching for their God. We'd see these men—always men, never women—and the better facet of Lenny's nature would surface and catch the light. The thing in him that had been hardened by years of struggle and fame. He'd kneel down next to them. Share a smoke with them. Break bread. As comfortable as warriors who hadn't seen one another since the Battle of the Bulge, who'd gone on to grossly different kinds of luck with life, but still shared a secret knowledge, a wound they couldn't explain to anyone else and didn't have to among themselves. He'd laugh with them and, remarkably to me, he never once sneered. Lenny, who sneered at everyone and everything. He accepted these guys in the place where he found them. They were courageous to him. He believed that the shame beaten into them was tragic. That it wasn't them but the people who'd put them there who should be ashamed.

A lot of what I remember about that last year is him not being there.

Just me and my mother. The security of knowing she was two rooms away, sipping her chamomile tea, cutting up a pear she'd later bring me as I sat on my pillow, six inches from the TV, entranced by the big eyes of Kimba of the Jungle.

I remember the limitless possible selves—each as kind and lovely as the others—that she urged me to imagine lying dormant inside me.

And special days, cradled in sunlight, when she put *Free to*

Be . . . You and Me on the turntable and we'd tumble into the all-accepting, gender-contorting, fantastically shame-free mirage inside that record, chanting along to "William's Doll" and "It's All Right to Cry," discussing the societal implications of "Atalanta" with the Talmudic fervor of true believers. The hope she worked so hard to instill in me, that cruelty was a crime that could be overcome.

Me and my mother, navigating the streets of the city together. My little hand in hers. My head in her skirt. Running errands. Getting bored. Lenny's presence felt only in its absence.

The bandshell at Tompkins Square, empty in early-morning fog. The fragility of the morning rituals of the people waking up on its stage.

The warmth of her arms across my chest as we sat on the grass and watched a squirrel tussle with an empty Fritos bag.

Her scent, cottage cheese and jasmine. Sometimes a strong tug of iron in the lower registers. How tightly these smells wrapped themselves around me.

I remember the psychedelic colors that swirled and blurred as my mother and I pushed past storefronts—the gaudy brightness of everything—chipping in places, growing old. The sense that beneath this thin layer of paint, the city was crumbling, rotting away.

And joyful marches. Her face flushed with life. Me helping her hold up the sign we'd made. She seemed to always know everybody there. They gave her the megaphone. Let her lead the chants. She was special to these people, desired, and since Lenny wasn't there she belonged to me. Only to me.

There was this one wizened little man who peddled ideology from a card table on the sideline of every demonstration. I have no idea why he's stuck in my memory, but he is. Vividly. His hundreds of buttons, one for every issue and every point of view on the left side of the scale. A cacophony of dissent pinned to his felt vest, strung like jewels along the brim of his Greek fisherman's hat. I remember there was something sour about him. Ageless and embittered. He could have been imported under a bell jar from 1890s Grozny, or just as likely, gotten lost en route to some Trotskyite gathering on Orchard Street where everyone spoke Yiddish and still thought it was 1952. Nobody ever said a word to him and nobody ever picked up any copies of the socialist papers he hawked.

The sounds. The music everywhere. Bands of traveling minstrels strumming esoteric instruments, looking like they'd just tumbled out of a horse cart from the twelfth century. Their lace-up boots and tunics. The wineskins slung over their shoulders. Hippies dancing barefoot in the streets. Women with hairy legs twirling and folding themselves in half, swaying, their heads upside down between their legs, their misshapen wide-brimmed hats falling into the gutter. Their laughter. How they flipped the hats right back onto their heads, not caring what sticky sliminess might've accumulated on them.

Hippies with their hands out, asking for change.

Non-hippies too, asking for change. Black people. Brown people. Native Americans or, anyway, people dressed up like them.

We paid our tithes and kept moving.

The sense that something was always happening but nobody really had anything to do and that when and if Mom and I chose to step out we'd be wanted somewhere.

There was a period during which the television was always on. Men in horn-rimmed glasses leaning into microphones and droning on in flat, tedious voices. Sometimes my mother turned the sound down, played music, barely paid them any attention. But we couldn't turn it off. I wasn't allowed to watch *Sesame Street* or *Kimba* or *Mister Rogers*.

I learned to hate these men. It was their fault my pleasure had been denied. I didn't understand—I couldn't fathom, even with Lenny Snyder as my father and Suzy Snyder as my mother—why a bunch of clean-cut dudes in ugly suits were more worthy of attention than the shows I liked. The little I understood about Lenny and Mom's ethos, the one lesson I'd learned, was that you should *do your own thing*. Live the reality of your own choosing. Fuck everything else. Just ignore it.

But here was Mom, subjecting herself to hours and hours and hours of the very people she hated. They droned on and on. All they did was make her mad.

The music. When Lenny was home, we listened to acid rock. 102.7. WNEW. The Doors and Hendrix and Jefferson Airplane. The Dead. His favorite, the Steve Miller Band. When he was gone, Mom turned to the AM dial. Cat Stevens. Carol King. Harry Chapin. Quiet songs that sometimes carried her off into a god-haunted place where I couldn't reach her. We'd twirl around together singing along to James Taylor's "You've Got a Friend." Falling into each other. She'd touch the tip of her nose to mine. I'd pretend not to notice how sad she was.

The things he'd say to her if she dared play this stuff while he was home. The wars they'd have.

Nixon's face melting on the TV as Lenny, my mother, and I watched in charged silence. His stiff, hunchbacked body. The air of momentous expectation, like a victory was about to be declared. The constricting tension. Nixon said something and Lenny lunged to his feet, hooting, clapping, howling. My mother fell back like she'd been holding a massive weight above her head and was all of a sudden free of it, like she was exhausted but also elated. "Yes," she said. Then, at the top of her lungs, "Yes!" Out the open windows, somebody picked out "The Star-Spangled Banner" on the electric guitar. People shouted, yodeled, celebrations breaking out up and down the block.

Then the phone started ringing. Short calls. Lenny's friends. And from the way he gloated and strutted around, I gradually realized they were congratulating him.

The war was over. One of them anyway. He did this. Or, as my mother would say, "We all did this." But it was mostly him. Lenny Snyder got the glory.

The look on my mother's face while she watched him. Like a butterfly spreading its wings for the first time. Like she'd decided to let the beauty pour off herself and cascade all over her husband.

"You know what would make this moment even sweeter?" Lenny said into the phone. Who knows who he was talking to. This was the tenth or twentieth call he'd taken. "If I'd really fucked that prig Tricia like I told the *Post*. That bird has flown. She must really hate me now." A cackle. He was cracking himself up.

My mother folded in on herself. Her lips pursed and she drew a shroud over her beauty. I felt like I was on a river, riding a raft that was splitting in two, unsure which side to hold on to through the rapids.

I remember a new kind of hope in his presence, a longing to play with him, a feeling that he might be willing to play with me. An adventure might've been planned for the day, an expedition to the park or maybe a birthday party for one of my little friends—though I don't recall having any friends. Maybe we'd take the subway out to Brighton Beach, where they'd strip me naked, set me loose in the surf. Whatever it was. A day organized around celebrating me. I remember my mother reciting the whole list of things we would do. Making promises about the fun we'd have. I remember an outlandish feeling of excitement. An expectation as big as the wind.

And I remember that this expectation revolved around the fact that Lenny had chosen me over his work, that he'd said no to the action and the accolades to take part in this kid-sized fun with me. He was the hinge. The door to all this joy my mother had laid out in front of me wouldn't open without his involvement.

Maybe it was just that once and I've embellished around the experience, extended it into a persistent pattern to quell the possibility that what happened next was more than an aberration. That the mask had been lifted and I'd caught a glimpse of the thing lurking, always, beneath it.

What happened was that we didn't go to the beach or the park or the party or whatever it was we'd been supposed to do.

I remember lots of sunlight. So much that instead of streaming in the windows of our railroad apartment, it seemed to radiate from the walls of the living room itself, up front, facing the street. My mother was there. Me. Lenny was not. He was at the other end of the apartment, past the series of entryways that led to darker and darker rooms the farther back you went.

And that's why we weren't going. Because Lenny was back there and we were up here. It wasn't my fault. My mother made this clear. But why, then? Because, that's why. But why because? Because we can't, that's why. She wouldn't say it was because there was something wrong with Lenny, but I knew this was the reason and her refusal to say so made the darkness engulfing him all the more menacing. It was like the darkness was emanating from him. Like if I could only bring him up into the light with us, everything would be fine.

So I ran to him, and when I got to the last doorway it was so dark back there that I could barely see, but I could feel his presence, his heat, his . . . I want to call it fear. Vacancy. Something altogether different from the rage and pixie dust that motored him out into battle. He wasn't moving. Not even breathing, it seemed. Just there, buried in the deep hole of himself. I can see him to this day. The shadow of him, the shrouded fact, the faint light in those eyes that didn't seem to register my presence.

One glimpse and my mother guided me away. But it was enough. Some portion of Lenny's fear—the failure, the premonition of failure, that's what it was—had pierced me and dispensed its poison into my blood, and this was more terrifying than any extravagant act of vandalism, mayhem or destruction Lenny might have exposed me to out in the world.

And back in the sunlight of the living room, I wanted to ask my mother why again, but I knew I couldn't. And anyway, it was a different question now.

. . .

And then nothing.

The glory days were over. He'd aged out of the fight. I'd say he reached the heights of celebrity from which he was paid just to exist, but we never had any money—or none I ever knew about.

There was no more kicking up trouble, getting righteously arrested, racing off somewhere to raise hell for weeks on end in some other state, some other country. Now when he wasn't home he had no excuses.

His new job seemed to consist of wandering around and joking with people on the street. Sometimes, very rarely, he'd drag me to an office, this tiny room above a boot shop on Bleecker. Always empty except for us. A desktop made from a piece of warped plywood propped up on sawhorses. A wall of filing cabinets with so many papers and overstuffed folders stacked on top that I was sure, each time we went there, that they were going to topple down on me and flood the room. He'd run a flyer through the mimeograph machine—hundreds of copies on colored paper—and leave most of them there, taking a few to pass out on his patrols through the neighborhood.

Once in a while we all sat around together, him and me and my mother, stuffing envelopes—making sausage is what he called it. But this wasn't frequent. He sometimes managed to bag an interview. To talk about himself and the things he'd done back when he still had things to do. There were a few special days when he was called up to play himself on the nightly news, but that didn't happen too often anymore.

He was writing a book, a guide, as he described it, about how to be an outlaw in the new America. A follow-up to his notorious grifter's handbook *Burn It, Break It, Steal It.*

I remember Sy coming to visit in a suit and tie, preposterously clean-shaven, his arrogant cheekbones bloated on his face. And me shrieking with delight like four-year-olds do, not recognizing him, refusing to believe this was the same man I'd known all my life. I demanded to know, "What'chu do with him? Where'd you put him?"

．　　・　　•

I remember the dense funk that hung in certain corners of the park, at the walled ends of alleyways, under stairwells, anywhere the breeze caught and eddied. Stale piss and spilled beer. And poured over this like syrup, penetrating everything, the sweet tang of marijuana. Repulsive smells that you long for after they're gone.

And a new presence on the streets, younger and harder to comprehend than Lenny's winos: Junkies. Living statues. Bodies void of souls. You put in a quarter and they danced for a moment, a few jitters, a brief stirring of consciousness, before returning to a state of blessed, terrifying emptiness.

I remember Phil's voice outside the apartment door. "Lenny, please, l-let me in. Let me t-talk this through with you. I've got wine, man. Chianti. I'm your *friend*, Lenny. Don't do this. Don't be like this, man."

Lenny's body wedged like a chair against the door, him leaning his whole weight into his shoulder, like somehow shambling, passive Phil might bust through the fifteen dead bolts he'd installed in his paranoia. He was shirtless, barefoot, free-balling it in a pair of bell-bottoms that hung off his hip bones and expose the top fringe of his pubic hair. I remember the sinews of his shoulders and biceps flexing like angry eels under his skin.

"I'm on to you, Ochs, you fucking cocksucker. Take your Chianti and go the fuck home."

The stringiness of him. The coil of his rage. His whine, his sneer, a scratching needle of complaint. Him pounding the door. Leaving dents.

Later, Lenny slumped on the floor. The black and white tiles, cheap and worn out, the dirty pink construction paper showing through in spots. His energy gone. The kitchen less crowded now without his hot air.

Then, later still, even his body was gone. I'd draped myself in a chair with my feet in my mother's lap. The nubbly texture of her burlap dress itched pleasantly at my ankles. She was drinking red wine out of a chipped coffee mug. The table wobbled every time she set it down. Phil was there too, standing, his ass to the counter, drinking his wine straight from the bottle—one of those decorative jobs, like an ancient urn wrapped in macramé. I wanted to smell it. Phil's face was puffy. His eyes, especially. They were talking, but it was all too subtle and complicated for me to understand. What I got was the tone, the soft goodness of it. Such concern. Such comfort. I felt safe. Protected. I wanted to pat Phil's head.

And even later, Lenny came back like a flash flood and then my mom was shouting and Lenny had Phil by the shirt, grappling, shoving, pushing him back, back, out onto the landing, where Phil missed a step and tumbled, sprawling, down the stairs.

More and more, he hung around with Ronnie Walker.

Mostly, I remember Walker by what he wasn't. He wasn't a Panther. He wasn't a poet or musician or artist. He wasn't into black nationalism. Not a card-carrying anything, as far as I could tell. Just a guy. A city dude. Raised uptown. Harlem or the Bronx. A vet, I think. There was this Asian woman I saw him with sometimes. Maybe his wife. Maybe a prize he brought home from the war.

He might've been down with the politics of the time—it seems like I saw him sometimes at rallies and fund-raisers and other events Lenny and my mother dragged me to, but he existed apart from the buzzy closed network of organizers and their egos. Never on the stage. Half the time, not even in the room. Out on the street, hanging around the stage door looking to catch Lenny for half a second, whisper in his ear, slap a low-five. Conspiring.

I remember he liked to wear a black watch cap low on his forehead, over his ears. And one of those green army field jackets— maybe that's why I thought he was a vet.

I remember . . . not a lot.

I remember Lenny telling my mother, once, "He's the real deal," and I remember not understanding what that meant.

. . .

More tests:

"It's all in how you play it," Lenny told me. "Be cool. Walk right in and check out the goods like you intend to buy everything in the store. Pretend you've got a wad of cash stuffed in your pocket. Fifties. Hundreds. Only the big bills. Feel it there. The weight of it. All rolled up inside a rubber band. Run your thumb along the edge. Feel the ripple, how it gives. Fresh bills. Never used before. Breathe in that new money smell. Make it real. Believe it. Who's ever seen so much dough in one place? Well, you have! This is chump change. Walkin' around money. How's it feel to be so rich? How's it affect your posture? Your heart? Your cock?"

He watched me shift my weight, shoulders rising out of their insecure slouch. He nodded encouragement. It was a game we were playing. A lesson built into it.

"Now go get 'em, kid," he said. "Take 'em for all they're worth."

And he shoved me through the door of the corner bodega.

I wandered the aisles, looking for some impressive thing to steal. Cool. Just a kid popping in on his way home from school. Never mind that it was ten in the morning and I wasn't even old enough for kindergarten. I fondled the chips. I waved to the guy who ran the place, towering there behind his high counter.

"What you lookin' for, papi?" he asked, friendly. He knew me from around the block.

"Nothing," I told him, and in an instant I felt the confidence— the arrogance—flush from my body. He was watching. He was on to me. He knew there was no roll of cash in my pocket. I ducked my head and continued through the aisles, feeling the heat of his sus- picion press down on me. Time ticking away. Lenny was outside, waiting. Calculating the ways I was fucking this up. I was thinking I should just give up now. Spare myself the hassle of being chased from the store.

"Your moms send you for something? Bread? Sugar? Tell me, I'll find it."

I shook my head. The piss began to burn in my bladder.

The counter the guy sat behind consisted of a grid of see-through cubes, each filled with a different brand of candy.

"I just want some of that," I told him, pointing at the Tootsie Rolls, not the brown ones but the green and pink and yellow ones. I had a quarter in my pocket and I held it up to him. He had to stretch his whole girth across the counter to reach my hand. Then he gave me five Tootsie Rolls—six—one for good luck.

Back outside, I showed Lenny what I had, pretending I'd stolen it. A transparent lie. The candy was in a brown paper sack.

He shot me this tight look, bafflement, disappointment, scorn, all bound together in the flick of an eye. "Not cool," he said.

And he was off. Walking fast up the avenue. I struggled to keep up. A few paces on, and he turned to me again.

"Not fucking cool."

Anger wormed through his body and I thought for a moment he was going to hit me, but instead he grabbed the bag and whipped it into the street, candy flying from it as it spun, dinging off windshields, flattened under wheels.

For the next three days he pretended I didn't exist.

The lesson was, he'd rather I'd been arrested.

The ragged people you sometimes ran into. Weaving along the avenues.

Men in torn dresses, sometimes flapping under cracked biker jackets—not drag queens, not subtle, not elegant. They reeked of brutality. Had no sense of irony. Or too much of it.

Women with open sores weeping on their cheeks.

Dudes out in the freezing cold in filthy T-shirts. Immune to the weather. Flying on something, reeling, crashing, burning. Combat boots lurching on and off the curb. Arms and legs and shoulders swinging like clubs. Mouths raw and wet like fresh wounds.

Half the time Lenny knew them, but when we saw them like this, we kept our distance. "Give that one some space. He's had a bad night," he'd say. "All you can do with a guy in that state is to watch out you don't get hit when he starts flailing."

They didn't frighten me. They were too familiar to make me flinch, just another part of the fabric of the city. At war with something, sure, but I knew it wasn't me.

There was this one cop we used to see around. Not a beat cop. He was higher up than that. He held himself differently. Cooler. Less bluster. His power lived in his shoulders. His heavy feet. He'd learned how to contain it. He had nothing to prove. A big guy, pink and doughy like they all were, but smarter than most of them— more refined. And tall. The orange in his hair fading like the cover of a paperback left on the dashboard. Something about him said he wouldn't beat you down. His shirts were always ironed. He never seemed to sweat.

We'd spy him through the window of the Odessa diner. Eating alone. Always Odessa. Always alone. Lenny'd see him there and a kind of joy would take over his body. We'd go flouncing in to pester the guy. The cop. The sergeant or captain or whatever he was. Lenny'd drape himself over the booth and tap him on one shoulder, come up on the other. Whoop—made ya look! He'd grab the cop's cap, twirl it in his fingertips, put it on his own head, put it on mine. He'd steal a pierogi off the guy's plate. Fucking with him. Laughing in his face.

And the guy, this cop, he'd just sit there and take it.

This one time, Lenny slipped over to the counter and ordered us a meal. Potato pancakes. Cherry cheese blintzes. "The pig's paying," he told the waitress. "Put it on his tab." Doing whatever he could to incite the guy. But this cop was unflappable. He just didn't care. "We'll take it to go," Lenny told the waitress.

And as we tumbled toward the door with our bag of food, Lenny patted the guy's shoulder and thanked him and, even through that shouty Brooklyn whine of his, he came off as genuine. Not a hint of a sneer.

That was Lenny. That's the way he was. But there was something else about his games with that cop. This sense that they were both in on the joke. Sometimes the cop seemed to struggle to keep himself from laughing. His mouth would be twitching, holding back a smile.

Then later the same day, Lenny'd be leading mobs through the streets, chanting "Fuck the pigs," chanting "The only good cop is a dead cop."

So . . . you know?

Lenny was always bringing home these metal contraptions, all screws and steel plates and tangled wires. Spitball boxes, he called them. Electronic devices jerry-rigged to communicate with the dial tone in beeps and blurts so you could save your quarter and beat the system while you talked on a pay phone. They did other things too, supposedly: transfer your long distance to Manny Hanny, scramble the circuits and override any taps that might be on the line.

He scored them from the phone freaks and most of them didn't work. They fell apart in your hands. Emitted squeals like knives slashing at your eardrums. Overheated and spontaneously combusted. He was crazy for them, though. They were going to take us, literally, off the grid.

Mom indulged him. She'd pound the flat of her hand on the box, willing it to work, cursing the thing, cursing Lenny, smashing at the thing until it cracked.

I remember her fielding calls through one of these spitballs, late in the game, during the last few months before the arrest. Always the same conversation no matter who she was talking to. "How the hell should I know where Lenny is. He's off somewhere with Walker. He could be dead for all I care."

Walker. Always Walker. I remember my mother's resentment of him more than I do the man himself.

Lenny in the living room, spread-eagle on the couch, jabbering at Sy, who was reclining on the throw pillows on the floor, casual in a pair of green short-shorts, his hairy dwarf legs stretched out in front of him, one ankle crossed over the other. Lenny was doing his intense, pissed-off number, chiding and sneering and accusing him of abandoning the cause just as they'd begun to win. Sy just fiddled with the mirrors sewn onto the pillows. Barely listening. No longer taking Lenny seriously. They'd been through this before.

"You won't even defend yourself," Lenny said, like this proved something.

"There's nothing to defend."

"Says the guy who just bought a house in Scarsdale." Lenny hunched over the coffee table as he talked, separating the seeds from a cluster of marijuana.

"I'll have you to dinner. You can tour the wine cellar and pick out any bottle you want."

"You got any Ripple down there?"

"Fuck no. I'll tell you what I do have, though. A walk-in humidor. You think this shit's good"—Sy motioned toward the pot on the table—"wait till you get a taste of the sweet mercy I've got warehoused down there. Bricks and bricks of it, wrapped in tinfoil. Compared to that, this here is skunk weed."

And like that, the tension between them evaporated and they were cracking up like it was old times.

I had no idea what was at stake, of course. To me Sy was the dude who used to wear a loincloth and now sometimes came around in suits and ties, boasting about all the cash he was raking in. He was the weirdly straight guy in Lenny's crowd.

What struck me that day was that Lenny treated him like an equal. He actually wanted Sy's approval. And he'd never fully receive it—I saw that too.

At dinner one night in a restaurant. It seemed fancy to me, but it probably wasn't. Fancier than a slice of pizza is what it was. A wooden-table, plates-that-could-break, real-silverware type of place.

I ate only pickles. My go-to dish. Breakfast, lunch and dinner, pickles were it and I was content 'cause this place had them and they'd brought me a whole bowl.

There was wine on the table. And crispy bread sticks. The place couldn't have been that fancy—the napkins were made out of paper. Expensive paper, hard to rip, but still paper.

We were there with other people. A man and a woman. They were serious—or I mean, they took themselves seriously. A strong-willed, iron-eyed black couple who understood power and were comfortable with it. They were the kind of people who, even if you didn't know who they were, you knew you *should* know who they were. They held their space with a kind of relaxed command, like they knew they wouldn't be pushed around. Even I could sense it and I was just a scrub who knew nothing about nothing. The man had a thick face, a few freckles on his cheeks, and massive eyes, wet and heavy. They projected compassion—what others might dismiss as dignity. But there was something else about him too. A tough-ness. A forbearance. Like he knew how harmless he appeared and he'd learned how to use this misperception with great ferocity. But he wasn't the real force in this couple. His wife, with her jangle of bracelets and her violet eye shadow and her skintight leather pants, did all the talking, and by talking I mean speechifying.

My mother was impressed with them. She leaned in almost half-way across the table to keep up with the conversation. She kept saying "Mmmm" and closing her eyes, like she was trying to dem-onstrate how much she savored their wisdom. She articulated her own points in a way that didn't sound like her at all. She was defer-ential and more eager than usual to prove how smart she was.

Lenny, for the first time I could remember, was out of it. Not groggy. Not stoned or tripping or hiding in the dark but cut out. Irrelevant. This was Suzy's stage—or the bracelet woman's. They paid as much attention to him as they did to me—zero. He was restless. He was bored. He kept staring at the woman's sweater, at her tits, like he was daring her to notice, like he wanted her to tell him off. She just kept on talking. Sometimes, when she made a particularly emphatic point, she clutched my mother's hand and squeezed. Lenny stole food off my mother's plate—a breadstick, a carrot, something—held it to his lips like a cigar and waggled it. No response, just a slow glance from the man with those eyes. He took a bite. Petulant. Put the uneaten portion back on the plate. A little later he ran his finger along the lip of his wineglass, trying to make it sing, but it wouldn't and he gave up. He was getting antsier and antsier. He started making jokes. One-liners. Irrelevant comments that nobody laughed at. He danced the wings of the chicken he'd ordered back and forth across the table, kicking the legs like deep-fried Rockettes. *I* laughed, at least.

"You like that, kid?" He did it again, glad somebody'd noticed but disappointed it was just me. He lobbed one of the wings onto my plate. "What's the matter with you?" he said. "Eat."

And then he turned back to the woman, studying her. Her afro. Her cheekbones. Her long, tapered fingers. He was playing with his napkin under the table. Folding it. Folding it. Folding it again. A tear here, a twist there. When he revealed it, the napkin had become a brassiere. He plopped it on the table between Mom and the woman.

Finally, attention. The woman stopped talking to examine his work. "Nice, Lenny," she said. "You should do children's parties."

She handed the bra to her husband and shifted in her chair to block out our side of the table.

The husband made a face and set the bra in front of Lenny, watching him like a teacher poised to catch a kid cheating on a test.

Lenny liked this. He arched one teasing eyebrow, tipped his head this way, tipped his head that way.

"Watch yourself, now," the man said.

"Always on my toes." Lenny snatched another napkin, dropped his forehead to the table and began working on it.

At this point, everybody had an eye on him, but it was subtle. The man had placed his hand lightly on his wife's neck, resting it there, reminding her that he was nearby. Mom hunkered down inside the conversation, willfully refusing to acknowledge Lenny. "It's all so interesting. Tell me more," she gushed. The woman did. There was a weaponized edge to her speech, like she was aiming it at Lenny—*don't fuck with me, boy.*

He came back with a new specimen of origami, twirling it between his fingers. An elliptical shape with an opening on one side, folds like petals shrouding a delicate gap. "An oyster," he said.

He flicked it like a paper football at the woman. Waited while she examined it. Finally he'd impressed her, but in the wrong way.

"Open it," he said.

When she did so, distastefully, she discovered something written inside. She handed the note to my mother and she read it too. Something seeped from her body. Her lips set tight. She locked eyes with the woman, then with Lenny, who snickered and said, "What?" Eyelids shut like in prayer, my mother waited for the heat to pass through her before handing the note back to the woman. The man read it too. They all had these looks on their faces, the kind Lenny had taught me to recognize as the pinched constipation of the oppressor.

"What's wrong?" he said. "You're not into free love? I thought you guys were radicals."

Everyone waited for what was next.

"Well, that was a success," my mother said finally.

The night was over. Even I knew it. Nobody, not even Lenny, was happy.

Later, walking home, my mother said, "Great job, Lenny. Really. Stellar."

Later still, Lenny swiped a pebble of concrete out of a shattered section of sidewalk and lobbed it at a street sign. "Fuck 'em if they can't take a joke," he said.

Neither of them said another word to the other for the rest of the night or for the next I-don't-know-how-many days.

I remember them after that in separate rooms, radiating contempt for each other.

Near the end, he was out more than he was home. He was vague on the details, smug, gloating over his secrets, barely there when he did show up, popping in for a clean shirt, to grab a book or some cash or to swipe my yogurt from the fridge. My mother never asked where he was going. She knew better than to tell him to be safe.

She'd nod goodbye with a jut of her chin and not even bother to watch him go. Then she'd stare at the door after he slammed it like she hoped she'd never see it open again.

Or she'd ignore him completely, just sit there in our dilapidated green armchair and pretend to focus on the feminist tracts and pop psychology she was into. Living her own life. Trying to, anyway. Working toward the personal transformation she hoped would maybe solve all her problems. Making it clear to him—though he wouldn't notice—that the new self-actualized woman she yearned to become would have no need for a raging, reeling fiend like him.

And the sense on some nights, after Lenny stalked out, that the walls of the apartment were incrementally collapsing, so slowly that nobody noticed but me. One day they'd fall in on us—me and my mother—and we'd be buried in the rubble, crippled and bleeding, our skin caked white with plasterboard powder. We'd never recover. We'd limp through the rest of our lives in a fugue state, somewhere this side of death but far from alive. I remember staring at those walls. Boring holes in them, marking their warps and angles against the floor, trying to pin down some sign of weakness there that I could show to my mother as proof that this pit needed to be fixed. She could solve the problem. I knew she could. If only she'd bar the door and lock Lenny in with us. 'Cause I understood what was happening. The walls weren't falling in for no reason. They were gravitating toward the empty space, the dark, vacant nothingness left by Lenny's absence.

Mom didn't seem to care. He's researching his book, is what she told me, as though that explained his rage, his furtiveness, his jitters, his being almost always anywhere but home.

This was before the shit at the Whitmore Hotel.

"Tonight it's just you and me," she'd say. Like that made it special. Like that made it different from any other night.

And behind her, the walls would buckle that little bit more.

.   .   .

I remember wandering west one day, cutting across the avenues, taking a diagonal path away from home. "Go get your ya-ya's out and leave me alone," Mom had said as she shuttled me to the door. I was angry at Lenny for being gone again. I was angry at her for letting him go. The fortress had been breached.

The world wasn't as free as Lenny and my mother made it out to be. Zones of relative freedom—of familiarity and intimacy—nestled inside each other. The apartment, where we could do whatever we wanted, lounge around naked gorging on ice cream, or—less fun—watching my mother trip and paw at phantoms in the air. The block, where we were known and tolerated, where people called our names when we went strutting by. The neighborhood, that span of blocks bound by 14th Street to the north, Houston to the south, Third Avenue, the river—inside this grid, you always knew where you were, what to expect around the next corner, how to play it, when to be cool and when to run. Each zone was contained within an invisible barricade, walls you passed through, if only psychologically, as you moved on to the next slightly less secure pasture.

Even at five, a kid could navigate the terrain alone.

I remember passing the landmarks I knew. St. Mark's Church. That square of sidewalk that had been painted to look like an all-seeing Masonic eye. La MaMa, where the theater freaks hung out, sometimes literally, swinging from the windowsills, singing experimental show tunes. The Catholic Workers building where, Lenny had told me, if I ever found myself in trouble, I could get a hot meal and a shower for free. And then I was at the edge of the known world. The Bowery, with its converging, dividing lanes of traffic. Its SROs. Its junkies and drunks, so different from ours, drabber, sadder, older.

Up the avenue, dropped in the middle of the street, stately Cooper Union. Who knew what was beyond it. I'd been to the other side lots of times, but never alone. I'd tagged along behind Lenny or my mother when they went to visit friends and collaborators. I'd marched up Broadway with the angry mob. But the material particulars of the landscape whisked by me, barely noticed, streaks of color and form, leaving me with just a sense of their weight, their

light, nothing more. They belonged to strangers. Different ken, not
to be trusted.

I crossed the street, expanding my territory. A conquest. Owner-
ship. A grabbing hold of a new swath of city. Showing my mother—
and Lenny too—that my New York wouldn't be defined by them.

Going nowhere, just away. I believed I was taking steps toward
myself. What did I know? Not a damn thing, that's what.

I headed up to Astor Place, walked up and down Broadway. I
spaced out for a while outside a church, watched a squirrel dig
through the leaves in an empty fountain. I meandered from street
to street, taking arbitrary turns based on the walk signals. Seeing
things now. The buildings were shorter, sturdier. There were fewer
shadows. People wasted less time here—expending their energy
on specific, measurable goals. They glittered like mirrors in the
sun, unfettered, confident in both their industry and their leisure.
Most of them. Around the edges, working the newspaper stands
and hawking baubles, power-spraying the sidewalk, lurking in
doorways and subway entrances, the unglamorous thick-tongued
hordes watched and waited, encroaching, threatening. I remember
wondering which tribe was mine, certain that Lenny would say
"Power to the people" but knowing, also, that we were separate
from these people, special, famous, more daring than them.

Eventually, it occurred to me that I had no idea where I was anymore. Behind a green gate, there was a quaint little alley, cobblestones and gaslights and ancient brick houses. A single strip of life
that the city had forgotten to carry into the twentieth century with
it. I wandered in and the gate clicked shut behind me. I'm positive
I heard it 'cause I wasn't sure I could get out again. The spookiest
part was that no one was here. Just me and the ivy, so distant from
the city, yet smack in its center.

For a while I dawdled, examining the slate stoops, flaked away
from centuries of use, running my hand over the iron horse heads
on the hitching posts. I tried to ignore the tug of worry over what
that click I'd heard might've meant. I was pretty sure I'd trapped
myself, and the more I tried to avoid thinking about this, the more
convinced I became that, absolutely, no question, I was trapped.

I fucked around with the lid of a rotting wooden box attached to one of the houses. A coal shed, maybe. Or a potato bin. I was guessing. I had no idea what it had ever been used for. I picked off some of the flakey powder-blue paint. Tapped with the toe of my sneaker at the soft spots rooted in the dirt. Swung the lid open and shut, open and shut until the hinge snapped in half.

Panic cut across me like a riptide. Not that I was going to get in trouble, more that I was going to be stuck in this alley forever. I curled into a ball and wrapped my arms around my head like a nuclear bomb was crashing down on me. Stayed like that for I don't know how long.

Past the echoing in my ears, I made out the sound of the gate creaking open. The click of the latch again. Shuffling feet.

It was Phil Ochs. He crouched next to me and placed a hand between my shoulder blades. Held it there, firm but gentle, until I calmed down. And without asking what had happened, why I was there, if I was scared, without asking any of the questions that might have exposed the brute childish truth of my predicament, he navigated me home.

When we reached my front stoop, Phil wouldn't come up. "I'm not w-welcome there anymore," he said.

He lingered like he was waiting for one more thing. He flicked his head to keep the hair from falling into his eyes and gave me a complicated, sort-of-sad smile. Then, like he'd just remembered why he was there, he reached into his pocket and pulled out a guitar pick. Kneeling in front of me, he held it out in an open palm.

"F-From the great Phil Ochs," he said, cutting the self-aggrandizement with a lopsided smirk. "You can tell people he was once your father's friend." Standing back up, he dipped his head and touched two fingers to his temple in a halfhearted salute, a familiar gesture, perfected through years of signing off with it from the stage. "I'll see you around," he said.

And with that he lumbered off, back the way we'd come.

And of course I remember Lenny's coke jags—it never occurred to him to hide them from me.

White powder dusted over album jackets. He liked to use the Dead for this. Him pushing it around with his old Brandeis ID, maneuvering it into finicky lines, cutting them in half to create even smaller ones, bringing a meticulous concentration to the task, rationing the stuff so it would last all night. He'd chatter at me between snorts. Labyrinthine monologues, rich with righteous zeal. He was still a fanatic, even by his lonesome. I couldn't follow him. Most of what he said was nonsense. What use does a five-year-old have for Marcuse? How did he think I was supposed to comprehend his intricate theories about Zionism and its corrosive effects on the Jewish character, say, or the race war that he envisioned erupting the day we finally elected a black president? Not that it mattered. He was talking to himself. Or rather, the coke was talking through him.

And where was my mother during these binges? I don't know. It seems, in my memory, that she'd ceded the apartment to Lenny at these times.

And when she was there? He'd flee with a pocket full of oranges.

I remember Ronnie came to our apartment once when Lenny wasn't around. He pounded on the door. "Lenny, man, it's Walker. I gotta talk to you."

My mother made me keep quiet. I held my breath. Pretended we weren't home until he stopped banging and went away.

Sometimes Lenny would come home with a bloody lip, a black eye. We never asked what happened. I wasn't allowed to, and Mom was sick of the burden of knowing, sick of the boasting and scheming and constant bullshitting. Sick, mostly, of him.

Every new hustle he got himself into took him further away from her.

I remember the fear that one of those times he'd be gone for good. And that Mom would be relieved. That whatever was taking him out into the world—his book, always his book, his running with the bikers, drug traffickers and bank robbers who'd populate his grand subversive opus and justify the dank adult urges he'd never learned how to say no to—was just an excuse, a way to rationalize walking out on us without having to cop to what he was doing.

The sense of unwantedness. Of being a burden.

Walker.

We ran into him once, Lenny and I, hanging out in Tompkins Square. Boosted up on the back of a bench. A cluster of six or eight dudes around him. Tough in a different way than the kind of people we spent our time with. Hard. Untempered by idealism. As he pulled himself away from them to talk to Lenny, there was nodding and whispering. Giving fives. Low and slow. Conspiratorial shit.

He knelt in front of me and made some token chat-with-the-kid small talk, and all I could think about was that every time he opened his mouth he managed to blow smoke in my face and why did he have to do that?

And then he took Lenny by the shoulder and led him off behind a tree so they could discuss whatever it was without me hearing.

That last night with mom. This is when my memories really start popping.

She liked to think she was psychic—two parts Carlos Castaneda hokum, three parts sensitive girl-child fantasy of a world where dragons and gnomes still roamed the kingdom. Auras and vibes, blessings, curses, she took these things seriously. She listened for whispers reaching through the darkness, teased meaning from rustlings at the edge of her hearing. Mostly it was just fun. A casual, playful way to dance around the cold prison of rational thought. A whimsical nod toward the sacred.

It was August, that night when it all went down, the 14th, a Tuesday. She sensed a bad mojo in the air: a smell, like rotting mushrooms, a phantom stirring in the beads that separated their bedroom from the rest of the apartment, a spot of chill hovering where it shouldn't have been cold, subtle signs embedded in the hidden fabric of the moment. She kept picking up the phone, not calling anyone, just listening. Checking the dial tone. Pressing the clear plastic cylinders that opened and shut the connection. Listening some more. Slamming the current spitball box against the countertop. Swearing and shouting at the federal agents she just knew were listening in on the line. Placing the arm back in its cradle and walking away and returning to check the dial tone again.

Eight, nine o'clock, she leapt into action. She had me by the wrist, pulling me barefoot down five flights of stairs. The nighttime was prime time on the Lower East Side. It was getting dark, so things were starting to hop. The sky streaked with color and the low summer light soaking into the brick façades, making everything look like it was glowing from the inside out. Transistor radios propped on every stoop, a turf war of tunes and textures. People hanging around—on milk crates and beach chairs and the hoods of cars, drinking beer out of brown paper bags. The streetlights were on and we dodged and wove around the freaks and stoners and the extended Puerto Rican families, the transvestites and punks and Ukrainian toughs, all making their parties right there on the street. We marched around the corner to Avenue A. Every door was flung open, a cacophony of restaurants and bars, their light flooding the sidewalk, a hundred different unrelated societies superimposed on the same strip of land. She rushed us to a dim, overstuffed storefront called Holy Ablutions and bought a bundle of sage. All this time, not saying a word to me. Dragging me like dead weight. Ignoring my alarm and confusion.

Back home, she threw all the windows open. She held the sage to a burner on the stove until it started smoking. Then she danced around the apartment chanting who knows what, speaking in tongues and waving the sage all over the place. She turned on the radio—Bob Fass—and we listened to him rap about the Rockefeller laws that were—and this is important—due to kick in at midnight, the structural injustice embedded within them, how they were one more front in the war this country was waging against the poor and powerless. Throw everyone in jail for victimless crimes, that's one way to ensure they don't rise up against you. She sat in the window listening to this, sipping peppermint tea late into the night and smoking dope to take the edge off until the street outside grew silent—the only life still stirring out there, a periodic siren, the addicts, the homeless, and the charity workers passing out PBJs.

What she'd been doing was sitting vigil. And just this once, her haphazard fidelity to superstition had happened to align with the ferocious goings-on outside her knowledge.

Later, she'd place great significance on this—what, coincidence? She sentimentalized it and swore she'd known without knowing that wherever Lenny was that night, whatever he was doing, she'd foreseen it and—but for her stupid pride, her arrogance and jealousy and resentment—should've been able to stop it.

Never mind that by then their marriage was a joke.

Never mind that when it came to Lenny, nobody could save him, especially not her.

So . . . the bust.

What can I say? Facts are facts: At 10:30 p.m. on August 14, 1973, Lenny entered the lobby of the Whitmore Hotel on the corner of 29th Street and Ninth Avenue. He was wearing a fake mustache and wire-frame glasses. He'd brilloed his hair and roughly parted it on the side. He carried an overstuffed bag of groceries from Gristedes, bananas and sliced bread sticking precariously out of the top. And lodged in the bottom, three pounds of cocaine wrapped in plastic and tinfoil. The desk clerk reported that he was sweating profusely, shifting the bag from arm to arm as he called up. He gave his name as Benny Schechter.

The power grid had been sputtering all summer, particularly on hot days, and Con Ed had implemented a schedule of brownouts to forestall a catastrophic failure. The elevators at the Whitmore were out that night, so Lenny took the stairs to the eleventh floor.

Waiting for him in room 1102 were two undercover New York City police officers—later identified as Thomas Keene and Frank Giordino. Giordino had been in contact with Lenny before, having presented himself, depending on who you believed, as a heavy from Bayside recklessly stepping out, hoping Lenny would provide a conduit to a new supply chain unknown to his bosses; a tweaker from Rockaway, squalid, stupid, looking to score; or a middleman for the IRA, PLO, RAF, ANC, PPK, take your pick, hoping to work with Lenny to establish a reliable street-level cash flow with which they could support their constant need for arms. Which cover Giordino had actually used would later become crucially important. Each implied a different motive on Lenny's part. What's incontrovertible is that the two of them had been introduced three months earlier, in early May, by an Afro-American man whose name was never revealed to the press.

When Lenny arrived in room 1102, he was manic. He wouldn't stop yapping about the room's shitty décor. The worn, discolored carpet, ominously stained in places. The bug-infested curtains. He took a backward leap of faith onto the bed. "Too soft, you couldn't even fuck on this thing." He fiddled with the Magic Fingers coin box attached to the headboard. "You guys got a quarter? I'm tense. Does this really work?" Then he reportedly said, "This place, it's too perfect. It's like somebody called central casting and ordered up one fleabag hotel! The seedier the better. Make it look like the only possible reason you'd rent a room is to carry out a half-cocked drug deal." He riffed about what they were about to do. "You guys go with the suitcase or the old duffel bag? The bag, am I right? 'Cause, look at this place!" Hopping around. Rubbing his greedy hands together. The sweat pouring off him like he'd burst a pipe.

Giordino and Keene thought he must have been high, which, of course he was. But it's not like he'd have acted differently clean. Anyone who knew even the least thing about Lenny understood that these antics constituted the basic core of his being. The thing that would have been odd was if he *hadn't* been both high and high-strung that night.

"Check you two out," he purportedly said. "You in costume? You sure? Am I supposed to ask if you're cops now? That's the game, right? That's how it works in the movies."

But he *didn't* ask if they were cops. Instead he rolled on with his rat-a-tat-tat. "*I'm* in costume. I always am. I'm not who I say I am. Who is, right? But seriously, Benny Schechter? You gotta be kidding."

The cops, by now, were losing their patience. Keene would later tell the *New York Post* that it took everything in his power not to slap Lenny upside the head, to say, "Give it a fucking rest, already. You're giving me a headache." He claimed never to have been involved in such a bizarre bust. "It's like the guy *was trying* to get caught," he said.

And maybe Lenny was. Or maybe his ego and insecurity were just too wild to tame.

"You don't recognize me?" he said. "Maybe I'm famous. What if I told you I was Lenny Snyder?"

It was then that the cops decided they had to act before Lenny's ineptitude blew the whole deal. They professed never to have heard of Lenny Snyder. Wouldn't know him from Adam. Which might've been true—two guys from the Catholic precincts of the outer boroughs, what did they care about the glamorhounds fetishizing poverty in the fantasyland that was Manhattan below 14th Street? It's not like Lenny's movement had threatened them. Their children were too young to know from dropping out. On the other hand, they were there in the room; they'd gone to great lengths to coax Lenny toward this particular juncture at which law and order might finally reveal that the great radical prophet of global revolution was and always had been nothing but a hustler, a two-bit criminal who'd finally overstepped his bounds. Is it really possible that they'd stumbled on him by accident? I think not—but, then, I've got a vested interest. I think they were hitting him where it hurt. Stripping away his last vestige of pride.

They asked to see the product. He asked to see the dough. A duffel bag—yes!—was hauled out from under the bed, thrust open to reveal thirty grand in marked bills.

Lenny unpacked his groceries, still at it with his manic jokes, wagging bananas like cigars in front of his face, popping a can of nuts open with a fake flinch like he thought snakes might leap out the top, placing each item primly on the dinged-up desk the hotel had retained from a better era. His hands shook as he lifted the coke from the bag, and when the crucial moment finally arrived he went dumb, tongue-tied for maybe the first time in his life.

Keene and Giordino could barely contain the urge to laugh. "Never would've guessed the guy would turn out to be such a pussy," Keene said later. And for what? When they proceeded to taste the product, the final step in this pantomime, it was shit. Baby laxative, baking soda. So stepped on that they wondered who was conning whom. It had to be considered. Maybe Lenny'd marked them for cops all along. Maybe this was a PR stunt, another piece of theater constructed to make the police look ridiculous.

Possible. But likely? Depends on who you ask.

In any case, it was too late to change the plan.

"We good?" Keene said.

"Sure are," Giordino responded.

And the second after the money touched Lenny's hands, the blues hiding in the bathroom, the closet, the hallway, sprang into the room, all guns drawn and leveled at Lenny's head.

He pissed his pants. The great Lenny Snyder. He fell to his knees, hands raised above his head, blathering nonsense about justice and fairness, and as their sights closed in on him, half step by half step, he lost all control of his muscles and bones. He slumped to the carpet, his fear secreting from every orifice. A pathetic specimen of a perp. Not even brave enough to face what he'd just done.

So said Thomas Keene and Frank Giordino. Lenny would dispute this in a hundred different ways, adjusting, refining, launching sarcastic challenges to the public record, often contradicting claims he himself had made.

Unlike the facts, the truth was mutable, dependent on hearsay and rumor—on each individual listener's willingness to believe this side or the other's coloring of events. Everyone involved had an interest in convincing the world that his version of the story was true. The cops had their own petty egos to protect. Their visions of commendation and raises and slaps on the back. Free rounds at Dempsey's. The wanton expressions on their wives' faces. All this because they'd pulled in a big fish, played the hero, protecting our way of life, faith and family and all that crap, the very essence of America, from the existential threat of Lenny Snyder. They were helped by the exhaustion of the populace, the desire among the hoi polloi for a simple, exculpatory explanation for everything that had gone wrong since the psychedelic '60s had slipped into the drab, oily puddle of the '70s. People wanted order. They wanted sense. Anything but the ruin and chaos that surrounded them. How helpful, then, if Lenny—chaos incarnate—turned out to have never been anything more than a dirty Jew, a fast-talking petty thief finally exposed to have built his whole career on the exploitation of their children's sweet, wishful dreams. Look! This man was no angel of light! He never intended to lead you back to Eden! This is who he is, who he's always been. A stooped, hook-nosed creature on the make for a big score.

This was the story told by all the papers and broadcast on all the nightly news programs. This is what was codified and pounded into the consciousness of our culture at the time.

Or, more kindly, if he wasn't a fraud, he was a cautionary tale. What happens to a person when the culture changes, abandoning him and all he holds dear? What becomes of the idealist in a cynical age? What pits of desperation will a man wallow in, what acts of self-destruction will he reach for as he tries to save himself? Without challenging the facts the cops claimed were true, you could argue that Lenny's was a tragic tale. He'd been a flawed messenger for the change he'd advocated. Too arrogant. Too out there. Too ready to confuse himself with his message. Is it any wonder, when the revolution finally didn't come, that he'd cracked just like his enemies always said he would, drowned himself in delusions and drug abuse? Yes, you could argue this, and some people did. Those same movement leaders he'd warred with throughout his career, those same politicians and bureaucrats, who'd shown from the start that they cared more about the system in which they thrived than the ideals they espoused, claimed Lenny's fall as proof that they'd been right all along.

Remember, though: He'd been writing a book. For a year and a half he'd been in and out of the hinterlands of Idaho and Northern California, hanging with the militant remains of communes in Texas and Minnesota, taking notes on how gangs of all sorts—from the Angels to the New Lords to the Innombrable to a myriad of lesser-known outlaw groups—were creating their own economies and codes of honor, using illegal, underground activity to carve out places of freedom far from the reach of the laws of America. Isn't it possible that he was trying, however amateurishly, to enter and understand his subject? That he got in too deep? That the forces that had been after him for years would use his haphazard attempt at gonzo journalism as a justification for taking him down? Isn't it possible that he was still a threat and the powers that be seized their chance to shut him up?

Everything depended on interpretation.

There were rumors later that he'd been running guns. That the coke was just a way to raise money for *la causa*. Rumors that the drugs hadn't belonged to him. That he'd had no idea what was in the grocery bag. A splatter-shot of rumors. Lenny spread half of them himself.

His favorite, the one he eventually worked into his myth, was that he'd wanted to orchestrate his own martyrdom. To bring down Nelson Rockefeller's odious new drug laws. What he'd say was that he'd *intended* to get arrested, to force an outrageous maximum sentence and spark a revolt among the chattering classes. 'Cause it was one thing for some poor black sucker to be put away for thirty years and an altogether different thing for them to do this to an icon of the culture. Who better for the task than Lenny Snyder?

Honestly? I don't know why he did what he did. I have my opinions, but they change all the time. Sometimes I wonder if he'd just been bored.

What I remember is seeing the photo that ran in all the papers the next day.

On every front page—and there were a lot of them, the *Times,* the *Post,* the *Daily News, Newsday, The Washington Post,* papers from Chicago, LA, San Francisco, Boston, even London—the same shot of Lenny, cuffed, haggard, drenched in sweat, looking like a porn king in a bad suit. He'd been arrested. He was in jail.

Big deal. It was his job to get himself arrested. His favorite sport, when sizing up a new audience, was to boast about all the ways he'd been busted. A good bust. A bad bust. A hard bust. A bullshit bust. That time the pigs laughed and refused to bust him. "It's not your turn, Lenny. You didn't do nothing wrong." Goosing him. Shrugging him off. Till he marched down to the precinct and grabbed a folding chair and smashed up the trophy case they kept in the lobby. "Now I've done something wrong. You gonna read me my rights, or what?"

This was different. But how? Not in form but in content. The photo on the cover of the tabloids told the tale. Lenny's stunts had lost their humor. Now *he* was the spectacle. No righteousness here. No confident defiance. He was stooped and tired. Not even resisting. His dress shirt soaked in flop sweat under a rumpled suit jacket, he hung like a rag from the hand of the pig still clamped to his bicep. And his eyes, avoiding the camera—they contained something new. Fear, yes. A blunt, stupid fear. But also shame.

He'd been cut down to size. He was just a man now.

I remember my mother on the phone in the other room while I stared at the photo. Talking to Lenny's lawyer, the legendary William Kunstler. Or talking's maybe the wrong way to put it. You didn't talk to Kunstler. You endured him. You sank under the weight of his monologues and said fine, sure, fine, whatever, when he finally got around to asking a question. He'd been calling all morning to relay new facts: the barrage of charges, where Lenny was being held, what time and where he was going to be arraigned. "They've been after him a long, long time," he told her. "They're not gonna let this one go."

And she said—and this might be where the fixation started—"Whatever this is, it's Ronnie Walker's fault."

I'd learn all this later. Right then I was heaving, clinging to the photo, vaguely aware of the muffled sounds of her cursing and spitting in the other room.

When she returned to the kitchen, my mother was dressed, playing it straight or as straight as she could. She'd thrown on a frock that ran halfway down her shins, one of those printed muumuus even women who weren't fat wore in those days, and sandals that wrapped right up to her knees. She was in a state, ruthlessly focused in the way she got when she was about to take to the streets.

"I'm off to the Tombs," she said, not to me. To the ceiling, the door. I'm not sure she even saw me.

And I remember, without her, the apartment grew very quiet.

Something welled up in me. A ballooning agitation. I flailed. A diarrhetic stream of kid terrors raced through me. Spasms. A child's mind in meltdown. Until, finally, I threw myself on the floor and sprawled there, quivering, entirely spent.

For I don't know how long I just lay there, pressing my forehead into the linoleum, thinking about that photo. The expression on Lenny's face. That horrifying shame. I still didn't understand what he'd done. Didn't want to. Didn't need to. It was too much just knowing he could be made so small. Him! Lenny Snyder! My terrifying father. The man who, more than the rest of them combined, had yanked the fedora off the country's head and exposed the scrambled, incoherent psyche hiding beneath it. That's what I'd been taught. That was who he'd been throughout the five and a half years of my life. Not this embarrassing sweaty schlemiel.

How? How, how, how, how could this have happened? Lenny'd had a gift for controlling the optics. For seeing every possible version of the story, the way these variations would play in the press, and how those reports, analyses and think pieces would be understood by the always-underestimated man on the street. He dealt in symbols. When they worked—and for a long time they did—his message stood like a beacon on the hill, casting its light over everything below. A burning dollar bill held up to the cameras. A chorus of children singing songs of peace, their shirts and faces slicked with blood and coal. There was always something out there in the world to justify his grandiose self-promotion. But that Lenny and the Lenny in this photo—they were incompatible human beings. Whatever kind of asshole Lenny might've been, he wasn't a man to be caught reeling, falling, pissing his pants.

I refused, I just refused to believe it was true. And if I lay there long enough, grinding my head into the grubby tile floor, maybe, just maybe, I could make it not true. Which is what I did. I could have laid there forever. It wasn't like anybody cared anyway.

All that was left to do was wait. And then, or so it seemed to me at the time, to die.

Instead, I fell asleep.

He was arraigned on charges of narcotics trafficking—a class-A felony—by a judge named Preston Eggleston, an unimaginative soldier for the status quo that Lenny and his scruffy pals had tried so hard to replace with, as Lenny liked to say, "the status quid." Eggleston, out of spite or because of the authoritarian's natural instinct to punish, set Lenny's bail at $100,000. A sum that made a statement. Street dealers, Hells Angels, serious pushers like those Lenny'd been researching for his book were getting slammed for five, ten grand, twenty at the most.

So the fix was in. Everybody knew it.

In Kunstler's calculation, this was a good thing. During the quick walk-and-talk he allowed my mother as they left the courthouse, he flashed confidence. "They're sitting there thinking, 'We got him good this time. No way we're going to let him go.' And the more they overplay their hand, the better this is going to be for Lenny. We've got precedent on our side. There's a clear path—not without risks, mind you—and we're going to follow it."

When my mother asked for details, he waved her off.

"Trust me. I have my ways." Pulling off toward the taxi stand, he called back to her, "You worry about making bail. I'll worry about the rest."

And worry she did. Because, even with Lenny's book deals and college tours, even with the big coke he'd supposedly been slinging, we didn't have anywhere near that kind of money.

In earlier times, when Lenny's arrests were freighted with political righteousness, there'd been systems in place, well-funded organizations willing to come to the aid of culture warriors. That was a different era. Now Lenny was on his own.

And bail bondsmen wouldn't deal in figures that high. Or they would, but not for Lenny, who'd warned his readers in *Burn It, Break It, Steal It* to stay away from them. "They're the seedy underbelly of the court system," he'd written. "Capitalism at its most usurious extreme. Get involved with them and you're dealing with a much more dangerous adversary than some two-bit sheriff with a huff in his puff. They'll break your legs, crush your bones and keep you in hock for the rest of your life. Would you get into bed with the Gambino crime family? Neither would I. So borrow some bread from your great-aunt Esther, instead, the one everybody hates. That way you won't get hurt and you won't feel guilty if you jump bail."

What Lenny wanted was for my mother to crawl home to her estranged mother in Long Island and beg for a slice of the fortune my grandfather had left behind. He'd died of a sudden heart attack in the pool at the Roslyn Country Club. In the thirty-two years since he'd fled Austria and come to this country, he'd worked up to senior VP and then president of Harman Kardon, the high-end electronics company, and he'd invested well. The dough was there somewhere, if she could just access it, which would've been easy if he were still alive—they'd adored each other—but the thought of approaching my grandmother paralyzed her.

Days passed as she agonized over what to do, ranting to anybody who'd listen—mostly me.

In the seven years since she dropped out of Mount Holyoke to join the revolution, she'd only seen the woman once—at the funeral.

"It was horrible. You don't even want to know," she told me, or herself, since I was just a mirror for her thoughts. "Horrible. Just horrible," she said again. "You weren't there. We left you with Judy"—whoever that was—"because it was enough trouble, given all that was going on, just to bring Lenny along."

And she proceeded to rattle off—not for the last time—every detail of the story she'd claimed was too horrible to tell: The service at the Jewish funeral home on Minneola Avenue, officiated by a rabbi they'd never met before. The glow boxes behind the podium, lit up to look like stained-glass windows. The small gathering of devoted friends and colleagues, all those men itchy under the ill-fitting yarmulkes they'd fished from the tray at the entrance to the chamber.

The homily, boilerplate: "We're here to mourn the passing of"—Rabbi Joe-Shmoe peering at the card on which he'd written down the names—"Arthur Morgenstern"—glancing at my grandmother to be sure he's got it right—"cherished husband of"—the card again—"Estelle, and father of"—one more time—"Susan." He went on far too long about the honorable man Arthur Morgenstern had been—"his love of skiing, his pride in his role as provider"—his voice growing thick, like he'd known this man or cared about this family, as if any of them had ever been members of his congregation.

Then the dedications from Arthur's brother, his boss, anyone else who'd asked to speak, except of course his loving, free-spirited daughter, who'd been forbidden by her mother from "making it all about her."

Restless, on guard, cynical about the virtue of hollow ceremonies, my mother and Lenny battled the urge to criticize the paltry good-enough-ness on display. Failing that, they glanced around the room, taking it in in all its cheesiness, counting all the faces they didn't recognize. One in particular. A man of a certain build. A certain stripe. Wearing a certain kind of flat, sturdy shoe. FBI. Overseeing the proceeding. Taking notes. Padding his dossier on Lenny, even here.

Then, later at the house, after Lenny skipped on home, his support not worth the tensions his presence would create: My mother and grandmother, separately mourning on either end of a long, low mid-century sofa. Legs crossed identically. Each refusing to look at the other. A stalemate broken, again and again, by the complaint and accusation Jews confuse with love. "You never call. You never visit." "Oh, *now* you want to hear from me." "I didn't say that. Think of your father." "I am, Ma. On today of all days, he's all I'm thinking of." "I didn't mean like that. I meant—oh, forget it." "I'll have you know, Ma, that we talked every week. Dad would call me from the office. He just knew better than to mention anything to you." Pulling back into their corners, for a time, until some new resentment thrust them forward again. "Did you have to bring that man?" "You mean Lenny? My husband?" "Oh, is there another?" "Shut it, Ma. Really. Don't start with me." "Susan—" "I mean it. Don't start." And again and again until the guests, proud to flout the kosher laws even at a shiva, began arriving with their shrimp bowls and rugelach and chicken hearts wrapped in bacon, and then the two of them were compelled to circulate through the house, accepting condolences, pretending to be gracious, keeping the coffee flowing while my grandmother searched for every opportunity she could find to take veiled swipes at her daughter. "This one ran off to change the world, like what we'd given her wasn't good enough, like the safety and opportunity this country's provided is something a person can just take for granted. How he worried! How many nights he paced the halls, unable to sleep, convinced she was locked up in some jail somewhere or worse. I'm not saying she killed him, but . . . He was too anxious. High blood pressure is what it was. The Morgenstern curse." Argument as a proxy for mourning.

And Mom whispering back, as she squeezed past her toward the kitchen to refill the tray of deviled eggs, "I didn't kill him. If anything, you did. You and your all-encompassing, overwhelming fear." Compulsively bringing in all the childhood experiences her mother never talked about: Saarbrücken, the Brownshirts, the never-healing wound. Taking it too far, like she always promised herself not to do before going ahead and doing it anyway.

The guilt and shame that sluiced through her after that. This was no way to honor the beloved dead. The kindest thing to do for her mother was to flee, so she did. Let her mother think the worst, which of course she did.

What was the use of asking for a favor now? What, realistically, were the odds of receiving any sympathy? If she couldn't forgive herself, she knew, her mother had no reason to do so either.

So she put it off and off. She visited Lenny as often as she could, left me home with the boob tube and a bag of chips. And she did what she could to avoid the topic. When he asked about the money—"your inheritance, it's owed you"—as he did each and every time, she'd mumble and pretend she hadn't heard him.

Meanwhile, the celebrity muckraker Ricardo Polente did a two-part exposé on Lenny's case, calling it the scandal of our time, which didn't mean much, since a journalist of his caliber would've happily devoted a prime-time special to proving that hangnails were the scandal of our time if he could've found the requisite footage to carry him through forty-two minutes of airtime.

He filled a whole hour with obfuscating details, details that cast doubt, details he could only have gotten from Kunstler. He noted the mysterious break-in six months earlier at the clubhouse-cum-office-cum-printing-press on Bleecker—everything rearranged, nothing stolen. "It's the kind of thing that just makes you wonder, how long had the FBI been surveilling Lenny and how legal was this sting operation? Isn't it possible that Lenny's not the drug kingpin he's been tarred as, but rather, another casualty in our government's ongoing persecution of the Left?" He hammered on the size of Lenny's bail, poked holes in the narrative the police and, up to that point, the press had built around the arrest, pointing out how lame the coke Lenny supposedly sold had been, less pure than the dust you'd find on the toilet tops in the bathrooms of most Manhattan dance clubs. "What he'd sold these guys was baby laxative, plain and simple. Mannitoil's. That's what it was. But the joke was on him. And why?"

He made his viewers wait until the next night to find out.

"Get it together," Lenny told my mother when she visited the Tombs to report in. "Call the old lady already. She owes you. Make her understand that."

In any other context, she would've hit back with everything she had. Instead, she kept calm and allowed just a touch of sarcasm to curl through her voice. "Easy for you to say. She's not your mother."

Never one to let a cheap shot pass him by, Lenny responded, "My mother's dead. Pops, too. What're you saying?"

"Forget it."

"Just ask her."

"I will," she said, but when she got home and tried, she could only stare at the phone and moan, "I can't do it. I can't. I just can't do it."

Polente used the second night's broadcast to gloss through Lenny's most celebrated stunts and replay old clips—the march on Washington, hippies flashing peace signs and twirling to the Dead, the flowers, the tie-dye, the trippy bubble letters falling into each other. Telling a story of harmony and hope that already played like the chorus to a song you've heard so often it tortures you in your sleep. "Oh, how the mighty fall. Oh, how ideals curdle," Polente said, as the images took their familiar turn toward darkness. Fire hoses aimed like battering rams in Birmingham. Cops pummeling youngsters in Chicago. The flash of a knife below the stage at Altamont. Charlie Manson's smiling face. Hendrix coaxing the flames from his guitar. "Are the sordid allegations against Lenny Snyder yet more evidence that the Age of Aquarius was and always had been a sham? Or do they forebode a new dark chapter in the history of our country, one in which our freedoms will be systematically trampled and any who dare to rebel will be sent to the gulag? The answer depends on your point of view. But one thing is indisputable. Whatever your feelings about Lenny Snyder, he surely deserves a fair hearing in a court of law, just as any other citizen of our great nation would receive. There shouldn't be one set of rules for him and another for you and me. Not in the America I know and love." His mock profundity leading him, as it always did, into a prim sanctimoniousness.

For a moment it seemed the scandal might turn. The tabloids buzzed for a day or two. The barflies argued. Seizing on this pressure, Kunstler got the bail cut in half.

And still my mother couldn't pick up the phone.

And Lenny remained locked up in the Tombs.

The time had come, she knew, to confess her failure. Let Lenny curse her out all he wanted. His abuse had nothing on the mindfuck of speaking to her mother. Once there, in the Tombs, seeing his hopeful face, though, she lost her nerve again. She was afraid for him, afraid of becoming yet another of his problems. She didn't have the heart to fight back right then. Like all the best ranters, she could mostly only summon her Sturm und Drang at a safe, cushioning distance from her tormentor.

"I talked to her," she said, leaning in toward the glass. "She told me we could go fuck ourselves." Not really a lie if the essence was true.

Lenny just smirked. All that anguish for nothing. "So we'll do this the hard way," he said. "Start a group. Get organized. You can call it the Lenny Snyder Defense fund. LSD for short."

Ha! He could still make himself laugh.

So she did what he asked.

She harnessed her will and, with Kunstler's help, called up a couple of the more visible movement figures—Leslie Ritchler and Preston Hammington, old-timers whose bitter memories of McCarthy would, she hoped, lead them to overlook, this once, their profound distrust of Lenny and his motives. She convinced them to take out a full-page ad in the *Times,* an open letter arguing that Lenny's arrest was an embodiment of the class warfare at the root of Rockefeller's new drug laws. What they drafted said everything Lenny would have hoped for: That he was a serious man committed to the people, to the cause of freedom; that these new laws were a manipulation of the American justice system meant specifically to target black folk and the youth; that Lenny's arrest under these laws and the outrageous size of his bail were a transparent attempt to make an example of a controversial public figure. A short, forceful statement of outraged support signed by 126 notable leftists: Noam Chomsky, Dr. Spock, the Brothers Berrigan, and Lenny's old mentor at Brandeis, Herbert Marcuse. Ginsberg signed it. Mailer. John and Yoko. Marlon Brando. A glittering list. Every loudmouth from here to the Hollywood Hills—except for Phil Ochs, who to his great distress hadn't been told the letter existed, and Sy, who'd given no explanation, traveling or something, my mother rationalized, unreachable.

Things seemed almost to be going well.

"You remember when everybody wore those buttons with the little fists on them?" she told me, explaining the logic of what she was doing. " 'Free Huey Newton'? Remember? We went to DC for that rally? Lenny gave a speech. Or John Sinclair? Remember 'Free John Sinclair'? No? It's a thing you can do. Applying public pressure. We'll have fun. It'll be like a crusade for justice. For Lenny. What do you think of that?"

Great, I thought. Yay. I imagined a parade.

She marched me around the corner to drop in on Marcus Kirsh, an old trickster and the irreverent publisher of the underground rag *The Conformist*, who'd had his rifts with Lenny like everybody else. It was ten in the morning. Kirsh had just dropped acid. "You want some?" he asked like he was offering tea.

"Sure," my mother said. "Why not."

He showed her what he had. "Wicked witches or golden tickets?" The witches were stamped with pointy green hats. The tickets had been dyed a bright canary yellow. She chose the ticket.

"That's what you need, isn't it, pard'ner?" he said, winking, his face open like it had never known fear, like the laughter never stopped under his skin. "The golden ticket. It's all that's gonna save Lenny now." He turned to me. "You want one?"

"He's good," she said. "Nobody does LSD anymore, Marcus."

"Right. It's all about the cocaine," he said darkly. "Thus . . ."

He pulled two mismatched chairs up snug together and seated my mother across from himself. Their knees touched. They couldn't escape each other's focus.

"Can we talk?" she asked.

"I already signed the letter."

"We need money."

He gave her the bug eye and laughed himself into a ball on the floor. Just when you thought he was gonna pull it together, he convulsed again. Three or four times, this happened.

My mother kept a straight face, serious, waiting. When he finally took his seat again she was back at it. "Will you help us?"

"With money? Look around." His apartment was the size of a rabbit hole, virtually empty except for the old and new copies of *The Conformist* warehoused along the floor, the cartoons and articles mocked up on the walls. "Wait till this acid kicks in. Then we'll talk."

They sat in silence, staring tediously at each other. My mother's expression held tight, somber.

Kirsh did some hoodoo-voodoo with his bony arms, twirling and chopping them in front of her face. "I can see the gray death creeping across your cheeks," he said. "The cannibals are massing outside the door." When he saw she wouldn't play, he said, "I wrote a piece. It'll run in the next issue. The hundred-odd people who still listen to me will read it. What else can I do?"

"A poster," my mother said.

Something sparked. "Free Lenny Snyder!" shouted Kirsh.

And Mom allowed herself a small, determined smile. "Precisely."

By that evening, Kirsh had designed and printed 250 posters in large-scale black and white. A mug shot of Lenny, not the pathetic one from this arrest but a sexy-crazy one of him in his heyday, a corona of wild hair framing his face. A black eye. A leering I-dare-you smirk. The dimple in his chin, the cut of his cheekbones, all reinforced in dark inky ink. He'd never looked more alluringly dangerous. Stamped across this image in blocky stencil: FRAMED. And below: FREE LENNY SNYDER.

We spent the night tumbling giggling through the streets. Or they did. I spent the night wheat-pasting. Kirsh's acid kept them spinning as I tugged them by the hand from wall to plywood wall, a daisy chain of freaks led by a barefoot child. It was no big thing. I'd done it before.

Each time my mother thought she was coming down, a new surge of fantasia cascaded into, over, around, and about her. The colors! The sounds! The world born anew! She and Kirsh kept forgetting what mission we were on. They buried their arms to the elbows in the glue and snickered at each other, "Oh, wow . . . It's like . . . I don't even know."

But we got it done. *I* got it done. By dawn every empty space south of 14th Street had been plastered over with Lenny's likeness. I navigated my mother and Kirsh through the morning fog, dragging our mops and pail home through the sunrise, and the three of us all collapsed on the futon. Exhausted and inspired by our achievement—really, *my* achievement and their giddy vision quest—we slept the day away.

It felt good, but nothing changed. Lenny was still locked up and within hours the posters were defaced with graffiti, messages from the new wave of nihilists taking over the hood. *Die Hippie Scum,* they said.

Mom pressed on.

People owed Lenny favors. Some she knew, some she didn't.

He'd been keeping a list, apparently, reciting it in his cell, memorizing and adding names to it each night. He rattled them off for her during the next visit, gave her notes on the right tactics for this or that person. A whole plan of action. Every detail mapped out. Just looking at it she could see it was more grandiose and wishful than practically useful. But hell, wasn't that his way? Didn't he have a long, successful record of making the impossible seem inevitable?

She met with various cells and contingents. Maoists. Anarchists. Black nationalists. Folks who'd excised themselves from the lives they'd once lived to hole up in farmhouses without running water, or various anonymous communal spaces where they criticized themselves in the name of purity. Trotskyites. Disciples of Che Guevara. Saul Alinsky. Ideological pedants and those opposed on principle to ideology. Extremists and incrementalists. The old left. The new left. The violent, the benign. All those proliferating factions that had burst out of the old coalitions. You have to understand, even when they'd been working together, these people had seethed with spite for each other, and particularly for Lenny, who along with Sy always gobbled up the press and never followed the script.

Of course, they had questions. They couldn't help themselves. Theory was realer to them than flesh and blood. And what better time than now to make Lenny pay for his logical inconsistency? 'Cause, really—no, really—who exactly was Lenny hoping to help? Besides himself?

They could go on and on, and would and did, pulling out all the tricks they'd learned in debate club, citing whichever sacrosanct notion that momentarily flitted through their minds, baiting my mother to respond so they could trip her up and score yet another Pyrrhic victory.

And Mom being Mom, she took the bait. Didn't he risk an awful lot defending your violent means to the press? He gave his royalties for *Burn It* away—remember? Well, you should! He gave them to you! He was there in Chicago during the Days of Rage getting bludgeoned right next to you. I know, I was there too. 'Cause Lenny and I *organized* that shit. We came up with the motherfucking name! Not that you ever gave us any credit. Without us it would've just been called Those Assholes Are Rioting Again. You're telling me he still needs to do more? You're telling me he hasn't proven himself to you over and over again already?

Yeah, but. Yeah, but. There was always a retort. Some esoteric quote from their pet theoretician to dismiss her charges and justify their refusal to help.

She'd come home from these appointments hopped up and indignant, all the things she should've said in the moment now bouncing in her brain like popcorn. Then she'd settle into a doobie and a pot of chamomile tea and, most crucially, total silence—the only way she knew how to recover. "Don't start with me, Fred. Mommy's head is exploding."

She reached out to his old comrades and hangers-on, folks who used to linger around the apartment worshipping at his feet and fetching him beer.

I remember we visited the Fag. Ray Garrett. It was an open secret that he'd been born to money. And he'd funded many an action in the past. Then one day in '69, he'd vanished, only showing up to preach from the stage when the crowd was massive enough to make it worth his while. We tracked him down in the West Village. He was as tall and graceful as I remembered, though he'd traded his flowing linens and beads for thigh-hugging bell-bottoms and a jersey shirt festooned with an iron-on rainbow.

It turned out he'd never been as amused by Lenny's pet name as he'd let on.

When my mother asked where he'd gone, what'd happened to him, he said, "I guess I found some other fags to hang around with." The bitterness lingered there, heavy on his tongue, throughout the rest of their conversation. He'd found better things to spend his money on. The Gay Liberation Front. A bookstore on Christopher Street that he and his new friends were in the process of opening. "I'm supporting fags like me," he said. "But I'm sure Lenny can find some kikes to bail him out this time."

"Come on," my mother said. "Lenny's always been a friend to the gays."

He smiled, quicksilver. "And what a night that was. Give him a big sloppy kiss for me."

One way or another, we reached out to and were shot down by

most all the various people who'd signed the *Times* letter. We got maybe fifty, a hundred bucks, chump change, I don't even know from who. Their logic was unshakable. By the standards to which they held themselves, they had an obligation to oppose injustice but a personal desire to see Lenny suffer. Everyone had some grudge or other that they'd been clutching tight for so long it had become a part of their soul. Those who didn't despise him resented him. They blamed him for their splattered ideals.

And the consensus—but of course!—was: guilty as sin.

We expanded our reach. We'd talk to anyone, whether we wanted to or not. Kunstler gave us names and we'd go knocking, and we'd call him again each night with a full report.

Why, you might ask, did my mother take orders from Kunstler? Why did a liberated woman like her, with years of experience mobilizing people, need to be micromanaged by Lenny's showboat lawyer? It didn't take a weatherman to know which way the wind blew, and maybe she already suspected, in her heart of hearts, that this time she'd bound herself to a genuinely lost cause.

I remember weeks and weeks of slogging around the tristate area, every day a scramble to the bus, the subway, the PATH and the Penn Central, sometimes followed by a brisk walk through the tall grass along the highway toward some Jersey suburb, some hilly Town-on-Hudson's cul-de-sacs of condos, the stately campus of this or that college where tired, aging leftists now taught at the very institutions they'd once protested against. We searched down every lead, but whether we chose to admit it to ourselves or not, we already knew they'd amount to nothing. The goodwill for Lenny Snyder had been all used up, and whatever moral authority he'd once held had disappeared like a line of coke up his nose.

And with every new disappointment, psyching ourselves up again became harder and harder to pull off. What had been advertised as a fun crusade to Free Lenny Snyder had turned into an exercise in humiliation.

And eventually, we just ran out of options.

Kunstler, of course, had decided the news should come from my mother.

"We struck out," she told Lenny over the phone. I listened, as I so often did in those days, at her feet.

"With everyone?" he said, his bark so abrasive that it cracked through the kitchen like he was right there.

"Basically, yeah."

"Even Mailer?"

"Mailer threw twenty bucks at me and claimed he's broke."

She let him digest this news.

When he spoke again, he said, "Fuck 'em. They're a bunch of cowards." He was silent for a moment, then he said, "You gotta talk to Sy. He's a lion. He'll come through."

And knowing how hard it must've been for Lenny to swallow his pride and make this request—as hard as it was for Mom to call her mother—we did as he asked. We trudged down to the Financial District. If I remember correctly, we even took a cab. It was one of those damp days when it's not really raining but it's not *not* raining either.

Sy had rented an office in the World Trade Center, which had just barely opened—not even fully. One tower had begun taking in tenants, the other still had contractors stalking its lower levels, checking the wiring, doing damage control.

As we walked up the staggered platforms leading to the plaza, each one as wide as a city bus, pinpricks of rain smacked against our cheeks and lodged in our hair like diamond chips. It took forever to get to the top, like climbing a mountain, and on the last rise, in the plaza between the two buildings, the wind gusted with such force you were sure it was going to blow you right back down. We stood there for a moment, like you had to on your first visit to the place, staring up at the sky, at the optical illusion of the towers seeming to bend on each side of us to meet up there somewhere beyond the clouds. It made my stomach swim. I felt like I was going to fall upward, into the chasm of air between those two monoliths.

My mother felt it too, but she wasn't as spellbound by the experience as I was. To her the buildings were a symptom of a larger sickness. And like leftists everywhere at that time, she was repulsed by the garish aesthetics of the place, so blunt—"there's no subtlety"—

and so arrogant. She and Lenny had discussed it a hundred times. They were like enormous tombstones erected by high finance over the graves of everything good and right in this city. Bye-bye, culture. Bye-bye, art. See ya later, alligator.

And now, here, faced with the physical mass of the buildings, seeing close up how truly immense they were, she couldn't help herself. She brandished both fists over her head and flipped each tower its own individual bird. "You've finally done it, Sy," she shouted into the wind. "You must think you're king of the fucking world."

Then she tugged me by an arm toward the revolving doors.

On the twenty-third or twenty-fourth floor—anyway, high up there—we found Sy behind a door festooned with the words HOLISTICS, INC., the name of the venture he'd left the cause to found. He was happy to see us, warm, eager to show us this new revolution his life had taken.

"Supplements," he said, sweeping his arm in front of the hundreds of bottles stacked on shelves that filled one entire wall. "Vitamin C. Iron. This one's"—he checked the label—"magnesium. Want one? Here, Freddy, catch!" And he lobbed the bottle into my chest.

He asked about how Lenny was holding up, and he leaned in, soft, intent, flush with compassion, as my mother told him.

"You know Lenny," she said. "He's a fighter. He keeps on keeping on."

Their joint history—that of Lenny and Sy—seemed to hang there between them. They'd been a symbiotic pair. Sy knew how to survive. How to sustain relationships and build something from nothing and sustain it. Lenny was a scam artist and a street fighter. Together, they'd made each other better. Sy could explain Lenny to the movement people, and Lenny knew how to goad Sy into the reckless mind-meld that churned out their best, most memorable accomplishments. They'd been bound by the ten thousand things they'd done together. The hours of brainstorming that often led nowhere. The nights with no sleep. The panic and frustration and intense despair that required such faith—such unqualified trust—that nothing about one remained hidden from the other. They each knew how the other took his coffee and what sandwich to order for him at the deli. They'd covered for each other's failings and experienced each other's sorrows and they knew the joy of watching each other soar, understanding that they'd still be earthbound if they'd tried to fly solo.

"We're on different paths now," Sy said, not without sadness.

I couldn't get over how doughy he looked. How well fed.

Mom and I both knew the moment had arrived. The only thing to do was to put it to him straight.

"He needs your help," she said. "We can't make bail." She locked eyes with him for a moment and then looked away. Ashamed? Maybe. But I couldn't say if it was of having to ask like this or because of the gross difference between our fate and his.

He took his time formulating a response. Folded his hands and plopped his arms on the desk. Breathed deeply and loudly, a deliberative sigh. Then he said, "Let me ask you. Would Lenny do the same for me?"

There, in that one searing moment, I really, truly, fully understood what my mother meant when she talked about her head exploding. The steam hissing from your brain. The fire burning in your eyes. The lava hanging on your tongue.

Sy just watched us.

He had some advice for me as we left. "Drink a lot of wheatgrass and think for yourself." He slipped me a copy of *Anthem* by Ayn Rand as Mom pushed me out the door. By the time we made it to the elevator bank, she'd peeled it from my hand and slammed it in a trash can.

And that was that.

"So he'll rot in there," my mother said as we descended. "Honestly? It's his own damn fault."

She took me down to visit Lenny one morning. Whose idea this was, I don't know. The Tombs in 1974 was no place for a child, no matter how much his father missed him.

Just three years earlier, the place had been like something out of a medieval nightmare. Overcrowded, with four, five, six inmates to each six-by-ten cell, floors pooled with raw sewage for days on end, shit streaked across the walls, even the ceiling in places, where inmates desperate to prove to themselves that they still existed, and lacking any other instrument with which to make their marks, had flung it or used it to finger-paint their names, their sexual organs, the crude shapely bodies of imagined goddesses, legs splayed to reveal cunts as big as their heads. It was never hosed down. Nothing ever washed away. Just years', decades', worth of accumulated filth. Bedbugs and lice and fleas, carpets of cockroaches, swarming in such large colonies that they ruled the place like gangs, boldly leaping from bunk to bunk, attacking in the dead of night, showing mercy to no one, black nationalists, white supremacists, Irish and Italian street thugs, Puerto Ricans and Dominicans and Triad kingpins—if you were in the Tombs, the bugs made you their punk, and quick. The only gang more dangerous than them was the guards, the COs, who would smack you down for smiling at them wrong, poke one eye out for breakfast and the other for lunch, knock the wind out of your lungs and, if you still had the strength to gasp, gag you on their batons until you went unconscious.

Guys were killing themselves to get out of there. Two weeks inside were worse than a lifetime in the fed. There'd been riots. Five COs had been held up with shivs fashioned from bedsprings—pig stickers they were called, and in this one instance they earned their name—taken hostage in the barricaded seventh floor and treated to some of their own medicine. The inevitable exposés started appearing, punny *New York Post* covers, *New York Times* editorials, and eventually the city caved and announced they'd shut down. Inmates were shipped to Rikers, to Attica, where a few months later they'd riot again.

By the time Lenny got there the place was like Auschwitz after the war but before liberation, emptied of nearly all its population, about to be abandoned but as gruesome as it had ever been for the couple hundred souls still trapped behind its walls.

And it was into this horror that my mother dragged me.

I remember us walking down from the Lower East Side, her chattering like mad, to me, to herself, it was hard to tell which. "Fucking Walker. Fucking Kunstler. Fucking Sy. Fucking Garrett. Fucking motherfucking fuckers. Some fucking community." She pulled me into traffic, heeding no lights, her hand cuffed around my wrist, yanking me along. I had to two-step to keep pace. Across Canal, delivery trucks inched up on top of us. "Hey! Asshole! You got eyes? You see the child with me? No? Fucking no? You gotta be kidding me." So focused on the anger seething inside her that when the city crashed in it was just more raw noise. "You were supposed to be smart, Lenny. That was the deal. You were supposed to make sure shit like this didn't happen." Definitely not talking to me. "So what's the play, Lenny? I'm out of ideas." Saying all the things she'd have to suppress later. She didn't always deal with pressure very well. Her anxiety had a way of spilling all over me, thrusting me forward, aloft, like I was caught in the turbulence of a wave.

And then there we were, outside the prison. An art deco box, but without the graceful curves, stripped of everything but the spikes and angles so you felt pinched by its constricting geometry. Its grand entrance was for upstanding people, not us. We had to circle around to the side and find the hole outside of which visitors were made to wait in shame.

When our turn came, before she wrestled open the levered door, she knelt on the sidewalk in front of me, braced my hips and said, "This is going to be . . . educational, Fred. Lenny needs to see that you're brave. That you still believe in him. Remember that. The bonds of love are stronger than any prison."

A nice sentiment. She must have read it in some book.

Inside, the walls looked like they weighed a million pounds. Walking down the hallway, you could feel them swallowing you up. Even the waxy lead paint they used seemed heavy, like it was pulling the whole of the building down.

We were accosted by an endless string of guards. One to sign us in, another to escort us through reception, a third to buzz us into the air lock, a fourth and fifth to pat us down and root through my mother's fringed bag. Then at the second door, another to lead us through the maze of corridors to the room that housed the visiting berths. And each of these guards, no matter his shape or size, gave off the same aura, like something rancid, something toxic, was oozing out of him. I'd noticed this in low doses in cops before, but never encountered it in such concentration. Scorn. Loathing. Utter revulsion. For my mother, for me, for any and everyone who wasn't them.

An education. Well, here was the first lesson.

For six years I'd been surrounded by Lenny and his carnival of malcontents, soaking up their opposition to power. I'd experienced their theatrics as a kind of pageant, a story they told the world to entertain themselves. They compared arrests like baseball cards, comic books, things they competed for and collected. They were cool. They were hip. They were at one with their times. The big police riots were long in the past and whatever moral seriousness still lurked in them, whatever sacrifices and risks they'd taken, seemed hypothetical, unrelated to their lives. Even the episode with me and that tree—it was a joke, an anecdote to be trotted out at parties. There was rarely a sense that the danger had been real, just occasional glimmers, encounters with people whose eyes told of hard secrets, stories about certain legendary actions when the air changed and a depth charge of terror plunged through everyone's gut, but even then—the way they told it—they always won.

Not so in the Tombs. There was no winning here. No escape. No joy. No glory in revolt.

As we were shunted deeper into this fortress, the mechanisms of control grew more pronounced. The place was designed to disorient you, hallways turning and doubling back on themselves, rooms with too many doors to keep track of, the same floor-to-ceiling tiles on the walls, all painted the same pissy prison-yellow. Noise assaulted you from every direction. First the clang of reinforced steel doors. Then what sounded like sledgehammers pounding on iron pipes, an almost musical rhythm except for how it skipped every time you caught the beat. More. Scraping sounds. Screeching sounds. Yowling sounds. Echoes. The rattle of steam heat bucking through faulty pipes.

We went through one last door and were handed off to yet another guard. These guys, they all blurred together. Bulky white dudes in uniforms that made them look like blobs, their faces hardened with the pinched menace of stupidity.

This specimen consulted his clipboard and barked us toward one of the booths lined up like door-less toilet stalls on the other side of the room. "Snyder," he shouted.

And Lenny's cracking voice beckoned us forward, warbling "So Lonesome I Could Cry." Was it campy? Yes it was.

We couldn't see him. In my memory, he's not seated behind glass but walled up behind a solid steel panel, painted that same yellow and fitted with a slot—like a mail slot—that was sealed up with bulletproof plastic.

He launched into a new verse—"Did you ever see a robin weep, when the leaves begin to die"—and my mother nudged me half step by half step toward his stall.

"Kid, is that you?"

The tin bench built into the wall had lost half its screws. It hung there uselessly, unable to take even my minuscule weight. I shifted on my feet, not knowing what to do.

"It's him," my mother said.

Simply being there—us on this side, him on the other—communicated the whole message. I studied the graffiti scrawled and scraped all around me. So many illegible names. Such deep gouges.

"Listen. Kid," Lenny said. "You bring the cupcake?"

"What?"

"The cupcake."

I glanced at my mother but she was no help.

"Remember? We discussed this."

"He doesn't know what you're talking about, Lenny."

"Sure he does. The cupcake. Remember, kid? You promised to bake me a cupcake."

"I did? Uh . . . I don't know how to bake."

"Sure you do. You go to the store. You buy a box of mix. You read the directions. The cupcake's crucial, kid. You don't remember any of this? Next time bring the cupcake. Lemon crème's my favorite. And add that something-special to it just for me. That something I might not be able to get here on the inside."

"He's joking," my mother said.

I didn't get it.

She went on. "He's joking and these assholes are listening—you know they are, Lenny. They're just looking for an excuse."

"Hey, kid. Come here."

I stood on my tiptoes to try and look through the slit. Behind the scribbles etched into the plastic, one eye peered out at me.

"Don't listen to her. She's just jealous."

"Lenny, cut it," my mother said. "I'm serious. We don't have time for this."

"I've got all the time in the world, baby."

"He's showing off for you." She leaned back against the stall and bit at her lips in exasperation. Given how wound up she'd been all day, I doubt anything Lenny might have done would've pleased her.

Still, somebody had to say something, so I tried. "What's the joke?"

"The joke, Fred, is that you bake a file into a cake," said my mother, "and you deliver the cake to the person in jail, and after they eat the cake they can use the file to saw through the bars and break themselves out. It's a cliché and it's not very funny. And"—

she turned toward the steel plate—"you're not fucking Cool Hand Luke."

"I'm trying to talk to my boy," Lenny said, a new tone, almost a plea, tugging at his voice.

"Fine."

"So let us talk."

But she wouldn't. Not yet. She'd spent too much for too little reward. "You want to know how it's going out here?" she asked, flat and sarcastic.

"I already know," he said softly. "I talked to Kunstler."

If she'd expected this, she didn't let on.

"Hey, kid," Lenny said, bouncing back. He dipped his head around, ducking here and there, trying to make me out through the distressed plastic. "You know what they did? You're not gonna believe it. Can you see me?"

"Sort of." All I saw were shadows, color shifting behind the scrim.

"They cut my hair. Shaved it right off. Crazy, huh? It looks pretty good, though. I think I kind of like it."

"Why'd they do that?"

"You really want to know? It's . . . well, it's kind of heavy."

Before he could go on to describe how the COs had pulled him from his cell, bucking and squirming, a guard on each leg, his arms locked behind his back—and the suddenness of it all, the way their violence had erupted out of nowhere, the poodle-shears scraping crudely across his scalp, catching sometimes in his tangle of curls, yanking it out by the roots—my mother cut in. "Lenny—"

"What?" he snapped.

The viciousness that passed between them in that instant. It said more about the bonds of love than either of them would ever have admitted.

She let him sit without an answer for a long minute before saying, "We have to go."

Something like panic roiled on the other side of the steel plate.

"Wait. Kid. Freedom. One more thing. I gotta tell you." He was scrambling. Revving himself up. "This place is a joke. It's all a fucking joke. And I'm not the guy they're trying to turn me into. I'm this guy. I'm Lenny fucking Snyder. Don't forget it. Whatever they do to me. Whatever they do to *you*. I'm Lenny Snyder and you're my son. And Freedom is a state of mind."

A lesson there, too. But I was, at the time, entirely unequipped to comprehend it.

So anyway, that's where we were.

By now Lenny'd been locked up for months and the trial was still more than half a year away. LSD consisted pretty exclusively of Kunstler and my mother and, for what it was worth, me. There was nothing doing. We'd pretty much given up. And out of nowhere we got a call from Bob Fass at the leftist radio station WBAI. He hadn't forgotten Lenny's many appearances on his show to announce this or that public rally, free concert, mobile soup kitchen or spontaneous protest at x-y-z time in such and such a place, all those instances when Lenny had called in from pay phones in the middle of the chaos to describe what he was seeing and provide essential details—where exactly the cops had assembled, how many people they'd beaten and hauled away, which streets were still open to intrepid listeners who might want to venture out to the barricades. Don't forget your bottle of water. They've got the tear gas flowing.

"Lenny's a compatriot," he told my mother. "We need him. How 'bout you come up to the studio and make a pitch."

He'd read Kirsh's screed in *The Conformist*, which turned out to have framed Lenny's incarceration in a sweeping argument for the legalization of everything from pot to angel dust to bennies to H, since losing your mind was the only sane response to an insane world. And though Fass couldn't get past his skepticism as to how this might lead to a better, more equitable and accountable system of government, his feeling was, hey, everybody makes a mistake now and then.

"What matters is that Lenny's an important voice," he said. "And now that so few voices are left, it's crucial we get him back. Don't know why I didn't think to do this earlier—well, I do know. But that was *my* mistake. We'll rectify that."

The thing to do was to pick up on the insinuations Ricardo Polente had thrown around on his televised exposé. But minus the leer. To appeal to people's sympathy, not their lust for scandal. And the path toward sympathy, Fass and my mother agreed, led through me.

They knew I could do it. Lenny had dragged me up to 'BAI to be interviewed by Fass once before. A stunt. I'd be the voice of the *new* youth generation. Four years old. Not a hippie but a bippie—coming to you live from the papoose. He'd asked me intricate, serious questions. Did I believe violence was a rational response to the irrational policies of the US government? In light of what the Pentagon Papers had revealed about the depths of mendacity and subterfuge in the Defense Department, should a criminal investigation be launched and, if so, who should head it? Did I stand with Shirley Chisholm on the ERA? And I chirped out my answers. All very cute. Nobody comes between me and my mom's boob. As for the Pentagon Papers, what was there to say except that even a child could've seen it coming. Never trust anybody over six.

At the end of the session, Fass asked, "What do you want to be when you grow up?"

"Free!" I said. I'd been heavily prepped for all these questions. "But what does it matter? If we don't unilaterally pull out of this unjust and illegal war in Vietnam, I won't even have a *chance* to grow up."

Apparently, I killed. Who knows.

All I remember is the hot light over the table, the mic suspended in its cage like a leg in traction, the massive plate-glass window that took up one whole wall.

The idea was that we'd repeat this performance, but instead of being interviewed, I'd just tell my story, like a tiny professor bringing the news, the secret history, to the masses waiting out there to have their minds blown.

It was supposed to be fun. That's what my mother kept saying. "You like telling stories, and God knows you're a ham. Pretend you're talking to me. You'll be fine. I promise. It's no big deal."

But it was a big deal. She spent days writing and rewriting the script. Anguishing over it. Squeezing her eyes shut and chewing her pen. She'd started smoking again. Mores. Filling mason jars all over the apartment with those thin brown butts.

I asked her, why couldn't I just say I missed Lenny and talk about all the stuff he'd done and whatever? Just be myself?

"That's exactly what you're gonna do," she said. "But you have to do it effectively. That's why we have a script. So people actually want to give us money. Like I said, no big deal."

And the less of a big deal she tried to make it, the bigger the pressure on me became. We'd rehearsed and rehearsed, me stumbling over the words I didn't know, working them out phonetically.

Would you believe this was how I learned to read?

At night, I'd sit there in the dark, listening to cop cars whine through the neighborhood and I'd play out fantasies of all the ways I could fuck up and instead of saving Lenny, condemn him to an eternity of . . . what? Piercing cold and darkness and sinister strangers. Somewhere along the line he and my mother had made the mistake of letting me watch *Nosferatu* on *The Late Show*. The creature, that gargoyle with its long eerie fingers and its taste for blood mixed in my mind with the junkies who'd taken over the hood. I saw them crouched in the shadows, watching Lenny, not me, waiting for the right moment to stab their needles into his neck. He'd be in howling pain. On his back. Naked. And they'd be shaving his head again. It would be my fault. Every time. Whatever scenario spooled through my mind, it always ended up being all my fault.

I was getting headaches. Boxing matches were being fought in my stomach.

By the night of our appearance, I'd wound myself up so tight I could hardly look at my mother without hyperventilating. I was ticky. Twitchy.

She must've noticed, but her response was to deny my fear and drive me harder toward our objective. "Remember. No big deal. Just do what we practiced. It's in your genes. You just have to channel Lenny."

In the cab to the station, she kept touching me—my hands, my shoulders, my hair, my cheeks—saying, "Breathe. The key is to breathe. Because remember what happened this afternoon? When you started rushing? And losing your place? That's what happens when you don't breathe." A pat on my knee. A deep inhalation to show me how it was done. "I'm not saying you should worry about it. Just be aware. You'll do great. I promise. You're going to be fantastic." A squeeze of my arm. "Just remember to breathe." A pause. She squeezed my fingers so hard they cracked. "Okay?"

We got to the station and Fass was easy, level. He looked like he should've been working for Boeing. Heavy black glasses. Short blond hair, parted on the side. But he had the kindly bedside manner of a TV priest.

"How's our boy?" he said, killing time in an industrial hallway that doubled as the station's greenroom while we waited to go on the air.

Before I could answer, he crouched to my level, a hand on each knee, and rolled out an anecdote about a bizarre experience he'd had, "a few days ago," while sharing a meal with some friends. "Just as we cut into our chicken française, a mouse came racing up the length of the restaurant, right there in the aisle between the tables. When it got to the door to the kitchen it froze, confused, its little head poking back and forth like it couldn't decide which direction to go. Just for a second, but long enough for everybody to notice it was there. Then it turned around and scurried back the way it had come. And then the oddest thing happened."

He went on to describe how instead of leaping on their chairs in alarm the patrons calmly worked with the waiters to coax the rodent into a box that the owner, a sweet guy, then carried out to the street where, surrounded by the waiters and kitchen staff, as well as all the people whose meals had been interrupted, he set the box gently along the curb and let the mouse poke its way to freedom.

"Everyone applauded. And when it disappeared into the sewer grate, we all went back inside and finished eating. It was remarkable." He shook his head with something like awe. "It's enough to give you hope for humanity."

He must have told this story a hundred times before. He had all the beats and inflections down, like he knew exactly how each moment would land. It was his go-to warm-up to put his guests at ease. And it worked.

"Are you sure it was a mouse?" I asked.

"You're right." He chuckled. "It might've been a very small, adorable rat."

By midnight, when Fass's show started, I'd forgotten all about being nervous. Whatever happened in there, I knew, this man would cradle me through it.

The three of us made our way into the booth and adjusted our mics. Fass fiddled with the levels on the soundboard. And just as we were about to go live, my mother started touching me again, rubbing my back, ostensibly to calm me down, but actually transferring her anxious energy into me.

"Breathe," she whispered. "Don't forget."

But it was hard to breathe. The booth was tight, barely room for the chairs in among all the equipment. And before I could find my equilibrium, Fass had done his intro and given me my cue. The red on-air light mounted above the door glared down on me, and in the silence of that moment, I realized suddenly that this was real, this was now, and I was in no way up to the task.

"Freddy," my mother said, "it's okay. Go ahead."

I had to say something, so I said, "Uh . . . hi."

The thing to do was to dive in, like at a swimming pool. I burrowed into the script.

"I don't . . . I don't want to talk about Lenny today. I want to talk about a guy named Geronimo. An Indian. Or I mean, a Native American. Let's call him an Apache, because that's really what he was. A Chiricahua Apache of the Bedonkohe band. A great warrior and freedom fighter."

My voice caught as I swallowed back the knowledge that these words were, in fact, absolutely about Lenny. Every time I looked up I could see my panicked face in the glass of the booth. I told myself, Ride the rails of the script, bounce along with it, don't let yourself fall off the track.

"Geronimo came from a little village in New Mexico. But it wasn't New Mexico then, it was just Mexico. In this village, people shared everything. The old wise men, the little children, the fathers, the mothers, the young scouts, everyone. They cooked big communal meals called potlatches, and afterward, they liked to sit in a circle around the fire, laughing and telling stories and playing games with sticks.

"These villages, they weren't like our cities and towns. The Apache, Geronimo's people, had a different relationship to the land on which their villages were built. They believed it was more powerful than they were, that they were only one little part of the wild, mysterious life of the land. They didn't try to own it. They didn't try to control it or manage it or make it do what they wanted it to do. Instead, they listened to it and responded to what they heard it say. Sometimes they moved their village from one place to another. They could do that because they lived in houses called teepees that were made of long poles covered with animal skin. The family could take its teepee down and pack it up whenever they wanted to—like when we put our clothes in a suitcase and take a trip, Geronimo and his people would carry their whole house with them. When they got to a new place, they'd unpack the teepees and build their village again. They wouldn't think about who might come and stay on the land where their last village had been because they'd never thought of the land as being theirs to begin with. Nothing was theirs. Nothing belonged to anybody—that's how they saw it. The great gift that was the world was too beautiful to keep all to themselves. They shared it, just like they shared their food and everything else—not just with each other, with the animals and the trees and the rivers and the wind. Everything was shared by everything else. The Earth was an endless continuum and they were just a small part of it, grateful be included.

"And think about it. Wouldn't life be better if we all thought that way? Isn't that how life's supposed to be? Geronimo thought so."

Mom nodded along with me, sometimes mouthing the words. And I guess she was charmed when I stumbled over the more difficult passages, 'cause for the first time in months there was no tension in her face. It flickered with light, with encouragement. I was doing okay. The power of the story had taken me over.

"One day, Geronimo and all the other men went away on a hunting expedition. They were gone six days, tracking deer and buffalo. Collecting prickly pears and stalks of aloe to use as sunscreen. And while they were away . . ."

Here's where things got tricky.

"The white man came and burned their village to the ground."

My mind began to wander off and affix itself to the parallels between Lenny and the story I was telling. I wasn't supposed to be thinking about this. I knew that. But I couldn't stop. So I told myself, Don't think! Don't think! And the more I did that—the more I thought about not thinking about Lenny—the harder it was for me to focus on Geronimo and the words I was supposed to be saying.

"When Geronimo and his hunters got home, he jumped off his horse and ran through the smoking ruins and called out for his family, but it was too late."

The fear, the horror, came racing through me.

"They'd been murdered. His mother. His wife. His little girls."

These people were us. Me. My mother.

"He fell to his knees and looked up at the sky, blind with sorrow and rage. Then he held out his arms, begging the world to explain what he'd done to be punished like this."

And I slipped. Reading the next sentence, I said, "When Lenny—"

The room shrank around me and I seized up. My mother's palm was suddenly glued to my shoulder. She pantomimed breathing.

"What happened next?" purred Fass. "You're doing a great job. We all want to know."

Stammering, struggling to find a way to press on, I said, "Geronimo, he . . . I mean . . . uh . . . and the white man . . ."

My mother's finger on the sheet of paper showed me where I was in the script.

"He opened his . . ."

Focus.

"He opened his mouth to howl and his soul flew out. His heart, all the goodness that had been in his life before this day, it rose from his chest like smoke and escaped into the air. A voice . . . a voice came to Geronimo. 'No gun will ever kill you,' it said. 'I will take the bullets from your enemies and I will guide your arrows.' He stood tall. He imagined a movement and gathered people around him and inspired them to believe that he could lead them. And he fought back. Just like—"

And this time the transference was in the script.

"—Lenny Snyder, my dad. Geronimo—and Lenny, too—did the thing you're not supposed to do. He refused to submit.

"In Geronimo's case, he and his band of warriors took to the hills. They ambushed stagecoaches and wagon trains. They fought off US Marshals and cavalrymen who had been sent to track them down. They held out for ten long years, living off lizards and rattlesnakes, hiding like coyotes among the desert's craggy boulders, clinging to the hope that one day they'd win and their people would be free.

"And . . ." I knew what was coming. I'd read the script a hundred times, preparing for this moment. But still, the pale bony fingers of Nosferatu came inching out of the dark places in my mind. The specters with their scabs and bruises and bleeding sores—all those deathly visions I'd imagined turning on Lenny, chewing him up—it all flooded over me.

"L-Lenny . . ." I stammered. "My dad . . ." My voice cracked.

Airtime moved at a different pace from real life. Slower. Every fraction of a second more pressurized. Tick. Tick. Tick. Time narrowing around me. And I wasn't ready for the effect of a live audience. Even unseen. Even theoretical. The idea alone of tens of thousands of people, a multitude of invisible witnesses, craning their necks toward the radio, waiting, wanting to hear what I would say next—I fell completely apart.

"And . . ."

Lenny's voice came down from on high. *Don't be a pussy. Politics is no place for the sentimental. You need a gut like iron. A heart made of fire. Never, never ever let them see you cry.*

"They . . . they took . . ." We were failing. I was failing. Just like I knew I would. "They . . . took him . . ."

And then I was sobbing. Snot bubbling from my nose with every word I pushed out.

"Just . . . 'cause . . . like . . . Ger . . . on . . . i . . . mo . . . and . . ."
I couldn't go on.

All I could do in that moment was look at my mother for for-giveness. What I got from her instead was horror. I'd let her down. Never mind that I was a child. I'd failed. And as the recognition of all this twisted through me, my body tightened and I couldn't find my breath, she must've seen me, how small I was, how desperate. 'Cause her horror shifted. It turned inward. And she broke and she—for the first time in I don't know how long—she was just a mom, all arms and protective, possessive love, reaching out to me, the tears coming to her eyes too.

In the midst of all this, Fass somehow kept the show going. He understood that it was better for the pitch to let us wallow. He slid the script from me and adjusted the mic. "They're having a moment, folks. What you're witnessing here is the human cost of our nation's draconian drug laws."

He let our sobs carry over the airwaves, milking our sorrow for all it was worth, until my mother was ready to disentangle herself from me and pick up where I'd left off. "Like Geronimo," she said, "Lenny Snyder has sacrificed everything to stand up to the powerful factions in this country and say No! No more slaughtering our chil-dren. No more worshipping at the bloody altar. No more oppress-ing your own people to make a quick buck.

"If you listen to this show, I don't have to tell you what he's done for the cause. You've been there battling by his side. You know what it means to say 'Power to the people.' And you know how selfless Lenny's been in the fight to make that slogan more than just words. You were there in Chicago. You were there at the Penta-gon. In Berkeley and Madison and Detroit. You were there in Ohio when your comrades fell. In Newark and Watts when your cities burned."

The strength pouring out of my mother buoyed me. I sniffled. Incrementally getting it together in gulps and shivers.

"What you might not know is how Lenny's suffered for his brav-ery. Like Geronimo before him, Lenny is treated like an enemy of the state. For years now, Lenny and I and little Freedom here have been living under siege. The FBI watches our every move. They come into our apartment when we're not home and put hidden microphones in the walls. They listen in on our phone calls. They get people to pretend to be our friends and report back on every little thing we do. That's what happens when you have the gall to stand up for what's right.

"And now he's in jail on trumped-up drug charges. He's accused of things that the Lenny Snyder you and I both know would never do in a million years. All because he refuses to shut up. They're afraid of him. They're afraid of you. Of us. They're afraid of what we can do if we all come together and raise our voices against them."

She looked to Fass, who took over for her. "He needs our help, folks. Right now, bail is set at—"

My mother leaned in and said, "Ten thousand dollars."

"That's a lot of dough for someone who's spent his life forsaking money. So please. We're making a plea right now, live from Radio Unnameable. If you care at all about the important work Lenny Snyder has done on your behalf, open your wallet. Contribute five or ten bucks, whatever you can afford. Let's get this great American patriot out on the street again."

He passed the mic back to my mother. "We'll take cash or checks, but if you write a check be sure you make it out to the Lenny Snyder Defense fund—LSD for short. Oh, and whatever you do, don't mail it. They confiscate our mail as well. Bring it to the Namaste Bookshop on 6th Street between First and Second. Ask for Ted Barrow. The password is 'Do you know the way to San Jose?'"

"Or you can bring it here to the 'BAI studios and I'll make sure it arrives in safe hands."

At the end of the segment, Fass slouched back in his seat and gave a little nod. "You did good," he said. "You made some money tonight."

When we stopped by the bookshop the next day, though, Barrow told us nothing had come in.

We went back morning, noon, and night. Barrow was always there. He lived in the back, in the cell of an office, just him and his turtle and his research on alternative forms of consciousness. He'd hear the wind chimes on the door tinkle as we entered and he'd shuffle out to meet us, leaving 90 percent of his mind behind.

"*Nada,*" he'd say, introspectively running his hand down his droopy, tongue-tickling mustache. "But not *todo por nada.*"

Two, three days of this. Back and forth, back and forth. We might as well have lived there, we made the trip so often.

And then one evening we popped in around closing time and Barrow was waiting for us up front.

"Well, look what the cat dragged in," he said. He unraveled the wire specs from around his ears and wiped them clean on the felt vest he wore every day. "*Todo con todo,*" he said, and with two fingers, he slid a fat manila envelope across the counter.

Inside, the full ten thousand in hundred-dollar bills and a note, hand-scrawled on a sheet of blue-lined paper.

Two words: *Sorry, Phil.*

"That fucking guy," Lenny said when he got out. "Probably thinks he did the world a good deed."

At home: his moods. His scabby buzz cut. The way he stalked the apartment, silent, radiating heat.

I was scared of him, scared of what he might do.

My mother tried a few times to sit him down, to get him to focus and work on a plan with her. She'd taken notes, procured documents, clipped all the press, done each and every thing Kunstler'd advised. She spread this information across the living room floor, a timeline, a map, a narrative of that night. What was missing was Lenny's version of events.

She called on him to help her make sense of it all. "If we're gonna win, we need to prepare ourselves."

He'd just stand there and stare at her, at all her diligent work, his eyes sunken and black, like he couldn't fathom why she'd think all this had anything to do with him, why she'd be so naïve as to believe she was helping.

He looked at me the same way. As if we were both too much for him. As if more than anything, he wanted to be released from the annoying, oppressive sight of our love.

He locked himself up in the cubby behind the kitchen, that same room he always disappeared into whenever his mood turned too heavy, the one where we threw empty boxes and random junk we didn't know what else to do with. He spent his days looking out into the air shaft, studying patterns in the snow and soot caked to the bricks of the building behind ours. Even that was too much light. He blacked out the window with greasepaint. Sat there on the floor. Or lay there. Sweating in the dry-steam heat of winter, braced for the moments when the chill outside broke through. Staring down the darkness. He didn't bathe. He didn't eat—a saltine here or there; that was about it.

My mother kept me away.

He called for her sometimes when he needed something. They'd whisper behind closed doors.

"He's working," she said when I tried to peek in on him.

"On what?"

"On what's next."

Which . . . in retrospect—maybe he was.

I've reached the age now where I can, I think, understand what he must've been thinking. Not that I forgive him, but I can understand.

An accounting was in order. At thirty-six, he was an old man. He couldn't comprehend the person he'd become.

He ached for those days, those years, not so long ago, when he'd open his mouth and the words that tumbled out came from some cosmic authority beyond his control. When just being himself had made him righteous. People'd see him on the street and say, That man is free. They saw him on television and their first thought was, Hey, dig it, what if I was like that, too?

And whenever the beast tried to chew him up, he just had to cackle and throw on a costume, commandeer a TV camera and tell people, Look! This beast's made of paper. It's a piñata. Grab a stick. We'll smack it. We'll break it all to hell. Then we can redistribute whatever falls out.

It hadn't just been him. It had been his friends too. Sy and Garrett and all the rest. Suzy, of course. Even Phil in his way—their minstrel, telling the tale.

And they'd done it. They'd bludgeoned that beast till it tore apart. Candy flew everywhere.

The nation looked like them now. The most popular character in the most popular comic strip in the country was a zonked-out pothead who talked to plants. Whole swaths of New York were perfumed with skunk weed. Even oil men and congressional aides were growing their hair shaggy over their ears, letting it touch past their collars. Suburban housewives were fucking their neighbors and their husbands were sometimes fucking each other, everyone getting together afterward to discuss the joys of an unconstrained eros. And look at all the people who'd wandered off to the forests of Northern California, the hills of upstate New York, the vast empty plains of Kansas and Nebraska, the rocky beaches of Hawaii and Mexico, erasing their footprints behind them, changing their names, declaring free zones no government could reach, in India, Denmark, Thailand, Costa Rica, embracing a grubby communion with each other. Buildings were being liberated all over New York, reclaimed by force of will from a city that had let them rot. And everyone was poor, so everyone was equal—or more equal than they'd been in a long, long time.

So where was the candy now? Or maybe the better question: Why was the candy still worth anything? Why was everyone hissing Gimme, gimme, gimme, gimme, gimme more candy? It's mine! It's all mine!! As though the goal all along had been to join the ranks of the powerful, not smash the power structure to smithereens.

Lenny, the consummate hustler, who'd scammed a whole nation into changing its dreams, had been hustled. The people'd abandoned him. It was inexplicable. Inconceivable.

And, look. Moles and agents provocateurs had squirmed their way into each and every leftist faction. Everyone and his sister hunkered down in this or that liberation front, each condemning the other for counterrevolutionary thought. The black nationalists refused to truck with whitey. Radical feminists and womyn's libbers castigated the movement and all it had achieved for being just another, groovier iteration of the same old patriarchal bullshit— smash it, they said. Even the vegans had grown militant. The trip went on and on and became very strange indeed.

Paranoia wafted through the streets like tear gas. With smoke in the air and the wind in their faces, the legions of the Left fragmented into a hundred warring tribes, all defining themselves down to a hundred competing, essentialist dogmas each of which had only one belief in common: that to be free you had to strap on a straightjacket. They didn't seem to understand that there was no way to reach for their precious candy if their arms were constricted inside that straightjacket. Who cares if they sewed the jacket themselves, they still weren't free now that they were strapped in.

Nobody could take a joke anymore.

Fuck 'em. Fuck 'em all, if that's what they wanted.

'Cause, what, really, was winning if it looked like this? It was just an illusion. An impossible pose. Another something to smash for the hell of it.

Which is why he'd made the trek to the Whitmore Hotel. To remind them what freedom—*real* freedom—looked like. Or that's how I sometimes think he justified it. He'd done it to show the world that he could.

And the world had come back and told him, no, he couldn't.

Winning might not be real, but losing had consequences. Whatever he really thought about candy, there'd be none in prison. In prison he'd die. He couldn't go there. Not like this. On a coke bust. He still had his honor. His name still stood for something, didn't it? Wasn't he still Lenny Snyder? The danger of building your identity around your enemies is that once they surrender, you lose track of who you are. The crazy inside you starts leaking out. Something perverse in him had wanted to get caught. *Needed* to get caught. Did that mean he'd won? Did it mean he'd lost? When had all this shame replaced his joy?

And here he'd get stuck again and cycle back to the beginning.

Until—at least the way I remember it—he strode out one morning singing Sinatra songs, peeled off the filthy underwear he'd been wearing and pulled himself into his best pair of cords, the short-sleeved shirt from an NYPD uniform he'd salvaged from some surplus store for one of his antics, his cowboy boots and hat, a whole get-up designed to convey that his strut was real and the time for self-doubt was over. Primping in the mirror. Blowing himself kisses.

We gaped at him. Alarmed. Relieved. Both.

Clapping his hands like he was trying to corral cats, he turned on us. "Anybody else want a hamburger?"

We said sure. We grabbed our parkas.

And sitting in a booth in some diner on Third Avenue, he chowed down and informed us, not pausing to swallow, that he'd made a decision. He was innocent. Morally innocent. Dig it: In this tattered new America, where it was all you could do to scrape up enough cash to cover your rent, maybe once in a while float the base payment on your overdue electricity bill before they turned off the lights, it was better to join the shadow economy than enslave yourself to the system of exploitation that was finally, thankfully, breaking down. Heating up his rhetoric, even just for us.

My mother glared at him, growing impatient. "So you're saying you're guilty."

"Naw."

"Coulda fooled me."

"I'm saying the law's at fault. Drugs should be legal."

"But they're not. You know? What's that they say? If wishes were fishes, we'd—"

"And I've got Kunstler."

She smirked. "Right. Okay. Let's go talk to Kunstler."

So that's what we did. We marched right up to his office, unannounced.

In all the months of trying to secure Lenny's bail, and all the previous instances in which Kunstler had shielded Lenny's right to play the fool, I'd never once been inside his office. We'd meet him on street corners or a bench in Union Square. Sometimes my mother and I rode the dark whining elevator up to drop something off or exchange information too sensitive for the phone. Even then we'd be there for maybe two minutes, quick drive-bys during which she and Kunstler closed themselves off behind his thick oak door, ditching me in the reception room with his bull of an assistant. He never had time for meetings. There were too many press conferences to hold.

Now there we were. Lenny and my mother and me. Kicking the slush from our boots and refusing to move until he dropped everything and gave us a hearing.

Well, that's what Lenny was doing. My mother was making helpless faces at Kunstler's assistant. And I, as usual, just stood there, dumb and nervous.

"You have no appointment," the assistant kept saying. She spoke with a raspy accent, like her tongue was made of sandpaper. "To see him you must make an appointment."

"We'll wait."

"So wait. He won't see you. You have no appointment."

"Tell him it's Lenny Snyder. He'll see me."

"You could be the prophet Elijah. With no appointment, he will not see you."

But nothing could harsh Lenny's buzz. He said something in Yiddish, something charming, I guess, and for a second it looked like she was about to laugh, but she caught herself and soured and said again, "You must make an appointment."

From the doorway behind us, Kunstler broke in. "No need for that, I've got the time now."

Who knows how long he'd been there, leaning against the doorframe. A tremendous shambling stork of a man. Kunstler was awesome in a way people aren't allowed to be anymore. He looked, even then, when it wasn't yet noon, like a tornado had just plopped him down where he stood, his greatcoat flapping, even in the stale air of his office, his tie loose around his neck, his long hairy fingers curled around a greasy brown paper bag, a hundred scraps of loose paper tumbling from his pockets, cocktail napkins, torn corners of envelopes, receipts and jagged strips ripped from yellow pads, each one containing a crucially important note to himself.

He tipped his head. "Come. Come-come-come." And he marched us past his assistant and her stink eye.

Inside, he nodded us toward some dilapidated chairs and plopped himself down behind a massive, distressed, old insurance desk. It looked like him—I mean, it had the same spirit. An avalanche of paper spilled over its surface, folders splayed everywhere, legal pads and streaked sheets of mimeograph paper. Stacks of briefs and memos were lined up on the floor, lodged on windowsills and guest chairs.

I guess they talked and I guess I listened, but I have no memory of what they said. What I remember is the ceremony of the occasion. How Lenny collected himself under his cowboy hat. How my mother ran her pinky along her heavy eyeliner.

I remember Kunstler pulling apart the croissant he'd been carrying in the bag, unwrapping it like a package and placing strands of the flakey bread on his tongue. Once it was gone, he reverted to flipping through his three poses: the listener, fingers teepeed under his nose, glasses clamped like a ten-year-old girl's hairband across the balding dome of his head; the exasperated parent, physically blown back by the degree to which his kids wouldn't listen; the expounder, when the glasses would come off, pinched between two fingers to be used alternately as a prod and a chew toy—one, two, three, bite, bite, bite, like an automaton.

They were debating—or Kunstler was debating himself. Running through scenarios. Parsing Lenny's chances. And I remember the sense of how big the stakes were. He was asking, I think now, which was more worth saving, the man or the myth.

He went on and on and Lenny actually listened, tense, perched like an insect against the boot he'd dug into the leather seat of his chair, leaping up sometimes, not very often, to interrupt, to pound on a point, to protest.

And my mother off to the side, her kohl-blackened eyes smoldering, sending up smoke signals the men ignored.

Me, I glumly pulled at loose threads in the beanie she'd shoved on my head as we left the house, picking it apart, destroying the fucking thing. That's what I remember. Being bored. Getting frustrated by the endless details. Struggling to follow them. Lost in their meaning.

I remember certain repeated words and their inflections. Entrapment. Criminal conspiracy. Prove it. Evidence. Bleecker Street. Wiretaps. COINTELPRO. Extralegal. COINTELPRO. NYPD. COINTELPRO. They're still at it. They say they're not, but they are. Prove it. Skepticism rising off of every one.

Even if the details were beyond me, I understood this conversation wasn't going anywhere near the way Lenny had promised. More and more, after popping to his feet, he'd take a couple steps, make like to speak, and then stop himself. Him! The great Lenny Snyder! With nothing to say! Suffering under Kunstler's stampede of logic and law, his mood slowly turned. And finally, he darkened and shut down, slipped lower and lower into his chair until, unable to sink any farther, he heaved himself up and began slipping all over again.

And I remember, at one point, my mother interjecting, finally having had enough, "What about Ronnie Walker? We should be talking about him."

Lenny's look then. The spinning wheels in his head. "Ye*ah*." A slow drawl. "What about Walker?"

And the others—my mother, Kunstler—waiting for him to answer his own question. It seemed so important, the key to the whole thing, and I know he went on, fierce and adamant, but I don't recall the substance of his response, just the look on his face, like he was chasing dragons.

Then Kunstler, exasperated, rubbing his eyes. "I'd advise you to cop a plea."

Something broke in the air—I couldn't say what, but everybody was angry and I was scared.

Lenny popped up again, enraged, and slammed his fists down on Kunstler's desk. "So fuck the facts. Like Suzy said, it wasn't my cocaine. I'm innocent."

"Are you?"

"Yeah. And morally, too."

And Kunstler teepeed his fingers under his nose and considered Lenny like he knew he'd never see him again. He rolled back in his chair and said, "I can only advise you about the law. What you choose to do against my advice is . . . well, I have no control over that, do I?"

Something passed between them, some meaning beyond words.

Lenny glanced at my mother to see if she understood. He shot me a glance too. "But also," he said, turning back to Kunstler, "you'll do everything in your power to keep me out of jail."

"Of course," said Kunstler.

And that seemed to be that. Kunstler high-stepped over his maze of paper and propped himself against the lip of his desk. Gnawing on the arm of his glasses, he studied me. "How's our little man?" he said.

I picked at my hat, trying to give him nothing.

"I've got news for you," he said. He dug in the pockets of his suit jacket, patting himself down until he finally found what he was looking for. A lollypop. He crouched over me like a kind of hipper, suaver Frankenstein and held it up between us—a green wafer of sugar on a teardrop-shaped stick, the type of sucker's gift you'd get from a dentist. It had been in his pocket a very long time. Lint clung to the wrinkled cellophane. The candy inside looked like it had freezer burn.

I must've made a face because he shoved it toward my chest. "It's all right, Freedom. Take it. It's for you."

But the more he insisted, the less I wanted the thing. 'Cause he wasn't just being friendly. This lollypop was some sort of booby prize, meant to distract me from whatever it was that had just happened. He was trying in his awkward, tone-deaf way to console me. He wanted the lollypop to mean more than it possibly could. And I remember feeling like if I accepted it something inside me, I didn't know what, would be made smaller in the transaction.

Lenny flashed alive. He slapped the lollypop out of Kunstler's hand and sent it ricocheting into the depths of the office. "Christ, Bill, leave the fucking kid alone. If he doesn't want it, he doesn't want it. Right, kid? You don't want it, right?"

I might have shaken my head. My "No" was barely more than a whisper.

One more thing about that day.

As we trudged home that icy afternoon, my mother folded her fingers around Lenny's arm and clung to him. Comforting. Protective. A sly, private smile flickered across her face. "I'm not gonna say I told you so," she said.

And he cackled, just like the Lenny of old. He pulled her close. "But you did tell me so," he said, bumping her with his hip.

And right then, in that instant, with both of them trying so hard to be happy, they seemed unfathomably sad.

Just so damn sad.

What's funny is, after that, everything got better.

Lenny, well . . . I remember his gaze. Intense as ever, but now leveled on me. Taking me in. Lapping me up, whatever I might do.

I liked to babble. Goofy nonsense from my head, fairy tales, tall tales, learned from the water-stained books my mother'd scored in the Astor Place thieves' market, and that in my telling flew into the absurd reaches of my imagination. I played air piano—'cause *everybody* played air guitar—especially to the Wings album that was in heavy rotation on our family turntable. I close-lipped my Kool-Aid for optimum mustache. Kid stuff. Inanity. Things I'd never stopped doing, even in the tense times, because it was like doing nothing at all. All of it was suddenly marvelous to him.

Like he was in love.

Like I was made of some magic he'd never encountered before.

We did things. Extensive, ever more complicated breath-holding competitions. Funny-face games. Egg creams at Gem Spa almost every day. Hot dogs from Papaya King, washed down with piña colada. Pulling the doors off the kitchen cabinets so we could cart them to the park and use them as sleds.

When we raced down the block, he always let me win.

Lenny and me. And my mother, too. The three of us. A unit.

Packing in all the stuff we'd never bothered to do before, those experiences you could take or leave, the tourist traps, the shit you took for granted 'cause you were busy actually living.

The Empire State Building. The Met. The New York Public Library. All those institutions of culture, where money went to mellow out and change its features, where power masqueraded as a shared heritage available to anyone who didn't question its intentions.

The Cloisters. Standing in front of the tapestries, him and my mother each resting a hand on my shoulder. Listening to their art talk. Check out the peasants trampled underfoot. Me rolling down the hill again and again while they lay in each other's arms sharing a joint.

The Staten Island Ferry—an inane trip to nowhere.

Or mucking through the slick and sludge to the Statue of Liberty. We paid our fare and climbed the steps up, up, up through the endless gray chute, and when I began whining that I couldn't go on, he sat next to my crumpled body and said, "You sure? We're almost there. Look. You can see the light." Which was true! Three, four landings up, the staircase opened and the prize, the view from the crown, shone in. But no. I was done. I didn't care anymore. "Whatever you want, kid," Lenny said. My mother, with a maniacal determination, teased us. "Men. Typical. Go ahead, puss out. But not me. No-ho. A woman finishes what she starts." And she clomped up the final few flights. While we waited for her to return, Lenny pulled out his Swiss Army knife. "Here, let's mark the spot." And we carved into the paint.

Freedom Was Here.
Nice Rack, Lady Liberty—Lenny Snyder.

I didn't go to school. I'd never gone to school.

Lenny and my mother had loudly advocated against what they called the get-'em-while-they're-young-and-get-'em-good system of American education. They'd given speeches. Attended rallies. Worked up a whole shtick, one part vaudeville, two parts dogma, that they performed, ad hoc, whenever they found themselves in front of a live camera. Lenny stabbing at my mother with an imaginary cattle prod. Zap: She'd jolt like she'd been electrocuted, make staticky sounds and bark out her lines. Zap: "American exceptionalism." Zap: "Manifest destiny." Zap: "One nation under God." Zap: "The only good commie is a dead commie." Zap: "Support the troops." Zap: "They're fighting for your freedom." Zap: "Support the government." Zap: "It's working for you." Zap: "Vote!" Zap: "Your vote matters." Zap: "Take part in the system." They could keep this up as long as the cameras allowed them to. "The patriarchy! Women, stand by your man! Respect your elders! Pull yourself up by your bootstraps! Strive! Strive! Strive! Buy! Buy! Buy! Fear! Fear! Fear! Obey! Obey! Obey!"

Mom launching into her husky alto: "My country tis of thee, sweet land of liberty, of thee I sing." Her hand mounted on her forehead in a slapstick salute.

No way were they gonna let me be brainwashed. They homeschooled me.

But they were too busy agitating for the new consciousness to bother with the hard work required to provide me with a counter education. So homeschooling meant that they let me run wild and pick up what I could on the sly. The school of life, not only without walls, but also without a curriculum. I learned my ABCs from *Sesame Street*. Learned to count from the corner boys. It's a wonder I leaned anything at all . . . well, that's not true. My mother spent hours guiding me through the workbooks she'd acquired, patiently showing me how to sound out words, organizing carrots into separate piles and nudging me to add four plus seven. Let us now praise mothers and all they do.

Lenny sometimes contributed too. Civics. History. Those were his beats. We'd sit with their massive flimsy atlas and pore over the page with all the flags at the back. "They're symbols, kid. Let's learn what they really mean. Great Britain: Overreach. Imperial power. Ireland: Resistance and Catholic guilt. Switzerland: That's where the money lives. South Africa: Illegitimate power. Zaire. Liberia: Self-determinism. The people rising up to take what's theirs. China: The birthplace of civilization. Riffing. Entertaining himself. Israel: Where Jews—your people!—go to prove they can be as thuggish as anyone else. The United States of America: A dream of liberty floating on a sea of blood." When he got bored, he'd wander off and leave me to muddle through these lessons alone. He didn't have the patience to whack all the weeds growing in my child's mind.

But still, I look back on those months after he got out of jail and I think Lenny really was trying to teach me something.

A crash course on him. So I'd know where I came from.

He sat me in his lap on the big mirrored throw pillows and read to me. *Howl. King Lear. The Wretched of the Earth.* Books that mattered to him. And though I could hardly follow a single word, they mattered to me too, in those moments.

"You wanna know how important you are?" he said. "This man, Allen Ginsberg, the most important writer in America, wrote a poem about you on the day you were born."

Which . . . that's not exactly true.

Ginsberg did write a poem—more a diary entry—on my birthday, but it was mostly about the washed morning light outside his window on 13th Street and the HATE sign that had been painted over the entrance to the Free Store after Groovy Hutchinson was murdered. The creeping malaise—the doldrums—that he'd been unable to shake that day no matter how many sutras he recited. I was mentioned once, obliquely. "And Susan on 7th Street still dreams of giving birth to Freedom."

Still . . . nice to have. Nice to see Lenny show such pride in me.

He took me to a Knicks game. "Don't believe what they tell you, kid. Baseball's all right. Football, sure, if you're cool with overt pageants of militarized aggression. But basketball's where it's at. Basketball's the true American sport. Invented by the Aztecs. No lie. It's truly indigenous. They've been playing this game right here on this land for five hundred years. It predates the white man. It'll outlast him, too. There's a reason the best players are all niggers and kikes."

From the cheap seats, you could hardly see the floor through all the smoke. I have no idea who they were playing that night, but it didn't matter. These were the '74 Knicks! Earl the Pearl! Dollar Bill Bradley! And most especially Clyde Frazier and Dave DeBusschere. Whoever they played, they were gonna slaughter them.

"Teamwork, baby," Lenny said. "They look like they're all just running around but they're not. They're finding their marks. They're setting picks and reading the defense. Reacting. Watch this. See how Clyde adjusts? How the rest of the team responds to his change of plan? It's like they've got one mind—one united consciousness— and their bodies are vehicles for its perfect expression."

He used to play, he said. This was news to me. Another discarded part of him that he now needed to retrieve. To hold. To hand over. He'd been a forward, like DeBusschere, first at Tilden High and then, because he was good but not disciplined enough to be really great, as a walk-on at Brandeis. Two years of that before, in one grand gesture, he threw both his career and the Brandeis season away, taking bets on his own team, running book-rackets out of his dorm room and, lo and behold, beating the spread, if not the other team, in each and every game. Didn't take long for rumors of what he was doing to trickle out of the mouths of his duped and embittered classmates. And though it wasn't provable—he kept the numbers in his head—the Judges judged him unworthy of standing by their side.

"Story of my life," he told me that night at the Garden. "Never met a system I didn't want to fuck. Watch Clyde, now—one, two, three around the horn to DeBusschere and . . . there. Soft off the backboard. Far out, hey?"

He showed me how to shoot. The fingertips loose on the leather, the impossible, awkward positioning of the elbow if you wanted to line up a straight shot. "Watch the basket, not the ball. And don't push it from the shoulder, use your elbow as a fulcrum, extend and release.

"Here, try it again."

All morning like this at the courts down by the river. I'd shoot an air ball and he'd chase it down, give it a dribble or two and then pass it back to me.

Again. Again. Again. And again.

I was hopeless. My eyes didn't focus like they should. But somehow he resisted calling me out. Kept the trash talk in check for once. Pretended—and this must've been excruciating for him—that with enough practice I'd amount to something.

Coney Island. All the way out on the F train. A chilly, misty day. The place was a ghost town. All the stalls shuttered. All the rides closed down. The only thing open was Nathan's, a bright fluorescent box in the rain, bustling at 10:00 a.m. with kids from the projects out on Surf Avenue. I remember wandering through an empty parking lot and spotting a dead, mangled animal. A dog? A raccoon? Some sort of possum? Its fur was peeled off in places, eaten away. Maggots squirmed on its soggy bloodless flesh. Lenny shielded my eyes. "No need to see that."

We meandered along the boardwalk and watched the raindrops pelt the sand, the gunmetal waves, so consistent, so small, washing over the shore. And I remember noticing that we had the same gait—tense, forward-leaning, hands shoved habitually in the front pockets of our jeans, making ourselves thinner to cut through the air—and thinking he never taught me this, it's just how we are, embedded in the genes, thinking that's some profound shit, but not sure why or how.

"I used to come down here. As a kid," he said. "We'd take the trolley down Flatbush. Wander over. Look for trouble." Just that. Nothing more. He left it to me to imagine the rest. Something I couldn't do. It didn't seem possible that he could have ever been a child.

And the concerts! How many concerts, I can't even count. Folk, blues, rock. Nothing glam—glam confused him. Ideologically he was all for it, but in practice he wondered where the humor was.

We saw Neil Young, electric, coked out of his mind in a dark little cavern off Great Jones Street.

Dr. John and Fairport Convention and Steve Miller—oh how he loved that dude—and George Harrison and Bread and J. Geils. I'm forgetting some, I'm sure. Most all at the Bottom Line, where we never had to pay because Lenny knew the owners from back when they'd organized free shows in Tompkins Square together.

Jackson Browne at the Beacon.

I was his buddy, his partner. He brought me along to each and every one. Not just me, my mother, too. We were a hip family stepping out in the city. Joyous times. We'd vibrate as we walked home, our muscles still coursing with the electric current of the music, our ears ringing so loudly that it was like someone had slapped bells over our heads and persisted in clanging them, enclosing us inside, separating us from the rest of the world. We'd be shaky on our feet.

He got us backstage passes to Jefferson Starship. We wore them around our necks and watched from the wings. It was hard to see. Everything back there was speakers and curtains. I remember Grace Slick had on a see-through blouse—a billowy thing that glistened like mother of pearl. She came right for me when they finished their set. Knelt down in front of me. Said, "Here's the real rock star. Freedom, what did you have for breakfast? Was it good?" She took my hand between her palms. Touched a finger to my cheek. Then, to Lenny, "He's a charmer. You sure he's really yours?" A wink to my mother and she was gone, folded into a caravan that, this time, didn't include us.

Springsteen and Marley and who all else at Max's, which I hated 'cause there was always a massive scene and Lenny always joined it and I always ended up forgotten in the back of some slippery booth, nodding off, head drifting toward the table with its shellac of spilled drinks, bounced awake again and again by the maximum sound blaring through the space.

We saw the Dead, oh, I don't know, four times that spring? They annoyed me. A Dead show meant another long night of pussyfooting around him and my mother, guessing—double-guessing—what would and wouldn't bum them out as they tripped their asses off.

We saw Joni, or my mother and I did—*Court and Spark*. Lenny skipped that one. So maybe that was later. After.

Anyway . . .

Come April he took me to a Yankees game. Why? Because he was a Dodgers fan. "Know your enemies, kid. Study them. One way or another, they'll tell you who you are." The Yankees were the team of the plutocrats, with their dress codes and company rules about facial hair. The team that survived when the Bums were thrown out. And if sports are an elaborate analogue for the sociopolitical emotions of a people, the Yankees' triumph—bought and paid for and legacied—over the Dodgers, and now that they were gone, the Mets, the scrappy bumblers across the river, signified the true beliefs of this city of ours. Give me your tired, your hungry, your poor, I'll offer them the moon and pay them slave wages, I'll cultivate their dreams and then confiscate them. There! You really thought you could win? In this town, nobody ever wins but me. "We're here to root against them," Lenny told me as we bounced through the crowd into the stadium. "We watch the Yankees to burnish our hatred. Note that. Don't forget it. Hatred's the one emotion stronger than love."

Also, the tickets were cheap if you sat with the drunks and the slobs in the bleachers. Which, where else would anyone want to sit?

We nabbed the front row, right above Bobby Murcer. I don't remember a thing about the game, who they were playing, what the score was, who pitched, just the spirit in the air, all that rambunctious energy swirling like a wave through the stands. The hoots and jeers when somebody bungled a play. The same hoots and jeers when somebody made one. Everybody shouting at the players on the field. Everybody sarcastic, every one of them a critic, even the folks rooting for the Yankees. And Lenny's whip-crack voice rising above the rest. "Come on, Murcer. That ain't a throw. My six-year-old can throw straighter than that." They could hear every word—Murcer and whoever else was out there. They could look you in the eyes and say go fuck your mother. That's how close the bleachers were to the outfield. Sometimes a chant would go up, the whole section punching the syllables. Mur-*cer*. Mur-*cer*. Until he turned and raised his glove to acknowledge us. And as people got drunk and the game went on and on a tedium set in—the truth rhythm of the game. You became more aware of the assholes sitting near you. The statheads and the dagos and the odd little guys who, even now in late middle age, looked like their mothers still picked out their clothes. Their restlessness, their crankiness, their distaste for one another. Words were spoken. Beers were spilled. A couple times, chests were thrust and fingers jabbed. Now, instead of shouting or pleading for the players' attention, people threw things at them—cups, crumpled popcorn cartons. I got into it too. A carton. It didn't make it past the warning track.

Lenny leaned in at one point and wrapped an arm around my neck. "There you have it, kid," he said. "Baseball: organized boredom punctuated by brief thrilling moments when the fact that something, anything, has actually happened tricks you into thinking you're not just wasting your time. It's like life, that way."

As though to prove his point, a streaker leapt out of the stands along third base and high-stepped it into the outfield. Thirty thousand people rose to their feet, pumping their fists, giving their best Bronx cheers. The guards trailing after him, chasing him in circles, loop-di-loops, figure eights. And Jesus, the speed of that guy. Like a running colt. The way his hair flowed behind him. His bony white ass. The tangled dark mess clustered around his dick as it slapped back and forth. The excitement that lingered in the crowd, even after he was carried away, kicking and flailing his arms.

I can only think of a single time my parents argued in the five months we spent together that winter and spring.

We'd received a manila envelope. Official correspondence. Our address hand-lettered on the label under Carnegie Hall's simple, elegant logo. Inside, three tickets to an upcoming show.

A note: *We're sold out! Hope you can make it! Phil.*

We should go, was my mother's stance. We owe it to him.

But Lenny was adamant. "Fuck that fucking guy. What do we owe him? Not a goddamn thing, that's what."

"He adores you, Lenny. He looks up to you."

"Not my problem."

"And—"

"And what? He ponied up?"

"When no one else would."

"Did I ask him to do that? No. I did not. And it's just money. I've burned it before, I'll burn it again."

"The money doesn't matter. What matters is what it bought."

"My freedom? Ha. Kunstler would've thought of something."

"Oh?"

He turned dark. "We're not going."

And the look on my mother's face—not anger but concern. A sad, protective impulse stopping her cold.

"You go," he said. "Take the kid. Sing along to all his pretty lies. I'll be interested to hear how that goes for you. Me, I'll stay home and watch *Kojak*."

Suffice it to say, we didn't go.

I remember my mother riding him for weeks to take me out to Flatbush where he grew up.

"Why would I do that? There's nothing left," he'd say. Or, "The past is dead. Let's not sit shiva for it." Or, "You want him to learn his history, take him to Long Island. Let him meet your mother. See? Not so much fun when it's your own bad trip."

Sometimes he'd launch into an extended harangue against the very act of remembering. Crying over the never-was, he called it. And what do you end up with? Fascism. The worship of a mythic, long-ago time ruled by a vengeful tribe with a reverence for might. The complete inversion of everything that has made our people unique—our restlessness, our wandering souls, the nimbleness that comes from centuries of living and dying by our wits. "Nostalgia's a killer. The present, that's where it's at. The wide open world." Not that he necessarily believed all this. He was testing hypotheses.

Rolling ideas around, raging for the pure joy of hearing himself rage.

Because one afternoon he took me on a subway ride that seemed to last forever. He stood the whole way, too agitated to keep still. Shifting from foot to foot. Reading the tags sprayed and sharpied on the car aloud. Cackling. Joking. Sparked with nervous energy.

"Listen," he told me at one point, "as far as your mother knows, we never did this. *Capisce?* Don't go ruining my reputation."

In Brooklyn, where the train lines converged to snake out in new configurations, we transferred and rode on until we rose from the tunnel and stopped above ground.

"Come on, kid, quick-quick!"

We stepped into a kind of enclosed amphitheater above the street. I was all turned around but Lenny, who hadn't set foot here in years, pushed ahead like he'd never left, like he still knew every rivet in every steel girder holding up the elevated platform. I wouldn't quite say he was excited. More like he was on a rush, like he'd reentered the rhythms of his childhood and was moving instinctively in all his old ways. He'd positioned us in the car closest to the turnstiles and before I could glance around or take anything in, he had us clanking down the steps to the street.

"Where are we?"

"Sutter Avenue," he said. "Can't you smell the aspirations? Come on. This way."

He led me into the shadows under the tracks and as we jaywalked, weaving around double-parked cars, he launched into a rap about how this was where the dirt poor went to wallow in the mud. How the Jews and the blacks shunned even by their own people washed out here to stoke their resentment in half-collapsed buildings and scheme, separately and together, about leveling the world. "Heaven," he said. "It was fucking heaven."

Walking and talking. As long as he stuck to the long outrageous con called civil society, he was in his element.

We moved from street to street with no clear destination. Past I don't know how many boarded-up buildings, I don't know how many mountains of trash, houses with cinder blocks where their front stoops should've been, around corners onto commercial strips lined with so many street hawkers you couldn't find the storefronts behind them. The smell of those strips—incense, frankincense, sandalwood, rising from bundled sticks mounted under rocks on tables; fish frying in open kettles filled with oil; tins of cocoa butter and vials of essential oils stacked around arrangements of geodes and precious stones, sending up a sweetness so strong it clogged the nose. The colors—the emaciated wooden figurines lined up like judges with their deep hues of brown, mahogany and black; the racks of shirts and dresses bursting with negritude. The stacks and stacks of socks that had fallen off trucks. People tumbling over the sidewalks into the streets; life like you didn't see in our part of the city. Then, around another corner and the street would be empty except for one lone kid riding his bike in circles over the broken pavement.

"It's just about the same. Except the Jews are gone. Look, there's Herzl Street."

"So you grew up there?" I asked.

"Fuck no. Even when this place was teeming with Jews, Pops thought he was too good for it."

Wherever we went, whatever turn we took, we were conspicuous. Dudes with picks in their 'fros propped on the hoods of cars followed us with their eyes. Old men sitting on milk crates in front of tenements muttered under their breath. Women in hijabs, pulling carts of groceries behind them, crossed the street to avoid us. "Don't worry about it," Lenny said. "If you lived here, you'd be suspicious of us too. 'Cause, look. We're not priests. We're not social workers. What the fuck are we?"

"I thought we were going to see where you grew up."

Lenny threw a shoulder, shrugging me off. He peered up the street—one way, the other—stalked partway down the block, looked around, stalked back. Searching for something. Unable to find it. We moved on, farther down the main thoroughfare, past faded old furniture stores with broken windows and empty showrooms, storefront tabernacles, vacant lots, the odd art deco fortress.

"I *am* showing you where I grew up. You wanna know what made me, it was more this place than that back there. I liked it bet-

ter over here. More action. More trouble. You wanna know the difference between a gangster and a radical? The gangster takes your
money and then demands more. The radical burns it and offers you
some soup. Brownsville had both. You could hop between the two.
Pick-up basketball at the Boys Club, then dice in the alley behind
the candy store."

Another turn and we were back in the shadows of the elevated
train tracks. He gestured toward a park built into the hill above us.
"That's where I smoked my first joint. Made my first girl." And turning again, he said, "Here you go, kid. Flatbush. Canarsie. Crown
Heights at a stretch. This right here is the no-man's-land where all
those hoods blur. This is where the fun stops. Over here, you're an
alrightnik. Back there"—he jutted his chin toward the other side of
the tracks—"that's Pigtown, where you're a nogoodnik."

"So—"

"'Cause, what's the fun in being an alrightnik? Really, kid. Have
I taught you nothing?"

He wandered on, turning into the residential streets with their
rows after rows of peaked Archie Bunker houses. His chatter trailed
off. Eventually, after we'd walked for forever, we came to a house
that didn't look like the others. No bricks. No balcony. No striped
plastic awning. Just a squat two-story box covered in rotting yellow clapboard siding. "There. That's where Pops and I lived. On
the second floor." He let me study it for a while, let me try to imagine him into it. The darkness. The difference from the cozy homes
around it. "Before Fred Trump came in and built the bungalows,
the whole hood looked like this. This and empty fields. Dirt roads."
He sat himself down cross-legged on the sidewalk and, remarkably,
left me to think my own thoughts for a moment.

I look back on it now and I wonder why I didn't ask him more
questions. What he meant by alrightniks. What he meant by
nogoodniks. How his father had managed to hold on to the house
when everything around him was being rebuilt into what at that
time must've seemed like the future. And why? What pride or fear
or necessity led him to cling to this tumbledown shack instead of
moving up to a house of solid brick? I knew he'd been a merchant,
a step above a peddler, a buyer and seller of this and that, though

what exactly he sold remained forever amorphous—abstract—as if the goods themselves were meaningless, cheap excuses for the transaction, the deal, the movement of money from one place to another, the accumulation of respectability. And so why had he and Lenny stayed in the oldest, saddest, least respectable home in Flatbush, a place that, for all his striving, embodied the poverty he'd tried to escape more than the wealth he'd believed was his destiny?

I should've asked Lenny about all of this. But I didn't have the wits yet to know how to do that. I was too young. I understood that this experience was profound, but why that might be was beyond my comprehension.

It's easy to psychologize. To see little Lenny learning how to resent the man, traveling back to the rougher streets in Brownsville that his father had fled and throwing himself into the fast-talking, shit-kicking trouble he found there, the people he could identify with because, whatever their race or creed, they were all as poor as he felt himself to be. You can imagine Lenny cultivating the chip on his shoulder there. Learning to love it. You can imagine how these early experiments set the stage for the rest of his life. The secret message he was sending his old neighbors when, in '67, in response to the tour buses of thrill-seeking squares trolling along St. Marks Place, he'd organized his own tour of hippies to ride in the backs of borrowed pickup trucks through the placid streets of deep Brooklyn and Queens, their faces dripping with day-glow colors as they gawked and pointed at the Trump bungalows. The personal motives behind the chaos he'd unleashed at the Stock Exchange, showing the world—and the spirit of his dead father—what he really thought of the old man's dreams.

I think about how he sat in front of his old house that day, silent, not moving, coiled like a snake, and I recognize that this place held some key to who he was. But to say it summed him up would be too simple. He'd outgrown that house. That place. He'd liberated himself. Made something new—the famous Lenny Snyder—out of the scraps he'd been given.

For years afterward, right up to the day he died, I held on to a desire to return to Flatbush without him, to ask him the questions

I should have then. When we were apart, I'd contemplate all the things I didn't know. I'd make lists in my head, tell myself, Next time you see him, remember, get answers. But then, in his presence, there was always something else stealing my attention, some crisis, some passion, some new circus of his that overwhelmed everything, and I'd forget, or I wouldn't know how to assert myself. I'd feel that familiar urge to flee and hide. He was too much trouble. The only way to carve out any room for myself was to cut myself off from him completely.

The one thing I did ask, right then, right there: "Where was your mom?"

He ignored me. Acted like he hadn't heard what I said. But a few seconds later he hopped up like I'd broken him out of a trance and he was off again, wandering, leaving me to catch up or not.

What was a kid to do?

I followed him.

No matter which way we turned, we passed the same oppressive bungalows, endless lines of squat red huts set back from the street behind tiny strips of lawn. Sometimes they had green awnings, sometimes white, or no awning at all. They felt like places where you might get lost and forget who you were. On the corners of the avenues, larger tenements and apartment complexes loomed, build-ings with names like the Lincoln, the Alford, the Bertha, the only things tethering this nearly suburban landscape to the city.

And the quiet. Block after block, we hardly saw a soul. Those few people we did see seemed isolated, out of time. A bum picking through a trash can. A girl with pigtails and glasses playing with a stick. Some dude cracking his screen door to scowl at us.

We could've been walking in circles for all I knew. Once or twice Lenny stopped to stare, to hawk a loogie into the gutter. Then we'd keep moving.

Finally we reached an area where the streets widened and the houses fell away entirely. In their place, a crumbling brick wall held together with moss and brassy yellow lichen. Above the wall, a chain-link fence topped with razor wire.

"There," Lenny said, throwing a thumb. "That's where my

mother was." The first words he'd spoken since we'd left his old house.

I peered over the fence, through the brambles and bushes, but I couldn't see anything except darkness.

We kept walking. Past a massive derelict smokestack, the trees thinned out and revealed what might have been a prison or a poorhouse back in the day, a hulking old fire-scorched complex of buildings where you just knew nothing good had ever happened.

"What is it?" I asked Lenny.

"Brooklyn State Hospital. She was in Building G."

"What happened to her?"

He ignored my question and walked on, pointing at the sprawling prefab school across the street. "You see that? Wingate. I got my high school degree from that joint. Never set foot in a single classroom. Dig. Pops said, 'Go ahead. Ruin your life. What do I care?' Which meant he cared too much about all the wrong things."

Typical Lenny. Intriguing me with the seed of a story while skipping the details that might allow me to comprehend what the hell he was saying. What he wanted was for me to ask. So, something had gone down between his father and him. Okay. But we'd been walking for hours and I was still hooked on the mystery of his mother.

Anyway, he couldn't handle the silence. Wait him out long enough and he'd rush back in with more.

"They'd built the place when I was a sophomore to warehouse the overflow from everywhere else. A weird mix of kids from all sorts of hoods. An experiment in integration that I was supposed to take part in. But as far as Pops was concerned I spent too much time hanging out with the *shvartzes* already. Tilden. That's where it was at." He gestured toward some faraway place. "The white school. The Jew school. He worked like hell to keep me in Tilden. Harder than he ever did to keep my mother out of the nuthouse. Even tried to bribe the school secretary. Guess he succeeded because I did stay at Tilden. And irony of ironies, the place was crawling with pinkos. He'd have been better off letting me go to Wingate. Maybe then I wouldn't have spent my high school career writing anti-McCarthy diatribes for the student paper. Maybe I never would've applied to Brandeis, where revolution was the only game in town. He definitely wouldn't have had to endure the shame of my refusing to sign the loyalty pledge Tilden shoved down our throats, or of being told that as punishment I wouldn't get my diploma, or the irony of having to scramble to work out a deal to let me graduate from the very school he'd tried so hard to keep me out of." He grinned at me. "So fuck him and the horse he rode in on."

We'd moved deep into some new neighborhood where the houses had driveways and sprawling wooden porches. Grand old Victorians. Actual trees. A foreign country.

I worked up my courage. "That place back there. Where your mother was? That was—"

"Building G. I told you. They don't get any nuttier."

"And she lived there?"

"Until she got shipped out to Kings Park."

We took a turn and the city swallowed up the genteel precincts we'd just gone through. We were back to tall buildings. To bricks and graffiti and faded signs.

"You ever met someone who's batshit crazy?" he asked. "They're lovely. They're alive—until the lobotomy. Check it out. That's the armory." He jutted his chin toward a red stone castle that took up a whole block. "That's where they'll come from when they hunt us all down."

And just like that, we were back on the boulevard and down in the subway and on our way home.

One final thing I remember from this time.

A new restaurant had opened. Fancy. Uptown. It had gotten all kinds of press. Famous people hung out there. Not like us. Legit. Born to it. The Jackie Onassises of the world. And Lenny got it in his head that we should go.

First we had to outfit ourselves for the part. Jackets. Ties. For my mother, a pair of real heels. We hit every thrift store on the Lower East Side, ventured all the way over to Bleecker in our search. You'd be surprised what people threw away. By the end of the day we'd cobbled together what could be called somebody else's Sunday best. A lot of somebodies. We looked sharp. My mother wore lipstick and eye shadow, probably for the first time in my life. Understated but elegant. Her hair up in a loose knot, a few key strands dangling to frame her face. She hadn't forgotten the principles drilled into her by my grandmother. She'd found a proper gown and a string of fake pearls. It was the first time I'd ever seen her dress up in anything other than patterns or exotic prints. Lenny played it straight too. His hair was still short enough to pass. All three of us. We looked like we'd just come in from Paris or Milan. "Dress the part you're playing," Lenny said. "The rest will come. People see what you tell them to look for."

Off we went to the meal of our lives. To peek, ever so briefly, at the life those who would rule us took for granted.

You'd think I'd remember the name of the place, but no. I can tell you that the chairs were uncomfortable and the tables were packed too close together. And that what I ordered didn't end up being what I'd expected, and there were some chuckles and knowing conversations with the jolly, gruff, thick-accented owner when he learned I'd had trouble choking it down. I do remember that the whole place was overstuffed, too much gold and too many mirrors, too breakable. And not knowing where to look. But liking that the dinner came with not two, not three but four desserts. And truffles, whatever those were.

And how happy Lenny and my mother were. How they gazed at each other, moony, in love, sharing off each other's plates.

Like they knew this night would have to stand for much more than itself later on.

What I remember most: Near the end of the meal, Lenny ordered champagne. He told the waiter, "Let's get a flute for the kid too." When it came, we all raised our glasses over the table.

"To freedom," said Lenny, and I thought he meant me.

Then, after I'd eaten all the bread I could hold and my parents had eaten not only everything on their plates but also most of the food on mine, Lenny presented the owner with a letter, typewritten on heavy bond paper. I have no idea what it said, but I do know this: After the guy read it, silently mouthing the words, his already obsequious attitude turned brighter. He clapped me on the shoulders, both hands heavy, squeezing from behind. "Monsieur," he said, "I hope your meal with us met your standards."

"Exceedingly," Lenny said, and the man beamed like he'd been touched by God.

"You understand," the man said, "that I cannot under any circumstances accept payment from you. It's a gift simply to be able to provide you and your charming family with hospitality. A great pleasure."

"The pleasure's all mine," said Lenny.

And as we fled we managed to refrain from giggling until we were down the block and around the corner.

Later that night, three or four in the morning.

I was woken up by what sounded like mewling. A low, mournful fugue like the alley cats made when they were in heat, but much closer, inside the apartment.

I slid out of bed and waded through the dark toward the sound, and there were my mother and Lenny, upright on their futon, wrapped around each other like vines. It was hard to see what they were doing. They blurred. Shadows within shadows. But they were fully clothed. They weren't having sex. I watched them for a long time, and finally, I understood. They were crying. But more than that. Something beyond crying. These sounds. They were the guttural rumble of despair.

That's all I've got.

After that, poof. He was gone.

[III]

THE WILDERNESS

I could . . . well, okay. Let's start here. The next morning.

What I remember is my mother explaining that Lenny had slipped off to a place called the Underground and not even she knew where that was.

"He's safe," she said. "Here with us, he was in danger."

"Are we in danger?" I asked.

She had no answer for that. Instead she said, "The bad guys won't know he's gone for months and a lot of people are helping him."

"Are we in danger?" I asked again.

And I remember she touched my chin with her thumb. Held it there for a second and then said, "We're fine. You and me kid, we'll ease on down the road, just like we would if Lenny was still here."

That was the extent of it.

That and the water gun, the AK-47 she fished out from on top of the kitchen cabinets. A parting gift for me from Lenny. A consolation prize. Except for the red plastic plug in the barrel, it looked exactly like the real thing. In true Lenny fashion he'd attached a note, scrawled like all his other missives in a big, loopy, ego-projecting cursive on lined yellow paper ripped from a legal pad.

Hey kid, it said. *See you on the flip side. Use the gun to protect your mother.*

No signature. No sign-off. No proclamation of love.

Reading over my shoulder, my mother snatched the note out of my hands. "That's a joke," she said. "I don't need protecting. Neither do you." Something about the way she said this, though, made me think that it now fell to me to crack her up and distract her from the taste of iron in her mouth.

First thing I did, I filled the AK's banana clip with water and

stomped through the apartment, pounding out a war dance, toma-
hawk chopping and thrusting my gun around like I'd seen soldiers
do on TV. I incorporated karate moves, kick-ass Bruce Lee shit,
elbows out, legs high and stiff. And I imagined Lenny surveying
all this from wherever he was underground, cackling, cracking up,
giving a single clap of his hands, less for me than as an exclamation
point on his pleasure. I saw him leaping in and gleefully narrating
my demonstration of martial prowess with the standard one-two of
a bad overdub.

It took time, it took coaxing, but my mother joined the fun. She
slammed her bare feet against the floor, shaking the foundations,
sending tremors through the building until the downstairs neighbor, Fran Wronski, a devout Polish hausfrau who hissed at us in
the stairwell because she thought we were Satanists, and whom we
suspected but couldn't prove had been feeding the feds lies about
us for years, pounded the ceiling with the blunt end of her broom.
Fists on hips, triumphant, my mother shouted at the walls and the
ears lurking there, "That's right, motherfuckers, he's not here! Oh
no! Not today!" Falling to her knees. "He's gone!" she said. "You
hear me? He's gone to Disneyland!"

She flopped onto her back and closed her eyes. Took a deep yogic
breath.

"When will he come back?" I asked.

"That's a secret, Freddy," she said, suddenly tired. "Nobody
knows. But he will. I promise." Then pounding her fist against the
floor to let old Fran know she'd heard her and didn't give a shit, she
shouted, "You hear that? He'll be back, you fucking cocksuckers!"

She heaved. Laughing. But, no. Sobbing.

She crumpled like a used tissue on the floor.

Leaving me to carry on alone.

AK strapped to my shoulder, I circled her in full guerrilla mode,
my finger pulling rapid-fire on the trigger as I took aim at every
target the apartment offered, the beaded curtains we used as doors,
the wavy-gravy posters commemorating my parents' coups in
drippy, melty words, family photos going back to the old country, to Ephraim Snyder, the cantor, and his wife, Fanny, paintings

and lithographs, their McCarthy peace poster and other movement memorabilia, Lenny's signed copy of *Sgt. Pepper,* the button-eyed doll he'd kept to remember Snick and Liberty House by, the ferns and ficus trees and creeping ivy strung with bright flowers that my mother had painted up the walls and across the ceiling, the books and pamphlets stacked all over the place, the framed photo of me chained to that fucking tree, the whole history of the times they'd lived through and influenced and hated and loved, all hoarded like memories in our cramped tenement apartment.

It felt good to soak the place down. Such power. Such release. Such cathartic vandalism.

I remember my mother telling me that before he fled Lenny had said to her, "I refuse to let you suffer for my sins. I want you to stay free." Like a mandate. Like a dare.

We took him at his word. We believed him.

If Lenny was free, we'd be free too. We'd enter the new world. No bounds could restrain us. We were free! Finally! We were truly free!

But what did that word even really mean now?

It meant constant vigilance. Knowing, at all times, that someone was somehow trying to ascertain just how free we were. There were ears in the walls and eyes in the windows. We kept the blinds down, the music always cranked up. Lenny's spitball box remained attached to the phone, hissing and screeching, inserting a scrim of ones and zeros between us and anyone who tried to call.

On Mondays or Tuesdays, if we'd been out of town, we played a game called Find the Bug in the early-morning hours. We'd tear the apartment to shit. Flip the pictures hanging on the walls. Roll up the rugs. Stick our heads inside the TV set. We never found anything, but you know what the thin man says: Just 'cause you're paranoid doesn't mean everyone's not out to get you.

Eventually we got used to it. Vigilance became a habit. We assumed the narcs were living among us.

Anyway, what more could they do to us? We were merely the survivors.

Freedom meant a thousand other adjustments too.

It's easy to espouse free when you've got an income. To give the Panthers twelve thousand bucks when you know another check's in the mail. Lenny'd been less free folk than urban raconteur. His book was a bestseller. His speeches drew thousands in protest and support. Worse came to worst, he could always extort the local businesses that got rich off the movement he'd started. Before he went on the run, we'd lived like exiled kings. We had a color TV, cab fare if we felt lazy, all the Gem Spa egg creams we could suck down.

Now all that was gone—all except the TV.

So, freedom meant learning how to scrounge for cash.

Mom tried hawking candles she'd hand-dipped in wax warmed over the stove, colored with the same DEP packets she used for my tie-dyes. Spindly things. The wax soft as putty.

She moved on, jewelry twisted out of wire and rhinestones. This seemed like a sure bet. Back in the day she and Lenny had raked it in just by stringing beads on strips of leather. Nobody was buying that crap now. You needed semiprecious stones. You needed designs that looked less like crude weapons. You needed talent. That's what she was told.

"I've seen people sell worse shit than this in the parking lots at Dead shows," she told these skeptics.

"Then go join the caravan, if that's what you're into."

It wasn't. She didn't.

One night she found a sewing machine on the street. A sign from the cosmos. How hard could it be? Well, it took her almost a week to figure out the machine had been thrown out because it was broken, and another of struggling by hand over a single blouse to realize tailoring clothes was hard as fucking hell.

Getting a normal job through the normal channels—running a cash register, answering phones, temping, like the great masses she'd dreamed of saving—this she couldn't do. She'd rather die than be a slave to the system that she still, despite everything, wanted to destroy.

So instead we suffered for our freedom, which of course, ironically, proved we were free.

Freedom meant the sharp blade of poverty slicing away at our thoughts, keeping us jumpy, obliterating our concentration. It meant a constant tightness in my stomach, the tension of my body eating itself. Mom's anxious fingers tapping constantly at her lip, twisting, picking, her voice sharpening and stabbing if I ogled a candy bar. We subsisted on peas and lentils. My Kool-Aid was replaced by hibiscus and chamomile, bought in bulk from dark, musty Chinese joints under the Manhattan Bridge, boiled and strained and left to cool on the windowsill.

Freedom meant spending afternoons at the food pantry in the basement of St. Mark's Church, not as volunteers but as supplicants. It meant learning not to whine about the tasteless mush my mother cooked or the sludge it turned into when it hit my bowels. We learned how to scavenge the dumpsters behind Met Foods, how long after closing time the rejects were thrown out: perfectly good boxes of Raisin Bran magically transformed into trash by the date stamped on their sides, or fruit—browning bananas, bruised apples, plastic containers of strawberries, just fine if you ignored the couple of moldy ones at the bottom. Sometimes we'd snatch bread. White bread. Wonder Bread! We weren't too proud to eat mass-produced garbage. We'd cart it home with the rest of our haul, and since the toaster had broken in a hail of sparks and fire, we'd brown slices over the burners on the stove, gorge ourselves on a whole loaf in one sitting; if we were lucky, with butter, too.

We never blamed Lenny for our hardship, not even on days when we didn't eat at all. We knew that whatever pain we were going through was nothing compared to his life on the run.

Besides, just as often, we'd have ground beef or sliced cheese that Mom had smuggled out under her dress. I got in the game too. Hot dogs, polish sausages, snaked down the leg of my jeans. Those old lessons in thievery finally sinking in.

On Tuesdays we stood in line at the Catholic Workers building—the very one Lenny had taught me to rely on if ever I found myself truly in trouble—waiting for our stew thick with pasta and potatoes. We'd sit at long foldout cafeteria tables with the other hard-luck cases. We were them now. We were free. This was what freedom meant.

On Sundays it was Sister's, the little spot on Second where Sister herself—helped by a scrappy collective of no-bullshit women—

made one dish a day in bulk and fed whoever walked in. Pay what you will, no questions asked. We ate for free those nights. Roast chicken. Three-bean chili. The best mac and cheese the world has ever seen. Sometimes we paid a quarter, plucked from the street. Or we'd help with the dishes after Sister locked up.

On certain days, when nothing had worked out, we trudged over to Dubrow's Cafeteria and piled our trays high with saltines and ketchup, free for the taking from the condiment rack. We'd crumble the crackers in a heap on our plates, slather on the ketchup. Add enough salt and pepper—free too, in their paper two-tubes—and if you squinted, if you held your nose, you could almost convince yourself it was spaghetti marinara you were eating.

Other nights, we found ourselves reduced to scavenging in the garbage cans along the avenues for pizza crusts and half-empty containers of fried rice.

Freedom meant learning quick who your friends really were.

It meant strained relationships, a fraying of the networks in which my parents, at another time, might have shared a meal or caught a film or just bounced through time, wasting the day away. Now my mother and I had nothing to contribute to these potlatches. Show up empty-handed often enough and you eventually stopped being invited over. Your poverty is interpreted by others as an affront to the concept of sharing. Movies, wasted days, these cost money too. We tried to be graceful. We tried gently demurring and ducking the fun. But how many humiliations does it take? How many evenings of listening to your friends grumble about the price of gas to Woodstock, where they were overseeing the work on their country house—A shack really, they'd say, it's falling apart so we got it for next to nothing. But when it's done? Man, we're putting in solar panels and a Japanese rock garden and a skylight, and hey, did you try the shrimp, Suzy?—how many nights like that before you felt yourself screaming inside, What's the matter with you people? I can't afford a subway token. You really think I give two fucks about your koi pond?

The networks fell away. Or we did. We couldn't keep up.

This was city living, not Black Bear or Drop City or whatever commune with its homemade bread and evening hootenannies and fifteen-hour discussions of any and every minuscule infraction of the public peace. Its commitment to all going down together. We hadn't rejected this society, exactly. We'd sunk into the concrete and gotten our feet stuck.

The squatters living in buildings Lenny claimed to have liberated back when they were called crash pads, even they abandoned us. Those people didn't trust us. Why should they? To them, Lenny and my mother were charlatans. Fixers cultivating powerful connections they didn't want folks on the street to know about. The squatters came to us for help, not the other way around.

At first my mother tried to keep playing her old role. I remember her dragging me to a women's lib meeting. Some church basement. Me squirming on the folding chair next to her, slipping to the floor. My mother's legs. Her clogs. Her flared jeans. All the other legs under the table too. Muscular, hairy legs. Black legs and brown legs and white legs. Legs draped in cotton printed with African and aboriginal patterns. A multitude of legs concealed under dirty jeans. They all belonged to women. I was the only child there. The only male.

The tension in the air when my mother said, "I could be a great asset to you."

"Could you?" The derision in this woman's question. Such antagonism. I didn't understand.

"I've run national campaigns. Maybe you're familiar with a few of them. The March on Washington in '70. The May Day Draft Dodge. We got thousands of people in sixteen different cities to burn their cards on the steps of city hall. Lenny and—"

"See, I'm going to have to stop you right there." This was a different woman. They were taking turns with her.

"Why?" my mother asked, bristling. "Because of Lenny? He's my husband. We're partners. *Equal* partners. The work we've done, the things we accomplished—"

"You keep saying *we,* but all I ever saw was him."

"He's the public face."

"And you're apparently okay with that."

"Yes!" The vehemence squeezed into this one little word. The fierceness. I stopped moving under her feet, paying close attention now.

"Well, we're—"

"Some of us aren't—"

They all started talking over one another.

"It sends the wrong—"

"—structural imbalance—"

"—didn't hear him giving you credit too often."

"I've been a little busy raising a child lately," my mother said.

More commotion. More interruptions. More talk of "structural imbalance" and "conforming to society's expectations" and also "maybe *he* should be the one staying home." I remember almost laughing at that—word still wasn't out that he'd gone on the run.

"Look, I came here to help," my mother said. "I know all the players. People who could be very useful to you."

"Men, you mean."

One lone voice defending her: "Come on, Renee, that's not fair."

And we were out of there.

I don't know how many of those meetings we went to. Was it one? Two? Not many. I remember my mother grumbling about them, "The problem with those girls is they have no sense of history. They want power, not equality."

It's not for me to say if this was true. What I'm sure of is she felt rejected by them, and part of her believed she deserved their condemnation.

Because here's another thing freedom meant. It meant that despite my mother's tendency toward riot, despite her proud stances on abortion and equal rights and sexual liberation, she couldn't escape being seen by the world—and secretly, by herself—as, more than anything, Lenny Snyder's wife.

Now she was struggling, unsure who to become.

She started smoking again for the umpteenth time. Mores. Then More Menthols. Then Virginia Slims.

She threw herself into one thing after another. Learned to cast tarot. Studied astrology. Chinese herbal medicine. Macrobiotics. *The Teachings of Don Juan*. Each new passion consumed her for however long it lasted, a month, a week. As if macramé owls—

another lightning obsession—were capable of transforming the soul.

She spent two and a half days at Theater for the New City building giant Easter Island heads out of refrigerator boxes. Then she quit in disgust when the director suggested that maybe she should let another assistant—one who knew what he was doing—teach her the right way to construct the things.

There was one jag during which she became a Buddhist. Chanting nam-myoho-renge-ko for hours at a stretch. Praying for wealth.

None of it worked.

The truth is, she was desperately lonely.

How she clung to me. Arms around my belly. Face in my neck. She'd breathe me in, not so much showering me with love as burying me in it. She constantly asked for my advice. What should I wear today? What should I do today? Why don't they like me? Why won't someone help me?

To which, how was I supposed to respond to that? "I'm a kid, Mama. I can't help. Don't you see? Mama, please." But I couldn't say that.

She'd say, "Sing me a song, Freddy. I'm sad."

So, I'd sing,

> Sing. Sing a song.
> Sing out loud. Sing out strong.
> Sing of good things not bad.
> Sing of happy not sad.

Sometimes a flicker of relief or distraction—let's say love—would shoot like a falling star across her face. Just long enough for me to notice when it was gone.

I'd sing,

> Oh, baby, baby it's a wild world
> It's hard to get by just upon a smile
> Oh, baby, baby it's a wild world
> I'll always remember you like a child, girl.

And she'd join in sometimes and we'd sing together, tracking the melody in each other's eyes, both thinking our own secret thoughts about Lenny, about each other, about how hard it was to be the person other people needed you to be.

She had two friends. Cindy Belloc and Isha Ali. They lived worlds away—the Upper West Side, Harlem—and I only remember visiting either of them three or four times apiece, but the way she talked you'd have thought she saw them every day.

Cindy was glamorous in a low-key way. Pantsuits and defiantly flat hair. She carried herself with an air of self-possession that recognized empathy as a function of self-confidence. Sipping tea from real china, not even chipped, in her classic six, we felt almost dignified, flattered to be treated as equals.

She'd been in the movement, peripherally, back when she'd dated Sy. Now she worked for *Redbook*. She'd published a couple articles my mother had written, heavily edited—I mean, rewritten from scratch. But still, a byline, an opportunity to present the new consciousness to the great underestimated nation of women, just waiting for the call to find one another. We ate well for a few weeks after those checks came in. We put a tiny dent in our back rent.

Kindness can cut deep when you're in real need. My mother must have known she'd been given these gigs out of Cindy's sentimental loyalty, a kind of philanthropy intended to absolve her guilt over abandoning the counterculture when things got too hot, but Mom started dreaming that she could be a writer and bombarded Cindy with half-cocked pitches. How to recognize the chicest clothes at your local thrift shop. Eight surefire self-defense tactics for when you find yourself alone on the streets at 3:00 a.m. How to kill a rat. And of course, Lenny, Lenny, Lenny, his tribulations. Topics that might've worked in *The East Village Other* but would seem bizarre to the happy homemakers who subscribed to *Redbook*.

Cindy must have braced herself every time the phone rang, dreading my mother's impossible dreams. Anyway, she stopped answering. Stopped inviting us over.

Isha Ali, though, she was hard as cut diamonds, hot with love and discernment. No pretensions given or accepted. If she liked you, you sensed, she'd take you in like a sister, but if you crossed her you just knew, whoa, she'd scar you for life. Like the real thing my mother feared she could never be.

Isha's husband, Calvin Williams, had been shot dead in his sleep by the cops in Philly, another martyred Panther to add to the list. And though compared to this Lenny's self-sabotage looked like a bad joke, she was wide-minded about it, open to paradox. She cared more about the circumstances she and my mother shared than the righteousness or not of the men who'd caused them.

The two of them had been to the wars. They were battered and struggling now to fend off the crush of poverty while raising their little boys alone. They laughed a lot together—full-bodied, unguarded—and bemoaned the fissures that had opened up all around them.

"That's what happens when the Left starts winning. Rich liberals take what they want and exploit it. The rest of us gouge each other's eyes out for the scraps."

A chortle.

"We—and by we I don't mean you and me—only know how to lose. We *want* to lose."

"We want each other to lose. We—again, not you and me—want to win at everyone else's expense. Women, black folks, the gays, everybody. They're just out to get what's theirs. When they say 'solidarity,' they mean step in line."

A rueful snort.

"We want the poor to lose. Is it any wonder that they killed Martin right after he announced the Poor People's Campaign?"

"Well, we—and by we I *do* mean you and me—have already lost. All that's left is the dying."

A contented smile. With Isha my mother felt seen, finally, and understood.

Meanwhile, in the other room, Isha's son, Amari, was grabbing my toys, claiming them as his own and stiff-arming me so I couldn't take them back. He'd give me the stink eye. He'd taunt me. "Reparations, motherfucker!"

Good times.

But Isha too often kept her distance. She had to be careful not to be seen with kikes like us. Her militant patrons wouldn't tolerate it.

Most of the time, Mom felt forgotten. Isolated. All she had was me.

She took comfort in men and, a couple times, women. I don't judge her. I understood, even then, that whatever she got from these strangers in my house could only ease the burden on me.

Anyway, freedom meant it wasn't my decision.

They never lasted long, these love affairs, with their queasy mix of tenderness and pity. A day, a week, and Mom would recoil, disgusted by her weakness and hateful toward the good intentions that clung to these shmucks. Their compassion couldn't equal Lenny's fierce, frenetic propulsion.

What could?

What ever would?

Freedom meant watching as my mother dissipated. As she sprawled on the couch with a forearm thrown over her eyes, her tea getting cold, the day blurring into night. Signs of weakness beyond comprehension. Moments when I'd done some foolish thing, drawn on the walls, broken a glass by mistake, demanded breakfast when I knew there was no food, poked at her, poke, poke, poke, vying for attention. She'd snap at me, "Cut it. Get lost. Scram."

I'd bop from foot to foot, not sure if she was serious. Sometimes she'd melt and remember I was a kid. *Her* kid. She'd pull me close and suffocate me with her remorse.

More often, she'd tighten, fuming, and I'd flee and blame myself, not her, for my banishment. But I'd be angry too. Shaking out of my skin. Because she'd failed me. She and Lenny both.

Freedom meant drifting through the streets in search of any reason not to go home.

Everyone lived on top of everyone else, like layers of paint splashed over the same wall. You had to know your faction and you had to know the others, how they lived, how they thought, their proverbial POV, what would make them laugh and what would get your ass kicked.

It meant wising up to the dangers that lurked in the battlefield we called a neighborhood. You learned to read the signs, the cut of his leather—tailored and sleek like the Puerto Ricans' or distressed and worn like the white boys'? And what secondary evidence could be found? Patches meant Angels. Buttons meant the new white breed called Punks. Either could fuck you up, but since the Angels lived by a code, they might just protect you instead.

There were others: Freaks like us. Trash superstars—the remnants of the Factory, glamorous in their glitter, rags and rubber. Queers and artists (often the same thing). Black kids from the projects out by the river. That confederation of anarcho-nihilists who called themselves the Pedophiles. Old-timers, the Jews and Poles and Ukrainians, what was left of the original ghetto, those who refused to ghost away; they lived in a society that had long been out of date. They endured the rest of us, waited us out, and their kids were the toughest motherfuckers on the block.

Some people—well, Lenny—could talk to everybody. But I was no Lenny. I had to be prepared, on any given day, to be shoved hard enough in the back to go sprawling. So many skinned knees I stopped wearing shorts. I learned to notice when people around me shifted pace, when their hands lingered a tick too long in their pockets. I traveled with my keys splayed through my fingers like brass knuckles.

Freedom meant shit happened. You couldn't control it.

A fight would break out. Preening. Scuffling. All of a sudden, a fist. Sometimes you knew one of the people. You might even know his name. You'd seen them all around. But you kept on walking. You didn't stop to watch.

One day, a junkie stoop-sitting on St. Marks became so offended by the sight of my tie-dye that he ripped the shirt right off my back, leaving only the collar around my neck.

Some kids once pinned me to a curb over on Stuyvesant and tried to shove a dead pigeon down my throat. When I flailed, one of them aimed a feather at my eye and threatened to poke it out if I didn't stop. I went limp and he said, "What's the matter, pussy?" They acted like they were just being friendly.

I carried my AK with me everywhere I went like one of the crazies lost in his own myth.

Random things caught fire. Trash cans. Tires. Second-floor apartments. You never knew who did it or if it was on purpose.

Freedom meant not caring, trying not to notice.

It meant turning yourself into the deviant creature you imagined might be hiding under your skin. That is, if you had the stomach, the balls, to do so.

But also, it meant a throbbing boredom.

I remember long tedious afternoons, nothing on the tube, Mom off who knows where, and me baking in the sunlight that poured in through the windows, wondering where Lenny might be at that moment, what he was up to. Some thrilling adventure. I remember feeling him nearby sometimes, secretly watching, urging me to survive.

"It's important, what we're doing," my mother told me on low, slow days when I asked her if this was what it felt like to be dead. "We're refusing to break. One day history will write about our courage and sacrifice."

Notice the assumptions hidden in that statement. Getting arrested was something to be proud of. Losing your father was cause for celebration. Even when we felt small and insignificant, we did what we did for the public record. Because, of course, the world revolved around us. Or if not us, Lenny. We basked in his glory.

She did what she could to try to distract me. We'd go to Tompkins Square and I'd hide under benches, stand stiff behind trees, race around, dodging the hippies, the homeless, the junkies. I'd spin figure eights around the Hare Krishnas with their jingle bells and sitars and filthy blackened feet. And she'd hang back behind me, pacing herself, making sure not to catch up, her arms out stiff and her fingers splayed like claws. We called the game Fugitive or sometimes just Lenny. It never got old. She'd chase me until she collapsed. Or we both did. Her tumbling over me, tickling. Our small joys.

And then we'd feel close to him for the rest of the day.

Renewed.

We could go on.

One night, I remember, I was outside someplace and the streetlights weren't working—on the fritz or smashed or maybe there weren't any. I was near the river. The air had that salty weight to it. By myself. No Mom. Just me and this eerie, silent pocket of city.

For once, I wasn't scared.

I remember not wanting to return to the fray, the blinking lights, the noise—I can hear it now, muted, a distant party.

Footsteps tapped toward me along the cobblestones. Male, I could tell by the cadence of the sound.

And I remember thinking, maybe I'll die here. Maybe it'll take forever to find me. And maybe then my mother's life will be easier.

A dude came into view. Kind of a young turk. A white guy in all black, flashing chrome and steel. Just strutting along. Attitude rising off him like diesel fumes. It had to be midnight, and we were in the shadows, but still, he was wearing his sunglasses. Oblivious to me, or so it seemed.

When he was right on top of me, he bobbed his head and pivoted on the balls of his feet, smooth, almost dancing. He shimmied his shoulders. Leaning in, invading my space, he clasped the sunglasses between finger and thumb, pulled them from his face and revealed his eyes, and there was something about him, a moxie that registered in my young mind as a new, rage-free form of confidence. It's stuck with me all these years. This random guy, showing me a brief glimpse of his playful machismo. The joy bursting out of it. He swept his palm out flat like he was displaying the world to me. Then he slipped the sunglasses back over his eyes and kept on going like none of it had happened, like the whole encounter had just been a figment of my imagination.

For a long time, I was sure this had actually been Lenny, coming to me in one of his disguises. To buck me up. To scare the dogs away. To remind me that one day he'd return to us.

We just had to hold on. We had to have faith.

'Cause, really, in essence, that's what freedom meant.

It meant wasting away. Lenny's last true believers.

There were times when the pressure let up and I'd catch sight of the life I'd have if *I* were that solitary young turk. For a minute, an hour, I'd experience the luxurious sensation of floating unencumbered through time and space. Just reading a book in the afternoon sun. Throwing a tennis ball against a wall and conjuring more and more complex rules to keep myself entertained. Traveling through boredom to that place beyond, where everything suddenly became interesting.

So this was what other people meant by "normal." They meant unafraid. They meant having no need to strike a defensive crouch.

It only happened when I was alone, when my mother and her moods were far enough away to seem abstract and not quite real.

I remember one afternoon—it must've been June; the kids were still in school but it was hot as shit. And me, I spent the whole time rooting around in the dirt in Tompkins Square. I had a magnifying glass. I'd found an old dead leaf. A sunny day. Perfect for starting fires. I remember how pleasurable it felt to concentrate on channeling the sun's rays. How I could get the light to focus and make it dance and navigate it around my nest of dirt, but holding it still on the skin of a leaf, that was tricky. Addictively frustrating. Almost, but not quite, impossible. My arm would get tired. I'd shake it out, start over.

All that existed were the glass and the leaf, and me lost in them. The other people in the park, whatever they were doing, the dogs, the squirrels, the rats, everything had faded and fallen away. So when a girl—Rosalita, that was her name—raced over and stole the glass out of my hand, she seemed to come from nowhere.

She was one of the squatter kids from up on 13th Street. Tough.

With stringy dull hair and mean dark eyes and the ghost of an old scar running down her cheek.

"You're doing it wrong," she said. She posed, hand on hip, waiting for a reaction. "You're not even trying to burn something worthwhile."

On another day, in another context, bunkered inside the family paranoia, I might've responded by shrinking and willing myself to disappear. Instead, I challenged back. "Oh? What's something worthwhile?"

She marched my magnifying glass over to the buckled trash can that had been plunked next to a string of concrete ruins that had once been benches. Shoving the glass into her back pocket, she studied the garbage. Tracking something. Up and down, over, around. Tracing its path. Her hands poised and ready to grab it. Then clapping. "Fuck." More clapping. "Shit, damn, fuck." Her head bobbed and twisted. I could almost see the dotted line trailing behind the path of her eyes.

I wandered over. Not to help. Just to see if she'd succeed.

As I got closer, she sensed me and flapped her hand. "Get back."

Her focus narrowed on a fly resting for a moment on a banana peel, twitching, running its front leg over its head, cleaning itself.

Another clap, but she missed again and the fly flew off. "Why'd you do that?" she said.

"Do what?"

"You chased it away."

I could've argued but I liked her. I liked the way she'd taken charge. I said, "Sorry."

"Don't do it again."

To prove myself, I went off to find my own flies. I searched the overflow, the snowdrifts of crap that piled up in the corners and along the pathways. They were drawn to the spots where the junkies hung out. They liked the stench of urine.

And—wait, wait, wait . . .

There.

"I got one!" I shouted.

Rosalita came running. The fly ticked around inside my cupped hands, batting its wings against my palms. "Show me," she said. So demanding.

"If I show you, I'll lose it."

We negotiated a transfer, hands on hands, each gap shut tight. She bossed me around and I did what she told me.

Then, the fly in her hands, we returned to my station—the light was pure there—and she tightened her palms until she had the fly pinched between her thumb and her forefinger. She placed it in the dirt, holding it tight by one wing, and pulled the magnifying glass out of her pocket.

"See, this is how you do it," she said.

And with a flick of her finger, she crinkled its wing.

We were, both of us, sprawled on our stomachs, propped up on elbows. Two kids being kids, impervious to fear. Nothing existed but us. I remember realizing this. It startled me. That we'd fallen into this intense communion. What I'd always longed for. Still do.

We watched the fly hobble in circles, flicking its good wing, trying to get away. You could hear the whiz of its struggle. It seemed to know it was wounded. And after a while, it exhausted itself and gave up.

Rosalita worked the angle of the sun through the glass. She was better at it than me.

She had a steady hand. Once she'd grown her bead of light, she led it to the fly—it was docile now. We waited for something to happen. The fly glowed. Its eyes and torso shimmered like steel, orange and purple and green. And then a little stream of smoke rose out of it.

She nudged the carcass with her finger. There was nothing left inside. Just a brittle dead shell.

She grinned at me, all teeth, one of them chipped. "See?" she said. "That's how you do it." She hopped up and handed me the magnifying glass. Still grinning. Proud. Like she'd even surprised herself.

I felt bad for the fly but I tried not to show it. I probably mumbled something. I don't remember what. What I remember is this feeling: Don't go.

"You want to kiss me?" she said.

I threw it back at her. "Do you want to kiss *me*?"

"Maybe."

There was menace inside her, coursing through her blood. It couldn't be repressed even in her kinder moments.

I positioned myself in front of her and waited and we stood there clueless, not knowing what to do next.

"You have to be closer," she said, so I took a step toward her and puckered and clenched, my eyes shut tight.

"You know what?" she said. "I changed my mind."

And off she ran. And I remember wondering, is this what it means to have a friend?

My mother and Lenny worked out ways to stay in touch. They couldn't call each other. Our phone was still tapped. We were being watched or, anyway, Fran downstairs still had one eye fixed on our movements, and who knew who she might be complaining about us to. What they did was they sent letters back and forth like contraband. My mother's contact was Ted Barrow, our drop spot the Namaste Bookshop.

We avoided the main entrance and went in and out via the basement, squeezing through the stairwell stuffed with warped and faded ten-cent remainders and into the dark hoarder's nest of brittle paper where Barrow kept his overstock. The place spooked me. It was unfinished. So dank. So many secrets. The one time I went down there the mildew creeping through the stacks so overpowered me that I could feel the spores coat my body like the black death. The gateway to the Underground is how I imagined it. Who knew what monsters lurked there waiting to pounce. Smackheads and bloodsuckers and Nosferatu.

After that, my mother mercifully set me up to stand guard outside. I remember poking around out there, my nose level with the sidewalk like a troll, checking out the shoes that wandered past, seeing a pair, sometimes, that shouted narc. Feeling proud of myself, ready with my gun.

On a good day, my mother walked out with a manila envelope full of letters that she'd carry around in her fringed shoulder bag for the rest of the afternoon. They'd stick out, just a corner, their open flaps exposing our secrets to anyone who might want to hurt us. We'd poke through the neighborhood doing this and that and I'd be sure everyone—good, bad or indifferent—could learn everything they wanted to know about us in a glance.

She didn't care. She was cool.

Except when she wasn't and she pawed at the envelope, caressed it, riffling the edges of the smaller ones inside, guessing at their contents, knowing she had to be careful about where and when she opened them. An exquisite torture.

And I knew this meant that when we finally got home, I'd be entertaining myself all night while she communed with the scraps Lenny'd sent her of his life.

It's been years since I've looked at those letters. They're painful. They pull me back into the paranoia that I've spent my life learning how to avoid. Call it denial. Self-preservation. When you're raised in a cult, you develop tactics. So you can survive. So you don't get sucked back in.

But lately, you've got me thinking about this stuff. Last week I fixed my truck and drove up to Brandeis to look at the papers Lenny sold them before he died.

They surprised me. I hadn't remembered them being so . . .

Well, here. Listen to this:

Penelope—
    The first thing you'll want to know is if I made it.
    I did, and how.
    Dig it:
    Mario and Gypsy met me in the movie theater, as promised. It was a heavy scene. They sat a seat apart from each other in the back row, and I entered late after the lights dimmed, squeezing through and taking the seat between them. They were so well disguised that I was convinced I'd fucked up and that they were the wrong people for the first twenty minutes or so. But then Mario got up to use the john, and there on his seat, voila, the envelope. Their people came through—those Weathermen are pros—and before you could say "your mama" I had a new name and a ticket to Somewhere in my hands. (I can't tell you where, of course; all will be revealed one day when they write my story.) Gypsy

gave me a hard look. "Now we're even," she hissed. "Ask for anything else and you won't get a response." She watched the movie for another half hour and then she slinked out too.

And get this: The movie they picked was *The Way We Were*. So maybe they've got a sense of humor after all. I stuck around to watch the whole thing. Research. It's a good flick. There's a character based on me.

Then I checked myself into a fleabag motel near the airport and dyed my hair. I'm a blond now and what they say is true: I'm having much, much more fun.

I'll let you in on a secret: Anonymity's a drag. I'm just another shmuck now. Not even you would recognize me. I've got a new nose. Well, almost: It's still healing. I'm working on my walk. A clean passport and legal driver's license. My new name's growing on me day by day, even if I still forget to answer to it half the time. The only real question left to figure out is, who do I *really* want to be?

It's exciting. I'm ready to commit to whatever comes now.

The hardest part was letting go. I could have stood in the dark with you, watching the kid sleep forever. You know this. You were there. Whatever goes down from here on out, whoever I become, however far away from each other we travel, please remember this.

There will be times when you won't hear from me. The danger might be too high. The ground too uncertain. You'll hear rumors. Kvetching. Disinformation campaigns. Ignore them. You know how these motherfuckers like to talk, and the same agents provocateurs who claimed I stole SDS's lunch money back in '68 are still spreading lies and trying to discredit me.

Teach the kid who his daddy was. Don't let our enemies do it for you.

I'm counting on you, Suzy-Q. Have faith. Think of it like this: I'm taking the long way home. Wherever I go, whether you know it or not, I'll be carrying the two of you with me.

—Odysseus

She never knew when these letters would come. She'd get six in one week, two months' worth of one-sided conversations detailing his private obsessions. Then she wouldn't hear anything from him for months and she'd be left to wonder if he was in danger, if he'd been found out and forced to change his hair color and hop on yet another bus to nowhere.

Here's another one:

Luna,

Had a dream last night. The two of us on a boat. A little dinghy that looked like it was barely seaworthy. In my dream-logic it morphed into a luxury yacht when we boarded it. The beauty of the sea on a calm sunny day. Rocking. Floating. Far off at sea. And in this dream we were surrounded by a tremendous radiating sensation of peace. We sat on a blanket laid out on the deck, eating fresh-cut apples and honey-drenched cheese. Warm, doughy fry bread like we used to get at Curry Tandoor. We lazed around and napped and fucked—oh, did we fuck! The rocking of the boat. The rolling of our hips. The waves lapping up against the hull. We were in tune with the sea and the earth and the universe. Cosmic fucking. That's what it was. The kid was there too. Serious like he sometimes gets. He sat on the prow watching the horizon through a golden periscope. Not moving. Navigating us toward dry land. Safe haven. I don't know. Our destination was hazy. What was clear was that we—you and I—were in his hands and that we both knew with that deep certainty one accesses in dreams that he was leading us toward a better place than the one we'd left behind. For a long time we floated like this. A light rain fell. A sun shower. And then the kid shouted, "Land ho!" and we followed the seagulls to a rocky beachhead we'd never seen before.

I woke up slowly, not wanting to leave, feeling like I could choose between that world and this one. But of course I can't.

Eventually there I was again, blinking on the couch in the chilly, damp basement of the safe house where I'm currently shacked up. Barely recognizing myself.

I've been thinking about this dream all day. Is this what they call a dream of escape? 'Cause it feels to me more like a dream of what could've, would've, should've been. Like the truth is that you and the kid are on that dinghy without me, sailing off to new frontiers I'll never see.

There's so much I'm missing.

Send word.

—Sol

Her letters to him were . . . less interesting. Or that's not true. What they were was too close. To me. My experience. Even now, I feel like I need to protect her.

I found this, though. She got me to perform for him sometimes. To improvise stories into the tape recorder so he could hear my voice and feel like he was still part of the family. I'd forgotten all about it.

Listen:

LADIES AND GENTLEMEN!

WELCOME TO THE STORY OF THE FREE LITTLE PIGS!

Once upon a time in a kingdom way far away there were free little pigs named Joe and Bo and Stinky who all wanted to have their own houses. That was because they had growed up all together in a teeny-tiny pigsty. It was a really tiny and muddy and yucky pigsty and the free little pigs got stuck and bumped into the other free little pigs when they tried to turn around sometimes. They were very very sad, and they, even though they loved each other very much, they sometimes wanted to be alone and not have to share their toys all the time.

And they lived with the mean farmer too, who always spit at them and called them names. He was big and fat with the overalls and the hat, like the farmer hat, and he smoked cigarettes and didn't look both ways when he crossed the street and all kinds of stuff like that. And he was the one who made them live in the pigsty. He did all the things that bad people do. He chased them around with the poker thing and he didn't fix the heat in the winter.

So one day the free little pigs ran away from him. They moved out to the faraway country to make their houses and meet the big mad wolf.

When they got to the country, they played. They, like, rolled around in the mud because they were free little pigs and they liked that. And they played tag too, but the one pig, Stinky, didn't want to because he always had to be It and he was way slower than the other pigs so he couldn't ever catch them and they made him cry. And what else? They played cops and robbers and keep-away and, um, and they got to go to their dad's house sometimes because he lived there too, and they got to play with him. And, you know what? They never ever ever ever ever ever had to go to Amari's house and eat nasty rutabaga stew while their mom did grown-up things without them 'cause they cramped her style.

Their dad was a nice dad. He played with the free little pigs and he didn't ever yell or make fun of them because he was so busy playing with them. And then, after a while when he usually gets all like HUMPF, HUMPF and making I-don't-want-to-be-here noises, he didn't do that either because he still, even after all day of playing, he wanted to play with them some more. And even then when it got to be bedtime, he didn't want them to have to go home.

Then at home, when it was late at night and they were sleepy from playing all day at their dad's house, they couldn't sleep. It was too dark and scary and they missed their dad. And it was really cold . . . and really dark . . . and . . . just really, really cold . . . and it got rainy sometimes and people shouted outside their window at night.

And monsters—there were monsters there too. They couldn't see them too good.

The monsters sat way far away in the woods—they were so big, like this big—and they had little tiny heads and big sharp teeth that flicked around on snake necks. They would fly their heads up to the free little pigs and say really quiet and whispery, "DON'T GO TO SLEEP OR ELSE I'M GOING TO KILL YOU!" And then when the little pigs looked to see them, they'd pull their heads away really fast and be like ghosts. The free little pigs were so scared they had to give each other big hugs all night long.

They wished they were still at their dad's house.

Then it got to be morning and the monsters went away and then they made their houses!

The first little pig made his house out of straw. And the second little pig made his house out of sticks! And the third little pig made his house out of bricks!

Then they were happy because they had their houses and it was warm inside.

But then the big mad wolf came!

"Little pig, little pig, let me come in!"

"No!" shouted the free little pig named Joe who lived in the straw house and . . .

Anyway, you get the picture.

It's strange. I've got a shitload more, but I don't remember making a single one of them.

Three months after Lenny went underground, almost a year after the bust, on an early August night in 1974 not so different from the one that had sent him rushing deliriously into the Whitmore Hotel, a night that, more crucially, marked the end of the day before the trial was set to begin, my mother went at it with the sage again. We lit candles—massive things, the size of moon rocks, with five or six wicks apiece. Clutching my AK so tightly my fingers went numb, I squirreled from post to post around the living room, patrolling, my eyes on the windows or the shadows in the hall, while my mother hunched next to the radio, focusing in on WBAI, on Fass or sometimes when he went on a tangent, on Vin Scelsa, spinning the dial back and forth, anxious for news of Lenny that no one was interested in broadcasting anymore.

I think we thought he'd come back. That he'd show up at the courthouse, despite the risk, and vindicate himself like he had in the past. He'd somersault down the steps, crack that famous grin for the cameras and drawl, "Shucks, boys, what did you expect? You can't catch me. I'm the gingerbread man."

I think we thought he'd send us a signal that night telling us to get ready for him.

The last thing I remember is being sprawled across the throw pillows and that it was real late and I'd been watching the candles swallow and drown their wicks.

I woke the next morning to the scream of the door buzzer. Then the phone started ringing too, and I realized this had been going on for who knew how long, that I'd been hearing it in my sleep, stitched through my dreams.

It was late. After nine. The sun sliced a rectangle around the closed blinds.

The buzzer screamed again, longer, angrier this time.

I was discombobulated, trapped in my mother's arms on the futon in her room. She must've carried me in there after I passed out. The way she curled around me now—clinging, almost peaceful, her breath coming in with soft milky pops—I wondered how she could sleep like this, so still when whatever was about to happen was right here, right now.

I squirmed out of her arms and padded off to see who was at the door. Odd things were happening inside my head, like déjà vu but more uncertain. Like the future—the immediate future, the next few moments—had already spooled out in some other dimension. I could feel its momentum, I just couldn't see it. I remember this great dread about who might be out there. A fear that it would be Lenny and also that it would *not* be Lenny.

The buzzer again. The phone. The jackboots of doom kicking at our door.

Balancing on a kitchen chair, I peered through the peephole. All I saw was hair, fish-eyed and magnified out of proportion.

"Lenny?" I said.

The guy shuffled, didn't answer. His hair wiggled and bent. I heard mumbling. Or whispering.

"Who's there?" I said.

An eye. "The name's Douglas Horsley."

"Uh . . ."

He backed up so I could see him. Then he grinned at the peephole and waved. A total square. "Are your parents home? Be a good boy and fetch them for me."

We had rules for what to do when cops came to our door. Protocols. Steps to take. Legal rights to assert. Fuck if I could remember a single one.

I hopped off the chair and ran to my mother, calling, "Should I let him in?"

She rolled onto her back. Blinked. Stalled. "No," she said wearily. "I'll do it."

The phone rang again. The buzzer buzzed.

When the ringing finally stopped, my mother gathered herself up and rested her forehead on her knees.

"Mom?"

"I said I'll do it." It was like I'd joined her cadre of enemies.

Up then, and marching toward the kitchen, she made no effort to prepare herself. Her hair hung like a geyser, black curls and stray locks spritzing out all over the place. The shapeless tie-dye she'd worn to bed rode just below her hips, not quite covering her naked ass.

And though she was no prude—nudity, like everything else, was a political act to her—this . . . it seemed dangerous. Reckless. She'd been having premonitions of Armageddon. And now the federale was lurking in the hallway. The phone was ringing off the hook. Who knew what else was coming down on us. She and Lenny had warned me this day would come. For years—my whole life—we'd been waiting for the moment when the feds would bum-rush the place and extract their payback for all the times Lenny had made them look like fools. Now here it was. She needed armor. Sturdy shoes. To protect herself so she could protect me.

Or not. There were ways of wielding power I couldn't yet imagine.

She flicked angrily at the various bolts Lenny had installed on the door. Turned the gear on the crossbar belted above the knob. Kicked the iron rod from its groove in the floor. Then, throwing the door open, she blocked Douglas Horsley with her hairy bush.

Did he blanch at her pudenda? You bet your ass he did. He went further. He gawked. Studied its curls and folds.

"Up here." She snapped her fingers in front of his nose. "Warrant?"

Amusement played on his face. "What do you think?"

"Let me see it."

He slapped a sheaf of papers against his open palm. Held it out. Pulled it back. Cat and mousing her. Flirting. The stairwell behind him was crawling with cops.

As she looked over the warrant, the phone rang for the hundredth time. She swore. "Jesus fucking Christ." She spun away, leaving the door open, stomped down the length of the apartment and then she was swearing at and pounding on the spitball box while Douglas Horsley and I stared at each other like bozos.

"We need to talk to your daddy," he said, saccharine, faux. There was something of the used-car salesman to him.

I backed up a step.

"Is he here?" He mugged, peering under the table. Grinned at me like this was some children's game. Like he was a paid entertainer here to beg for laughs. "Is he back there? In the closet? The bathroom?"

I said nothing. Took another step back. My head clicked with calculations, the reverse chronology of lost and found that, I hoped, would lead me to my AK-47. I'd had it the night before. I'd put it down. But where? If I only had it now, I could be brave.

"What's your name, kid?" the guy said.

He'd cornered me. He was squatting, split-legged. His pants strained their seams. "You're scared. It's okay to be scared sometimes. I've got a kid just about your age. He gets scared too. The world's a scary place."

Something crashed against the wall—another spitball box biting the dust—and we heard my mother bark from the other room, "What part of go fuck yourself don't you understand?"

The guy peered down the chain of rooms at my mother on the phone, checking on her, or checking her out, a little bit of both.

And I suddenly remembered. The throw pillows. Somewhere on the floor out there. Unless she'd put it away somewhere. But that wouldn't have been like her.

"Looks like she's left you in charge," he said. "You can handle that, right? But you know, that means you've got a big decision to make. You look like a nice kid. You look like a kid who tries not to get in trouble. And hey, right now, you're not in trouble. You should know that, okay? You can keep it that way too. It's easy. I just need to know what happened to your daddy. Does he call to say good night? Go ahead and tell me. I'm one of the good guys."

Like I was a chump.

"The thing is, if you don't tell me—well. There's some things you should know. Different kinds of trouble. 'Aiding and abetting.' 'Harboring a fugitive.' Ever heard of that?"

I tried to summon Lenny. What would he have done at a moment like this? I couldn't remember.

The cops were inside now. Some of them. Log-jammed around the door. The whole squadron seemed to have been called up. Here and there I recognized a face among them—guys who'd been friendly back in the day, guys who'd acted like they were in on the joke. And maybe they had been. Maybe it was their joke all along and Lenny and his movement had been the punch line.

Everyone watching me. Waiting for me to say something. I felt hot. I couldn't think.

And then there was my mother, palming my head, holding me steady. Guarding me. She'd wrapped herself in a caftan and she was holding my AK. "Lenny's not here," she said. "But you know that."

"I know nothing," said Horsley. But he stood up and backed away from me.

She sucked water out of the barrel of the gun, drinking from it. A bluff. Asserting her unflappable cool. "Sure you do. This is harassment. Our lawyers have been informed."

"Mind if we have a look?"

She pointed the gun at him for half a second, casual, almost like she didn't mean it. Just a prop, a baton waving him on. And off he went to ransack the apartment, his police escort trampling after him.

While we waited them out she sat behind me, bracing me tight between her knees. She kissed my neck—the soft spot where everything converged. "Don't be scared, little man," she said. "This is progress."

Later, after they left, having discovered nothing, not even a stem, not a single seed, she explained herself. "Wait and see, Freddy. It gets better from here. Now that everyone knows he's gone, we can start fighting to get him back."

"And?" I said.

"And what? That's it."

And wandering off to hop in the shower, she left me there to stew.

It wasn't enough. The world had promised us something. Or Lenny had. I couldn't say exactly what that might've been, but I knew it was far from the life we were living. Nobody even really talked about it anymore. And look, our apartment had just been totaled. Posters torn from walls. Files and news clippings scattered everywhere. Shoe prints on the plasterboard where the cops had kicked at phantom secret compartments. Lenny's famous American flag shirts—this I remember particularly clearly—littered everywhere, ripped to shreds. It was hard to make the leap from this ruin to something as nebulous as hope. The best I could do was give in to my clenched urge for order and try to put everything back in its place. I folded afghans, stacked books on shelves, sorted ripped paper into color-coded piles, cleared a shotgun path down the middle of the apartment. Did it help? It did not.

There was more buzzing at the door. People rallying to the cause. Well, one person anyway.

"Ochs here."

I peered through the fish-eye. He looked older than he had the last time I'd seen him, fatter, bloated. He was worn out. Half-faded. "You're not supposed to be here," I said. But I opened the door, hating myself and my weakness even as I did.

He stuttered—or no, that's not quite the right word. More a whisper of an echo of doubt in his voice. "W-Will you let me in?" And before I could answer he ducked inside, his arms overloaded with newspapers.

What struck me was that, under the fat he was the same old Phil he'd always been, wearing the same old uniform—that pale blue work shirt, those grease-stained chinos, the work boots laced tight around his ankles. And that same melancholic determination—let's call it idealism—weighing him down like a hair shirt. He seemed harmless. A fern.

I wanted him to leave.

He spilled the papers all over the kitchen table and started opening cupboards. Shutting them. Opening others. "Where's the coffee in this place?" he said.

"Where's anything?" I said back.

He moved on to the fridge, shuffling shit around to see what might be hidden in there.

And done with her shower, now dressed for battle, my mother appeared and leaned against the doorway, where until that morning a beaded curtain had hung. She watched him, impassive, glancing my way once so I'd know she was pissed.

When, finally, he realized what was going on, Phil flopped into a chair and squinted up at her. "Hey," he said. "Suzy." Soft as a sponge.

They stared each other down, weighing implications, silently negotiating terms. His compassion must have enraged her. It must've looked like pity.

"You don't know, do you?" he finally said.

"Know what? Has he been caught?" she said.

"No."

"Then of course I know. He's been gone for months."

"You should've told me," Phil said.

"Oh? Why?"

He gaped at the floor.

"Whatever. I don't have time for this." She stepped past him and made for the door. "He's your problem now," she said. Not to Phil, to me. And off she went. To see Kunstler, I found out later. Paperwork. Reporting. A private mea culpa. The beginnings of a public record meant to prove we'd known nothing, been abandoned, were eligible for welfare.

With her gone, the fear tightened in my chest. I ached. Everything inside vibrated, unstable. This was how it would be. This was forever. That's what I kept thinking.

Not knowing what else to do, I threw myself back into my quest for order. The trash can—I tipped it upright and piled in the garbage. Lemon rinds, orange peels, cakes of loose tea, napkins, everything nasty, damp and sticky. The beads from the curtain in the kitchen doorway. There was crap everywhere. I'd start on one project that seemed almost manageable and in a panic switch to another. Righting tipped stools and retrieving stray coupons and refrigerator magnets wedged under the oven, the fridge.

Phil—a sucker for the tragic, good with helpless things—just watched me, sad, caring. It was intolerable.

I went at him with all I had. "Why are you here, Phil? Why'd you come? We don't want you here. You think you're helping? You're not helping. Nobody asked you to come here. We don't want your help. We don't want your newspapers. Or your stupid . . ." I looked for some weakness I could exploit. ". . . shirt. Go write some songs, or something," I said. I wasn't good yet at school yard taunts. Couldn't think on my feet. "You're stupid," I said. "I hate your stupid face." I told him my mother and I could take care of ourselves. Said, "We're tough motherfuckers. Tougher than you."

And he just took it. Passive resistance on an intimate scale. Slouched there with his shoulder to the wall, clear-eyed, patient, waiting, waiting, waiting me out, not even trying to comfort me so I could push him away again.

When, finally, I was near tears, he tipped his chin and said, "You find that coffee yet?"

I blinked at him.

"You really want me to leave?" he said.

Too proud to bend, I stomped off to find my gun.

For the next however long, he kept his distance from me. We camped out in different rooms. I listened through the walls. Cupboards opening and closing. The tap. The teakettle. The burner clicking and catching. I was glad he was there.

Eventually, a kind of numb normal settled in and I went off to find him.

You have to understand how large Phil loomed in my life throughout this time. He had a knack—he seemed to magically show up whenever and wherever I needed him.

I hovered and watched him in the front room, newspapers stacked in read and unread piles on either side of him. I wasn't sure yet if I'd be willing to speak, but I was ready to hover around him. I held my AK tight and edged closer, trying not to be noticed. He'd folded the section in his hands subway-style. I came closer. Just for a second, he held the hair out of his eyes, gazed at me and then went back to his paper.

"What's it say?" I asked him after a while.

Tensions in Chile. Some hotel bombed in Norway. Odds on the Foreman fight scheduled for that evening. People had been born. People had died. Another day. The world was full of news. "Take a look out the window," he finally said.

A crowd had convened. Ten or twelve shabby men in sloppy

clothes. The press. You could see it in their posture, in the hollows of their eyes. They were dressed like anybody else, a little sharper around the edges, maybe.

"Tonight, tomorrow, it'll be nonstop Lenny. Exciting stuff. In England they call it taking a runner. You could make a statement. Then *you'd* be the news."

Lenny had warned me about these people. They lived in the country of cynicism. "Anytime you're dealing with a newsman," he used to say, "someone's gonna be the sucker. Your job is to make sure it's him, not you."

"What do they want?" I said.

Phil let slip an understated, private smile. He put down his paper. "What would Lenny do?"

"He wouldn't be in a situation like this."

"But he *is*. This is exactly the situation he's in. You are, too."

He was up. Pacing. That hand clamped to his forehead. Gears were grinding in his brain. He grabbed my mother's beat-up old guitar from where it lived, never used, in the corner. "We could write a song. All the news that's fit to sing."

Clamping a foot on the arm of the couch, he rested the guitar on his knee, tuned it in a flash and plucked out a few chords. Then he adjusted the capo and spun out a tune, fully formed, a ballad, faint echoes of the olden days lilting through it. Maybe it was new, made up on the spot. It sounded like all his other songs. The minor harmonies. The abrupt shifts in key. The tempo that slowed and sped up with the length of his lines. The rumbling on the strings as he took the song on its turn toward hope.

"Songs don't fix anything," I said.

This saddened him. Such a young kid, so jaundiced already. "You really believe that?" He plopped down on the couch, draped his arms around the neck of the guitar and stared at me, earnest, taking me seriously. "You sound like your dad now," he said.

"So what?"

"So it's interesting." Mounting the guitar like a cane between his legs, he leaned toward me. "Have you ever been to a demonstration? I know you have. I've gone to them with you. Used to be we marched side by side. So . . . so you know. It's the songs that unite and focus the crowd. Music gets them moving in the same direction." He contemplated what he'd just said for a moment. Then he added an amendment. "It's not the music Lenny lost faith in. It's the direction."

A few things here. First, assume this was all going over my head. And that Phil didn't think twice about whether or not I understood him. He'd stored this up for years and now he was making his case, if not to Lenny, then to the next best thing. Making peace. Making clear that whatever misunderstandings might've accumulated between them, his fidelity had never wavered. Second, don't forget how freaked out I was. And that Phil had promised some vague possibility of solace. So this wasn't helping.

He went on. "You know he's right, don't you? We've veered off course. Wh-Who knows where the hell we're headed now. Who's going to remember the place we were trying to get to? Who'll keep the record? I'll tell you. The singers. The troubadours. That's who. So . . . so music."

Something snapped in him and he realized he was talking to a six-year-old.

"Did Lenny ever tell you about the day we first met? I guess, no. W-Why would he? You should know this, though. Who he was. W-What he was capable of.

"So." Gauging my interest, pushing on. "Right around the corner. On St. Marks. Late September 1967. Not long before you were born, actually. I was on my way to check on Old Bull Lester. You don't know who that is. A foundational figure. Maybe the last of that generation of hobos who'd carried the sounds of the South to the cities up north. Folk and blues and a lonely wind in the boxcar. Not a thought of fame. Alan Lomax found him living in a cold-water flat on Avenue C. He recorded him, turned a few of us on to him. Eighty-four years old, arthritic and blinded by cataracts. But he still had that auld lang syne, as they say. He'd invented a style of double-fretting—unconsciously; he was entirely untrained—by which he could coax two different chords from his instrument at the same time and make them harmonize. We owed him, for this and a whole lot more. We revered him. On Sundays I took it upon myself to check in on him, learn what he knew, keep the old sounds alive, bring him groceries and that sweet red wine he loved. He's long gone now.

"Anyway. Fall '67. I was heading over to Old Bull's place, walking along under the elevated train past Astor Place, then down St. Marks toward the park. Halfway up the block, right near The Dom, I saw something was happening. A tight little knot of strife. People had congregated and stepped up on the stoops, straining to see.

"Th-This was a tense time on the Lower East Side. The tribes were in chaos, struggling to hold on to their turf and forge a new equilibrium. There'd been troubles here and there, ethnic sensitivities getting out of hand, the meddling cops exacerbating distrust. The Newark riots were fresh in the air, which just heightened the usual nobody-listening-to-each-other shit. I'd been noticing all this, wondering if this was going to be a moment of coming together or falling apart. I feared the second, which . . . I'll tell you what: Despair's never far away. It's always there, lurking behind the next hill."

He lost himself for a second. "If we were going to end the war, we . . . we needed each other. Anyway, it turned out some black kid—he couldn't have been sixteen—was in such a good mood he'd jaywalked. Then he'd hopped off a car bumper to slap a No Parking sign. And this cop in a bad mood had watched him do all this and now he was intent on ruining the kid's day. By the time I got there, the kid was trying to save face, pleading and jiving. So we know how that goes. It's always the cop who escalates the situation. He stepped up to the kid, pushed, and the kid went passive, stepped back, held up his hands. 'I'm cool,' he said.

" 'You're not cool,' the cop said. 'You've broken three—make it four city ordinances. And I'm of a mind to place you under arrest.'

"I was just about to leave, shaking my head in shame, when out of nowhere there was Lenny like some lunatic prophet, making a racket down the street, running a broken umbrella along the iron fences out front of the buildings, barking like mad. 'Crumbpacker! Hey! Hey, Officer Crumbpacker! I need some assistance over here!' That voice of his crackling like lightning in the air.

"I knew who he was, of course. He'd already made himself notorious by then. But I'd never seen him in action.

"'Hey! Officer Crumbpacker! It's an e-*merg*-en-cy! There's some peace being perpetrated over here. You gotta break it up. It's your duty. Hey, ain't you an officer of the peace?'

"Everyone looked. The cop, the kid, everyone.

"'Come on, man,' Lenny said. 'How 'bout you pick on somebody your own size.'

"And we all laughed, everyone but the cop. He was a little hockey-puck of a guy. The kid towered over him.

"Lenny had wandered into the street. He wove back and forth, holding up traffic, stepping onto the hoods of cars, leaping off them, doing a soft-shoe, Fred Astaire in army-surplus boots.

"Somewhere in there the kid ran off. But Lenny wasn't done. 'You want to arrest somebody, Crumbpacker? Arrest me. Look here, I'm jaywalking.' He twirled the umbrella like a baton. "Come on, people, you can jaywalk too. It's the fun new dance. All the kids are doin' it.'

"The cop, flustered, humiliated, was turning red.

"'Crumbpacker's bored, folks. Come on. Help him out. Let's give him something to do.'

"Lenny's eyes darted over the crowd, a thousand calculations flicking behind them. He saw me and called out, 'Hey, Phil! Phil Ochs, everybody. Give him a hand.' And I have to say, shameful as it is, I ducked when I heard my name. I wasn't ready yet to hear Lenny's message. He was too hip for me. I was still stuck in '64. 'Hey, Phil. You're an honest guy. Give it to me straight. Did you see that kid destroy any property?'

"'N-No.' I cleared my throat and said it again, louder. 'No.'

"'No'?

"'No.'

"'I didn't think so,' he said. 'Because . . .' And he had us now, the crowd, me, even the cop. Everyone. And what he did with this attention, w-well, he quieted himself. He made us wait. And wait. Until, just when he sensed we might lose interest, he planted a boot on the bumper of the very same car the kid had jumped off of, raised himself up and stood there. He took two steps and he was standing on the hood. His voice cracked out. '*This* is what destruction of public property looks like.'

"And suddenly he was in the air, both arms flexed above his head, clutching the umbrella, bringing it down just so, hooking the No Parking sign and yanking. The sign popped a screw and twirled, bent, on its post.

"Lenny landed on both feet, crouched, somehow directly in front of the cop. He smirked. 'Whatcha gonna do, pig?' he said. 'Jaywalking. Destruction of public property. I think you might get your arrest now!'

"And he was off, triumphant, cackling, bouncing through the crowd, waving for all the children to race along with him. He spun and backpedaled, calling out, 'Guess you're gonna have to add resisting arrest to that list.' And then he was gone around the corner of Second Avenue, the cop huffing after him, stopping, wheezing."

Phil flipped the guitar to his knee and plucked a few notes, hit a double chord. He watched his fingers as he worked, head bowed, hair drooping over his face. Giving not one sign of what I was supposed to do with this information. What it had to do with today. With me. I remember feeling it was all irrelevant. That Lenny was irrelevant. Not there. Not gonna save us. And I remember the shame that attached to this feeling. The sense that forsaking Lenny meant betraying myself.

Phil ran his hand over his head and brushed the hair out of his face. "Whatever people say about your father," he told me, "and they're going to say all kinds of things, hold on to what you know. He's not the person they claim he is." He went back to his strumming, pressed two fingers to the fret board and rumbled out a rhythm over a single chord. "It's a pretty good song, I think. Should we try it?"

He unhitched the accordion bars over the window and shoved them open, inched up the screen and ducked onto the fire escape, pulling the guitar out after him.

And what could I do? It seemed wrong to leave him hanging there.

He saluted the reporters with a curt two-fingered tap to his forehead. "Hi-ya," he said, calling on his stage voice. "Beautiful day." He cleared his throat. "Freedom and I—" He walked me forward so the reporters could see me, hooked my neck in his elbow, pulled me tight like a pal. "Freedom and I have a message for you." A shy chuckle and he added, "A different perspective. This is called 'The Clown with the Bomb in His Hand.'" With that, he began strumming, singing the same song he'd plucked out inside, softly at first, his voice swallowed up by the dense humid air, but building, accumulating power and speed as his conviction swelled.

And the people on the street, the reporters, yes, but also the folks from the hood, responded in just the way I'd thought they would. He got catcalls. People shouting from windows. *Shut. The. Fuck. Up.* One of the reporters, recognizing Phil, called out, "You baby-sitting, man? Is this what you've come to?"

Phil just kept on strumming. He knew from a tough crowd. He must've thought his belief would win them over like it had so many skeptics before.

But I surprised myself and aimed my gun and shot, raining water down in their direction, a weak spray that died before it reached them. And they laughed, so I grabbed a chunk of cement, a decorative molding that had fallen off the building's façade onto the fire escape. I whipped it, dinging a car. They laughed at this too. They were in on the same joke as the cops had been that morning.

When Phil's last chorus wound its way to an end and the final tremor of his song dissipated, the reporters broke into a round of applause. Ironic. Cruel. Humiliating.

Did he know this would happen? Maybe. It could be he foresaw everything that occurred that day. I imagine him, after a night of maintenance drinking, shuffling past a newsstand as he walked home at bar time and seeing the early edition, still bundled in its heat-sealed plastic strips. The pressure drop of recognition as he noted the date and thought of Lenny, his day in court, and Mom and me. I picture him, buzzed and sentimental, not thinking too hard about what to do next, just heeding the call. Faithful, as always, to his old allies, regardless of what they might think of him. Maybe he realized I wasn't equipped to comprehend the implications of what was happening. Maybe he knew I'd need someone to lash out at. Someone who would pretend to be more pitiable than me. And maybe he'd known that he and he alone was particularly equipped to be this person.

As we ducked back inside I reached out and patted his back like some sort of big brother. "Phil," I said, "it's gonna be okay."

The circumstances of my mother's and my life somehow became both more and less real after that. Everything changed by not changing at all.

We limped along.

The trash made it down to the street, most of it. Anything that couldn't be salvaged from the raid. "Stuff is just stuff," my mother said. "Artifacts of the past. Didn't anybody ever tell you history's dead?" For months, we picked scraps of paper—the remains of posters for long-ago events that my parents had thought would be famous forever—out from under the furniture, from corners and closets. Every once in a while we still slipped on those beads—there always seemed to be more of them.

You get used to it. You keep keeping on.

We found hope wherever we could.

One morning before dawn, my mother disappeared, leaving me to stew in the apartment with no idea where she was, sure she'd been stolen away by the pigs, while she waited in line at the welfare office and met with the caseworker and filled out the forms and got herself on the list that might, just might, give us what little security we needed to survive. When she finally got back at, like, eight that night, she was so pissed at the bullshit of it all that I couldn't say anything. I just had to swallow my fear.

But maybe things were looking up. Lenny was back in the news. The time was ripe for my mother to pounce like a good Yoko Ono. She pled Lenny's case one more time in *The Village Voice*, countering the narrative that had been building—Lenny the huckster, the coward, the fraud, he'd steal the lunch money off your kids if he could—with her own theories of government conspiracy, an invidious COINTELPRO, law enforcement used as a bludgeon to smash our constitutional right to dissent. She recapped Lenny's long history of harassment, the slanderous whisper campaigns against him and the Left in general, started by moles trying to knock the wind out of anyone who might dream of a better world.

Stuff was happening. I didn't know what it was, but I could feel her excitement. The flame in her eyes. She and Kunstler talked a lot about Ronnie Walker. They'd hired an investigator to map his life, look into who and what he'd ever been. They hadn't found anything yet, but they were close. That's what she kept saying. "We're close."

And maybe she was circling a mirage, but it kept her lively while it lasted.

She grooved around the apartment blasting tunes.

Sometimes she dragged me out into the sunshine. We hopped turnstiles and rattled up to the Sheep's Meadow—site of my conception. We'd hit a playground or two. Hang out with the rich kids who called Central Park their own. The two of us. Taking over. Or she'd take over. She swung higher than me, whipped faster through the monkey bars. I tagged along. On the teeter-totter, she'd use her weight as leverage and plant her feet in the dirt, anchor herself, suspending me way up high above the ground, and in a flush of delirious joy, she'd sing,

> Even though we ain't got money
> I'm so in love with you honey
> Everything will bring a chain of lo-o-o-ove.

The whiplash I felt trying to match her highs. The sense of responsibility and dread, knowing even at six that her joy, her hope, her belief in the possible—it would crash. That she'd look to me to rebuild it and I wouldn't know how.

See, that's what I mean about change. It wasn't material, but . . . I understood now what this chain of love implied. I understood who was supposed to protect whom.

Most of her energy went into doing what she could to bring LSD back to life.

Despite all the evidence to the contrary, despite her own experience begging for cash back when no one had ponied up for Lenny's bail, she convinced herself that this time—now that he was safely hidden away, living like the outlaw he'd always claimed to be—his old allies would rally to his cause. LSD would bring the movement back to itself. The tribes would gather again, rekindling the fires that had gone out in the years since everyone had fallen away. It would be a sort of revivalist event where everyone would lift a lighter and sing along to the old songs living in their bones. And Lenny would be the star leading them on, his spirit that much more powerfully there in the room for the fact that he himself was unable to attend.

She worried about it like you would any party to which you'd invited people you didn't trust. All day, before the first and, as it turned out, only LSD meeting, she futzed over the details, pulling the lava lamps out of the bottom of the junk closet, draping Indian-print sheets over the windows. Moving the furniture around just so. She stacked Lenny's favorite albums six-deep on the record player: Airplane, the Dead, Buffalo Springfield, Santana, Steve Miller, *The White Album*. She cued the first one up and flopped back on the couch and let its jangle and thump spill over her.

And she waited and waited and waited and waited for Lenny's champions to arrive.

Wanna guess who showed?

Phil Ochs.

No one else.

Just Phil, always a sucker for a cause. Give him your tired, your poor, your huddled masses yearning to break free and he'd write them a six-thousand-word paean for *The Nation,* organize a benefit concert on their behalf and get sloppy drunk at their birthday parties.

I remember him clomping into the room my mother had worked so hard on. In one hand, a whole mess of cheap Chinese. In the other, a couple of jugs of Carlo Rossi. He threw my mother a half-hearted two-finger salute, dropped into a folding chair in the corner, barely noticing the vacant seats around him, and set up shop. I remember a kind of awe at his obliviousness. It seemed like audacity to me. Confidence. And I remember how my mother scowled when she saw him, like he didn't count, like he'd crashed the party.

He fanned the cartons in an arc around his seat and methodically opened and ate what was in them. Sweet and sour pork clotted with syrup. Wilted string beans. Rice. Sesame chicken. More rice. Some sort of beef dish that glistened like an oil slick. Yet more rice. Then lo mein, which he shoveled up in bulging knotted mounds while he hovered over the carton and bit down on the stray noodles.

God, the sounds he made. Slurping and munching and grunting with pleasure. Yum, yum, yum. He ate with great velocity, spraying soy sauce all over his pants and the floor. Drowning each bite with wine straight from the jug.

My mother could barely force herself to stay in the room. He both disgusted and fascinated her. And maybe she was right to be disgusted. Maybe he was putting on a gross display of the sad, fussy glutton he'd turned himself into, but to me he sparkled with all the magic of an adult who's solved life's mysteries. I sat at his feet. Watched for what I could learn.

Eventually he glanced at her and, like he'd just noticed where he was, asked, "Where is everybody?" Talking with his mouth full.

She just shook her head. Bored holes in him with her eyes.

Lowering his chopsticks and carton to his knee, he held her for a moment in his pitiful, compassionate gaze. Then he gave a little shrug and went back to his feast.

My mother retreated inside herself after that. Soaking in the humiliation. She sprawled on the couch with her eyes closed, mouthing along to the music like it could somehow carry her off to paradise.

And I remember—and this seemed far more important than the party—how when he was stuffed and you'd think he couldn't eat another bite, Phil pulled two egg rolls out of his bag, one for him and one for me.

Understand: Egg rolls were among the few things we could afford. They cost forty-five cents. I ate a lot of them. And every single one tortured me. Did you take them out of their packaging and dribble grease down your arm? Or did you leave them in and end up with a sticky mess of duck sauce pooling in the bottom, turning the crispy parts soggy? Why, after one bite did the stuffing always fall out? Such a basic life skill. It shouldn't have been that hard. But I couldn't master it. No one had taught me how. I struggled, embarrassed and ashamed, with each and every one I ate. And Phil had noticed my anxiety. He understood.

"W-Watch this," he said, holding his egg roll up as an example.

He laid it, still wrapped, on his knee and grabbed the duck sauce. Pinching its sealed end, he shook the packet so the sauce would settle, and used the ribs cut into the end to tear it just slightly, enough to puncture the air bubble inside and create a spout. "It's easy."

All I'd ever managed was a long spurting gash.

Then he cupped the packet over the egg roll and spread a long spiraling ribbon of sauce across the tip. He did it again. Bite by bite. Ripping a bit more cellophane away each time. Everything contained inside right to the end.

It was a revelation. Such a small, insignificant lesson in living but delivered with such deliberate attention. Like he'd seen me. My needs. My confusion. Like I mattered. Like being baffled was a completely reasonable response to a mystifying world and a kid sometimes needed a little help.

It's stupid, I know.

But—and here's the thing—I remember that's when I understood he loved me.

And I remember, later, he and my mother got screaming drunk and feely with each other and he was there the next morning and many more after that and she never tried to hold another LSD meeting. She never even thought about it. LSD became another piece of evidence. More proof of the vast conspiracy against Lenny.

Here's another letter:

La Mer—

So much has gone down since I last wrote that I don't know quite where to start.

Maybe with an apology? I promised to write you each and every day, but over the past two weeks I've blown it. And for that I'm very sorry.

In my current circumstances, all I have is my word. It crushes me to think that I've broken it—and with you! Do me a favor, babe, and in your next letter, bring down the hammer. Snap the whip. Remind me who I am.

'Cause, babe, if you only knew the trouble I've seen.

I've had to pick up and flee again. By now I should know the signs. The spooky quiet that follows me around. The double takes on the street. The woman at the grocery store, usually so friendly, fumbling, unwilling to meet my eye. But apparently I've lost my Spidey sense. When the anonymous call came in telling me to run, it flattened me like an anvil. And as I hopped on the next bus to nowhere, I was shaking like a motherfucker. Half of me hoped they'd just catch me and put an end to the whole charade.

Well, they didn't, obviously. I've lived to fight another day.

Now I'm in another depressing factory town where the people are gray and washed out like the sky and the sidewalks are crumbling and gas costs a fortune. America! I'm seeing it through different eyes now—tired eyes—and it's a heavy trip. An angry, unforgiving place. From where

I'm sitting now, it seems impossible that we could have accomplished all we did just those few short years ago.

Were we deluded? I don't think so. I think we didn't take it far enough.

The truth is, I'm in a fragile state. I'm fucked in the head. I don't know how much longer I can live like this.

But, babe, please don't worry. It's not your problem. You've got enough on your plate with the kid. You don't need another infant to take care of.

I shouldn't even be telling you this stuff. I'd rather my letters were full of wine and roses. The good stuff. Only the good stuff.

And maybe that's why I haven't been able to bear putting the words down over these past few weeks. To do so would be to needlessly burden you.

Well, I'll say it right now: I officially and eternally relieve you of the burden that is Lenny Snyder. Promise me you won't let me take you down with me.

If it helps, there's a woman who's been traveling with me. She came into my life at the crucial moment when I was still learning how to be someone else. She's a deep soul. A shiksa with a conscience. I call her the Queen of Sheba. She hails from the kingdom of light. I trust her. There are no secrets between us. She's proven in a million ways that she won't betray me. And without her, I swear, I'd be dead by now.

So don't worry. I'm in good hands.

Be free!

—Your Lost Seaman

And, wait, there's this one too:

City Mouse,

The other day I went to a party, a small gathering of what I guess constitutes the closest thing this town has to a counterculture. They're theater folk, mostly. Eccentric amateurs. Secret homosexuals. Women too timid to seize the liberation they yearn for. They don't fit in here, but they still believe what they see on the CBS News.

Babe, it was a trip. The only thing anyone wanted to talk about was Lenny Snyder. The trial. All that jazz.

The upshot? Lenny Snyder's a fraud, and if he really believed half the things he claims to he'd have shown up in court to face the music.

I don't blame them. They have a vague sense that things aren't what they should be, but absolutely no means of accessing the truth. They've never been exposed to anything but propaganda.

I've gotten to know these people. They see me as a quiet, thoughtful man who's worked with his hands his whole life. It would blow them away to learn I was Lenny Snyder.

There was a copy of *Newsweek* with my mug on the cover right there on the coffee table and I kept glancing at it throughout the conversation, waiting for someone to put two and two together. Nobody did. I'm telling you, it was my most existentially challenging moment yet. One of the women—a sensitive older soul, churchy; in a different world she'd be out advocating for liberation theology—asked me what I thought and I surprised myself by saying they were right. Lenny was a coward. And the trippy part was that I believed it as I said it.

That's what this life does to a person. You have to channel yourself into the character you're playing. Change the makeup of your mind. It's method acting. You have to *be* this other person *entirely*. But somewhere inside some part of you watches this new you from the perspective of the person you were, horrified, defiant, punching at your brain.

Of course I haven't been able to move from the couch since, but that's a story for another day . . .

Much love,
Country Mouse

And there's this one. I've got a bunch of them.

Northstar—

Things have only gotten worse since the last time I wrote.

I went to another party a few days ago. A different scene. Heavier. It had a real Frisco vibe. Full of old compatriots and friends.

I knew before leaving the hotel that I shouldn't have gone. But fuck it. I didn't care. I needed the danger. To be, just for a night, reckless and alive again.

Anyway, it was a test. The person going to this party wasn't Lenny Snyder. He was the other guy. The one I've become. A friend of the Queen who was a friend of a friend of a friend of the host. And as I slumped along toward the club with my new gait, I felt pretty good about being this person. I felt healthy. Energetic. Light on my feet. I was excited to be out in the streets of a city, to see the trash on the sidewalks, the cigarette butts and broken bottles in the gutters, the cars belching their exhaust, all the hip, happening grit of life roiling around me, Ratso Rizzo barking, "I'm walkin' here." Young dudes with afros and Ray-Bans and terminally bad attitudes, jiving, "go ahead and try to make me move." All those different vibes bouncing off each other, negotiating their terms of engagement. God, I'd missed it. The city. It brings out the best and the worst in a person.

And just like that, the guy I'd been pretending to be, he just vanished. So long, my provincial rube. So long, shy dumpy boob. I was Lenny Motherfucking Snyder again.

Of course the Queen noticed the change immediately. She's got psychic powers, at least when it comes to me. She clamped me by the arms and stopped me in my tracks. "Don't do this," she told me. "Get it together." Her gaze burning through my eyes. "Right now. Or we're turning around and marching back to the hotel." The power this woman has over me. She's saved me a thousand times. I can't oppose her.

I reined myself in and we made it to the party. Somebody's birthday, I'm still not quite sure whose.

Hidden behind dark glasses, I played my role as the Queen talked to old friends. She introduced me around, or I should say, she introduced the person I was pretending to be, which was right and good.

One of the funny things about life underground is the difference between *pretending* to be someone else and *believing* you're this other person. When I'm pretending, it takes an extra split second to respond to my name. My accent slips—I start dropping my H's. It's hardly noticeable except to the Queen, and it kept happening at this party. Every interaction, no matter how slight, ended with her kicking my shin or pinching my elbow. But I couldn't stop it. The more I tried, the worse it got. Like trying not to think of the word "orange."

And of course everybody was talking about Lenny Snyder. Lenny Snyder this, and Lenny Snyder that. My name bouncing off the walls, echoing everywhere. Lenny Snyder. Lenny Snyder. Whispers and threats spurring my paranoia. Every glance thrown even vaguely in my direction accused and convicted me of being who I am.

I should've left then. Instead, I stayed and sank into the darkness at the edge of the room.

Eventually the Queen and I found ourselves sitting with a young woman with short blond dreadlocks, a poet, I was told. One of Ginsberg's ever-growing tribe of wandering souls. I don't know how she ended up at our table. She kept looking around the room, starstruck.

The Queen, in that gracious way of hers, coaxed this woman—really, she was just a girl, maybe twenty, still a child—into conversation and it turned out that she had a combative mind. Passionate. Engaged. Every thought on fire. The Queen is a master of small talk—it's in her blood. She kept it light. Current events. The boob tube. The woman's own poetry. Guiding her away from anything that might get her shouting.

Okay, cool. I did my best to tune them out.

But when Lenny Snyder's name came up, you better believe I shot to attention. And when the poetess got hot and said, "I don't know why we're supposed to have any sympathy for that guy. He's a misogynist and a creep. Where was he on equal rights? Where was he on black liberation? Nowhere and nowhere. He was against the war, but why? Because white guys like him were getting killed. When he talked about sexual liberation, you just know he meant liberating women of their right to say no when he wanted to fuck them." The same old tired line. And babe, I just lost it. I took off my sunglasses. I leaned in, and before the Queen could stop me, I told this girl, "Kid, listen, I love how primed for the fight you are. I love your spirit. But frankly, you need to learn your history. You have no fucking idea what you're talking about."

"Who the hell are you and who asked for your opinion?" she said.

And she might not've known it, but she'd caught me out. In that moment, I had been wholly and completely Lenny Snyder.

The Queen sees everything. She stated my new name like she was hammering a door shut. She recited my cover story and told the woman, "Don't mind him. He's not feeling well today."

But at that point, I was gone. "What do you know about Lenny Snyder?" I said.

"I know he loved to see his own face on TV and I know he gave up what little credibility he might've had when he got himself arrested for dealing coke."

Ginsberg and Ray Garrett had joined us at the table. I'd been so claustrophobic that I hadn't noticed them until this minute. "Is it the dealing that bothers you or the fact that he got caught?" Garrett asked. This caught her off guard. He went on. "Because I've thought about this a lot. You know, Lenny and I were friends. He wasn't perfect—who is? And he undeniably lost himself for a while there, but we all did."

She kept pressing. "Please," she said. "Lenny Snyder doesn't know the first thing about what it means to be oppressed. Why should it be okay for him and not, say, me?"

"But was it okay for him?" asked the Queen. "He got arrested. The only reason he's not in prison right now is because he went on the run."

"Unless he was set up," I said.

Garrett studied me. I couldn't tell if he recognized me or not. I had a beard and that new nose. Even in the dark I'd left my sunglasses on. "You and I both know he wasn't set up."

"Do we?" I said. "I've got it on good authority that he was."

For a moment there, it was like all my illusions had been stripped away. I couldn't have hidden if I wanted to.

"But that wasn't my point," he said, turning back to the poetess. "You can judge Lenny all you want, but I'll tell you what. If Lenny were here, he wouldn't judge you. He's the least judgmental person I've ever met. Well, except for Allen," he said, patting Ginsberg's knee. "But Allen's a saint. Lenny's a hostage to his emotions. If he were here with us tonight, hearing your outrage at the way men—even supposedly enlightened men of the Left—are still profoundly failing to respect women, he'd have only one thing to say. 'How can I help?' And he'd mean it. For all his faults, that's the kind of person Lenny Snyder is."

She took this in slowly. "Okay, white man," she said, and her posture, like a coiled cat, said she was prepping for her next lunge.

And you know Garrett. He fagged himself up. "Okay yourself, honey," he said, and he winked at me. And the Queen, who like I said sees all, capitalized on the moment to announce that we'd be leaving now.

I'd blown it. Taken needless risks. But I was beyond the question of risk at that point. My blood tingled radioactively in my veins. The person I'd become was gone and I was fully and completely and exclusively Lenny. I didn't care who knew it.

No, it was heavier than that. I actually *wanted* the world to know. I wanted to be found out, if not by Garrett and this strident young poet, then by somebody else. So I'd have proof that I still existed.

Babe, if only you knew. I've been watching the news of Lenny Snyder, turncoat revolutionary, discredited rebel, I've watched these claims wax and wane in the press and no one ever refutes them. No one lifts a finger to correct the record. And the myth morphs and mutates—it lives a separate life from me. I'm gone. The best me. The me who's Lenny Snyder. Obliterated. And sometimes it gets so heavy that I just explode inside myself.

That's what was happening at this party. I never should've gone. Never should've allowed myself to come face-to-face with old friends who'd remind me of my old life.

As I squeezed past Ginsberg he placed a hand on my arm. Up to now, he hadn't said a word to anyone. He'd just sat with us in that calm, alert manner of his, listening, betraying nothing. He motioned for me to bring my face close to his and I bent for his blessing, like I've done a hundred times before, like so many people do when confronted by his humbling presence, and dig this: He squeezed my shoulder and whispered, "It's good to see you." That was all. The look on his face said the rest.

It broke me.

But the Queen, she'd had enough. She hustled me out of there before I could even thank him. She threw me in a cab. Got me to the hotel.

And since then . . .

Well, I'll put like it this: There was a moment when she had to physically extricate me from the window because I was halfway out and ready to jump, shouting, "I'M LENNY SNYDER! I'M LENNY FUCKING SNYDER!" She bound my hands and feet to a chair. Call it my Bobby Seale moment. Now she's terrified of what I might do to myself. She's hidden all the knives and taken my pills from me.

Suzy, I'm cracking up. Hell, I've already cracked. I cry in my sleep. The Queen tells me I howl, "MERCY! MAMA! MERCY!"

But there is no mercy. There's just submission or refusal. I've spent my life refusing. I'm GOOD at refusing. Resistance is the very core of my being. No matter how dangerous it might've been, I was always right there on the front line, ready to sacrifice my body for the cause.

Wasn't I?

Suzy, tell me. Remind me who I am. Please.

'Cause I keep asking myself, when is enough enough? At what point does your God-given right to freedom succumb to the floodwaters rising around it? What's freedom worth when your life's a fraud?

—L.

He could be like that, and then he could be like this:

Esther,

I now hear from Kunstler that there's nothing more anyone can do until and unless I turn myself in. And I'm telling you, this news hit me like a punch in the balls.

My question to you is: What have you been doing? What happened to LSD?

I was relying on you.

But apparently you're gonna let me die out here in the cold. Maybe that was your plan all along.

You've betrayed me, Suzy. You've betrayed me and taken my freedom from me.

—The Wandering Jew

I remember when she got this one. How she tried to hide her emotions from me. She'd been standing in the kitchen, like always, two steps into the apartment, ripping open envelopes before even taking her jacket off. And I remember she stopped stone-cold. Just froze. She crumpled the letter in one hand and dropped it in the trash. Picked it back out. Read it again. And again and again. It was like the life force was seeping out of her. I asked, "What's wrong?" But nothing. The letter fell from her hands. She didn't say a word. Just shuffled away to sit in the window, staring out at nothing, done for the night.

I kept that letter. I flattened it out and folded it up nice and carried it around with me in my pocket. Taking it out every once in a while to remind myself that I had to do better. That it was up to me to fix our lives. How, I didn't know, but I was sure, if I worried with enough intensity, if I pushed my scheming mind deep enough into the white expanse beyond my comprehension, the correct course of action would come clear. It never did, of course. What did I know? But I gave myself stomachaches trying.

The key was Ronnie Walker. That's how I saw it. My mother hadn't mentioned him in months, not in the phone calls I overheard between her and Kunstler, not in the chattering and "processing" she subjected me to. It was like his alleged role in Lenny's bust had been completely erased. Nonetheless, I fixated on him. Everyone else might've forgotten, but I hadn't. I'd show them. I'd find Walker and save the day.

This was the sum total of my plan: somehow corner Walker and force him to confess. At gunpoint if necessary. I had my AK.

But wherever I looked, he was never there.

Okay, here's one from my mother that I'm willing to share.

After months and months the obstacles put in her way by social services, meeting with caseworkers, filling out the same forms again and again, receiving promises that were later denied or forgotten, but still, persisting, dogged, unrelenting, proving her poverty, she'd received a single misspelled letter in the mail, informing her that she'd been denied. No welfare for her. The reason, as stated: husband's assets.

What that meant remained obscure. Lenny'd brought in some dough from his book and his lecture tours. But her understanding was that this money was gone. He'd given it all away to the Panthers in a grand public gesture—cameras, flashbulbs, speeches, him and Huey Newton throwing a kamikaze flurry of black-power salutes back and forth until he ceremoniously lifted up an oversized, like, Publishers Clearing House–sized check and secured it in Newton's hands. That's what got reported in all the news outlets. It was what he'd told the IRS and what she'd then told the welfare office.

So was he holding out on her? Would he do that?

Didn't matter.

She needed to survive. And she was still his wife. For richer, for poorer.

So, she sent him this:

L,

Please don't take this the wrong way, but do you think there's still royalties coming in from your book, and if so, can I somehow access the account or the money? I spoke to Kunstler and he told me that he knows nothing about it. I called the publisher too, and they told me they

weren't authorized to discuss your finances with anyone
but you.

I guess what I'm saying is, can you help me?

I hate myself for even asking, but I've run out of options.
I've been denied welfare. I guess I could appeal, but that'll
take months, maybe another whole year (you know those
bureaucracies, they're there to kill you slowly) and the
writer's life is apparently not for me—Cindy Belloc won't
even return my calls. I'm a street fighter and a rabble-rouser
and, I fear, far too extreme for the story the liberal press
wants to tell. ("Unreasonable," they call me. Well, the Nazis
were reasonable. Would they rather that?)

Frankly, I'm tired.

Freedom has become a complete pain in the ass. I don't
blame him. I love him and this is all very hard on him. But
he sometimes goes for days refusing to speak, staging a silent
protest against your absence. Or he lashes out. He lectures
me like he's the parent and I'm the petulant, misbehaving
child. The other day he had the gall to say, "You don't even
try, Mom. If I was Lenny, I would've left you too." Can you
imagine? It took all my strength not to smack him. And then,
when I finally calmed down, it broke my heart. Poor kid. It's
not his fault the world's upside down.

To say nothing of the constant surveillance. I found
another bug in the overhead lamp last week. And the FBI
came knocking again yesterday. They still believe, despite all
the evidence, that I know exactly where you are. I told them,
"Look, I can't even find my checkbook. How do you think
I'm supposed to keep track of Lenny?" They didn't laugh.
They never do. Lately, neither do I.

It's getting very dark down here in the LES. I don't know
how Freedom and I are going to survive.

Faith, I guess.

And maybe some help from you?

I miss you more than God.

—Suzy

Reasonable?

Well, here's how Lenny responded:

Susan B. Anthony—

I hear you loud and clear.

What I'll say in my defense is that you knew this life would be tough from the day you first walked into the Free Store. And we talked at length about how much harder it would become after I went underground. You knew what you were getting yourself into. I wish I could say I'm sorry, but I'm not. It's the price of doing my business. None of this should surprise you in the least.

I guess I, maybe, thought you were tougher than you are. Well my offer still stands. Go ahead and file for divorce if you must. Tell the judge I abused you. Who cares if it's true. Ship the kid off to your mother if he's too much for you to handle. Move on with your life.

But don't blame me.

And don't say I ever wanted it this way.

See you around.

—Benedict Arnold

For months after that, through that whole spring and summer, my mother still trekked over to the Namaste Bookshop hoping to hear from him. She still positioned me out on the street. Still chatted with Barrow about whatever rumors he'd picked up. Faking it. Braced for disappointment but trying to show the people who mattered that she was as fierce as ever.

No one was fooled.

Each time she climbed up out of that dungeon, a darkness came with her. And there were jags after Lenny's letters stopped coming during which my mother simply disappeared into it.

His silence—the lingering burn of his scorn—was too much for her.

She'd be up. She'd be down. Either way, out of her mind. Moving the furniture. Moving it back. Gazing despondently out at the rooftops across the street. Studying the pigeons. Wishing she were one of them. Her body still shuffled around the apartment but there was no one inside. Maybe she was doing bennies. Or ludes. Or both. Who knows. Whatever she could get her hands on. She hated the sunlight. She seized up around other people, including me. Her hands shook.

For one long, disturbing week she obsessively repainted the walls of the apartment, populated them with flowers and vines and woodland creatures, rainbows, peace marchers, frolicking children, nude hairy people of all races and creeds tumbling around a maypole. She stayed up all night, then all night again, three, four, five nights in a row, painting over her work, reimagining it. The flowers got drippier. The dancers trippier. Her agitation worked its way into her brushstrokes, the violence and rage that the image denied revealing itself in the texture of the paint. Splatters. Thick streaks like exploding roman candles where smiling faces should've been. Fingers of paint sliding toward the floor; she didn't bother to wipe them away. Slashes of red. Inadvertent crime scenes. Hovering above it all, like Christ crucified, Lenny with his wild Jewfro, his tired eyes, his American flag shirt torn and billowing like Old Glory herself.

She was just thirty years old, my mother. Still so young, I realize now.

She stopped answering the phone. Stopped reaching out. Weeks went by without a word to Isha or anyone else.

Or, no—Phil still showed up at our door sometimes. He was like family by then. He had his own keys. He'd walk in with groceries, or sometimes with Chinese, and lurk around like he lived there. Not every day. A couple times a week, maybe. Just often enough to remind my mother that if and when she chose, she could take his hand and he'd do what he could to pull her out of the abyss. Until she did, he'd keep one benign eye on me and provide whatever guidance he could. Was it enough? It felt like it was at the time. He read to me. Shakespeare—I remember we went through all of *Julius Caesar*. Baudelaire. Walt Whitman. *From the Mixed-Up Files of Mrs. Basil E. Frankweiler. The Pushcart War.*

The way I deified him frustrated her. She'd tell me, later, "Look, it's not like he was in a position to save us. He could barely function." Which was true, undeniably, but I'd maintain—and still do—that at least his intentions were in the right place. To which she'd argue that he wasn't as selfless as he seemed. He got what he wanted out of the arrangement.

Well, I don't know about that. It seemed to me at the time that she barely noticed he was there.

She barely even noticed I was there.

Unless I was in the way.

I learned to keep my distance. To focus on the TV that, now, was always tuned to the same regimen of shows. *Joker's Wild* and *The Price Is Right* and *Days of Our Lives*. I'd sit on the floor two feet from the screen and stare at it until my vision distorted. A kind of vertigo. A falling inward toward the all-consuming sound and vision.

In the afternoon, cartoons came on. Ancient things. Black and white, sometimes. *Woody Woodpecker. Heckle and Jeckle.* If I changed the channel to watch them, she'd be right there flipping the knob back to where it had been.

So I'd watch what she wanted to watch. *The $10,000 Pyramid. Let's Make a Deal.* Anything as long as the drone didn't stop.

Sometimes just knowing she was nearby was too much. This person who had ostensibly dedicated herself to shielding me from and teaching me about the world, now buzzing in her shell, depleted by bitterness, incapable, for days on end, of even taking a shower—how was she supposed to take care of me?

I'd catch her, sometimes, gazing at me, semiconscious. This look on her face—what was it? Regret. But more than that. Helplessness. A fading recognition that her love for me didn't do me any good. And this . . . it was harder to bear than the times when she was just pissed.

I'd retreat to my room and fantasize about escaping, about joining Lenny in the vast Underground.

But the unknown out there terrified in its own way. The feds still lurked around. Or I thought they did. Watching. Tracking, maybe. Taking notes.

Or maybe they'd finally lost interest in us.

As time went by, they stopped knocking at our door. I saw less and less of them out in the streets. But I still felt them there, like ghosts in my peripheral vision. Blurry threats at the edge of my sight that vanished when I tried to catch them straight on, leaving me with nothing, just an ache in my neck from whipping my head around too fast. A constant tension I couldn't be quite sure was justified.

Some afternoons I did nothing but sit on the stoop fondling my AK-47 and watching the light bend. The shadows. I was standing guard is what I was doing. Fulfilling my promise to protect her. For hours, I'd watch the people out there, good folks and bad, living their lives. Old ladies pushing squeaky carts over the cracks in the sidewalk. Punks flicking their Zippos against the wind. Bikers on patrol, roaring their engines. Mothers, sometimes fathers, patiently coaxing their children from one distraction to the next, ready with a finger for the little tyke to hold, or else smacking, cajoling, laying down the law. I'd study these people for what I could learn. How the dude in the dog collar slammed out his door at exactly the same time every afternoon. How the big guy with his even bigger wolfhound appeared one day with his arm in a sling. I'd strain for insight, some glimpse of the larger fabric that might link these brief street scenes together, some means by which to understand my isolation as anything other than an aberration.

I yearned for things I didn't know how to name, for the confidence of that solitary man in black. Or for the bright aggressive energy of that girl Rosalita. He was a figment but she—well, she was *real*. Even if I hadn't seen her since that one day in the park. Just the thought of her posed a challenge to me; to become, to be, to toughen up.

Then, long after dark, I'd slink back upstairs to wait for the day to end.

My mother might be sitting at the desk she'd jimmied out of a discarded door, lost in thought, writing something in her nervous spikey script, another desperate letter to Lenny, another brave fable thrown into the void, rolling back the confession that had so enraged him, claiming we were all right, that I was growing, smarter, brighter, that she was thriving, self-contained in her power, that our greatest concern was for his safe passage. I worry! My mind veers to worst-case scenarios! Send word!

Whatever she was doing, it's safe to assume she was too addled to have noticed I'd been gone. I remember, so many times, waiting for her in the gloom, wishing she'd at least ask where I'd been. Then slipping off to my little closet of a room. It didn't even have a door I could slam. I'd sit there on the mattress and peel the lead paint off the wall.

There wasn't enough space to contain how I felt. More than resentment or anger or hurt—more even than terror—what I remember is the shame. The pity and the shame. Pity for her and her hard, lonely life. Shame at my inability to save her from herself. What won't a son sacrifice for his mother? What worth does his life have when his mother's in pain?

I'd exhaust myself thinking of all the ways I'd failed her. Then I'd sleep, and when I woke at three in the morning, I'd find her sometimes in the doorway, gazing remotely down on me.

"Here," she'd say, lobbing a couple Twinkies on the bed. "Dinner."

Eventually I ventured farther from home. Let my mother take care of herself for a change.

I'd head out mid-morning, stepping past her sleeping body, tip-toe to the stairwell and lift off down the stairs, take them five, eight at a time, barely touching the ground except to pivot on the landings at each new floor. I'd throw the broken front door open with so much force that it slammed and ricocheted back on itself. Down the stoop and out onto the street.

I ran. For the sake of running, I ran. For the brief sensation of total autonomy. I took off toward the river, toward the west side, uptown, downtown, wherever. I carried my water gun everywhere I went, slung over my back on a strap made of frayed hemp.

Any and all directions I chose took me past the landmarks of Lenny's fading influence. Boutiques and head shops, still hawking bongs, but now doing so with less groovy phantasmal joy. The Free Store, still boarded up, the word HATE spray-painted over the old LOVE above the door. Peace symbols had been replaced by circle-A's and swastikas. None of it mattered. What mattered was that I keep up my speed, keep moving.

Run. Run forever. Past the addicts and lost ones nodding off on their feet. Past St. Mark's Church. The Bowery. Past Ukrainian Row where the air, even at this early hour, smelled like boiled cabbage and organ meat. Past the old Chinese folk in the park south of Houston doing their morning tai chi.

I couldn't run forever, though.

Eventually, like anyone, I sputtered out. Doubled-over, hands on my knees, huffing. Kneading at the cramps in my side. Walking it off. The burn in my knees. The rawness in my lungs. The sweat chilling on my face.

I'd wander the streets. Wading through time. Searching for fuck-all. Not going anywhere, really. Just picking my ass.

Sometimes I spooked myself, convinced that every vaguely recognizable face I passed belonged to the surveillance team dedicated to torturing my mother and me. I'd feel their eyes following me, their hands wanting to reach out and graze my clothes. I'd wonder if this would be the day when they nabbed me and took me away to the sensory deprivation chambers where they'd spin me and starve me and hang me upside down, refusing to believe, no matter how I pled, that I knew nothing about nothing about Lenny or where he was.

Other times, I'd forget to be afraid. I'd slip through some filament in my consciousness into a less constricted state of mind. Then, wow. *Freedom.* I could get lost in that.

But also, I might not notice the dangers around me.

Like the time, while floating around in my head in the trash-strewn lot behind the Lafayette Street subway entrance, I snapped back to discover that some dude had joined me. He looked like an alien—that hairless, triangular face they always have. That freakishly thin neck. He'd pulled his legs up under himself like he was about to meditate but his tiny eyes were staring me down.

When he saw that I'd noticed him, a smile drifted across his lips like he'd remembered a secret. "Hi," he said.

My defenses shot up.

"How's it going?" he said.

"Fine."

The secret smile came and went. "Yeah?"

"Yup. Just fine," I said.

"You look . . . Whatcha doing out here all by yourself?"

"Nothing."

He grooved on this, his head bobbing on its thin neck, as if I'd said something profound. "Far out," he said.

He'd affixed a cluster of buttons to his jacket, ruining a perfectly good piece of suede. A smiley face. A United Farm Workers eagle. A peace sign. A platoon of slogans and puns.

"What's your name?" he asked.

"What's *your* name?"

"Rick." He gazed at me. "Whatcha running from?"

"Nothing."

"Well, that can't be true. You're running from something."

"How would you know?"

He peered across the street like there was something he needed to keep track of over there. "I saw you. Before. Up on the Bowery. You were moving pretty quick for somebody with nowhere to go."

"That's just how I walk. So, what? You've been following me?"

He reached into his pocket and fished around. "They call me the button man," he said, pulling a new one out. He studied it lovingly for a second, then flipped it around his fingers. "You want one?"

And there, under its plastic casing, Lenny's iconic face grinned out at me, black eye and all, the very same image my mother and Kirsh and I had wheat-pasted all over town, now superimposed on a pillow of blue and green letters: FREE LENNY SNYDER. I should've fled. I told myself, Get the fuck out of here. But something stopped me. Call it curiosity.

That secret smile again as the guy placed the button in my hand. "You know him?"

Savvy enough not to give myself away, I said, "I know who he is. Everybody does."

"It sucks what happened to him, huh?"

Lobbing it back at him, I said, "You can keep your stupid button. It doesn't even make sense. Lenny Snyder *is* free. He escaped."

The guy slipped the button back in his pocket and took out another one.

"You're a hip kid, huh? You know what's up." Studying the new button like he'd never seen it before. Waiting for me to ask for a look. "You ever wonder where he went?" he asked.

"No. Why would I?" Then, "You a cop?"

He waited a tick too long to say no so maybe it was true, maybe he was a cop. Or maybe he was just another creep looking to force a bond with a seven-year-old. But the coincidence was too great for me to stick around. I thought of the solitary man in black I'd encountered all those months ago, the strength he'd offered, the sense of possibility. I asked myself, What would Lenny do?

And hopping to my feet, I screwed on my best fuck you. "You're never gonna find him, pig," I said. Then, backpedaling, I flipped the guy a double bird.

Still, part of me was always on the lookout for Walker. Inspecting every light-skinned black man I came across for height and gait and general vibe. Like this would help. Like salvation was still in any way possible.

Some days I staked out the park, waiting for him and his posse to take over a corner of the bandstand. He never showed.

Well, once, just once, I thought I saw him ducking into a bodega. Same watch cap. Same army jacket. Same looseness to his step. I followed him in. Hid behind the aisles and spied on him. Watched him in the fish-eye mirror mounted to the ceiling. Tucked myself into a nook back by the service door while he rooted through the refrigerated case for his six-pack of High Life.

I tracked him out of the store. It was him, I knew it. He had those cheekbones. Those tiger eyes. I crept after him, from a distance at first, then daring myself to get closer and closer. He stopped at a light and I found myself right up on top of him and he swung around—he'd known I was there all along—and said, "Kid. What gives?" and instead of the basso I remembered Walker having, this guy croaked like a toad with a Dominican drawl.

I shrank away. I went back to running.

Sometimes I trolled the park for Rosalita. The swarm of kids from the squats who might've led me to her were always there, but it had been months since I'd seen her hanging out with them. I sat for hours on the lip of the bandstand, bouncing my heels against the concrete, thinking the longer I waited the more likely she was to appear.

Often the only squatter kid I saw was the bigger guy everybody called Lumps. He—oh, he must've been twelve or so. There was something wrong with him. Or maybe he was just mean. In retrospect, he was ahead of his time. He wore a uniform: all black. Jeans. T-shirts. Boots. Jacket. His head looked like he'd taken poodle-shears to it. Bald patches where you could see his nicked scalp between clumps of hair maybe half an inch long. A far cry from the mop heads everyone else had. And his hormones were fucked up—that's what Rosalita told me later. He had the body of an albino walrus.

If he looked like he might not try to hit me—if he wasn't carrying a stick, say, or destroying public property—I'd edge up and ask where Rosalita was.

"Fuck off." His catchall response.

"Have you seen her?"

"Go fuck yourself."

"You think she'll come out today?"

"Maybe you didn't hear me. Fuck off, motherfucker."

If I persisted long enough, if I didn't run away when he faked a punch at me, I figured he might tell me where she was, just to get rid of me. But he never did. It always ended up with me losing my nerve and fleeing.

One windy day in September, though, there she was, lingering by herself on the far end of the park, awkwardly watching the other squatter kids play Flinch, kicking at the dirt while they spoofed on each other, and blowing giant bubbles that popped and stuck to her nose. When I called out to her, she pretended not to notice.

She was there the next day too. Again pretending not to see me. This time I didn't call out. I just sulked and wondered what I'd done, why she didn't like me, pining, refusing to venture from my perch on the bandstand and risk the public shame of her disinterest.

And then again the next day. I ignored her this time and focused instead on fucking with the weeds growing out of the cracks in the bandstand's cement. And once I'd finally succeeded in forgetting that she was out there on the other side of the park, she showed up right in front of me, striking a pose, fists on hips, pelvis thrust forward, the all of her prickling with disdain.

"What's wrong with you?" she asked. "Don't you have friends?"

I scoffed, pulling my best Lenny. "Don't you?" I said.

And after that, it was understood that if I was there and she was there we'd be together, that I'd tag around behind her for as long as she'd let me and she'd be secretly happy about this.

Rosalita. She was fearless. In the best of ways, anything was possible with her. We did all the things kids do together. We built forts and played games with rules we made up ourselves, testing the bounds of logic, of our bodies, of the known world. We went exploring—spelunking through the subway tunnels, scrambling like rats through abandoned factories. She taught me how to smoke cigarettes. I taught her how to slide candy bars down her underwear without getting caught by the store clerk. One day, apropos of nothing, while we poked around in the gravel under the bridge, she roughly grabbed me and laid a kiss on my lips. *Mmm-mmm.* She made smooching sounds. Pressed her mouth to mine. It wasn't romantic, just surprising. Awkward. Two kids fucking around. Pretending we knew things. "Now French-style," she said, and she showed me how to stick my tongue out and flick it like sandpaper against her own. Another time—same spot—we dared each other to reveal our privates. Then to touch them.

But none of that was what drew me to search her out.

We shared our dark little dreams. And though I couldn't quite fathom what her life was really like, how she was related to the other kids in the squat—sometimes they were her "brothers" or "sisters" or "cousins"; sometimes they were just "those fuckers"—or if she had any parents at all, I felt I understood her. Her defiance. What it covered up. She'd much rather throw a sharp rusty pipe at my feet, daring me to flinch, than cop to any fear in her life.

A lot of the time we just existed near each other. Sitting around. Lying on the grass. Proximity was a form of intimacy. We had nowhere to go. Nothing to do. And even if we did, what difference would it have made? We were precociously cynical in that way so endemic to kids in the city. Unimpressed by the museums, the celebrity sightings, the concerts and monuments and free theater in the park. We were hip to the con. We knew that none of the cultural opportunities the city offered would lift us rank heathens up to the vague, genteel civic ideal they promised. That stuff wasn't meant for us. But also, we were unimpressed by the seedy thrills that the counterculture held out as an alternate path, the hard drugs and grifting and bodies for sale. The screaming guitars and hoarse rebel yells and clubs and bathhouses and everyone, everyone, even those in squalor, clamoring for fame. Nothing impressed us. Whatever lie we might choose to build our lives around, the truth would remain the same. The poor would be poor. The rich would be rich. And we'd still be alone with no real friends but each other.

Sometimes we touched hands as we lay there together. Sometimes the sun beat down so warm on our faces that we fell asleep.

When we talked it was with a sneering ticklishness. She taught me to boast and to lie. She'd say anything, whatever popped into her head.

"You know that pet store over on Ninth Street, the one that smells so nasty, like birds? The lady who owns it killed her husband, did you know that? She ground him up and fed him to the cats. It's true. She never got caught."

Or, "Did you hear about that artist guy with the beard? You know the one I mean? He's always dressed up like Jesus? He's making dirty movies now. He casts his daughter in them. I know because he asked Lumps and Paulie and Stinger if they wanted to be in 'em too. Would you do that? I'd never do that."

Who knows what was true and what wasn't. One day she told me she was dying. "There's a hole in my heart. It's a very rare disease. I've had it since I was born. One day I'm gonna drop dead. Could be today. Definitely by next year."

"You don't look sick," I said. "You don't act sick."

"But I am. What would you do if I died right this minute?"

"Nothing, 'cause you're not gonna die."

She had a particular look she threw when she was frustrated that lit up the pencil scar on her left cheek. "I *am* gonna die. At most in two years."

Best to just go with it. Anyway, she was more upset that I didn't believe her than that she was really going to die. "Maybe I'll die with you," I said.

"Would you? Oh my God." She launched herself onto me. Slaps and squeezes. "Dy-no-*mite*!" And she was up and off to scale the bridge, straining to pull herself from rivet to rivet, negotiating gaps barely as wide as her body. Reckless. Peering down at me still rooted in the dirt and mocking my fear of joining her. "Freddy, look! It's fun! Freddy! Or maybe you're just a pussy!" Like, whatever the truth of the hole in her heart, she was hell-bent on dying one way or another.

There was one time when she somehow got hold of a whip and insisted that we take turns using it to try to knock each other off our feet. The only thing that stopped us was, we were too small and the whip was too long for us to handle, much less snap. We couldn't even flick it to its full length; it just wagged there, limp, in our fumbling hands.

Another time she found a baggie of powder under a park bench.

"Let's do it," she said.

We didn't know what it was. It was kind of pissy yellow. Marked with a unicorn.

"No way."

"Come on. Nothing's gonna happen."

"It might be poison," I said.

She laughed. "So, let's do it."

I still refused. Visions of Lenny at his worst jittered in my head. Of my mother. Of the dead eyes you saw on nodding junkies. Of the naked duster I'd seen, once, fighting off a platoon of cops out in front of Cooper Union, shards of glass embedded in his chest, blood everywhere, trickling down his thighs.

"Do it! Do it!"

She poured the powder out onto one of the wooden slats of the bench and began cutting it into lines like she'd seen people do in the squat.

"We could die."

She glanced up and snarled. "So what?"

And as she struggled to roll a dry leaf into a straw, I panicked and blew the powder to the wind.

"Why'd you do that? I hate you. You're never any fun."

But she didn't hate me. Even if she screamed and swore and hit me all the time. I knew. We needed this tug-of-war. She'd pull toward destruction. I'd pull toward something else. Revelation. Release. That thing I couldn't name but just knew must exist.

By late September of '75, my mother realized that her life would be easier if I wasn't there needing things all day. She enrolled me in school. As long as I was someone else's problem, she no longer cared if I was indoctrinated or not. Anyway, even she was half-bored and exhausted by her screeds now. The politics meant nothing. All they did was increase her hardship.

So off I went to PS 64, where the dregs of the Lower East Side gathered and clotted in the drain.

The first thing that happened my very first day was the vice principal tried to confiscate my AK. He pretended to be nice about it. He told my mother, while she filled out my registration forms at the high counter in the office, "He can have it back at two-thirty when school lets out."

"Come on, man," she said, barely paying attention. "It's a water gun."

"It's still a gun."

She shot him a look. Continued with her forms.

"We've got rules, ma'am. Policies." A big hulking dude who, I'd discover later when I saw him patrol the halls, wore his pants too tight.

She stopped writing. Tapped the pen on the counter and stared at him. "You've got to be kidding."

"I don't kid. Would you feel safe knowing I let other children bring guns to school?"

"Water guns. That shoot water. Not bullets. You dig?"

"In this case, ma'am, that's a distinction without a difference."

"It's a toy," she said. "It comforts him." She shook her head in disgust, realizing she couldn't win. "You people."

Smiling at her, he said, "What people?" He was black.

More disgust, smeared with scorn. "Bureaucrats." She looked at me fighting back my terror, cradling the gun like I'd die without it. "This isn't going to work out well for you," she said, meaning the vice principal, but she might as well have been talking to me, since she caved and took the gun home with her, leaving me exposed, all by my lonesome.

I hated it there.

Already in second grade, the patterns were set.

The black kids—and it was mostly black kids—hung out with each other, vacillating between a resentful pliancy and rambunctious outbursts of coded disdain for the entire endeavor of public education. They knew the value of what they were getting and they gave it the same respect it gave them. Where they ruled was the playground. They stampeded down the slides, dodged swings, scaled the monkey bars and fences, reveling in this space where they were left alone, free of the assumptions the union-vested lifers teaching in the school threw their way—that they'd failed just by being born; that the harder they tried, the greater the joke on them would be—and also free of the humiliating condescension, the saccharine pandering of the younger teachers, those do-gooders who, still bucking the limits of good intentions, had made it their mission to prove the old-timers wrong. Sometimes I'd catch Dante Alexander—the kid who sat next to me—staring at his desk in an unending stone-cold rage and I'd think, I don't blame you. Your daddy told the truth. You're already fucked.

I sympathized. I was sure I was fucked too.

The white kids—Russians, Polacks, the offspring of the hippie artist-freaks and the wannabes who'd followed them to the hood, Jews of the old school and the new—none of them would have me. They stuck to their own just like the black kids and I reeked of something that wasn't quite right. They all wore the same jean jackets, festooned with the same buttons. The same floppy newsboy caps with the same shaggy hair winging out from under them. Whatever their obsession—comics, chess, magic, theater, movies, *Star Trek*, Hashem, the batting averages of long-retired baseball players—you got the sense that they were after the same underlying goal: proof that they were singular, meant for the best of the better things. Not having been schooled in the topics they cared about, I wasn't even worth dominating. What could I say to a Beatles fanatic as he proclaimed, for the ten-thousandth time, all his reasons for believing *Revolver* was their peak? My mom fucked John Lennon at an orgy once? He'd never believe me, but you know he'd hate me. And I'd probably have to explain what "fuck" meant. So, better to cede. To remain invisible.

The Puerto Ricans existed in a separate world, hidden from the rest of us behind a scrim of Spanish.

The Asian kids sat up front and talked to nobody, especially not one another.

Then finally there was that other klatch of kids, children of the impoverished gentry, journalists, actors and graduate students, painters and poets, photographers, a whole multiracial class of New Yorkers that was, then as now, low on cash but high on cultural capital. They'd been raised to embody their parents' ideals, a liberal humanism that, as they aged, was supposed to colonize the world. They transcended race and creed, were bound instead by their exquisite taste, their precocious facility with the language of art and fashion and cool. Their sense of destiny. In another life, they would've been my people. Instead all they gave me was the cold comfort of their knowing my name, what it signified, why they should snub me for it.

And this was the education you got at public school. Not reading or writing or arithmetic but a practical initiation into social theory. You learned to recognize your tribe and the danger of trying to transcend it. Stay in your box, love it, let it shape you. Hold your resentments tightly. There's power in the mob. Protection. Out on your own you're gonna get trampled. The one thing you couldn't do was think for yourself.

In that context, I was a tribe of one. A feral dog. I bit. I threw flailing punches, even at girls. Instead of fear, I provoked only laughter.

The administrators, that fucking vice principal and the social workers, even my teacher, Ms. Rice—not a cruel woman, just dim enough to confuse the existence of rules with their value—all of them at some point called my mother to discuss my unhinged behavior, to send me off with her and rid themselves of the problem. Sometimes she was home and sometimes she wasn't. When she was, she sometimes answered the phone. And when she did, she was sometimes willing to trek over and retrieve me.

Other times, she left me to sit in the corridor outside the principal's office with its three stiff chairs and giant clock on the wall. And then, when two-thirty came I might still be there for an hour or two more, listening to the sound of the other children rioting in the halls gradually thin to an empty echo, waiting for the moment when the office secretary finally released me so she could go home.

But maybe, just maybe, my mother would pick me up, listen to what I'd done and fight back on my behalf. "I heard you," she'd tell them. "You keep saying the same thing. He threw the ruler. What I don't understand is why. What did the other kid do? Do you even know? Freedom must've been provoked. Do you even care? You're treating the symptoms, but you know what, I think maybe you're the disease."

Oh, how they must have loathed her.

But not me. I didn't hold my mother's absences against her. Those times when she did show up and stand up for me were enough. Later, at home, I knew, she'd give me back my gun. She might even wrap me in her arms and tell me I was brave. That I was righteous. That Lenny would be proud of me.

Sometimes after school, I'd go outside and there would be Phil leaning against the sagging chain-link fence. No matter the weather, rain or snow or sleet or sun, he'd be dressed in his uniform, those old work boots, that stained blue shirt, that greasy jacket.

He'd wave me over and say, "Looks like it's you and me today, Freddy. Your mom got hung up. Let's make the most of it." He'd kneel down and reach behind my ear to flip out a quarter—something he'd learned to do in his lonely, sickly youth. "W-We could find some creative way to spend this," he'd say.

And we'd go to the Gem Spa so I could load up on candy. We'd run through the neighborhood, jumping in puddles if it was raining, letting ourselves get soaked to the bone. We'd cut through the projects on Avenue D, dodge traffic on the service road below the FDR, climbing the concrete dividers to get to East River Park where we'd stand by the railing at the edge of the river and watch the rain pelt the surface of the water.

Then, maybe the sun would break through and Phil would say, "Look at that. The forces of good strike again." He'd drop a hand onto my shoulder. "Let's go someplace warm where we can dry off."

What he meant, sometimes, was we were headed to his pad on Clinton Street, a third-floor walk-up looking out on the Williamsburg Bridge. We'd navigate the maze of newspapers he warehoused there—twelve years' worth, stacked like roman walls, dividing his apartment into smaller and smaller chambers. And we'd sit by the window on stools made of newsprint and watch the Brooklyn-bound traffic pile up and start to glow, listening as the horns and sirens punctuated the merengue that the Dominicans who ruled the block played as a soundtrack to their eternal stoop-sitting, dominos-playing party. The screech of city life.

When winter hit he'd make us hot cocoa, spiking his cup with vodka.

He'd leave me be. Let me rummage through the papers searching for treasure while he scribbled in his notebook across the room. When I fell asleep, he'd carry me home to my mother.

Other times, what he meant was let's find a bar.

Understand: We were living in seedy times. Kids I knew were skipping school to play the ringer in their uncles' three-card-monte rackets, happy to be paid off in sour-apple Now and Laters from the corner bodega. Kids whose landlords had cut the heat to their apartments hid out for weeks on end in the school's boiler room, giving the creepy janitor blow jobs in exchange for keeping warm through the night. They ran in packs through the shells of burned-out buildings, crunching over shattered glass until their sneakers were encrusted with razor-sharp shards, jumping from one rooftop to another until someone died. Compared to that, fucking around in a bar—picking at the duct-taped booths at Blue & Gold, say, playing elaborate games of solitaire with the pool balls, drawing pictures in my own mouth-steam on the mirrors—while Phil slammed happy-hour drinks was nothing.

So he was a drunk and a slob. So he was endlessly, fatally consumed with self-pity. So what? There was something luxuriously stable, more stable than anything else in my young life, about hunkering down for a two- or three-hour stretch behind the clouded windows of an empty dive with him. And I didn't know—I mean, nobody knew—how close he was to spinning off the edge of the world.

Think about what he'd been through at this point. A lonely kid whose parents had dragged him all over the place as they tried to outrun their secret selves. Never staying put long enough to feel like he had a home. But circling back, time and time again, to Columbus, Ohio. That's where he defined himself. So there was that kid. Sensitive, intelligent. Steeped in the lore of the American West, all those cowboys and Indians and railroad men and hucksters, speculators and miners and unions and union busters. A solitary Jew in a cold Calvinist place where if he learned anything it was that the mechanistic gears of society would grind you into sausage if you were at all different from those around you. Unless you were rich, and odds are you weren't. He wasn't. He spent his childhood hiding in the movie palace, projecting his own psyche onto the images of Brando and James Dean towering over him. Willing himself to one day be like them. Valuable, even in his insignificance. Necessary. An agent of change.

And he brought to New York what he had to give. An acoustic guitar. A whole lot of desire for something to believe in. Imagine the moment when he first stepped onto the stage at Cafe Wha? and gazed in terror at the strangers, all so much more worldly than himself, crowded around the wobbly tables in the dim light. He knew he was outmatched. But he steadied his nerves, mounted that guitar like a machine gun against his shoulder and let his thin baritone float into the room. A tragic sound. Someone cruel could have broken it like stomping out an ant. Instead, they listened as he earnestly crooned about the Cuban Missile Crisis. They heard the yearning in his voice, the pangs of longing for a society uncorrupted by the coercion of empire, and they knew he was naïve but they loved him for it. They saw courage in it. This naïveté, it had to be protected. Phil might be the one they'd been waiting for, the idiot savant who could march them back to Eden.

He cut an album. Then another. And another after that. He experienced the doubled, contradictory sensation of being celebrated—sometimes, it seemed, worshipped—for his humility before the cause. Hitching rides out to union rallies in Kentucky. Or riding the bus all the way down to Ole Miss to stir up support for Snick, strumming the whole way, leading the sing-alongs, getting that Greyhound to buzz with bottled joy. That's when he saw the real-world effects of his evangelism.

The problem with causes, though, is that they derive their meaning from what they achieve. The foot soldiers, those people whose aggregate passion fuels the change, might find satisfaction—or regret—after the fact in the roles they played in affecting this change, but they'd be wise to beware building their identities around the communal spirit in which the cause thrives. They might find themselves trapped, alone, in a movement that's vanished, wondering where everyone else has gone. Some people recognize this danger from the start. They ride the spirit of the age for all it's worth, taking what they can for their own gain. And by the time everybody else realizes it's over, they're already done and gone.

Dylan, that wily cracker, was one of these types. He and Phil had arrived on the scene at the same time. They were friendly, early on, could almost have been called friends. But what Dylan knew, and what Phil could not comprehend, was that they were rivals. Only one could win. Phil didn't want to win. He wanted to contribute. To the cause. The future. That thing greater than the self. He thought this was what everyone wanted.

When you're the rube in the presence of the cynic, you catch glimmers of the spite they harbor toward you. And as they keep succeeding and you stay the same, you begin to crave their approval. You give them your power and beg them to share it. But since they were never all that into sharing, they keep it and use it to make themselves stronger. Phil began molding his choices around the delusional idea that if he played things just right, he'd gain Dylan's blessing and be redeemed in his eyes. He gave himself away, allowed himself to become the supplicant to the more charismatic man standing next to him.

Always the believer but now no longer sure where that belief led, Phil cut some more albums. Less topical now. More darkly poetic.

He bound himself to Lenny and Sy and their kamikaze circus, took in their exhortations to be the change, to do the only reasonable thing this world allowed and reject all reason. He cheered them on as they declared the war was over. What war? There's no war. Make a wish and poof, it's gone. When they mounted a greased pig on the stage at their rallies and proclaimed, If the president of the United States is gonna squeal and smell like a pig, whaddaya say we go whole hog! Let's put this fucker in charge! Phil strummed along on his guitar, a one-man backup band. He was happy to be their bard. To wrap the belief—the hope—he still couldn't shake in their cynicism and absurdity.

That worked for a while, but we all know what happened. The jackboots were called out. Autocratic power, both overt and covert, kicked the life out of everything beautiful in the land. A lesson in raw political reality that Phil had ignored for far, far, far, far too long.

He lost his confidence. Dylan, then Johnson, then Nixon stripped it from him. The only one who never let him down was Lenny, and for reasons Phil couldn't fathom, Lenny had turned on him and closed himself off. By the early '70s, the movement was in crisis. Smoke and tear gas clogged the air. Community had fractured and hope had fled.

He tried throwing his energy into the conflict in Chile, inspired by Salvador Allende's refusal to be tamed, and more, awestruck by Victor Jara, the Chilean national folk singer. Celebrated. Worshipped. Most crucially, listened to. Like Dylan, if Dylan hadn't forsaken the movement.

In Jara, Phil saw a version of the person he could have been if the revolution here had succeeded. And in Chile, he saw a version of what America could've been if it had chosen the right singer to lead it into the new age. He met the man down there once, and the first thing Jara did was embrace him by the forearms and tell him he'd always preferred him to Dylan. That his music had been a great motivation to him, a comfort, keeping him warm, sustaining his faith through the cold, dark years before Allende's rise to power.

Imagine.

And imagine the associations that fizzled in Phil's mind when he heard that in the days after the coup, Jara had been arrested, that he had been taken to a soccer stadium along with thirty thousand other believers and paraded in front of them. *Here, gaze on your singer, listen to his song, hear how it speaks of your dreams, hopes and ideals, feel the emotion it stirs within you, now watch—closely—and learn.*

Imagine the lesson Phil took from Jara's death, how they'd prompted him to strum his guitar and sing, how they'd braced his hands on a table, and with a machete, sliced them from his body. *Here you see what good your song can do you. Here you see what we think of your hopes and dreams.* Instead of chastened, Jara was emboldened. He used what he had left. If he couldn't play guitar, he could still sing. So he did, and they shot him. He kept singing, and they shot him again. And still he sang. They shot him thirty-seven times until the words fell from his mouth in ribbons of blood, until he was dead, and with him Phil's last hope for anyone's redemption. He could trace the lines—he'd done so long before they martyred Jara. ITT, Bank of America, CIA, Pinochet. He understood that if they could do this in Chile, they could—and they would—do it here.

So where did that leave Phil? What was left for him? Where was his path forward? He suspected the answer was nowhere, nothing, nowhere. What do you do with the time you have left when you know your life's over yet you still have to go on living?

Everyone's an asshole in one way or another. Phil was less of an asshole than most. He was kind. He was patient with me. I didn't know from alcoholism. My parents were potheads. When Phil managed to keep himself half-sober, he took me to museums and talked about poetry. Mostly, like I said, we hung out in bars—the old Polish dives. Or Gerde's on 4th Street, where out of pity they let him drink for free. Sometimes we ventured into enemy territory north of 14th Street to hole up in one or the other of the Irish steam-table joints on Second Avenue.

He'd get a couple drinks in him—down a shot of vodka, half a second later a shot or two more, doubles probably, I was too young to tell the difference. And if he was in the mood, he'd wave me over to sit next to him, buy me a cranberry and soda and gaze at me, slack-jawed, a touch glassy already. This look on his bloated face, shy, like he was waiting for me to tell him my secrets. His eyes would drift off toward the bottles, his own distorted reflection in the mirror behind them, then on toward the ceiling, a slow floating away, before he combed his hand through his greasy hair and found his way back to me.

He'd tap the bar with his thumb, breaking the spell he'd put himself under, and report on where he'd just been, some instant retrieved from the long-gone decade when he'd been virile and relevant and happy to be alive. Telling his story. All the stuff I just told you.

Once in a while—well, maybe only once—he managed to coax himself out of the moist funk of nostalgia into an excitable urgency. It happened in an instant, like a gunshot going off in his head, a sudden edgy alertness that frightened me—so uncharacteristic of him—until I realized that this must've been the Phil he used to be.

"Come on, Freddy," he said, pushing off the bar. "I wanna show you something."

We lumbered out into the gray evening where the air tasted like ash and was too cold to smell. For a moment we stood there in front of the bar, wavering, unsure which direction to turn. The city felt timeless. A mist hanging over it. Steam leaking out of the man-hole covers.

Phil peered up 7th Street, first one way then the other. Off to the east, avenues away, he saw a minute flame. We trudged toward it.

Walk far enough, or so he must have thought, and we'd arrive at a campfire. All his past and future friends would be there. His compatriots. Huddled both for warmth and camaraderie around the blaze. They'd welcome him. Maybe even Lenny would be there, arms wide open, waiting for a rough slap-the-back hug. They'd ask him to sling his guitar off his shoulder and lead them in one more round of "I Ain't Marching," his anthem of peace, the one song everyone, even Dylan, had once revered. "Shucks," he'd say, feigning bashfulness. He'd tip his head, physically digging toward the tune, and scoop us all up with his song. And I, a child and not even his own, would be granted the inheritance he'd feared was lost for good.

By the time we arrived, though, there was nothing to see. Just another ash can filled with smoldering shit, a few scabby addicts poking around it, looking for a fix that wasn't there.

So I took him home. Just like every other time. Did what I could to repay him for all he'd done for me.

At some point, sometimes early in the evening, sometimes far too late, his eyes would turn to wax and his heavy body would lurch against whatever was next to him, and it fell to me to guide him to safety. In the best case, all I had to do was roll him into a cab, coax his wallet from his pocket and pay off the driver. "Twenty-four Clinton Street," I'd tell the guy. "Here's an extra five bucks in case he throws up." And I'd watch until they were gone down the avenue.

Often, though, he flailed and resisted. "No! Not yet!" A petulant toddler.

Or, if he was too gone to even get those words out, he'd jerk away, balancing on pins, and out of duty I'd trail after him. Listen to his babble. His conceptual leaps and drunken associations. Something about Marrakesh, maybe. About a boat. Some mystifying riddle about some long-ago promise he'd made to Lenny. All the while bumping him. Turning him. Tricking him in the right direction.

And because the bars were always closer to 7th Street than Clinton, and because he was drunk and four times my size, the right direction meant my mother and my place.

By the time we arrived he'd want another drink, a little nightcap, two fingers of vodka in the *Underdog* jar we kept just for him. More often than not, he forgot it was there before taking a single sip. He'd nod off in his chair. Turn into a bobblehead. Depleted, he'd have reached the point in the night, when what little consciousness he had left sent him reaching for my mother to wipe his sweats away and lay down next to him—not too close, just near enough to anchor him while the world swayed and spun.

She called him the Malingerer.

Like, "Ugh, is the Malingerer here again?"

Or, "Sure would be nice if the Malingerer moved his fat ass to the couch so I could finally get some sleep."

I can't say if she liked him. She endured him. She accommodated him.

I remember on one night—it might've been the same night we went searching for the campfire—he was wasted and she was exhausted and he pressed her too far.

The whole way home he'd mumbled about how "This isn't me. Don't see me like this. See me as . . ." Spacing. Unable to complete the thought. A blank where the self was supposed to be. Then rising anger. Not toward me. More a shallow belligerence. The drunk's frustration with the gaps in his continuity. He fell on the stairs, barely catching himself. Then he fell again, this time against me and it took all my weight to leverage him upright. By the time we were at the door, whatever self-control he had left had fled.

He lurched inside, saw my mother and yanked her by the hips, pulling her pelvis toward his own. He ground against her. Like he was in a trance. Lethargic, but pawing at her ass, her kidneys, her ribs. His head slumped on her shoulder. A heaving bear.

She'd dealt with him drunk before. She knew how to shrug him off, to laugh and walk him like a three-legged dog into some corner where she could dump him in a heap. "Go pass out," she told him. "Come on. This way, now."

He resisted. Pulled her tighter. He wouldn't let her go.

They grappled over who was in control of her body.

"Seriously, Phil," she said, "it's not even like you can get it up."

He mumbled, "Lemmeoldyou."

"Too bad." Placing a palm on his chest, creating space between them, she said, "It's late. Sleep it off."

As she pulled away to look at him, to make sure he'd heard her, he tightened his grip. He kissed her. Slobbery, messy with need. Missing his target. Bumping foreheads. Trying again. His mouth on her chin.

She couldn't wiggle away. Even drunk he was too much for her to handle. "Stop it." She said it again. "Stop it."

He fumbled at her breast. Slow half sentences oozed from his mouth, trailing toward nowhere.

Again, "Stop it. Get the fuck off me." And she sprang her body into a frenzy of motion, a mad spinning dance that culminated in her elbowing him in the face.

For a moment it seemed almost like something was dawning on him. But no, it was just the furry silence of the drunk hearing too many voices in his head. He collapsed on her, all two hundred and sixty pounds of him draped over her body. Clinging.

Then, somehow, he was crying.

He slid down her body and sank to his knees. Howled. Some guttural animal sound, like a wound deep in his bowels was releasing its stench.

"Why don't you love me?" he wailed.

Arms wrapped tight around her legs. Head tapping against her groin. Like she was a goddess and he was the wretched supplicant.

"Why doesn't Lenny love me?"

He was beyond tears now. Silently heaving.

And then, all at once, he toppled to the floor, out cold.

She stood over him, fumes rising off her. She went like to kick him. She was wearing her boots. And just at the moment when her toe touched his gut, she pulled back and slumped against the sink.

I gathered my courage. I asked her, "Why'd you do that?"

"He's a fucking idiot," was all she said.

She pitied him, but for all the wrong reasons. Something was wrong with him, sure, okay, but everyone I knew had something wrong with them. At least he'd remembered my birthday.

After that night, he never came back.

When I asked where he'd gone, she said, "Am I his keeper?"

"Are you mad at him?" I asked.

She said no. She looked at me like I was stupid. "Why should I be?" she said.

And that was that.

Without Phil to look forward to in the afternoons, I started skipping school altogether. Not every day—two or three days a week. I figured anyone who noticed would be happy I was gone. It's not like I ever got in trouble for it.

Somehow, on those days, I always ended up way out on 5th Street past Avenue C, wasting the hours away in a burned-out old Pinto there. My special place. Every kid had one. It had been there forever, just part of the landscape and somewhere along the line I formed a kind of intense sentimental attachment to it. There was just enough scorched vinyl left on the backseat to cover the springs so I could sprawl across it. Hidden. Invisible. Free to wallow in the honey-sweet muck of myself, the melodrama of my emotions.

The signs were all around me—Lenny's silence, Mom's withdrawal, Phil's abandonment, the prison pretending to be a school she'd sent me to, the post-apocalyptic turn the city had taken in which everything was either too hot or too cold, the violence everywhere, senseless, mundane, sometimes directed at strangers, sometimes at the self, sadomasochism on a governing societal scale—it all cascaded down on me, covered me like black snow. Eight years old and I knew hope was for suckers, I knew there was no future laid out for me, just scrabbling hunger. Picking through the ruins. A terrifying prospect. An overwhelming darkness. But here in my Pinto, my gun at my side, I felt cozy and safe.

As time went by I accumulated a parade of totems, each one carefully lined up along the moonscape that had been the dashboard. A purple-haired troll doll. A chunk of concrete shaped like a turtle. Buttons of all sorts that I'd found in the gutters. A white plastic Indian riding a horse, his bow drawn and aimed—my own Geronimo. Bottle caps I'd picked up on lucky days. All kinds of crap. To anyone strolling past it looked like nothing, but to me these items, like the car itself, contained drops of my more fragile emotions, the ones I was afraid might get beat out of me. They were sacred objects. They warded off the world. A tiny army protecting little me.

I'd leave this place feeling centered, grounded, like the Zen clichés my mother spouted just might have something to them after all.

And wherever I walked for the rest of the day, whatever new grotesque reality crossed my path, I was impenetrable, almost indifferent, able to observe it all from a distance. A junkie could nod off in the middle of the street, halfway through the crosswalk, like he'd forgotten he was going to the other side, and get hit head-on by a city bus trying to beat the yellow light; a man might be propped up against a brick wall, legs splayed out in front of him, arms limp at his sides, just hanging out, nobody paying him any mind, or so it seemed, until you saw the hole in his forehead, the trickle of blood crawling down the furrow between his eyebrows; a kid, a little girl, maybe, would be screaming at the top of her lungs, running frantically from storefront to storefront along Second Avenue, no parents anywhere in sight; whatever it was, it couldn't affect me. Or, if it did, if my heart reached out, it couldn't implicate me. I had enough bruises of my own not to take on more.

Eventually, I'm not sure how, I introduced Rosalita to my special place. Showed her my secret things.

"Bottle caps, huh?" she said. "Buttons? A hunk of cement picked up off the street?" If I told her they protected me, she would've laughed in my face, plucked them off the dash and thrown them down the gutter. Chastising my weakness. The garishness of my need.

"I like them," I said. "I've given them all names."

Deflection. Deniability. She could respect that. Eventually she grew to see their charm. How they guarded the compound. How behind the line, sunk inside the Pinto's charred and rusty carcass, you could almost believe you were in a different world.

We spent a lot of time in there. It got to be so that if I couldn't find her kicking around the neighborhood, I knew I could just wait there in the backseat and she'd show up. Maybe neither of us would cop to it out loud, but we depended on each other. My safe place became hers. That's how intimate we were.

Sometimes when we talked we'd expose our deeper selves. Or I did. I compulsively babbled about, oh, I don't know. How unstable my mother was. How impossible it was to be the boy she wanted when that boy was really Lenny and I'd never match him. How sad I was that he was gone. And Phil, too. What was wrong with me, with her? That we'd been abandoned? But what had we done? Maybe it was the fact that we existed. I poured out my maudlin, incoherent self to Rosalita. And maybe she stopped short of comforting me, but she also stopped trying to toughen me up. Her silence served as a kind of compassion. I felt, however meekly, like I was being held.

"He's gonna come back," I told her. More than once. "Lenny's gonna come back and get us. When it's safe."

And if I wondered about her reciprocal pain, well, she found other ways to communicate it to me.

"You know what the backseats of cars are for?" she asked one day.

"It's where the kids sit," I said.

"No, goof, it's where you get laid." This term was new to both of us. She used it lusciously, like a magical new toy. "You know. Like fucking." She made a circle with one hand and jabbed her finger back and forth inside it.

I must have looked dumbstruck in that moment 'cause she pressed on. "You wanna try it?"

Well, no, I didn't. But I couldn't turn down a dare—not from her.

We took our clothes off. In the tight confines of the car we kept bumping into each other, a foot to the shin, a shoulder to the gut. Down to our underwear, we both stopped. Partly, it was too cold. Partly, I don't think either of us was ready for whatever came next. We'd seen it done by grown-ups. That wasn't the problem. What it was, was it felt dirty, even for us, even though we'd seen each other's privates before, touched them even. This little space in the back of this burned-out car with each other—it was the closest thing either of us had to innocence. Reckless and stupid as we might've been, we knew enough to think twice about forsaking it.

So we shivered there, rubbing out goose bumps, not sure what to do next.

"Have you done this before?" I asked.

"All the time." Another boast. Who knows if it was true. "Lumps sometimes does it to me. And Stinger."

The other times, when we'd played doctor or whatever, we'd only shown each other quick flashes of ourselves. Now, seeing her stripped down to her Wonder Woman panties, I noticed scars along her rib cage, a string of circles. She must've seen me looking. She crossed her arms over them.

We sat like this for what seemed like forever. Getting colder. I think it even started to snow. I remember fiddling with my AK-47, flicking the plastic safety latch back and forth. Just something to do. A distraction from her. And eventually the tedium overwhelmed what had come before, and little by little we put our clothes back on and when we saw each other again, which we did, all the time, we acted like that day had never existed.

A secret. Something I could call my own.

There were casualties everywhere. Not just us. Not just the dead
rock gods. It was the spirit of the times.

Unless you got out like Sy or took off for the country to play
at utopia, you lived under siege. You lost track of all connection
between yourself and the larger movements of society. Within the
fourteen square blocks I called home, the concept of normal took
on a sickly shade. As long as I didn't leave, I didn't notice, but one
step west of the Bowery, one peek above 14th, and I was immediately confronted by the evidence of how alien and inscrutable I had
become.

You have to understand, we didn't realize we were casualties.
We thought—or my mother did—that the war was still raging, and
despite the overwhelming evidence to the contrary, we believed we
were still going to win. Like I said, we were under siege. We figured
we could wait it out, and once it was over, pick up the good times
right where we'd left them.

And maybe this was the freedom Lenny and my mother had
dreamed of, but it felt to me more like a wasting away into nothingness. At Woodstock Lenny'd famously told everyone not to eat the
brown acid. But we did. We all did. Someone had dosed the water.
A constant steady stream of psychedelic gibberish.

People who were there one day would be gone the next.

Sable, the tranny with shaky hands and cracked nails. She'd been
a lesser satellite in Warhol's orbit once. Now she lived in a dank
basement apartment on 11th Street, shooting speed and construct-
ing sad-eyed dolls out of burlap and cotton balls—intricate creatures with molded faces and hand-sewn gowns and hair clipped
from Sable's own head. They ached with something like a desire

to live. She carried them with her on her jaunts around the hood like they were part of her. One day, or so the rumor went, a couple of bridge-and-tunnel pricks snatched one of the dolls from her arms. Goaded her into a game of Keep Away. I wasn't there, I didn't see it, but word was when they got bored of watching her plead, one of them faked handing Sable the doll back, let her get hold of a leg and pulled like mad. The doll ripped apart at the seam. Stuffing floated off down the street. Sable screamed like she'd just witnessed a murder, which maybe she had. We all heard her shrieking, even from blocks away. And after that you just didn't see her anymore.

Or Moishe Kirschenbaum, a shell-shocked escapee from the Hasidic precincts of Brooklyn. He might as well have been from Neptune. He couldn't understand the most basic facts of secular American society. All he knew was that it must be better than the place he'd come from. A big motherfucker—six-six, thin as paper. In the '60s he'd been in a protest band. He played the jug. The kazoo. The Jew's harp. Now he pedaled around the neighborhood on his bicycle, all got up in costume—a Groucho mask pulled over his long donkey face, a shabby yellow leotard, rainbow-striped circus pants ripped at the crotch. I watched him scale the pedestal at the corner of Tompkins Square Park one morning and perch there, curled up like a praying mantis. I went to school. I came home. I went back out to the bodega for a Yoo-hoo. All day long, every time I walked past, there he was, not moving, not even blinking. Just one among a hundred bizarre things I saw him do. If anyone had cared, he'd have been carted off to Bellevue, but here, he was just part of the topography. Until one day, you asked yourself, where'd Moishe go? Feels like weeks since I've seen him. And you'd ask around and everyone said the same thing. And you'd be stuck with that question for the rest of your life.

Or Hank Palmer, the fat junkie who'd been eighty-sixed from the Angels for reasons unknown. He hung out at the St. Mark's Bar & Grill, where the Stones later filmed their "Waiting on a Friend" video. Took a hot-shot in the bathroom there and died. They couldn't get him out. He was too obese. Had to bust the wall down to make a hole big enough to slide his body through. The kids from the neighborhood, we all stood and watched.

Pastor Paolo, Rico the Ferret, Sally Sturges and Little Mickey Moonbeam. More. You heard about them all the time, out on the street, around the block.

Death was coming.

It would get worse, you could sense it.

Whatever was going right and whatever was going wrong, you'd look at yourself in the mirror and wonder if it would be your turn next.

I remember my mother staring down that question, struggling with her paltry alternatives.

She had no one to talk to, so she talked to me. Processing. Using the new lingo of self-improvement. "I've been working on getting in touch with myself," she'd say as she sat on her windowsill, toying with the leaves of the half-dead fern. "And I've started to realize, maybe I resent him. Subconsciously. Because . . . it's like this: We thought of ourselves as Bonnie and Clyde. That's what we used to say. 'Let's go down together in a hail of bullets.' Turns out we're not. We're just Clyde. Clyde and his sidekick. He can take her or leave her. And what's Bonnie supposed to do while Clyde's away? Change Clyde Jr.'s diapers. Keep the coffee warm. Spend her evenings polishing the gun she'll probably never use again. And I'm miserable, Freddy. You see that, don't you? I have no purpose."

It was no use to cry, What about me? What about being my mom? Isn't that a purpose? Isn't that hard enough? She wouldn't have heard me. She couldn't see me as separate from herself.

Who knows how high she was. She saw things most clearly while she was speeding. Or not clearly, lucidly. Her premises might be wrong but her arguments were sound, her conclusions compelling enough to spur her toward action. But when she did act, she behaved erratically. Grasping for reasons to justify her descent.

No, that's not fair. She really was, in her addled way, looking for something to throw her belief into. She'd built her faith around the revolution. She couldn't bear the thought that it had fallen apart.

More and more, she fixated on her friend Isha. They hadn't talked in months, hadn't seen each other since that tricky period before the world knew that Lenny had gone underground. None of that mattered. In my mother's neo-mythic imagination, she and Isha—they shared the same vision. Together they could launch a targeted assault on the unequal system in which they were both trapped.

She chattered about this too, sometimes when it was just us, alone in the apartment, waiting out the night. Making plans. Hypothetical. Notional. Fantasies. Nothing big. Nothing dramatic. The time for theatrical ploys was over.

"We'll start with small stuff," she'd say. "Things we can accomplish. Isha and I, these past few years, we've known how hard it is. We can use that. Our experiences as single mothers. And the two of us, the very fact of us—one black woman, one white, both fierce as hell—we'll remind people what the real issues are. Poverty. Poor women. The ones waiting all day at the welfare office. Begging the bodega guy to convert their food stamps into cash. Clothing their kids from the dollar store. All those women the rich, famous libbers mock with their talk of having it all. We'll hold teach-ins. We know how to do that. Community building. We'll perform street-level interventions, showing these forgotten women how to beat the system, and . . ."

Sometimes she'd lose the thread. She'd articulate stray ideas, complaints, sorrows. Like, "The whole conversation takes place within a value system that reinforces capitalist imperatives." Or, "I'm so sick of being told I've failed at life just because I'm not rich and liberal."

And then she'd wait like she somehow thought I had something intelligent to say.

Sometimes she got emotional, sentimental, like drug fiends do. She'd tear up. "Oh, Freddy. Oh, my sweet, kind boy. I'm tired. I can't tell you how tired I am. But"—a rally, the will to go on—"once Isha and I put our heads together, you'll see. It's all gonna work out."

At first it was just talk. Then she started calling. Impulsively.

At odd, inappropriate hours. Isha never answered. She was never home. Her son, Amari, he of the Fisher-Price reparations, picked up sometimes. He always had a reason she couldn't come to the phone.

Finally, one morning we marched up to Harlem to knock on her door.

I remember the tenement building they lived in, so much like our own, the same broken front door and the\same mounds of trash spilling out under the stairway. The hall lights were shattered. The windows cracked and painted over. Drips of orange-brown syrup clung to the walls. The steps were covered in black mottled scum. Except for the smells—fried fish, stewed greens, not a whiff of boiled cabbage—we might as well have been on the Lower East Side.

We curled up the stairs to the third floor. Knocked. Nothing. Knocked again. Still nothing. Hopped up, anxious, my mother put her ear to the door and listened. She knocked again, harder, using her fist, and finally someone responded. Amari.

"Whatchu want?" he said. He didn't open the door.

"It's Suzy," my mother said. "Snyder. Your mom's friend. I've been calling."

We lingered, waiting.

"Whatchu want?" Amari said again.

"I've got Freddy here with me. We were in the neighborhood. I figured we should stop by and say hello."

Another lag and then the sound of the locks shifting and the door opened an inch and pulled tight against its chain. Amari's amber eye, cold and wary. His ridged forehead. Sizing us up.

"See? It's us," said my mother. "Can we come in?"

"Mama ain't here."

Above us a door slammed shut and the energy in the hallway changed. It was like we'd transgressed and were about to be caught. We kept waiting. A pruned old woman in a housedress creaked down the stairs, bouncing a squeaky cart full of laundry in front of her. She glanced at us. Sniffed. In Harlem, as in Brooklyn, the only white folk who ever came around were nuns and social workers, cops, parole officers. We weren't any of those. We were intruders.

She walked on, hobbling, struggling with the cart on the steps, not saying a word, warding us off with silence.

"You sure your mom's not here?" my mother said. "I'd really like to see her."

"You callin' me a liar?"

"We could wait for her. How is she? Can you tell me that?"

"No."

They went back and forth like this. Around and around. The longer Amari lingered there, the more obvious it became that Isha was inside. I remember wondering what he was hiding, what he was afraid of, what darkness he was trying to protect. Casualties. There were casualties everywhere. The best minds of every generation. That's the way it goes. I know that now.

Years later, on the last album he dropped before he was killed, Amari recorded a song that laid it all out. A slow groove. Plaintive. Simple and direct. *Isha,* he said, almost but not quite singing. *It means purity, gift of god.* He used Marvin Gaye's "Mercy Mercy Me," with its exhausted air of defeat, for the hook. And rapping above the beat, he told the story of Isha's decline. How she'd run on the diesel of the black-power movement, holding steady through the fires on all sides. How when the pigs gunned daddy down, she refused to hate. *You taught dignity, stand tall, rise up, don't be swept away.* How he tried to take her word on that, *but Mama, it was hard to watch you turn it all back on yourself.* He talked about the rot deep in her bones. How she treated herself to the life she believed she deserved: hard drugs and harder dealers and open sores. *No more dignity left to lose.* She'd just been trying to survive. *Mama, you loved me.* His voice ached with emotion. *Oh mercy mercy me.* He'd tweaked the lyrics. *Things ain't how they s'posed to be.*

It struck me, that song. Just how much Isha and my mother had had in common. How similar their paths had been, though Isha's was worse. I think about it a lot.

And I remember, while we stood there outside their door, wondering what I'd do if Isha and Amari showed up unexpectedly at ours. Would I let them in? If it meant they'd see my mother bouncing off the ceiling? No. I wouldn't. I'd do the same thing Amari was doing. I was him. He was me. Both of us fighting to save our mothers. Neither of us equipped to even think about how to go about it. And I remember understanding, even then, that we'd never discuss this, never be allies, not even friends, any more than my mother and Isha ever would be again.

My mother, though, she couldn't see this. Her need was too great. She'd taken the risk to drag us up there and beg for the help she needed to save herself from herself. Having done so, she couldn't see anything except her goal.

She was pleading now. She'd jammed one foot in the crack to make sure Amari couldn't slam the door in her face.

"You got to *go*," he kept saying. "Lady, you got to *go*. Leave us alone."

And my mother, in response, said, "Just tell her it's me. It's Suzy. She'll understand. She knows me. Just tell her, please? You'll see. Please. She knows me. She'll want to see me."

Muscling the door. The two of them. Pushing and pulling until finally the chain broke or the latch came loose or something happened to it to send it flying open—Amari falling back on his heels, tumbling, trying not to lose his balance. And there was Isha, hunched on a sofa, watching it all through glazed eyes.

"She don't want to see you," Amari said. Now he was the one who was pleading. "She don't need no help from whitey."

The violence of the struggle, and the sight of Isha there in front of her, half-gone—my mother was stunned. Speechless. Unable to move. She saw now, with an indelible clarity, that she shouldn't have come here.

"Leave us alone," Isha said. "You've got nothing to give us."

She was right. My mother couldn't help her. She couldn't help my mother. Whatever had united them in the past was fractured now. Everyone was on their own.

We got lucky.

Seeing Isha like that rattled my mother enough to propel her out of the house in search of a job. Or a sort-of job. She volunteered at Sister's. Stood by her principles and bartered her labor for the greater good. Made just enough to cover the rent.

At least we had food now. It was better than nothing.

I remember nights at Sister's during those few good months, waiting around while my mother worked. Picking at the meatloaf she slipped in front of me. Making piles—the carrots here, the onions there, the mushrooms from the gravy far off to the side—until I could be sure my meat was pure. Then homework: workbooks for cursive and simple arithmetic. Rocking on the uneven legs of my chair until someone glanced my way.

The women at Sister's were all about mother love. They didn't mind my being there half the night. I was their pet.

Meg and Colleen and Nita and Violet. Billie, with the split ends, missing a bunch of teeth—you could feel the earth clinging to her broad flat feet, the old world rising through her, grounding everything she touched.

Misty and Juana, who might or might not've been a couple. They'd sit with me when it was slow and ask questions. "Whatcha learning? George Washington, huh. Whatcha think of him? You really believe he never told a lie?" Taking me as they found me and fawning over what they saw. "You're so smart . . . so sensitive . . . such a good boy. You take care of that old mother of yours, don't you?" Flattering me with their wishful assumptions.

I'd tap my water gun, there as always by my side, and say, "You betcha." My favorite phrase. I'd heard it on TV.

They'd tell me about themselves, about the lives they'd lived. How Colleen had gotten that scar on her arm. Why Violet left Detroit and the many stops she'd made between there and this final, unexpected destination. "It ain't much, but it's ours," she'd say, putting on a fake southern drawl to mock and camouflage the sincerity of her feelings. Then she'd laugh—sharp hiccups of sound—as though even that small crack had to be plastered over.

Even Sister herself—that's all anybody called her—kept tabs on me. Coming up from the basement with a tray of lasagna, she'd throw me a benign eye and tick her cheek, two clucks like a gun cocking, as she strode by. She'd lean back on the counter and smile, not so much at me as at the space she'd created. Like, *This, all this. It's my little miracle.*

And it was, I guess.

These women, each and every one of them, had lived hard. But somehow guided by Sister's vision, they'd carved out a space for themselves, a humble corner where it didn't matter what kind of messes they were. A cozy feminine benevolence pervaded, radical in its compassion and lack of judgment. They could heal, or not. Whatever they wanted.

My mother stood apart. Skeptical. She'd always felt she was more one of the boys. This squishy acceptance, it made her nervous. She wasn't so sure she wanted to feel safe.

I'd watch her run the register or work the slop station, holding herself that little bit apart from the others. They'd tease her—Juana or Meg, the cutups of the group—throwing an arm over her shoulder and striking a pose, waiting for her to seethe and tell them to buzz off. Or they'd ask about Lenny, had she heard from him, was he safe, had Kunstler worked his magic yet? "We don't know how you do it, believing in him like this, when the whole world's saying you should just forget him." They'd push it. "You've got a will of steel. We admire you. No way in hell would I wait for a man like that, but hey—"

Mom let them see her smirk. "Give me a fucking break," she'd say. "I'm an idiot."

"You said it, not me. But you know? Somebody's got to stand up for those oppressed men."

Getting to her. Playing their angles.

But they'd send pies home with us. Plates heavy with leftovers.

On my mother's thirty-second birthday, Sister baked her a cake. Angel food. Marshmallow frosting.

"I don't want this," my mother said. "I'm not going to celebrate."

"It's your Jesus year," they said. "Celebrate that."

"I'm a Jew. What do I care about that motherfucker?"

And knowing how to turn her frown upside down, Juana, or maybe it was Meg, winked and said, "You cared enough to kill him. Think about that."

So celebrate they did, blasting Aretha and Diana Ross late into the night, drinking too much cheap wine and watery beer. They weren't proud. That was their beauty and their strength. Even my mother danced—low, leading with her hips.

I watched that place do its work on my mother. Not quite softening her. More like surrounding her with softness.

And then, at home, all she'd do was complain about them. "It's like a cult. Don't you think, Freddy? All those good intentions? If I don't watch out they'll turn me into a lesbo. Hah. Well, no, but . . ."

She'd shake her head and glare at the floor and I'd know she was thinking about what champs they all were. Billie, with her ever-changing cast of violent men, and Colleen, skittish like a kitten lost on the battlefield, and Misty and Juana, so suspiciously happy. Sister herself, who must've reminded my mother of Lenny, a quieter, less grandiose version of Lenny. All of them.

It had to have been humiliating for her. She must've ached, seeing Sister hold tight to her irrational dreams.

But she kept going back. For the money, sure, what there was of it, but also for the friendship. For—and I mean this sincerely—the freedom.

She was getting herself clean.

Six weeks in Sister's care and she risked dreaming again. She risked thoughts of the future. Risked revving her engine just a touch to see if it still worked.

And that was when this came in the mail:

Petulant—

 Enough with the silence! It's unbearable. I've said it before, and I'll say it again, a hundred times, a thousand: you and I are the same person. The same heart. The same mind. If I can't bounce my sense of the world off of you, I'm lost.

 You understand me? I'm lost, Susan. Weeks go by and I remain catatonic. I can't write. I can't read. I can't even think. If the Queen weren't here, I most likely wouldn't eat. She makes me soups. She watches to make sure I get them down. They taste like bitterness. My own personal gruel.

I need you.

I don't know why you've forsaken me. Maybe it's just the distance and the troubling consequences of what must feel to you like a never-ending trail of government persecution. Maybe you lost faith and decided I'm not worth the trouble. I could understand that. It wouldn't be like you, but I could understand it. What I can't understand is why you'd cut off all contact with no explanation at all. Don't you realize what that does to my mind?

Is it the Queen? She's not a threat to you. Love's not a rare commodity like gold. It's constantly replenishing. The more you let it into your life, the more you have to give. Even if this weren't true, my heart's big enough to contain you both. You should be happy she's here keeping me alive. It's a helluva job and she's wondrous at it. She's like a custodian, keeping me oiled and running until you and I can be reunited.

I don't think it's this, though. We've shared ourselves with enough other people through the years that I'd know by now if you were the jealous type.

So what is it? The money? If I had any lying around, you'd be the first to know, okay?

Please, talk to me. Send me a locket of your hair.

—Your Ever-Loving Two-Hearted Fool

And this:

Olive Oyl,

Got the blues. Can't shake 'em. I'm not myself—don't know who I am. People talk about the legendary Lenny Snyder and I think to myself, do I know that guy? Feels like I used to. Would I recognize him if I saw him on St. Marks? Would he recognize me? He'd think I'm a square. That's the straight dope. Nebbishy, afraid. Some hick who couldn't possibly know the score.

I've lost myself out here in the high plains—and no, that's not a clue, it's a metaphor. Seems like this whole country is high plains nowadays. The air's thin. The war's far away.

I need to see you. I need to see the kid. See my face in his and remember who I am.

It's all I live for.

—Popeye

It was like he could sense her pulling away and he couldn't resist the temptation to remind her that her life had been indelibly marked by him. When he got no response from her, he upped the ante.

Daffodil,

Are you free the weekend of April 19? I am! And I want to see you!

Come. I don't care about the risk. Just come.

I've already worked out all the details with Kunstler. For obvious reasons, they're complicated. Among other things you'll have to find a car. Just ask him and he'll fill you in. In person! No phones!

Is that a yes I hear? Yes? Yes! YES!!

I'll see you then? Can't wait! And the Queen can't wait to meet you!

—Honey Bee
P.S. Bring the kid. I've got a baseball we can throw around.

I remember watching her after she read this. Her waving the sheet of yellow legal paper at me and jabbing at it with her finger. There was a violence to her excitement.

"What did I tell you, Freddy? Didn't I say everything would work out?"

She stomped off to the stereo and blasted the tunes. Collapsed on the couch with her head flung back, and let Richie Havens's frenetic guitar work carry her away to that fantastic future she'd almost lost faith in.

This was vindication. A big fuck you to all those people who'd tried to convince her to rebuild her life without him. The cynics and realists and pansy-ass healers. Hell, at one point, even Kunstler had suggested she give up hope.

Fuck them.

Fuck them all.

We were gloriously free.

Lenny had called us home. Just like he'd promised. Would we go? It wasn't even a question.

But first, one more thing about Phil:

There'd been times when I thought everything would be better if he'd just come around like he used to. But he never did. Not after that brutal night with my mother.

When I think of him now, I imagine him stewing in that apartment on Clinton Street, boxed in by stacks of *The New York Times*, taking slugs of vodka out of a chipped coffee mug. Drunk and sentimental, he'd swipe a paper off one of the stacks and gaze at the headlines. Watergate, My Lai, Gerald Ford. Dylan's second—or was it his third—comeback. They mocked Phil, these stories of power and import. Even when they revealed necessary truths, they distorted them. Bolstering the system that encouraged the corruption they'd been sworn to expose. Flattering—placating—the tone-deaf liberals who, trapped between their good intentions and their desire for comfort, depended on the paper for proof of their righteousness. *All the news that's fit to print.* Hah! The beautifully delusional arrogance of it all.

I imagine Phil stumbling around his apartment, thinking, to the degree that he could still think at all, that he'd had the wrong critique. Told the wrong story. They'd edited him out. Called him a buffoon—not even worth condescending to. And they were right. He knew it. He'd thought kindness was a virtue. As though something greater than his ego was at stake. He should've learned from Dylan, from Lenny, to use the machine, make it all about him, tie the drama of his own life to the message. He should've played chess with the world and never appealed to goodness. Goodness always loses. You lost, Phil, he'd tell himself. Got just what you deserved. Despising the game doesn't make you a winner.

I imagine him stumbling through that dark apartment, bumbling into the artifacts of his past. The notebooks full of old aborted ideas, the guitar, the newspapers, newspapers everywhere, warped, water-stained, yellow at the edges. Lyrics sliding around inside his brain, not his, Dylan's . . . *there's no success like failure and failure's no success at all* . . . They nicked and cut . . . *you got a lot of nerve* . . . *you had no faith to lose and you know it* . . . He knew them better than he did his own.

And I imagine him tripping over his own feet, falling into the stacks of papers. Unable to get up. Not even wanting to. If someone had to pull his body through another day, let it be somebody else, not him. I imagine him passing out, hoping he was dying, and waking up the next day as a different man, cynical, with a sudden will to survive.

That's what I think now. I don't know what I thought then.

All I knew was that he'd cut my mother and me out of his life, and missing him gnawed at me so much that one afternoon I marched down to Clinton Street and pounded on his door. One touch and it flew open. The place was gutted. A gaping emptiness. The windows had been thrown wide, the dark burlap curtains torn down and piled in a mess along the wall. The only signs Phil had ever lived there were a page from the *New York Post* shellacked to the floorboards and a putrid carton of lo mein in the unplugged fridge.

I blamed my mother. I ran home to scream at her. "Where is he? What did you do to him? I hate you. Bring him back. I hate you."

She tried to mollify me. "You know, Freddy, Phil's a busy guy. He doesn't owe us anything. When he wants to be in touch, he'll find us, I'm sure."

I wouldn't hear it. "No he won't. You did something. What did you do?" Shouting myself hoarse. I couldn't conceive of adult complication. Life was an all-or-nothing venture to me. And when things went wrong there had to be a reason.

"Should we call him?" she asked, amused by my strong emotion.

"We can't call him. He's not there. I told you already."

She went to the phone and picked up the receiver.

"He's not there!"

She dialed one number, then another, teasing me.

"Mom!"

"So you don't want me to call him?"

"He's not there! All his stuff's gone!"

"Well, there you go, Freddy. He's moved. Maybe he's gone back to LA." Gauging how well her gambit had worked, and seeing I'd been stung, she placed the receiver back in its cradle and watched me some more.

"He would've said goodbye," I said. "Why didn't he say goodbye?"

She knelt. She pulled me toward her. "It means he loves you. When you grow up, you'll see. People hate goodbyes. Goodbye means forever."

What she didn't tell me, what she'd been protecting me from, were the rumors she'd been hearing around town. How somebody had heard from somebody else who'd heard from somebody else right up the line that Phil had been spotted curled up in front of a basement storefront on Little West 12th, covered in his own urine, frozen half to death; how he'd been seen stalking McDougal with a hammer in his belt, accusing friends and strangers alike of having stolen something he called "the chimes," how he'd tried to bludgeon Sy Neuman with that hammer and, later, Marcus Kirsh and even poor old Pete Seeger; how he carried a guitar case full of cash around with him now, spitefully flinging it open, throwing bills in the face of anyone who tried to talk some sense into him; how, most recently, she'd heard he'd holed up in the Chelsea Hotel, refusing to leave his room for any reason, getting his vodka delivered by the case from the liquor store down the street while he recorded a grand, rambling theory of his persecution by the *Times,* by Bob Dylan and the CIA and Interpol and MI6, by General Robert McNamara himself, Henry Kissinger, Richard Nixon, LBJ, the whole kit and caboodle of pirate politicos, a frightening tale to hear, so said those who'd heard it, not because it was true but because of its pathetic logic, the hysterical reach of Phil's complaint, drawing connections between himself and Che and Fidel in the Sierra Maestra, the Rosenbergs, Emma Goldman, Leo Frank and more, James Dean and Marilyn and Edgar Allan Poe, Herman Melville, even Ralph Waldo Emerson, Guy Fawkes and Jean-Paul Marat and Joan of Arc, Robin Hood, Hassan the Assassin, Jesus Christ, a long continuous chain of martyrs tracing back to the days of Jeremiah, all of them blazing like heretics in the temples of the corrupt, all of them battling the same craven *machers,* all of them losing, but winning by losing, all except Phil Ochs, who'd simply lost by losing, so said the man holding court in his fourth-floor room in the Chelsea Hotel, which was why he'd had to murder that coward in cold blood and take over the job Phil had been too weak to finish. He called himself John Traine now—that's what she'd heard. And however sincere and generous Phil had been, Traine was just as spiteful and relentless. He'd transformed himself into a nasty piece of work whose self-hatred encompassed the entire world.

She told me none of this. Maybe, not having witnessed it first-hand, she refused to believe what they were saying on the street. Maybe she couldn't bear to contemplate the role she may or may not have played in bringing him to this state, couldn't face her culpability—if that's what it was. She was free, we were free, every-one else was free to travel his or her individual path regardless of the hardship they heaped on themselves, and this had been meant to lead to liberation, to an open society where every human being, even the most deranged, was accepted. Maybe, not knowing how to help him, she ached so much that she hid the depths of his pain from herself. She was a person who cared. She'd seen so many casualties. Maybe she refused to admit that Phil might be one of them.

Whatever it was, when word came down that he was doing a secret gig at Gerde's, she was reluctant to go. I begged and pouted until I got her to relent, which took less effort than it should have.

Typically, on the night of the show, she couldn't get it together to motivate us out of the house. She changed costumes three times and struggled to get her eyeliner just right. Then she couldn't find the keys. And the particular festive floppy hat she wanted to wear. She dawdled. Always one more thing to do before we left. This meant something to her too, seeing Phil again. Maybe she'd intuited that it was the end.

We made it finally out onto the street just to march right back upstairs and change into lighter jackets. Then, as we wandered across town, she decided we needed to eat something and she hustled me into a pizzeria.

"We're gonna miss it," I told her. I was hopped up. Anxious.

"Naw. These things always start late. And the cool kids know it's unhip to be on time. We're gonna get there right when we're supposed to, in the sweet spot when we'll look like we don't really care."

"But we do care!"

She leaned across the table and placed a finger to her lips. "Shh," she said. "That's a secret. No one's s'posed to know that." Teasing me. Happy. Joking around. She dabbed a napkin in her water glass and wiped the grease from my cheek.

When we finally arrived, the show had already started, maybe not on time, but more on time than us. People lurked in the dark just past the entrance, their backs to the door. Somewhere on the other side of their chatter Phil was strumming his guitar and muttering into a mic, but all we could hear from the door was the tenor of his voice, the rumble of sound when he dug rapid-fire into the strings for emphasis. The dude taking the money wouldn't let us in. "We're sold out. It's too crowded in there already," he said.

"We're on the list," said my mother.

"There is no list."

"Bullshit. There's always a list."

The guy shot her a look, two parts pity, one part fear, and we should've known right then how fraught things were inside. "Not tonight," he said. "Anyway, it doesn't matter. The kid's too young."

"We're friends of Phil."

He gazed at her, unimpressed, waiting for the point.

Phil was singing now, an old union song. His voice grated against the melody, more bark than tune.

"We're missing it," I said.

And my mother seized her advantage. "Look," she told the dude. "You're gonna make the kid cry."

He let us pass.

And there—once we got past the bodies crammed into the back of the club—was Phil. He was balanced unsteadily on a stool, holding himself upright with a stiff leg. Even fatter than when I'd seen him months earlier, in clothes a touch too tight, his work shirt unbuttoned out of necessity, his work boots untied out of neglect. He'd abandoned the union song. His head hung low, his chin tucked into his chest, his oily hair stabbing over his bloated face. Like he was too tired to play the role all these people expected of him.

He looked up at the ceiling and ran his hand through his hair, held it off his forehead the way I'd seen him do a hundred times before, and for a moment, the man I'd known came flickering through. The same, but sadder.

"Where's that drink, bub?" he said, peering out toward the bar. He strummed his guitar. "I can't do another song until I get that drink."

My mother and I had wedged ourselves between the standing-room crowd and the tables. Pressed in on both sides, we worked sideways toward the brick wall where there was slightly more space to breathe. We hadn't adjusted yet to the mood in the air. We sensed disturbance but didn't have enough information to comprehend its cause. All we knew was that people were riveted by something other than the music. And that Phil looked lonely up there, waiting for his drink.

Eventually a pint glass of clear liquid made it to the stage. Phil raised it like an offering and said, "Finally. The service here is for shit." He downed half the drink and dropped the glass onto a second, empty stool that had been placed beside him.

"Here's another one you're gonna hate." He picked out a few chords. "Straight from the prophet's lips." And he launched into a Dylan song. Groans and protests rose from the crowd. He ignored them, watched his fingers and rambled on until he stumbled over the lyrics and gave up. "Too many verses," he said, mumbling into the mic. "That man never knew when to quit." He slammed the rest of his drink and shot a look at the bar. "Another round for the troubadour?" he said. He strummed. He croaked out a few random lyrics. False starts. Aborted gestures. "There's no success like failure and failure's no success at all." A thought struck him and he paused to catch it. "He's a genius, though. No question. Always was better than Phil Ochs."

The crowd tensed. A call went out. "Play your own songs."

"Phil knew it the first time he saw him. 'Well then. I'm finished.' That's what he thought. I should've killed him right then and there."

More protests from the crowd. People pleading, shouting out titles.

"Those songs are shit," Phil said. "Phil made me promise never to play them again. He begged me. While I had my gun to his head. 'They're an embarrassment.' That's what he said. 'They're all lies. I'll let you kill me, Traine. I understand why you have to kill me. But once I'm dead, you have to start telling the truth. So, no more songs. No more false hopes.'" He went on and on like this, making no sense, not even pretending he planned to do anything more than chatter for the rest of the night. Sometimes he lost the thread and gazed off into the abyss. Then he'd grab hold of some new thought and chatter some more. A parable. A screed. A demand for more drinks. I didn't understand what was going on. He wasn't himself. I kept wishing he'd at least stutter. Something. That a crack would appear—a flash of light—and this dark creature who'd taken over his body would flinch and reveal the decent, sad, forgiving man I loved. I kept wishing this was a pose. But Phil had never learned how to separate himself from the illusion he presented to others. He was fatally, impractically sincere. This had been his gift. Relentless good intentions.

He was on to a new story now about some sort of bet he claimed to have made with Arthur Rimbaud. Something about Chinese checkers and whores and the profane secrets of the universe. And, of course, Dylan. Dylan and Rimbaud playing a series of games— best of five? Best of seven? If Rimbaud won, Phil Ochs would be plied with whores who would reveal cosmic mysteries to him. If Dylan won, Phil would be put to death. Or some shit like that.

I couldn't follow the logic. I'm not sure he could either. He kept backing up to clarify and change the story.

I asked my mother, "What's wrong with him?"

She gave me a look, weary, worried, fully of pity. "We should go," she said.

"But what's wrong with him?"

"He's—I don't know."

"We need to help him."

"No," she said, "we should go. We shouldn't have come to begin with."

"But he helped us," I said, "so we have to help him."

There was that pity in her eyes again. "That's not how it works." She squeezed my shoulder and tried to steer me back through the crush of people around the door.

And all I could think was, Phil hadn't seen me yet. And I had to say goodbye. It was important. Even if—especially if—goodbye meant forever. He was going on and on—the whores with their big tits taunting Dylan, hovering around him, pawing at his chest, trying to distract him so Rimbaud could win—and my mother was pushing me to leave and I was running out of time so I shouted, "Phil! Hey, Phil! Look! We made it!"

And he heard me. He squinted out past the lights into the crowd. "Who let a kid in here?" he mumbled.

"It's me! It's Freedom! We made it! We're here!"

"Freedom . . ." Holding the hair off his forehead, he tried to orient himself, to locate me in the darkness and remember who he was.

"Play that song," I said. "The one about Lenny." Who knows what I was thinking. I must've thought I was helping.

"Freedom . . ." A spark. "Right. Freedom. Lenny Snyder's kid. That guy's a secret agent. I have classified knowledge—documentation—that Lenny was personally involved in the murder of Che Guevara . . ." He gazed into the lights and seemed confused for a second. When he recovered, he said, "And he owes me ten thousand bucks." He chuckled. "A thief and a scoundrel, that's Lenny Synder, folks. But I got him back. I took my revenge. I cuckolded him. Fucked his wife. It was easy. Left her begging for more."

Maybe he continued. Some new diatribe. I wouldn't know. My mother had me out of there just like that.

She didn't say a word to me the whole way home.

We never talked about that night. What was there to say? Next we heard, Phil was dead. He hung himself in the doorway of his sister's kitchen.

And one more thing about Rosalita:

I had to say goodbye to her. There'd been times, over the past few months, when we missed each other. The snow was too deep, the air too frigid. One or the other of us flaked for whatever reason. There'd been weeks when, to appease my mother, I'd gone to school every single day, weeks when the chaos Rosalita never talked about in her life took her away to a heavy place that I knew not to ask about when I saw her again. It was no big thing. The thrill of waiting, not knowing if she might pop, scowling, around the corner, her hands balled in fists like she was off to kick someone's ass, the possibility, the fluttering chance of it, was enough to sustain me through the times when she wasn't there.

I'd flip through comic books. Daydream about the contents of the Wacky Packies she and I'd been sticking on the dash of the Pinto as reinforcements for my army of protective totems. I'd nap in the backseat.

One day she'd be there blowing bubbles, waiting for me with a whole mess of Bazooka comics.

"Where've you been," she'd say. "I thought you died."

And I'd say, "You're the one who went missing."

"Whatever. Look at this. And this one. And this one's the best." Feeding the little wax paper panels to me like they explained everything I'd ever need to know.

But lately I'd been waiting and waiting for her. A month—maybe more—had gone by. And sure, on some of those days I'd been in school, or at Sister's with my mother or just busy, but spring had blown in since the last time I'd seen her. The sun had come out of its hibernation, weeds had begun sprouting in the nooks and crannies of the car. Everybody else was out and about again. And still, I hadn't seen any evidence of her: no Tootsie Pop wrappers, no new Wacky Packies. Worry buzzed in my gut. The extravagant, hard-to-believe things she'd told me, they swarmed in my stomach. Maybe they'd all been true. I should have listened differently.

And now that the weather had begun to change, we were going away, my mother and me. We'd been plucked for selection. We might never return.

I waited in the Pinto for longer stretches. Whole days.

No sign.

I wandered the streets, searched under the bridge.

Unable to find her in any of the usual places, and worried that I'd never see her again, I started to construct a story in my head involving Lumps and Stinger and the other kids in her squat. Maybe they'd tied her up. They were doing things to her. What, I didn't know. The details were dark. But it was very bad and nobody, not even the adults in the squat, cared enough to do anything to stop it. She'd been right about her fatalistic vision of the future, but the hole in her heart was the least of her problems. Those kids would kill her before she had the chance to die on her own.

Our friendship existed in public places, semisecret pockets of the Great-Out-There where we could pretend to be whoever we wanted. I had no idea if anything she'd ever said to me was true. But the scars on her rib cage, those had been real. Someone had really burned her with a cigarette. They were doing it again. No one cared. Only me.

I had to save her. To try, anyway, so I strapped my AK-47 to my back and set off toward 13th Street.

I'd never been inside the squat. The closest I'd come was when I'd lurked outside—it seemed like lifetimes ago—while Lenny brokered some deal or other with the cannibals barricaded next door. The place had loomed there, frightening. The kids, maybe Rosalita herself, scurrying around in the shadows. Playing chicken. Violent, it had seemed. Capable of anything. Coming up on it now, those same trepidations surged in me. Those same old insecurities. I was too weak, too afraid. Doomed to fail. But somehow I managed to go up the three steps to the reinforced steel door pierced by two bullet holes, tagged so many times that it was now almost entirely coated in black. I pulled hard on the industrial handle screwed to the door and it flew open on its hinges. The lock—like every other one in the neighborhood—was broken.

Inside, the place virtually sparkled. It was so clean. So unlike what I'd expected. In its bones it was a tenement, just like the one I lived in, but instead of the rotting banister and wracked steps and brittle linoleum in clashing colors and styles pasted over holes in the floor, the squat had style, intention, an aesthetic sense that had been carefully considered and then executed to conform to a precise vision.

The floors were made of thick broad boards of wood, sanded and painted a slick black. The walls crawled with murals. Not the jittery dying flowers of my mother's walls but mythological creatures, giant sea squid and anglerfish, incandescent in dark water. Christmas lights snaked up the handrails. Work lights hung overhead. Extension cords, bundled into thick ropes, rode the edges of the corridor, neat, out of the way.

I listened. The first floor seemed abandoned. No sound or light. I took the stairs slowly. Wincing at each inadvertent sound I made.

Up out of the ocean, Viking ships rode the waves, their great sails straining against the wind. On the second floor, none of the apartments had doors. They just opened onto the hallway like a single maze-like dungeon. A continuous string of corridors and rooms.

Listening again, I still heard nothing. Or no, I did hear something. Faintly. A scurrying, like rats in the wall, but which wall? It all seemed very far away. I slung my gun around and held it with both hands and I crept like a grunt in the jungles of Vietnam through one doorway after another. Clear. Clear. Was that music? Someone picking at a guitar? But where? And how to get from here to there?

I slipped from room to room. My heart felt like it was being squeezed by an iron fist, which clenched more tightly with each corner I turned.

It was eerie how cozy, how warm these warrens were. Instead of squalor, I was confronted by comfort. Beds piled with blankets. Shelves filled with crates and boxes, each labeled and fitted and exactingly organized. Everything handmade. These people lived better than my mother and me. The place reeked of overwhelming attentive care. It upset me. Where was the rot? It had to be here somewhere. Rosalita's twisted way of confronting the world hadn't come from nowhere.

I kept moving.

I found the source of the guitar picking. A skinny white dude, maybe twenty-five, thirty, shirtless in a windowsill facing the air shaft. His hair hung flat and unwashed in his face as he watched his hands. He looked up when I entered. Pulled the hair from his face and smiled. "Howdy." Like some random kid skulking around with an AK-47 was completely normal.

I backed away.

Later, I caught sight of a ropey Asian woman with hair almost as long as her African-print dress. I watched her from two or three rooms away. She was standing over a chopping block in what must have been a kitchen. Open canning jars spread around her on the counter. The radio quietly playing NPR. I didn't come closer. I chose a different route.

Up the stairs to the third floor. Past more elaborate creatures on the walls. Phoenixes, dragons, griffons, unicorns.

There were more signs of life up here. A TV was on. Or a record player. Richard Pryor's voice cracking as he whimpered, in character. A rustling of life around the first doorway. Flattened against the wall, I strained to hear. The milky pop of an inveterate mouth-breather. Lumps. It could be no one else. I listened harder. A tinny clang and then a voice pleading. "Give it back." Was that Paulie? Someone else was in there too. I was pretty sure.

Before I bum-rushed the place I had to prepare myself. I fell back on the hundreds of cop shows I'd seen. The way Kojak or Rockford or the *Hawaii Five-O* guys would flex in the shadows. The exact stance of their bodies. Their spread legs. Their cocked arms. How they leapt into action and surprised the villains. That's what I had to do. Now was the time.

Maybe Rosalita was in there, maybe not. If she was, I'd run to her. Shield her with my body. Otherwise, Paulie and Lumps, Stinger, whoever I found, they'd know where they'd stashed her. I'd force it out of them. They'd pay. Oh, how they'd pay.

I flipped around the corner and there they all were. Lumps and Stinger and Paulie and others whose names I didn't know. Maybe eight in all. Boys of various ages and races. They barely glanced at me. One of them, sitting on a Big Wheel missing its pedals, tipped his head quizzically and plopped an M&M on his tongue.

"Where's Rosalita?" I demanded.

Stinger looked up long enough to hiss, "Shhh."

Richard Pryor said, "I was lookin' at this one titty lookin' at me an' looked like it winked at me."

They were, most of them, sprawled on the floor around the record player, listening. I didn't know what to do next. They were supposed to be shocked and disoriented by my arrival, to be sent into a frenzy of chaotic scrambling, covering their tracks, hiding their crimes. They were at least supposed to do something more than nothing. I waved my gun around, took a few steps into the room. Richard Pryor said, "I don't want to offend this bitch with this monkey foot, see?"

I was losing my nerve.

Someone had taken out the walls on this floor, broken down the barriers between the old apartments and turned the space into one massive loft. There were toys everywhere. Toys and picture books and art supplies. Anything a kid could want. Plop in the middle of the room someone had erected a modular swing set. I felt my anger turn, and not for the productive reasons I'd come here to fume about. No, I was angry at all this stuff. At the calm, attentive way they were entertaining themselves. I was angry at what they had and what I did not.

Even Lumps. Look at him there. He was barely sentient. A stunted troll. Stupid as a stone. Even he had more going for him than me. And he'd hurt Rosalita. And none of these fuckers cared.

"Lumps," I barked. "Where is she? What did you do to her?"

"Fuck off," he said.

"No, I won't fuck off. Tell me. Stinger. And you. You, the dumb

kid on the Big Wheel. Somebody tell me what you did with Rosalita." I pointed my gun at them like it would somehow scare them.
They went right on ignoring me.

I lurked. If they weren't going to give me what I wanted, I'd stick
around until they got annoyed enough to at least chase me away. I
stomped around the room. Peered in boxes of clay jam jars stuffed
with colored pencils, like I thought Rosalita might be hiding in
there. I kicked things. I climbed up on the swing and creaked back
and forth hoping the noise would be enough to piss someone off.

Nothing.

"I'm not gonna leave, guys," I said. "Guys?" I stood up. "Did
you hear me? I'm gonna stay right here."

Stinger pulled himself into a sitting position. "Do we even know
you?" He'd seen me a hundred times, out and about. In the park.

"He's Rosie's boyfriend," Lumps said. "They diddle each other."

And I lost it. I just lost it.

I shot my gun at him, but it was out of water. I'd forgotten to
fill it. So I lunged into the middle of their little conclave. They were
laughing at me now. All of them. Even the four-year-old on the Big
Wheel, though he might have been crying. I don't know. I went for
Lumps, clawed for his neck. He was twice, three times my size. One
swing of his fatty arm sent me reeling away into the record player,
into the Big Wheel. The record scratched and flipped off the turntable. I must've been screaming. That kid, whether he laughed at
me before or not, was definitely crying now. I threw myself around,
hands and elbows, kicking, swinging my gun by the barrel. Not
thinking about myself anymore. Consumed with thoughts of Rosalita, how she'd been abused, tortured, scarred, how I'd punish them,
all of them. Even if they beat me. I'd take them all down with me as
I fell. And the next thing I knew, I'd pulled that little kid from the
Big Wheel and straddled him, my hands around his ears, his eyes
bulging in terror. I struggled to smash his head against the ground.
I remember my own shock at what I was doing. The sense of yes,
wow, I was actually hurting him, but also the feeling that all this
was taking place somewhere far away, out of my control. I wasn't
really there. Someone else owned my body.

And I remember how odd it was. That none of the other kids in that room—bigger kids, stronger kids, kids who knew and supposedly cared for this boy—not one of them did a single thing to stop me.

I can't say how long this went on. Maybe no time at all. It felt like forever.

And then an adult voice, deep and black and unequivocal, said, "What the fuck do you think you're doing, son?"

And I froze and I looked up and there was Ronnie Walker. I don't know how I knew it was him, but I did. And instead of me catching him and saving Lenny or whatever I'd imagined would happen if I pinpointed Walker's location and turned him in to my mother, to Kunstler, to the cops, he'd caught me doing I didn't know what to a kid even littler than me.

I looked down at the boy. Somehow I'd already let go of him, risen up and stepped away, not altogether consciously. There was no blood. Maybe I hadn't hurt him. He curled in on himself like he thought I was about to kick him in the ribs. Sobbing so deeply that he made no sound. The tears vibrated in his body. His mouth pulsed like a baby searching for a nipple. So maybe I *had* hurt him. I've always wondered. Right then, with Ronnie Walker staring me down, along with these squatter kids who'd witnessed what I'd done, my power and how I'd used it horrified me.

"You hear me?" Ronnie said. "You gonna say something for yourself?"

All I could think to do was hug my gun, use it as the security blanket it had always been, but I'd dropped it in the chaos and Walker was waiting. His presence consumed the whole room.

I sputtered something half-formed. Just a sound, and Stinger, helpful, smug, said, "He's looking for Rosie. He's her—"

"I know who he is," Walker said.

And it was then that I realized Rosalita was there in the room with us. Or not quite in the room but hugging the doorway. She'd always been skinny. She was even more so now. Dark-eyed and hollowed out. Her hair looked like it hadn't been washed in weeks.

"What I don't get is why he's here." Walker looked at Rosalita as he said this.

She limped into the room. I thought she was headed toward me, and I reached out to hold her. To shield her. She walked on by. Wouldn't even look at me. She went to the boy I'd attacked. He'd pulled himself to the wall by then and, sickly as she was, she wrapped him in her arms, held him tight, comforted him.

"You think she's gonna choose you over her own brother?" Walker said.

Her brother. Her family. How, exactly, were these people connected? They weren't Walker's kids. Stinger was the only one who was black. Lumps—he was as pale as a Polack. They were a scraggly bunch of city kids who'd somehow all ended up in the same place.

"Just stop hurting her," I said weakly.

"Hurting her? Nobody here's hurting our Rosalita." He met my weakness with fury. Since I'd seen him last, he'd grown wild muttonchops and his hairline had eroded, all of which made him seem that much more bootjack and terrifying. He got right up in my face. Forced me back a step. "I'm gonna lay it down for you, kid. And you're gonna listen. Rosie over there's got some imagination. She sees visions. She gets ahead of herself. Ain't our fault if you fell for them. I know nothing about you, kid, and you knowing nothing about us, but I'll tell you this: The only reason I haven't thrown you out that window over there is that I respect your daddy. You understand me?"

It took all I could manage to nod my head. Rosalita still wouldn't look at me. She rocked her little brother in her lap like he was the single thing she had left in the world.

"I *said*, do you understand me?"

My internal organs were liquefying. But somehow I squeezed out one last spasm of resistance. "What about her scars?"

"Don't you worry about her scars."

"But—"

"But nothing. Shit, boy. Do I have to repeat myself?"

"But Lumps—"

"Lumps nothing. The kid is slow. Even you should be able to see that. Lumps didn't give Rosalita those scars. Not a person in this house gave her those scars. Hell. Use your head, kid. How do you think she got here to begin with?" Spit flew from his mouth. Tiny projectiles raining down on me.

He was right. I knew nothing about nothing.

Rosalita, she . . . it didn't matter anymore.

Reining himself in now, quiet, menacing, Walker said, "Why are you still here, boy?" If I moved I'd start crying and if I cried, I'd piss myself. "Go."

"Can . . ." I said, "can I get my gun first?" I'd dropped it in the scuffle.

Walker followed my eyes to where it lay next to the record player. He stalked over, picked it up, held it out toward me. "This?" he said. "This ain't a gun. This is a fucking toy." And then instead of letting me take it, he cracked it over his knee. I let out a shriek as pieces flew everywhere. Shards of plastic. Doohickies. Dropping the pieces still in his hands to the floor, he said, "This is a motherfucking gun." And he whipped a pistol out of his waistband and aimed it at me like he just might use it.

By the time I made it to the first floor landing, down among the fishes, I'd let go of all my functions. There was no me left to hold any of them back. I was the sum of my parts—tears and snot and piss and suddenly viscous shit. I tried to run the six blocks home but my feet felt like they were caked in iron. Each step more laborious than the last. I trudged. I staggered. I knew just how I looked. My piss-stained jeans chilled and began to chafe and I kept having to stop to wipe the mucus from my face.

Then, home, there was my mother like she'd been waiting for me. She wrapped me up. She cleaned me off. She didn't ask what happened and I didn't tell her.

In my memory, this all happened in the day or two before we left to visit Lenny. This and Phil's gig. The events tumble together. Blow after blow, slamming me all at once.

That can't be right, though.

There must've been some respite in there somewhere. Some moment or two of blank expansive safety. Of boredom. Of keeping on. Even now, when I'm trying so hard to remember, my mind's erased the happy parts of my past. To toughen me up. To help me survive.

The plan was, we'd go visit my grandmother. A family reunion. The old lady wished, finally, to meet the munchkin and maybe reconcile with her daughter. We'd get there. We'd endure forty-eight hours on Long Island. And happy to see my mom finally trying to make less than catastrophic decisions with her life, my grandmother would allow her to borrow the car. Then off we'd go on a trip to who-knows-where, somewhere far away, somewhere, maybe, Underground. Anyone watching would figure my mother to be another little girl lost in the spiritual morass of the 1970s. Yet another quester who, after years of chasing the dove of peace through the dense marijuana haze of her wasted youth, had finally realized she'd never change the world.

That was the cover.

The truth was, we were cold and weary and in need of shelter. My mother needed strength. She needed a car, sure, but also, she needed to see her mommy.

I remember the subway platform at rush hour. The smells—strong cologne, cigarette smoke, french fries and lingering urine. Rust. The vibrations of bodies up in each other's space. The globs of gum ground into blackness on the concrete. I remember the anxiety that surrounded me. All these people peering down the tunnel, searching for lights. My mother among them. Unable to stand still.

And the wind and the electric crackle of the rails and the mind-numbing roar and clatter of the train. The sudden crush.

"Wait." My mother held me back as the platform emptied out and the doors bumpered shut. The only two left were us.

I remember going downtown to go uptown. Climbing stairs. Switching platforms. Zigzagging around town until somehow we arrived at the maze of blind turns that was Penn Station. The flutter of the signs as they cycled through the schedule. My mother's hand clutching the collar of my jacket, tugging, guiding me onto a train.

We rattled through tunnels caked in dust and soot. Up and out in Queens, I watched squat brick houses flicker past, each one identical to the last. They reminded me of Brooklyn, of those sad streets Lenny'd dragged me down on that day when we'd gone searching for his childhood home. Miles and miles of these tiny houses. All the same. And then the brick fell away, replaced by a different kind of sameness. Larger houses, cleaner but less stable. The whole world suddenly brighter. Bleached. We were in the suburbs.

Then us standing outside the station in Great Neck, watching as shlubs in overcoats two-stepped toward the cars idling at the curb, toward their wives, their families, the rocks of their existence. And soon the lot emptied, leaving just us and a few stragglers, and then even their rides came, and it was only my mother and me again.

I remember her checking her watch, ticking her cheek, checking her watch again.

"Well, we haven't been followed," she said. "See? We're free."

I remember my grandmother's mud-brown Impala rolling into the parking lot, idling, not in front of us, but at the end of the station.

I remember my first glimpse of the woman. So tiny. Her head barely visible over the dashboard. Her two hands on the wheel, wringing it. And I remember the darkness that seemed to surround her. A stillness. Like she'd decided long ago to hold herself tight and shut everything else out. Her eyes were hidden behind thick round prescription sunglasses. I remember that as we made our way toward the car she stared straight ahead and didn't smile, didn't wave.

My mother threw the back door open and lobbed our duffel bag onto the seat. She gave me a nudge and I climbed in next to it. I remember a sense of dread, intimidation, like I'd entered an unknown, strictly controlled land. Twisting over her seat, not taking off her sunglasses, my grandmother scrutinized me. She reached out and measured my forehead with her fingers. Length and width. Even her smile was severe. "He has the Morgenstern forehead," she told my mother. "Very good genes. There's hope for him." She told me to call her Oma. German, like her accent.

Then, later, as we rolled toward her house, I remember the two of them bickering about why my grandmother had been late. "You said eight-ten." "No, I said, seven-thirty-five." Each of them was adamant about being right, intransigent about the other being wrong.

And I remember my entire body tensing up like it was tuned in to a new, anxious frequency.

In her house: a sense of mourning, of grief. The blinds all shut. The lights all dimmed. The furniture, even the massive boxy couch, was itchy and uncomfortable.

Her husband, my grandfather, had painted in his spare time. His artwork crowded the walls. Frightened faces, sadness dripping from their hair. Bodies struggling to break out of the frame. Even the landscapes were dark and brooding, every color tinged with blood.

The place felt old. It smelled like ancient paper. Powdery. Brittle. Slightly alkaline. Like weevils had gotten into the fibers and were slowly eating away at the foundation. When I think of it now, I see psychologists lurking in the woodwork, adjusting their pince-nez, saying, Ah, we'll always have Vienna. It was like she'd locked herself up in some ancient pain and nothing and no one would coax her out of it.

I remember one particular painting of my mother. Twelve, thirteen. Neither child nor adult. Her curls all in tangles. Her face turned away.

And dinner—was it that night or the next?—at some uppity French joint. Escargot. Steak tartare. The dour old-world elegance of it all.

The way my grandmother seemed to fit right in. She ate in silence, concentrating. Holding her fork like a pencil. Guiding her knife with one outstretched finger. Grim and determined. Like the repetitive action of stabbing and cutting, her body's requirement that she raise food again and again to her mouth for fuel, was a chore to be gotten through as quickly as possible. Like she resented having to do it every day. I remember, even then, at dinner in this expensive restaurant, she kept herself closed off behind her sunglasses.

I ordered the chicken. I remember because it came smothered in mushrooms. Revolting. And I remember my mother demanded I taste it. "One bite. That's all I ask. Then you don't have to eat any more." *What? Huh?* I thought. Whatever happened to doing your own thing? Who is this woman? What's she done with my mother?

It wasn't just that she was imposing new rules on me. I'd never seen her try so hard to prove she could be on good behavior. I remember—was it the first day? The second?—she packed away her scuffed jeans and peasant blouses and threw on an old dress from her high school years, conservatively fashionable in a muted, musty way. It came down to her knees. And a cardigan for the wind. Her hair pulled back in a leather thong. Her mules looked almost dignified under all that. Good enough to get by, to look like she'd tried.

And I remember my grandmother sizing her up, tipping her head at a certain angle—an invisible gesture, to me anyway—before finally saying, "You look very nice."

And unable to see the compliment through the sediment of a lifetime of criticism, my mother flashed. "Jesus. Here we go again."

My grandmother pled innocence. "What? I can't admire you now?"

"No. Because—no. I know what you're thinking. No bra. I'll sag. Well, fine. Everybody sags."

"Susan, it's the 1970s. What do I care if you wear a brassiere?"

"Go ahead. You tell yourself that. But you do care."

And my grandmother, showing some subversive moxie of her own, stared that much more pointedly, twisting a smile onto her dour face until my mother stalked out of the room.

Then, later, after they'd moved silently around each other, radiating warnings for what might have been an hour or more: my mother sprawled out on the couch, head thrown back, smoldering, staring at the closed blinds. How she seemed so comfortable there. So physically at ease. I could see her stretched out like this at various points in her life, as a small child, a teenager. Like she'd been here forever. Like it was the place she knew best. But also, roiling under her eyes, something else. Grievance. Affliction. The ghosts of past selves.

"I don't want to fight with you," she called out.

The answer, from behind a closed door: "So don't."

And then after another hour or so it was like they'd never argued at all.

There were no clocks. I remember being spooked and disoriented by this. Just one contraption under a glass dome on the table. A fortress of chutes and gears and levers and conveyer belts that shunted marbles around a track. It was supposed to tell time in some ingenious way, but I couldn't figure out how it worked. I studied it endlessly. Knelt on the floor and watched the marbles roll. To distract myself. To make myself disappear. Each gear spun at a different speed, pulling marbles to the top of the machine one at a time. They collected in lanes like race cars waiting for the starter pistol. Let loose at intervals, they'd slide down the various lengths of track and pool in stations at differing heights where they waited to be carted off by one of the levers or spun through a funnel and cycled back up to the staging area. The marbles that made it to the bottom sorted themselves out into numbered rows and these numbers, in conjunction with the count of marbles there at any given moment, would tell you the time if you could read them correctly.

She wanted something from the old lady. My mother, I mean. She didn't know what—or she did, but it wasn't something she could put a name to. It was too all encompassing, too deeply embedded in the essence of herself. And yet wanting it seemed petty. Childish.

They fed off each other. Like each of them was compelled by some power beyond her control to do everything she could to be disappointed by the other in all the same old ways all over again.

I've thought about this a lot in the years since then. How my grandmother must have read my mother's choices.

She'd come to this country at the age of sixteen, a refugee smuggled out of her native Germany at a debilitating cost to her family. Her father siphoned money from the shoe store he'd once owned but now only worked for, contacted second cousins he'd never met in Chicago, paid clerk after unreliable clerk for the documents and stamps that would allow her to travel to Britain, where it was up to her, harried, afraid, not speaking a lick of English, to find her way alone to the steamer that would bring her to the American Midwest.

This was 1937. Still early, but already too late for the rest of them. Her sister. Her mother. Her father. She waited in the care of these second cousins for word from the continent about where and how and whether everyone had escaped. None came.

And so she was stranded in that strange city. No connection to anyone except these confusing Americans, ostensibly family, who resented her presence more every day. They used her as the maid. They fed on her desire to show them she understood the sacrifice they'd made, her desire to contribute, to not be a burden.

Maybe it wasn't them who made her feel unwanted. Maybe she generated that feeling herself. They weren't bad people. They just hadn't seen what she'd seen. The broken glass. The fires. How they'd slowly killed her cat. Grown men punched in the head by boys no older than she was and, instead of fighting back, letting the boys maul them. Her own father. The sounds he made as he refused to resist, almost like he was relieved.

How to explain these things to the cousins here with their big bands and pot roasts and teenage crushes? They could barely find Germany on a map. Why should they understand her maudlin past? She deserved their neglect. This she knew in her bones. They were right; she should be happy, hopeful, like everyone else in this new country that would never feel like it was hers.

To escape herself, she went to the symphony. Not the real thing. Records. Once a month on Wednesdays, a listening party for refugees at the local Jewish community center. There she met my grandfather, elegant, capable, Viennese. He saw her isolation. It pierced his heart.

His people had been importers. Keeping the cafés flush with coffee beans. They'd been proudly assimilating for generations. Patrons of the city, by which I mean they once bought a half-finished Klimt sketch. They'd had the means and foresight to board the first train out, all together, on the morning after Kristallnacht. Losing nothing but their pride, they then dispersed to Palestine, England and Africa, where they were shielded by the connections they'd built through the years. When they finally reconvened here in the States, they set about re-creating the bourgeois lifestyle that had treated them so well in the old country. The cultural mores changed, but the aspirations remained the same. They simply transferred their allegiance to the American mode. Country clubs. Tennis lessons. Ski excursions.

My grandfather, the favored son, offered all he'd been given to this lonely, vulnerable girl from the JCC. He carried her away to New York, where he used his money and the opportunities it provided to build his castle around her. Let her venture out of the darkness or not, as she saw fit. Whatever she could muster on any given day.

I've wondered, in light of all this, what my mother might have been trying to prove by dedicating herself to Lenny like she had. Rattling the cage that had kept her mother safe. Was this how she showed her love? Or was there something more passive-aggressive at work, a need to punish that had been passed down through the generations?

I remember my grandmother breaking character just once. The sun had set but neither she nor my mother had bothered to turn the house lights on. A graying in the air. Them sitting apart in that woody room, each waiting for the other to break the silence, each resisting the impulse to do it herself. The way my grandmother looked at my mother then, remote and lonely. Needing something but unsure how to ask for it.

She'd been getting calls. Hang-ups, at first, and then silences, breathing. Eventually the callers actually spoke. They asked questions. What's your name? Do you live at 19 Coronet Lane? How long have you lived there? Mundane shit. Deep basso voices verifying the deets. And that night in the dark, she asked, pleading, "Who are these people, Susan? Why are they bothering me? I don't understand. Every day. Sometimes three or four times. And sometimes different people, too. Their voices are different. But they don't talk to each other. Or they don't take good notes. They all ask the same things. I tell them, I told your friend this yesterday. But do they care? They don't care. It's frightening, Susan. Did you know, one of the men asked if I play tennis every Tuesday morning with Rose Liberman. At eight-thirty, he said, at the club. Why do they ask such things? What do they want with when I play tennis?"

My mother, as always, attacking what she didn't want to hear. "It's the Nazis, Ma," she said.

And my grandmother, knowing this tactic, forgave it. "Hush." Then, "It's harassment is what it is. Preying on a defenseless old lady."

"They're gonna show up one day and repossess your tickets to the Philharmonic. New rules, they'll say. No Jews allowed in Lincoln Center."

"You think it's a joke."

"They'll confiscate your subscription to *The New York Times*."

"I should call the police and have them reported."

"Ma."

"That's what I should do."

"Ma."

"Don't you think, Susan? That's the right thing."

"Ma!"

"What? Why are you shouting?"

"Just stop answering the phone. These people calling you? They *are* the police."

She thought about this for a second. "I have to answer the phone. What if it was Alice Fein? How would I know who was hosting bridge?"

"Ma, *really*."

"What?"

"Think! These people, Ma. They're looking for Lenny."

The sound that rose out of my grandmother's throat then. Like every ounce of her being had clenched with scorn. A sound only an embittered Jew can articulate—obstinate, dismissive, cosmically aggrieved. "Ack," she said. "That man."

Calm now, calculating, my mother leaned in and said, "When was the last time you got a call like this?"

"A few weeks."

"A few weeks, like two? Three? A month? It's important, Ma."

"A while. I can't remember. What do you want from me, Susan? I don't keep track of every phone call I get."

"You should!"

And my grandmother, seeing her daughter's dismay, relented. "It's been four months. Maybe five? But, Suzy, what does it matter?"

A pause while they prepared to revert to form.

"You're impossible, Ma. That's the last thing I'll say." An answer that seemed to satisfy them both.

Whatever their conflicts, my grandmother wanted to show us off. We went to "the club," an exclusive manse of which she was outlandishly proud to be a member. Even there, on a slow weekday morning among friends and bridge partners, women whose husbands, like her own, had seized a place for themselves among the goys, she held herself apart, letting the conversation—the interrogation, really—of her wayward daughter flow past like muddy water.

They'd heard stories. Myth. Countermyth. In their eyes, you could see the questions they were afraid to ask. The awe. The nervousness. I heard you burn money. Money! What do you live on? Susan! Look at you! It's not like you can afford to burn money. What I've never been able to understand is, what did America ever do to you? Why the resentment? Why so much anger?

Instead they talked about the dangers of the city. The subway. The gangs. The *shvartzes* and their violent desperation.

My mother played along. She laughed. She treaded gently. She was oddly comfortable there with them. Even if she was faking it. In tune with the rhythms of the society she'd so fiercely and loudly rejected.

The conversation evolved. She remembered old friends. How's so-and-so? What's who's-it up to now? Exposing herself as a member of a tribe I hadn't known existed.

I was just a prop there to be seen and not heard. Superfluous, like I'd been throughout our time in Great Neck.

I remember fidgeting, looking around. Then wandering. All those blindingly white columns, white walls, white fences, not a smudge, not a fingerprint or skid mark anywhere on them, like the whole place was repainted each and every night. I remember gawking at the pool, its tarp winched tight like the head of a drum, all the towels racked up there waiting for summer. The silverware sparkling at the waitress station. Crisp starched tablecloths draped almost to the floor. And the women gathered in the corners, in the good seats in front of the windows, sipping coffee and orange juice, fingering their jewels. So well dressed and elegant, even in polyester. All these Jews living like gentry in the land of the free.

I remember the squirming sensation in my chest, like a baby animal clawing at the nest. And my wonder at the excess of this place. You are your context. This wasn't mine. But it could have been. Somewhere, in some past that had been denied me, it had once belonged to my mother. The shame. I made my way out of the clubhouse and into the landscaped area out front, two semicircles of lawn on either side of a hooded entryway where the extravagant cars these people all owned could lurch and idle while their passengers stepped onto the sandblasted cobblestone. I remember standing there next to a silver urn full of sand and cigarette butts, struck by what felt like a realignment of the physical properties of my being, a burning inside so powerful that it sparked along my skin, crackling, wailing, demanding to be let out. The rage. My life could have been safe. It could've been easy. I asked myself, what would Lenny say? *Eden is in your mind. Open the door and step into the garden. There's nothing less civilized,* he would have said, *than what we like to call civilized society. Our job is to expose it for what it is.* Lenny would've said I had a patriotic duty to cause as much mayhem as possible. And then they'd learn their lesson.

And Lenny would sense what I'd done. He'd just know. He'd be proud. He'd ask me to stay with him. Wherever he was.

The ashtray seemed like a viable weapon. I could wield it like a club, heavy end out, and smash some shit up good. Maybe throw it through a window. But when I went to pick it up, I couldn't lift it. All I managed to do was to tip it on its tripod and watch it crash to the ground. Sand and butts spilled out over the stones. Barely an act of vandalism. Could've been an accident.

Nobody saw it. This place didn't have valets.

I went back inside, looking for trouble now. Headed for the bar, or what passed for the bar. It was empty, of course. These Jews weren't really drinkers, not at this time of day. I ran my hand along the slippery polished wood. Poked at the holes in the high wicker chairs. Bars spurred thoughts of Phil, but he would have hated this place.

Next to a potted fern behind the service station I found a bowl of matchbooks, a hundred or more of them, stacked like party favors, engraved with the club's name in a busy cursive script. I grabbed one. I grabbed ten. Stuffed my pockets with them.

I wasn't really thinking about consequences. Like I said, I just wanted to light a fire. Get the burning inside me out into the open where I could look at it and somehow even the balance. Show these suburban grannies what a kid like me could do. Take my place as the rightful heir of the unbowed, unrepentant Lenny Snyder. And what would Lenny do? Burn the shit down. Burn, baby, burn.

As I race-walked out of the bar, hands dug into the pockets of my jeans to cover the bulge of matchbooks—staring at my feet, like, Who, me? I'm not guilty—I slammed into a dude barely bigger than me. A busboy or something. A midget with a feeble strip of hair above his lip, straining under a bin of napkins the size of his torso. They fluttered to the floor like dying doves.

"Thanks a lot, kid."

He didn't scare me. He was just some fifteen-year-old honky punk working in a country club. I was city tough. I was Lenny Snyder's kid. "Watch where you're going, motherfucker," I said.

And I left him there to wonder what the hell just happened.

Retracing my steps around and around the place. Nothing. Or nothing worthy of my purpose. Nothing that would make the dramatic statement I needed if I was going to impress Lenny. My mother was still out there with my grandmother's bridge buddies, smiling at the things they said, appreciating them. If she was unhappy, she sure didn't look it. Maybe this wasn't a cover at all. Maybe we were gonna stay here. Pull the ladder up after us. And then what? I'd spend my summers flailing around in the pool, holding girls' heads underwater, doing cannonballs, shouting "Geronimo!" midair. A shamefully easy, ignoble life. But what a relief it would be to relax for once.

What would Lenny say? What would Lenny do?

I was losing my will.

I fled the building and wandered to the far end of the pool, near the wall behind the lifeguard stand. I pulled one of the nubby white towels from the racks, unfurled it and stood there, legs wide, waving it in front of me like a flag. I started sparking matches—they wouldn't hold their flame. The breeze blew them out one after the other. But I stuck with it. Match after match after match. What would Lenny do? Lenny would be relentless. And finally I managed to get a flame going and I warded off the wind with my body and tipped the match to a corner of the towel, willing the terry cloth to catch. It did, weakly. I lit more matches, dipping them to the fire. Flares and sparks. Individual strands of thread burning up like wicks. The flame sputtered and coughed. It didn't want to take.

At some point I realized I'd succeeded at one thing. The whole club was watching me through the windows. I'd made myself the center of attention.

The flames grew. The towel was really cooking now.

Then the kid with the peach fuzz came racing toward me. He shouldered me in the chest, commandeered the towel and with a single snap snuffed the fire right out. He dropped it to the ground and I saw then that I'd barely charred the fucking thing.

My mother dragged me out of there, a walk of shame past the table where my grandmother's friends sat. Even from a distance I could see the effect my stunt had had on these women. They'd known I was no good, and hey, look, they were right. Closer up, nuance and variation was visible on their faces. Something almost lustful in the one who'd secretly loved witnessing my mayhem. Something sour in the one who was genuinely afraid of me. The itchy fingers of the gossips raring to spread the news.

And my grandmother, mortified, trying not to show it. She followed us out, betraying nothing from behind her dark glasses.

I remember, then, finally, at three, four in the morning, my mother shaking me to my feet and guiding me, sleepwalking, out of the house.

I woke the next day to learn we'd stolen the Impala and were rolling up a highway somewhere in Massachusetts.

If someone was tailing us, we didn't see them. We barely saw any other cars at all. It was just us and the highway and the FM dial. Cat Stevens, Harry Chapin, the Carpenters. Mom sang along. She'd gone batty with excitement. Linda Ronstadt, Wings, the Doobie Brothers.

I was hopped up too, reeling with all these fantastical ideas about what would happen when we got to wherever it was Lenny was hiding. Maybe he'd be clean-cut and shaved, his joy and his rage, always so bound to each other, sanded flat and smooth by the starched shirt he wore. Or maybe he'd be literally underground, living in a nuclear fallout shelter and eating pork and beans out of cans with his fingers. His hair matted in dreads. Cockroaches nesting in the kinks. His wispy beard not grown in but grown out, a patchy scraggle tailing off his chin like some Hasidic mystic, John the Baptist in the desert. He might be living in that clapboard shack I'd been imagining since the day he'd disappeared, dressed like an Indian, armed to the teeth, preparing for the moment when the pine needles rustled and he peeked through the slats to see flatfoots stalking among the trees, his final stand come at last. Maybe we'd get there in time to join the battle, me and my mother and the Queen of Sheba—what would she be like?—manning the barricades. If he'd have us. If we proved ourselves worthy.

"Will we get to stay?" I asked.

"I don't know." She gazed up at the bone-cold sky above the windshield and allowed herself a small selfish smile. "Maybe."

. . .

Hours later and we were still on the road, in Vermont now, off the highway.

"The Mad River Valley," my mother told me. "We're getting close, I think."

We bounced along dirt roads barely wider than the car, wheezed up impossible inclines through the mountains. Thick forest. Shadows and decomposing leaves. We saw deer, wild turkey. It was late April. The ground was still patched with snow and sometimes the road was so pocked with sinkholes that we had to drive around it, easing over rocks, scraping past brittle shrubs. These roads, they had no names. They weren't on the map. That's how we knew we were close—that and the spiking anticipation, the sense that the more lost we felt, the closer we must be getting there.

Sometimes we had to stop so my mother could consult the hand-scrawled directions Lenny had instructed Kunstler to send her. Turn right at the boulder. But which boulder? This one? That one? The one back there? She'd pass the creased sheet of legal paper to me and ask me to verify her instinct. We rode on faith, not knowing if the last turn was correct until we found the next one, not knowing if the next or the next was correct either. We went on like this, groping our way forward until we reached a turn that might have been a driveway—a stone wall, a lantern, a barn-door mailbox. There were posted signs: RESTRICTED USE. NO TRESPASSING. NO HUNTING.

We crunched up a gravel path, around a corner, up a hill and then we were in a clearing, staring at an old stone house. So maybe we'd made it. But there weren't any other cars in the driveway. No lights in the house. No signs of habitation.

I asked my mother, "Where's Lenny?"

"Sometimes appearances can be deceiving," was her answer.

We weren't ready. Neither one of us. We got out of the car and dawdled for a while. Digging in the trunk for stuff we didn't need.

I couldn't find my shoes. Sinking into the soggy ground, one socked foot lodged in the mud, I felt around under the seat and found one but not the other. More groping around down there. I could just touch the laces. Flicking a fingertip back and forth, I coaxed the shoe forward.

My mother, annoyed, took her anxiety out on me. "Quit horsing around."

"I'm not, it's stuck on the bar."

"Give me a break. It's not stuck."

"It is. I can't get it."

And she tried and she couldn't get it either.

"So go barefoot, Freedom. Take your socks off. Come on."

Off they went, and holding them by the stretched-out elastic bands I attempted to scrape the mud away with a stick.

"Just leave it. Here, roll up your jeans. Why'd you take the shoes off anyway?"

"'Cause—"

"No. Don't answer. I don't care. Watch the puddle, now. Let's go."

We marched to the door. Knocked. Rang the bell. We waited. Knocked again. Rang the bell again. No Lenny.

And I felt a sudden crash of panic: This was my fault. If he'd been caught, it was because of me and Rosalita and my moral failure, though I couldn't have understood it like that at the time, my inability to separate shame from duty, to understand things I didn't know, my deception, my betrayal, my—and Walker! I'd forgotten that what happened to me, what I did with my secret time, was always only a reflection of Lenny. "I . . . Mom . . . I . . ." I couldn't find the words to confess.

"What? Freddy, what is it?" Guilt torqued in my chest. She must've noticed: Her hands fluttered around my face but she resisted the urge to touch me. "We're there. What's wrong? Tell me."

"I did . . . something bad."

She flinched and I saw that she saw it too—the possibility of my having said the wrong thing to the wrong person, even if by mistake. "You didn't," she said. What she meant was, how could you?

That's when the tears came.

She walked me to the car and we sat there while I struggled with myself. She did me the favor of holding my hand.

"I have a friend," I said eventually. "She . . . I visited her once. She lives . . . there's this . . . Ronnie Walker was there."

If I'd been more aware, I might have seen her struggle to mask the amusement—the adoration—playing on her face.

"Ronnie Walker, Mom! I found him . . . and he threatened me, or maybe he didn't, or maybe . . . I don't know . . . he broke my gun and . . . Ronnie Walker! And now where's Lenny, Mom?"

I was cracking her up. "Oh, honey," she said. "Oh, baby." She drew me across the seat and nestled me under her arm. "You're cute." She gave me a little squeeze.

"I'm not cute. Because look, he's not here!"

"You're right. He's not here." She gazed at the dark house, at the empty muddy clearing, the ruts and divots where there should've been a car. "But I promise you, Ronnie didn't turn him in. Walker's fine. He's righteous. Kunstler's PI found him. He wasn't even hiding. He'd just been out of town. So . . ." She squeezed me again. "Okay?"

Well, sort of. 'Cause why hadn't anyone told me that? Why hadn't anyone thought I ought to know? They told me all kinds of other inappropriate things. My mother could go on about the Queen for hours. Were they trying to protect me? When had they ever done that? And what about the setup? Who was that other guy—the one they'd all talked about and who'd then disappeared? Had he even been there? What was and wasn't Lenny guilty of, exactly? Did it matter? It had to. They'd told me it did.

"Then why . . . Lenny said—"

"You know how Lenny gets when he's nervous. He'll be here. I promise. We just have to wait."

We sat there for hours. What else could we do? My socks dried and I picked off the crusted mud. We extracted my shoe from under the seat. Mom read a whole magazine, front to back. The ads, too. And then the sun set invisibly behind the clouds and the woods and the clearing and everything in it turned murky.

Later still, after dark, we saw a pair of headlights moving up the road. They turned in to the driveway—a station wagon. It circled the clearing, its lights skimming over us, shining on the house and then aiming back at the main road. The engine cut, the lights snapped off. Out stepped two people. A man and a woman. It was hard to make them out in the dark. They gathered a few things from the front seat. The man locked the car. He was doughy around the waist. When he stood up straight it was like he was still slouching, like life had defeated him. A shlub.

The woman called out to him. "Don't forget your camera, Nick." Her voice smoky and sharp with the diction of private school.

"Got it," the guy said. Not a hint of Brooklyn.

They trudged past us toward the house, two gentle people digging a pastoral rut. Seeming not to notice us sitting there in the dark car. When they reached the front steps, the guy stepped off the slate and found a switch hidden behind a bush. Now the house light came on, a globe above the door. They turned and waited, letting us stare. Posed there in silhouette, silent, tired, while we took them in. There was something ritualistic about it. A slow hello. Something almost Japanese.

"Well, you coming in, or what?" called the man. This Nick.

The woman nudged him flirtatiously with her hip. She called out to us too. "Welcome!"

My mother and I went through the saga of gathering our things again, self-consciously now, aware of their eyes on us.

As we picked around the puddles in the driveway toward them, the woman said, "We would've been here earlier but we were at a meeting."

Flopping his arms in the air, making fun of himself, the man barked, "Save the river!" and something familiar ghosted in this gesture. Lenny. But a Lenny who'd been pulled and stretched into someone else. Up close, I could see his nose was different, that honking Jewish bulb replaced by something flatter, not better, but stubbier. His Jewfro was gone—he was graying at the wings. And he had a beard now, sort of, unkempt wisps of hair growing in patches around his face. He didn't even dress like Lenny. Wide-wale corduroys in some dark shade of green. A duck-hunting jacket and a button-up plaid shirt. Lenny! In plaid! A button-up! And sandals! With socks!

He studied me, unsure of how to proceed. Then he hiked up his cords and squatted. Squinted. Judged. There was an element of spectacle to the moment; the women, Mom and the other one, the Queen of Sheba, who I'd thought would be black for some reason, deferring, looking on as we acted out our parts.

"You must be Freedom. Good to meet ya. My name's Nick Dixon." He held his hand out, but I was too confused to shake it.

"Really?" my mother said. "Nick Dixon?"

The guy threw her this look full of suppressed mischief. He winked. "Why not?" he said. And there was Lenny again, peeking through.

He clapped once like *ha!* and cackled and my mother laughed too, and something shifted and fell away. "Well, all right then," he said, pulling himself to his feet and giving me a noogie. "Let's get this party started."

And that was it. Lenny wasn't one for sentimental reunions. He'd rather be the poem, the joke, the threat.

He and the Queen led us inside and what I remember next is him showing us around. Or not us, actually, just me. My mother must've begged off, I don't know. Maybe the Queen had stage-managed the whole thing. Maybe there'd been some agreement between her and Lenny: educate the kid, bond with him a little while I charm your wife.

In any case Lenny dragged me from room to room, showing it off like of course I'd be impressed. And I was, I guess. Man, how that house reeked of money. Dusty money. Frayed, graying money. Money so old the blood had been washed away. Everything in the place was nicked and roughed up by history. Mirrors the size of New York apartments. Furniture mixed and matched from throughout the centuries, like we were in a way station for the favorite castoffs from generations upon generations of shifting fashion, every chaise, end table and Persian rug worth a fortune if appraised, but why bother if you could hoard it all here.

But none of this shit was important, not to Lenny. What he wanted to show me was the art. The mementos. The flashes of identity displayed on the walls. Things that would reveal just whose world we'd wandered into. He wanted me to see the mythology of the place. The leftist celebrity smoked into every crevice. Original Ben Shahns, Max Ernsts, a George Grosz cartoon of a baton-wielding pig—obese and deranged, all nostrils, fangs and blubber. A photo taken by Walker Evans of a kid sitting in the mud. A framed letter signed by Diego Rivera, written in Spanish so I couldn't read it; thanks for the hospitality or some shit. And the posters. A whole history of the Left yellowing on the walls. Pleas from the '30s urging people, through blocky constructivist imagery, to join the Communist Party. Spanish Civil War posters glorifying the anarchist POUM—¡BARCELONA LIBRE! Woodcuts of sombreroed skeletons hiding their faces behind bandannas, wielding guns—¡VIVAN LOS ZAPATISTAS! Interestingly, there was one we had at home—crude flowers and peace signs and musical half notes framing a funky, freaky list of promises. COME TO CHICAGO. FREE JAMS. FREE DRUGS. FREE CONSCIOUSNESS. DIG IT! A poster Lenny himself had designed. Up on the wall with the legends.

And photos too, telling the story. The same one dude I'd never seen before, accompanied sometimes by a casually gorgeous blonde. Dude with Eugene Debs. With FDR. Dude with Leon Trotsky. With Woody Guthrie and Pete Seeger. Fidel Castro. Che Guevara. JFK. MLK. Cesar Chavez and Harry Belafonte. Dude with motherfucking Gandhi. I tell ya, the guy was everywhere. In one dark corner under the stairs there was even a photo of him with Phil Ochs. And in the place of honor, above the downstairs toilet, there he was with Lenny—the Lenny I remembered, not this Nick Dixon—sporting a cowboy hat, a black eye, and a smirk, waving a North Vietnamese flag above his head.

Throughout this tour, Lenny kept up the façade of Nick Dixon and talked about himself in the third person. "That's when Lenny Snyder blew the cap off the Capital." "That's when they called in the National Guard to stop Lenny Snyder from crossing the Delaware." So proud to be on that wall with all the VIPs. "Someday you'll be up here too, kid," he said. "It's in your blood." A bid for connection, but instead of drawing me closer, it pushed me away from this place with its excesses and comforts, this man who both was and wasn't my father. I didn't see myself anywhere here.

The old dude turned out to be the Queen of Sheba's father. From the heretic strain of the Emerson family. She had pedigree. What they call progressive royalty. After flopping around Groton and disappointing his ancestors, living and dead, by betraying Harvard for Yale, he'd landed at Union Theological Seminary to study with Paul Tillich. Again and again in the decades that followed, he used his ecumenical humanism and the moral authority that adhered to his calling to press the social connections he'd inherited toward noblesse oblige, to bend the course of history toward justice, as they say. And when he died, he left his family's old country house—this house—to his daughter.

I'm sure he meant well. I'm sure he tried to do good. But the pride Lenny took in his connection to the man bewildered me. Because Lenny—the Lenny I remembered—never gave a shit about what anybody thought. Especially not the scions of power. You can't destroy the system and revere it at the same time. Or you can, I guess. If you're Lenny.

But really, you can't.

The Queen of Sheba's real name was Caroline. She was the kind of woman who never wore makeup. The kind for whom blue light filters were made. She came with a soundtrack. Joni Mitchell. James Taylor. Had that *I've-seen-fire-and-I've-seen-rain-I-met-all-my-best-friends-at-McLean* look. The worry lines around the edges of her eyes just made her that much more beautiful.

That first night, while "Nick Dixon" gave me my tour, she served my mother tea in the high style indicative of her class—matching china arrayed on a silver tray, Chessmen cookies fanned across a plate on the side. As Lenny led me from room to room, we walked past them, again and again, and there would be the Queen of Sheba, curled on the couch with her legs wrapped under her, self-consciously projecting coziness and trust while Mom remained planted like a gnarly mushroom on the pod-like chair across from her, glowering, smirking sometimes, resisting. Each time we passed through, the same tense summit.

Sometimes I heard them lob remarks across the distance between them. The Queen: "We're so pleased you could make it up. This whole ordeal has been difficult for Nick. You know how sensitive he can be." Or, from Mom: "You're everything I expected you to be." Remarks that fell flat, unreturned, making it that much clearer that no real connection would be possible.

"Nick" left them to each other. Let them fight over him, or not, either way.

What mattered to him right then was impressing me with tales of Old Dude's accomplishments. How he'd camped out on the mall in DC to show his solidarity with the Bonus Army. How he'd drawn up a risky, unpopular petition protesting the government's treatment of the Rosenbergs. How he'd walked by Castro's side in 1959 as the great man took his New York victory lap. How he'd been the single white guy in the room with MLK and the Southern Christian Leadership Conference as they planned the Montgomery Bus Boycott. And somehow, in the telling, these feats became Nick's own. More proof of his all-consuming importance.

That these stories bored me, that I was too young to understand their importance and would've been more impressed if he'd told me a knock-knock joke or pulled out a djembe and asked me to jam, or hell, if he maybe asked me a question, any question at all—none of this ever occurred to him. I was there to bask in his light.

And at that, I let him down. I resisted his control. While he went right on telling stories to himself, I tagged behind him thinking my own thoughts, barely hearing the words rolling out of his mouth.

Eventually, Nick noticed. He stopped showing me things. He circled back to the room where my mother and the Queen of Sheba were waiting. And seeing we were there to stay, they lit up like hostages glimpsing the sun. Lenny, now Nick, did a little dance, a few clumsy moves that might've been supposed to suggest the mambo. He waggled his fingers above his head, said, "Let's get this party started!" again—it must have been his new mantra, his new "Fuck 'em if they can't take a joke." And he plopped onto the couch next to the Queen.

He touched his lips to the nape of her neck and she—oh, what class—she patted his knee and drew into herself, wincing at my mother with an embarrassed little shrug. The women laughed the moment off, united for once in their willingness to indulge him.

Somehow, then, everyone focused on me. I remember the pressure of their eyes. How Nick Dixon's face seemed to change shape, the Lenny I knew rising to the surface. I remember the blushing sensation. The gratitude. But also the sense that they expected something I had no idea how to give them from me.

"How old are you now, Freedom?" Lenny said.

"You don't remember?" my mother asked him.

See, I'd already blown it. I burrowed into the beanbag next to her pod and hoped none of them could see my disappointment.

The Queen whispered in his ear.

"Eight," he said. "That's old enough to know a few things."

He pulled himself up from his crevice in the couch, gingerly, like someone much, much older than the man I remembered, and shuffled over to the bookcase, where he slid a massive book—*Ulysses,* I think it was, or *Moby-Dick,* the Bible—from a shelf, brought it back, plopped it on the coffee table, and flipped the cover open like a lid to reveal a plastic baggie full of marijuana. An impressive stash. Felony-worthy. And there sat Lenny, this triumphant expression smeared all over his face, waiting for me to collapse in awe. All I could think was: Really? In a book? Dude, you're getting soft. He'd never have chosen such a weak hiding place back in NYC.

"You ever seen this stuff before?"

"Um, what do you think?" I said. Ask a stupid question, you get a stupid answer.

"Nah, man. You think you have, but dig it. What you've seen is the skunkweed they sell in Tompkins Square. This is the real deal. One hundred percent Jamaican Kush. We got it smuggled up straight from Kingston."

"Okay."

"You know Bob Marley?"

"Sure."

"This is what he smokes." He glanced at the Queen as though for reassurance. "His pal Stinkeye Steven Braithwaite grows it *out de countreeside, ya?*"

"Okay."

"So, that's pretty groovy, ain't it?"

The harder he tried, the less I wanted to give. "Sure."

He fished a bud out of the tangled mess inside the baggie and held it up for me to study. "Take a look at that mossy shit growing on the leaves there. You see it? If you could get up close enough—here look, you see? Crystals. Pure THC. A hundred times more potent than what you get out here in our glorious land of the free. It's an organic hybrid cultivated by the CIA, but joke's on them, huh? It's in the hands of Nick Dixon now. And through him it's made its way to you, the one and only super-duper far out Mighty Mouse himself, Freedom Snyder."

I glanced at my mother, who grimaced back. Sarcasm or silence? Silence.

"So what do you say? Should I roll up a doobie?"

"If you want. I don't know. Yes, I guess?"

He didn't flinch. Outwardly, he didn't change at all. But I caught the warning he shot me. The rage flashing in his eyes like a light switch flicked on, then off. The violence clamped under his shuck and groove. His true feelings for me. How contingent they were. The need. The loathing. For the rest of his life, whatever we did, however well we got along, part of me watched for this tiger to bare its fangs.

It lasted just a second and then it was gone. It flew right past my mother and the Queen—or maybe they'd learned to take this aspect of his personality for granted.

He unsheathed a paper and folded it into a canoe. He sprinkled the sticky clusters of leaf inside, rolled it with his fingertips, then again in the flat of his palm, twirling the ends into conical swirls, not quite sealed. Gauging my impressions at every step, like, hey kid, dig this. You still watching? Tell me you've ever seen a more skillfully rolled joint. Holding it out for me to admire. Waving it in my face. "Textbook," he said. Then he fished a lighter from the pocket of his cords, held the joint to his lips and lit up and took a long pull.

Threads of smoke tumbled from his mouth then curled back in. He studied the cherry. Smiled at it. Took another pull, deeper, flexing his diaphragm. The weed crackled and popped. And then, satisfied, he held the joint out to me.

"If you don't turn on, brother, you can't tune in," he said, wheezing, holding in his breath, the smoke trailing out from between his teeth.

I appealed to my mother but there was no help there. She held herself tight, watching, taking mental notes, still too full of hope to admit sides were being drawn.

"Do I have to?" I said.

Lenny took another drag. "You don't *have* to do nothing," he said. "But, man, I heard you were Lenny Snyder's kid. Where I come from, that's supposed to mean something. I figured you for more of a cool motherfucker. Or at least not a pussy."

The Queen touched Lenny's knee like she was trying to silently remind him of something. He barely noticed. His everything was aimed at me. I ached for my shattered AK-47. "Why do you keep doing that?" I asked him.

"Doing what?"

"Pretending. Faking. Acting like I'm some stupid kid."

And my mother, after all those months of longing and lobbying on his behalf, of blind faith, abandonment and derangement, after having finally lost so much that she'd begun to slowly reckon with herself only to be called back by him with tantalizing distortions and the erratic possibility of hope, she did the only thing she could right then. She slid to the couch and placed herself protectively by his side. For the first time since this weird test began, she had something to say. "We talked about this, Freddy. How we were going to—"

"Faking? Pretending? I don't know what those words mean," Lenny said, waving the joint like a pointer. "Reality is a social construction. Dig? Reality's not real. It's all perception. You see Lenny Snyder when you look at me? That's your prerogative. I look in the mirror and I see Nick Dixon. Caroline, she sees Nick Dixon, too. So does Suzy." As he said each of their names, he put an arm first around the Queen and then my mother, pulling them close, bending them to his will. He leaned toward my mother, flexing his arm around her neck so he could take a hit off the joint he now held near her chin. "So, see? There's a perception problem here. We're all on one trip over here and you're floating around over there, all by yourself. Have fun with that. Or you could take the fucking doobie and join us over here in *our* reality. And I'm telling you, this place is a lot more fun than wherever the fuck you are." With insistence, menace, pulsing in his fingertips, he transferred the joint to his free hand so as not to singe my mother's hair and then disentangled his arm from around her neck.

What choice does a kid have in a moment like that?

Trapped in a foreign place where the dark woody walls are squeezing in on him and the silence outside stretches to infinity. Everything familiar miles away. And his mom—the one light, the little warmth he can be sure of finding, there in the room where he's being bullied by his father—not lifting a finger to intercede. He takes the joint. He holds it to his lips and inhales its musty scent, breathes the smoke deep into his lungs, coughs it back out.

"That's the spirit," Lenny said, snatching the joint back.

He turned his attention to my mother and the Queen, talking fast, working his patter, coaxing hees and haws out of them, while I sunk and sunk into the beanbag.

Wherever he got it—I'm sure it wasn't from Bob Marley—that pot was some strong shit. My vision narrowed. My secondary senses came alive. When I tried to follow the conversation, I found that I couldn't. Their voices came at me like tones on a musical scale, plains of sound, not human language, and I'd just barely decipher a thread of words—*pear tree down the hill,* maybe, *wild asparagus along the road*—when another thread would tumble over it, and then another, the language piling on top of itself like layers of tapestry thrown over my head, each one weighing me down a little more until, in order to breathe, I had to wriggle loose of them entirely.

The scents in the room came for me next. That crackly wood smell you get in country cabins. The smell of time, of history growing dry and stale. That and the pungent odor of Lenny, who, even here where he wasn't playing the hippie fool, still hadn't learned how to bathe himself. And the stink of marijuana floating over everything, carrying the adult voices back to me again, waves crashing down on me, pulling me under.

The only escape was to slip inside myself. Change lenses. Reset the terms of the experience. Instead of chasing sensation I darted after the strong thoughts rooting in my head. There was danger to this, too. Every thought had weight and import. Each strand of memory, each half-concealed concept, each fillip of logical reasoning, the strings of approbation and encouragement, they all recalled things Mom had told me, or Phil, or Rosalita, or, yes, Lenny too—the sum of my limited experience, undulating, iridescent, out of reach like the tentacles of some blind deep-sea squid. And I knew, I just knew, that if I could grab onto one of these flickering ropes, if I could hold it tight and climb it inch by inch, following the implications and resonances to the developing idea hidden within it, I'd arrive at the body from which it and every other thought sprang, the great tangled mess of meaning that would explain the secret of myself to me. But they moved too fast. They whipped through my head with such velocity that, when they slammed against my skull, they stunned me, left me dazed. Just when I sensed I was starting to understand, I'd realize I'd forgotten the central piece of information I needed to create sense. The solid thing I'd believed I held turned out to be a vast vacancy.

I fixated more and more on Lenny, stared at him as he cracked himself up. Nick Dixon. Lenny Snyder. Lenny Snyder. Nick Dixon. The same but different. Different but the same. He had a different nose but the same eyes. A different haircut but the same wiry hair. The scary part of him remained intact—the arrogance and self-regard, the omnivorous ego, the compulsive need for everyone, even me, to reassure him that, yes, he was the coolest person in the room. But that other part of him—the playful part, the reckless goofiness, the part that produced somersaults at the barricades and enabled him to sneer that, no matter how thick the locks on the jail cell, nothing, no system, no person, no bureaucratic machine, would ever separate him from his joy—that part was gone.

A flame sparked and died in my head. A flick of the Bic. A match in the wind. Delusional me, trying and failing to burn down the country club as though that would win his love, thinking I could look to him for guidance, for the key to growing up—as though he was capable of recognizing anyone as anything more than a groupie or a threat. And which was I? His son. I'd been ready to devote myself to him blindly, completely. But now? He'd flashed his rage. Made me the enemy. My mind constricted around this thought. Paranoia set in. A wave of sensation flushed through my body like ice water. I felt myself tense, relax, tense, relax. The flip of a filter. The lens changing again and again. Then the fear and palsy crept back in.

I must have been shaking because next thing I knew, my mother had me by the shoulders, holding me out in front of her so she could search for some movement behind my eyes.

"Freddy," she said. "Freddy, what's going on?" Then she pulled me to her breast and smoothed my damp hair.

And I remember Lenny watching, worried maybe, or ashamed, or just confused. And I remember him saying, "What?"—to the Queen? to my mother? To whichever one of them had thrown him a look. Almost whining. Pleading, How is this my fault?

This was just the first night. We stayed for four days.

The next morning, I woke up blurry and shuffled downstairs to find Lenny and the Queen of Sheba blasting Clapton in the kitchen, him yelping along, the both of them grooving, joyous, completely nude. They were making omelets, ostensibly. More like vegetables sealed in a laminate of egg. Onion and mushrooms, mostly. A country feast, they claimed. A display of the earth's bounty.

My mother was there too, wrapped in a caftan. She sat cross-legged on a chair out of their line of fire, cradling a hand-thrown coffee mug in her lap. She radiated beatitude. When she saw me blinking in the doorway, she beckoned me toward her and pulled me tight, coiled her arms around me so I could feel the tranquility vibrating in her core.

Sitting at the farmhouse table later, I picked at my food, searching for something edible. By the time I finished, I looked at my plate and discovered all I'd accomplished was to meticulously move everything from one side to the other.

"You're gonna hurt my feelings, kid," Lenny said.

I studied the slime on my plate.

The Queen, deflecting, talked about gardens.

Later still, my mother sat me down in the attic, where they'd stored us. "I know this is confusing, Freddy," she said. "But you know? Why try to make things worse when you could be working toward making them better? Give him a chance. Do it for me. I need this."

So I did. For her.

And I'll give him this—during the daylight hours, he and the Queen really did try. We were made to feel like guests at their country estate, everything stage-managed to show off the placid, idyllic rhythms of their lives. They took us on drives through the mountains, showed us the ski resort, just recently closed for the season, with its stagnant T-lifts and patchy mud slicks. They took us to lunch at a quaint one-room diner—one of those streamlined aluminum jobs—that took forty-five minutes to get to on back roads and made the same grilled cheese as anyplace else.

We went for a hike along a marked path up some mountain. Sometimes the Queen would hang back and let Lenny pad along next to us with his weird new gait. He and my mother held hands, awkward as innocents fumbling through a first date. What struck me was how they seemed not to know each other, how tender, how timid, they were. Like each feared the other was about to get crushed. There was no room for me in those moments. I'd fall back to walk with the Queen, watch her watching them. Her tolerance, approval, willingness to share.

When the sun began to set, they took us to the dump, where we locked ourselves in the car and watched the bears dig through the trash and gorge themselves on rotting vegetables and moldy sliced bread.

Those days—the first one, anyway. It was like music. Soft and sentimental. Leading me to forget what had happened the night before. Tricking me into thinking I'd fallen out of the world. Out of this world at least, with its grunge and sin and panic. That I'd slipped into an alternate reality, a place without strife that still smelled new, where ugly intentions hadn't been invented yet, a place that had always been there, hidden away, waiting for me to take the dare and leave my propriety and my possessions behind. All you—all *I*—had to do was embrace it.

And I did.

We all did.

Or it felt like we had.

Until night fell and I remembered that everything I'd brought with me—the things Lenny had and hadn't done, the fears and hurts and unanswered questions, the memories and their lingering effects—it was all still there, ineradicable, inescapable.

The second night, when the pot came out, I ran away. I hid in the attic with the lights out. Watched the shadows quiver. Willed the time to pass. No one came looking for me. What a gift. The silence, especially. The way every rustling came through more acutely. A chipmunk on the roof—I could pinpoint exactly where it was, when it darted and where to, when it picked at a shingle with its tiny claws. Hoots in the distance and right close by. Howls. Whimpers. The nocturnal world stretching its muscles. And two flights down, sometimes, the adults getting raucous, laughing, shouting for a moment before quieting down.

Then later, footsteps on the floorboards.

Something else, too. The sloshing of the water bed in the room below mine. A giggle—my mother's. More sloshing. She moaned, low like iron, and said something I couldn't hear. The movement of the water took on a tidal quality, wave after wave rolling up against the frame and tumbling over my mother's mewling. Then, Lenny's voice, sharp as a siren careening out of the city. He cackled. "That's my girl!" He sounded just like himself.

And floating in the darkness above them, I felt seasick and fled downstairs in search of anywhere, I didn't really care, just as long as it was away from them.

What I found was the Queen, set up on the couch with a flimsy copy of *The Nation* in her lap. She looked up at me with a kind of adoration. "Hey-ya." She held my gaze. So placid. Centered in that way white women aspire to be but only truly attain when they're both rich and damaged. Like the wind blew through her. An intense, overwhelming calm. I had no choice but to stay.

Sunk in the beanbag's intractable fist, feeling conspicuous and stupid, I waited for her to placate me in some barbed way.

"He's happy you're here," she said eventually. "We're both happy you're here. I've been looking forward to meeting you, but he's overjoyed. You're just about the most important thing in the world to him."

I could still hear the water bed's slow churn.

"It's been hard for him. Isolating. Weeks go by with him not doing anything but lying here on this couch. He doesn't speak. He won't eat. I bring him a glass of water, I say, Nick, please, we have to figure out how to go on with our lives. And he doesn't even see me. It's like he's not in there. Like no one's home. When I touch him on the shoulder he just turns his face to the cushions. But he's been on a high since your mother wrote to say you were coming. He's a whole new Nick. I like him better this way." She raised her mug to her lips and took a long meaningful sip of tea.

Upstairs, the water bed rattled like a torrential storm had attacked it.

"Are you having fun?" asked the Queen.

Fun. Not the word I would've used, but I nodded. There was only one answer.

"I'm glad." She gazed at me again, pushing for connection. "I'm hoping we can be great friends."

I could hear Lenny upstairs, yipping, now, like a fucking Chihuahua. The Queen floated that calming look of hers over me and said, no lie, "Don't worry about that. Your mom and dad are just showing how much they love each other." She smirked. "If we're going to be friends," she said, "it would be nice to get to know you."

There's nothing like kindness to send a weed wacker down your spine and clear away the spurs. My resentment melted. Heat rushed through my chest.

"So tell me," she said, "if you could snap your fingers and go somewhere instantly, where would you go?"

"Happy Wok Number Three." I was thinking of Phil.

"Oh?" she said. "Why's that?"

"They're authentic. And they don't use MSG."

"What do you like to order at Happy Wok Number Three?"

"Egg rolls. And sweet and sour. Mom makes me get the chicken, but the pork's better."

"I like moo shu."

"You have Chinese here?"

"Sure. There's Chinese everywhere. Chinese and McDonald's."

"Mom won't let me eat McDonald's."

"Chinese is better."

"Yeah." I felt mysteriously close to her now.

"We could go to the Chinese place tomorrow, if you want. Nick likes Chinese. He's just like you. Sweet and sour pork."

Just like me. I remember cherishing that. Despite everything. It was all I'd ever wanted to hear.

"Best New Garden. That's what it's called."

"Okay," I said.

My mother and Lenny and the water bed had gone silent upstairs. Except for the Queen and me, the house was silent. I hadn't even noticed.

"It's settled, then. Best New Garden for dinner tomorrow. We'll have a feast." She twisted her lip in a quizzical, almost flirtatious way. "But, Freedom, what if you could snap your fingers and go anywhere. Really *anywhere*. Even places you've never been before. Like, me? I'd go to the Galapagos Islands to see the Komodo dragons and the hundred-and-fifty-year-old sea turtles."

I tried to recall the names of those countries Lenny's friends were always running off to. "Liberia," I said. "Algeria. Uganda." This charmed her. We talked about these countries and what they were like. Why somebody would want to visit them. What they meant, symbolically, to the movement and the world.

All this time, half my brain lingered on what she'd said about me being like Lenny. Since the day he'd disappeared almost two years earlier, my sense of him had tilted and swayed, fragmenting and re-congealing into shapes that I clung to whether they were true or not. Essential illusions that reminded me of who he might be if he were with me, who I might become if I aspired to his shape. I'd emulated the person I'd conjured in my mind—not the real man but the one I'd needed, the myth onto which I'd projected my loneliness. He'd grown to totemic dimensions in my mind, become a creature of awe and wonder. That halo of unruly hair framing his face. The wicked bemusement—the cosmic joke of him—how, no matter what was happening around him, good or bad or peaceful or violent, whatever, his eyes darted everywhere, searching for the irony and the dramatic moment in which he could throw another tack under the wheels of empire. I'd loved him for this. I'd thought this must be what it meant to be an adult. Reckless. Relentless. Fearlessly embracing the chaos. To be like Lenny meant not giving a fuck. And I was too sensitive. I cared too much. But what if there was more to it than that? What if Lenny cared so much he *couldn't* give a fuck? Well, then, maybe I really *was* like Lenny. Or on my way to becoming like him.

But see, this is where things got complicated for me. Because Lenny'd abandoned me. He'd abandoned Mom. He'd put me in danger for the sake of a joke or to prove some fleeting point to the world. Just the night before he'd ridiculed me into submission and gotten me so stoned I was drooling, then he'd laughed so hard he had to hold his dick to keep himself from pissing his pants. I mean, one of the things Lenny didn't give a fuck about seemed pretty obviously to be me. I was the dog whose water dish he filled with beer. I wasn't sure I wanted to be like Lenny if it meant I had to be like that. Unless I did. And when the Queen put it so sweetly and matter-of-factly, then yes, yes, yes, I *did* want to be like Lenny. I wanted him to look at me and see himself and explode with pride and tell me, "I see you and you're a miraculous creature, and of all the things I've done with my life, making you ranks up there with the best."

I didn't tell the Queen any of this. Or, I did, but years later, when none of it mattered. That night it just bounced around half-formed in my head while I fell more and more in love with her. How could I not? She was patient and calm. She pretended to treat me like an adult. She listened.

What I did instead was ask, "Where were you? On Thursday, when we got here? Where were you?" A meeting, they'd said. But what meeting could have been more important than us? I couldn't accept it. I refused to believe it. "You knew we were coming," I told the Queen. "But nobody was here."

She waited a long time to answer my question. "You're right," she said finally. "We should've been here." She scrunched her eyes, letting this sink in. "I'm sorry. Nick's sorry, too. He's too embarrassed to say so, but he is. I promise you."

"But where *were* you?" I said.

Her lips clenched, just for a second, and she hid her face behind her mug, studied the drips of glaze lacquered inexpertly onto its surface, hoping, probably, that I'd lose interest, get bored, let her win. "We were at a meeting. Like I said." She glanced at the ornate grandfather clock standing against one wall of the room. "Some things can't be avoided. Life's bigger than you and me."

She might as well have slapped me.

Eventually, Mom came down wrapped in a towel and patted my hair and sent me off to bed. It was eerie, and, I guess, beautiful, how everyone seemed to be living and letting live.

The next day we wandered around Vermont some more. We took another hike, this time down a craggy canyon, so steep in places that we sometimes just slid from one gnarly trunk to another. At the bottom was a river, or a creek anyway, and for a while we sat around, dangling our feet in the icy water, eating gorp and admiring the patchwork of sunlight in the trees.

Then, later, we toured an alpaca farm and the Queen bought us hats that we'd lose before ever getting the chance to wear them. All day long I had the sense I was being watched. A pressure on my back like the baking sun. A quiet when I turned to look, quick glances, trying to catch peripheral visions that weren't there. I felt like I was being managed, like something was supposed to happen that day and it involved me but I had to be protected from it. A couple times, as we hiked back from the river, Lenny sidled up to me like he had some special, confidential thing to say, but instead of revealing whatever it was he'd come out with a joke. A priest, a rabbi and an alligator walk into a bar. That sort of thing. When I didn't laugh, he said, "Maybe back at the house we can throw the ball around. Whaddaya say? You can show me what you've got." A foreign concept, that. He must have known it, too.

We pissed the day away and then returned to the old stone house. We didn't get Chinese food or play catch. The three of them got stoned and I retreated into myself again. This time, when the sloshing started in the master bedroom, they all played together.

It's easier the second time around. You block it out. What I did was, I poked around in the darkness, soaking up the place. I left the lights off. Hovered in the shadows like a pickpocket. Getting to know the different rooms. Their smells. The musty smoked air of the living room. The cinnamon and soap of the tiny bathroom under the stairs. The textures and sounds. The wide planks under my feet, gouged and scraped from the old days of iron and coal. I tried to imagine living in this house. Really living in it. Like, forever. The long quiet. The lack of stimuli. In place of the hectic terrors of the city, I saw a big, blank, wide, never-ending boredom. My mother, the Queen, Lenny, they'd be my only distractions. It would solve many problems but create even more. 'Cause, where could I escape to? Nowhere, that's where. By some trick of the world, hiding out here in the country would make everything, even me, more conspicuous. Lenny must have felt the same way. Like he'd been condemned to being seen, even if the guy people saw was Nick Dixon. Like he'd lost control of the difference between his public and private selves. He was a city cat. And he'd shrunk out here. Maybe that was why he seemed so much more like a man than a god now, still terrifying and awesome, but also sadly visible, intelligible. He was turning into someone I didn't have to simply submit to, someone I could grapple with and, maybe one day, argue with.

I studied the photos he'd so proudly made me tour. All those important people. All their fading luster. Time trapped in gray scale, no longer teeming and boiling. Just mounted there, inert. Mementos of power struggles that no longer exerted any urgent pull on the present.

On the wall over the shoe rack in the mudroom tucked behind the kitchen, I discovered one Lenny'd skipped over. A Technicolor shot. Recent. Lenny—or with that beard, Nick Dixon—posed like a rock star and lit up in a blur of densely crowded lights. Pelvis thrust forward. Sunglasses covering up half his face. His arms were draped over the shoulders of two other guys in that sloppy carefree pose of men who've been partying late into the night. One of them might've been the sunflower dude who used to come over and eat all our peanut butter.

But where were they? And why? Well, I knew Lenny. I knew his habits, his needs. I didn't need evidence to see that they were in New York, not some distant town like the ones where I'd imagined him hiding out. Of course. And the disturbing thing—the outrageous thing—was, I wasn't surprised by this. It made perfect sense. Just like it made sense that he'd kept this visit a secret from my mother and me. He'd been too busy having too much fun to bother with us.

The truth pained me, sure. But not right away. It shot a capsule of resentment under my skin, a slow release that would take years to kick in. At that moment, all I really felt was alone.

The next morning, our last, we drove into the podunk ski town up there and ducked in and out of the various shops. Browsing. Looking at skis and jackets and more winter hats, at countless versions of the same landscape painting—birch trees and snowdrifts and misty moons. At muumuus and sandals and fondue pots. Blown-glass vases and hand-thrown pottery glazed with the same drippy patterns as the mugs back at the house. And maybe it was because I'd gotten used to the new him, but not once through any of this did I have the sense that Lenny was hiding. Except for the shlumpy posture and the flattened accent, he was the same old guy he'd always been. Bouncing on his heels, cracking up at his own jokes, making himself as conspicuous as ever.

The place wasn't built up like ski towns are now. There were only, like, six shops, all clustered into a single block. We ran out of things to do pretty quickly and ended up hanging around in a tiny café. Two tables, a counter, a crusty young dude pushing vegan scones on us.

I got the feeling again that everyone was keeping a secret from me. Every few minutes, Lenny hopped up to lean over the counter and talk to the dude, whispering, scheming, sitting back down just to hop up again.

"I'm bored," I said. "There's nothing to do here."

"You can look at the people." This was the Queen. "Imagine their lives. What do they love? Where did they come from? Why did they land in this particular place at this specific moment in time?"

My mother flashed me a smile—like *try, don't ruin it*—so I did, but there was hardly anyone out there and when somebody did wander past, they looked just like everyone else in this flaxen-haired, thick-blooded, boring old place.

"They're all the same," I said, but by now the Queen was up at the counter too, conspiring with Lenny and the dude.

Mom patted my hand, grimaced. She was as lost as me about why we were dawdling here, but she was more willing to let it ride. "There's a nest up there, see?" She pointed at the stoplight at the corner, where a tangle of fluff and twigs was wedged into the metal arms. "Interesting, huh?" We studied it for a while, waiting for a glimpse of whatever birds had made it, but there was no sign of life anywhere near it.

Lenny's whispers at the counter had escalated into commands. Something about the "schedule," about "Joel and Alice." He didn't whine, not like the old Lenny. He was a general now. "Where the fuck are they, Carl?" he said. "They've got the material. Did you call them to confirm the time? Carl? Did you do that?"

The Queen, Lenny's deputy, got in on it too. "We've got VIPs here for this one," she said.

My mother perked up. *VIPs.* She liked that.

"Carl," said the Queen. "*Carl.* People are going to be showing up soon. There's not even a bullhorn. They're gonna catch us with our thumbs up our asses."

When Joel and Alice finally arrived, they were pulling a red wagon behind them, loaded with what must've been "the material." They bumped slowly toward us, struggling over the uneven sidewalk. I remember their sturdy boots—hiking boots—and the wool socks pulled up over the cuffs of their jeans. I remember thinking, they're so straight. It's bizarre. What happened to the freaks?

Lenny, the Queen and Carl stopped bickering and took themselves outside. My mother and I stayed put, hunkered down, skeptical, feeling left out.

We could hear them through the window. Negotiations. Complaints. Lenny poked through the shit in the wagon. He picked up a cardboard tube and tested its weight. He dug through a box and pulled out a T-shirt, held it up to his shoulders, modeling it. SAVE THE RIVER, it said. White letters on blue cotton. Some ripples below the words, signifying, I guess, water. He made a face. "Pretty good, huh?" he said. And Joel and Alice grinned and they all went back to plotting.

More people arrived, two or three at a time. A small crowd slowly gathering. Good normal people. They could've been anyone.

They kept glancing at us, pretending they weren't. And each look they gave us, my mother threw back at them. She still, despite everything, lived for the fight, and I could see the old excitement churning inside her. Defensive and eager. Impatient. She was growing less and less confused by the second.

"You stay here," she said and she stalked out, leaving me to watch through the window as she tried to capture Lenny's attention and coax him away from his new herd of followers, to confront him, remind him that she'd always been his most intimate and motivated confidante. She hung like a shadow apart from the crowd, both there and not there, a spectacle of silence. I was just glad she wasn't making a scene.

Lenny was now passing out the shirts. He lobbed one at my mother—"Hey-o!" Wink, wink. "Eyes on the prize." That's the closest she got to him. The Queen, his deputy, guided her across the street so they could talk. She was hot, my mother, provoking and indignant, talking with her hands, leading with her shoulders. And the Queen indulged her. Warm, imperturbable, she absorbed my mother's agitation. Just like she'd done with me. Like maybe she did with Lenny. That woman had powers. She was calmness incarnate. By the time my mother came back inside, she was mollified, if not quite appeased.

"Come on, let's go," she said.

"Where?"

"Out there. To save the fucking river."

By then, thirty people or so had shown up. They wore their T-shirts stretched over plaid shirts and sweaters. Some were taping handmade signs to the cardboard tubes. Others had their signs hoisted on shoulders and were fanned out along the curb, little clusters of folk, awkwardly catching up like they only knew one another so well, reading the puns and the wordplay on the signs, the movement clichés they were so proud to have discovered for themselves. It was like the good old days had come seeping out of the mud, but instead of revolution, it was nostalgia in the air. And Lenny shuffled around embracing them, dancing his fingers in front of their babies' eyes, dipping his head to listen to their concerns. He didn't flash fire like back in the day, didn't sneer, didn't joke. He was steady Nick Dixon.

That's how it felt anyway, as we watched him and the Queen conspire up front, sending Carl on errands, assigning Joel and Alice tasks, leading the chants, coaxing the march forward. They worked together in a way their flock must have admired—such trust, such understanding, such a beautiful shared vision. Meanwhile, my mother and I, when we joined the parade, lingered in the middle, anonymous, and let ourselves be pushed forward along the route by the winds shifting around us. We were just two more bodies, no more special than the rest.

The march took us through town along quiet streets, past Victorian houses and trees that had lived so long and grown so large that they'd begun to shove the sidewalk around. We passed the strip of stores again. We passed a church, a park. It was a short walk. And we ended up on the lawn of the town hall, a single-story gable-roofed building with a spire that you could imagine the whole village erecting together sometime in a previous century. It was shuttered, vacant, like so much else in that place. Seems we were the only people out on this fine day, or maybe the whole town was here marching with us. A symbolic action, wholly useless. But it brought people together. Lenny gave a speech—I don't remember about what, saving the river, presumably, how inspiring it was to have such support; you have the power to remake your world if you exercise your rights as citizens of a free society. A chant: "The people united will never be divided." A boilerplate pep talk. Organizing 101. What I remember is his demeanor up there. Earnest. Humble. Insecure. There was no dig this, no dig that, nothing was groovy. It was like all this was new to him and he'd only found the courage to stand up there because the cause was just so fucking important. Like none of the things he'd done in his life had happened.

The Queen took the bullhorn. She was the same onstage as she was in private—entrancing, so secure in her right to claim her place that when she gazed at you like you might be her equal you felt as if you'd been given a benediction. "Look around," she said. "See how many of us there are? Word's getting out. We're growing. We'll win this fight. If we keep—look around again! Look at yourselves!" She made eye contact with a few people in the crowd, modeling what it meant to look, to see. Then, raising her arms above her head, she yelled, "How can we lose? The Army Corps of Engineers has nothing on us!"

Applause. Cheers. She silenced them with a wave.

"You want to know how widely the word is spreading? You all know who Lenny Snyder is. Well, he obviously can't be with us today, but his wife, Suzy, and their son, Freedom, they're right here. They came all the way from New York to show their support." She shielded her eyes with the flat of her hand and searched the crowd for my mother. "Suzy?"

My mother floated her open palm above her head, and everybody turned and gawked at us—well, at my mother, mostly. They wanted something, some vision of the past, some thrilling surge of danger.

"Come on up here, Suzy," the Queen said. "Inspire us."

Lenny puttered next to her, half-watching his feet, nodded like a sage. He leered at us. "Yeah, hey, bring the kid up here too."

We hesitated. This person they expected my mother to be—had she ever existed? Did she exist now? I remember being afraid for her, afraid she wouldn't be able to meet their expectations. When she grabbed my wrist and marched us up to the front of the crowd, I could feel the violence of her emotions seeping through her finger-

tips into my body. We stood there next to Lenny and the Queen—
Nick and the Queen, let's say; he was too remote to be Lenny
anymore—and we scowled out at all these good people. My mother
had that look she sometimes got, like she was still at the barricades,
behind a great wall, armed and waiting to knife anyone who came
too close.

And then . . . Well, first she glanced at me, all wry and witty, like
she was reminding me we had our own secret. She squeezed my
hand. There was a sudden softness to her touch. And she took the
bullhorn and gave her speech.

I don't know what the crowd thought they would hear. Some ode
to Lenny. To the movement. Platitudes and bullshit. Inspiration.
Hope.

What they got instead was this: "You know . . . there was a time,
not so long ago, when Lenny and I thought we were on the cusp of
history. We could feel it, a vibration in the air, like every second was
momentous, like each tick of the clock was going to change everything. And well . . ." She drifted, considering where she wanted to
go with this. "I guess we did change a few things. We caused a few
disruptions. But not in the way we thought we would. We believed
too strongly that we were righteous. We thought we, ourselves, were
the cause. That it was about *us*. That somehow, eventually, we'd
pull off a transformative coup and absolutely everything would be
different. We thought we could win, is I guess what I'm saying. But
listen. No one wins. You can do some good things. That's about it.
And when we realized this we got a little lost." She went on. She
let her defenses down for those few minutes, just long enough to
show these people she'd survived, that she was capable of survival.
She and Lenny both, wherever he was. "And who knows," she told
them, "maybe you *will* save your precious river. I hope you do. I
admire you people. But even if you don't, you'll still have to look
yourselves in the eye." She glanced at Lenny like she was about to
confront him, then changed her mind and turned away from him.
"Can you?" she asked the crowd. "'Cause what I want to know is,
what kind of you can you bear to live with? Fight for that. It's the
only question that really matters."

Then she lobbed the bullhorn to the Queen and, as fierce as

Lenny Snyder had ever been, maybe fiercer, she dragged me away through the crowd.

Later, the Queen took us, as promised, to Best New Garden.

Not just us. Joel and Alice came too. And Carl. Everyone huddled around the too-small table.

I got my sweet and sour pork and an egg roll that I ate in the meticulous way Phil had taught me. No one noticed. They were all too busy talking. Unwinding. Walking through the merits of the demonstration, the size of the crowd, the new faces that had shown up, as though this tiny march with no press and no opposition had actually achieved something. They were absurdly proud of the T-shirts. They're so nice. They look so good. Lenny was gracious about Joel and Alice's fuckup that morning—apparently Nick Dixon knew how to let things go.

Sometimes Joel or Carl or Alice made awkward stabs at connecting with the strangers at the table—my mother and me, their guests. What grade are you in? What's your favorite subject? Condescending questions. They weren't really interested in the answers. How long are you up here for? Isn't it beautiful? You should see it in the autumn, the leaves. So magnificent.

They were impressed by us. A little awed by my mother. Weirdly oblivious to the fact that Lenny was sitting right there with them. And my mother, she played it cool. She was in her power.

When, eventually, one of them—Joel—worked up the courage to ask her a direct question, he said, "Where'd you meet Caroline and Nick?"

"Oh, around," she said, winking. "All us lefties know each other somehow. You?"

Alice placed her hand on top of Lenny's and gave a little squeeze, a cozy gesture, small-town good intentions. "Joel married them," she said. "And we slowly became friends."

What I remember is my mother blinking. Joel and Alice, Lenny, the Queen, everybody just blinking, blinking, blinking at each other.

And the questions screaming inside me. *What's wrong with you people? Why's everybody acting like this is normal?*

. . .

And I remember we didn't stay the night. We packed up our shit and got out of there. Forgetting things. Socks. Those stupid alpaca hats. My mother's fury evident in her willful refusal to make a scene. What more was there to say to these people? Not much. Not right then. Everything was known.

I remember feeling that our lives had changed, even though they were still the same as they'd been before.

We climbed into the Impala and drove away. I read her the directions through the back roads, reverse-engineered from the sheet Lenny'd sent us. We drove and drove. Both of us quiet. Synched.

It got dark in that way gray days do, a shifting of shades, a growing gloom. By the time we hit the highway, night had fallen.

I remember how tightly her hands clutched the wheel. The whiteness of her knuckles, squeezed of blood. And I wanted to say something. To comfort her. But I didn't know what, or how. It was just an itch. Something under my skin that kept moving every time I thought I'd found it.

Finally, I located the words. Then for a long time, I was afraid to say them.

"He's not a good person. Why didn't you tell me that?"

She just kept driving.

A while later, I don't know how long—I don't even really know where we were—she impulsively pulled onto an exit ramp.

"Where are we going?" I asked.

She looked at me. She might have smiled. "I don't know," she said. "Where do you want to go?"

I answered right away. "Anywhere. Everywhere."

And that's what we did.

We were tough. We didn't believe in anything anymore.

[IV]
INVISIBLE ANIMALS

I've been thinking I should tell you about the time Lenny propped me in front of an electrical outlet and—using the little bit of knowledge he'd gained from watching his father tinker with their house in Flatbush—opened the plate, dislodged the cartridge and stripped off the wires, broke the thing down until all that was left was a hole in the plaster, black and red and yellow wires snaking out like vipers, and him cackling in that gleefully cruel way of his, babbling on about the wisdom of elders, how the things they know have a way of disappearing and you don't know what's been lost until, one day, the roof caves in and the past is dead and you're shit out of luck, standing there in your upstairs neighbor's sewage. How he coaxed me to experiment with the hardware, play with it, study it, figure out how it worked.

"Lesson one," he said, "put this outlet back together." And he wandered off and left me to it.

First thing that happened, I grabbed the wires and was shot through with current, hovering off the floor like a Looney Tune. I couldn't let go. It was like my hand had been soldered to the fucking things. Buzzing, actually buzzing—*brzz, brzz*. Sparks crackling off my body.

And did he help me? Did he show concern?

He's the one who'd turned the breaker back on. He laughed so hard he gave himself seizures. "Lesson two," he said, "don't believe a fucking word your elders say." Pounding the floor with the heels of his Beatle boots, grabbing his dick like he was choking off the fucking Hoover Dam. "And don't stick your fingers in electric outlets unless you wanna get fried."

.   .   .

Or I could tell you about the day when I was twelve and we had maybe an hour to connect before he was whisked away to another safe house. I hadn't seen him in over a year. And what did he want to do with this hour? Not learn about me. Why bother with that when there was so much to say about himself? He carried this shoe box around with him, held together with duct tape, so beat up it was more tape than cardboard. A soft gummy rectangle of silver that he placed on the table between us.

"Open it," he said.

I thought maybe there'd be a present inside. Stickers for my skateboard, something like that, like maybe he'd spent some time trying to understand this kid he barely knew. The way he snickered at my trepidation, though, made me think it was another trick. A scorpion, a cobra, something writhing and poisonous and poised to strike.

"Christ, kid. It's not gonna bite you," he said.

He pulled the top off, and what was inside? Photographs of all the women he'd fucked. White girls and black girls and Asian girls. Native American girls, hippie chicks, existentialistas and debutantes courting exotic thrills. One dumpling-shaped girl he claimed was an Eskimo. All of them naked, posing for his camera. Spreading their hairy pussy lips for him, pushing their nipples toward their out-stretched tongues. Grinning at the camera sometimes, a strained, nervous despair caught in their eyes.

"Go ahead and stare," he said. "The human form is a beautiful thing."

I wasn't squeamish about the fact that they were naked. I'd seen naked women before. You don't spend as much time as I did mixing it up with the radical fringe without gaining an exorbitant famil-iarity with the nude body in all its blemished glory. Hell, before she went straight, I'd seen my mother naked more often than I'd seen her clothed. What I was, was annoyed, exasperated by the, by now, completely expected irony of this icon of anarchic freedom, this dude who'd famously said, "Follow your bliss, and if any-body tries to take it away from you, piss on 'em," forcing his will on me.

He rifled through the box looking for his favorites. Whenever he found one, he took it out and gazed at it like it held the key to eternal youth. Then, handing it to me, he'd tell me about what crazy tricks this girl could do with her tongue or how she later guzzled a vial of liquid acid and turned into one of the moons of Jupiter.

He wanted my approval. A pal, a confidant. He wanted me to pat him on the head.

"When I was your age," he said, "my father took me to a whorehouse and told me, 'You're a man now. Go crazy.' I ain't down for that. For one thing, though I've got nothing against whores, until they rise up and start forming cooperatives, they're being used. I can't be party to that. For another, love is free." He fanned a new stack of photos. "I'll tell you a secret, and your mother knows this: Throughout your life there are going to be women who want to please you. When this happens, you'll feel a kind of moral conflict. You'll worry about what your girlfriend will think. You'll worry about hurting the people you love. I'm telling you now, don't. Just do your thing. Free your mind. Be the revolution. If a girl wants you to make her, go ahead and make her. She's giving you a gift. It's your duty to accept it. Each one who gets away will haunt you forever. You don't want to be that pathetic old shmuck doddering around in an apartment stacked floor to ceiling with newspapers. I'm telling you, Freedom, learn what that means. Do it. Go make the girls." He punched me too hard on the arm and said, "All right. End of lesson. I gotta make like a banana. Here. Take a souvenir." He handed me a photo.

When I looked at it later, I discovered it was a picture of my mother.

Or maybe you'd like to hear more about all the cocaine he did off the kitchen table while he was supposed to be babysitting me.

Or the time he spiked my Hi-C with acid.

There's the time he tried to hide me in his luggage so he wouldn't have to pay for my ticket to Nicaragua.

There's the time he took me up to the roof on 7th Street so the two of us could piss over the edge onto the undercover agents hanging out on our stoop.

The time he dressed me up like a Hasidic Jew and paraded me through a KKK rally.

You want more? I've got a million of them.

What I really want to tell you about is the time *Life* magazine flew him and a bunch of the other radical celebs from that period down to Miami for a kind of reunion. It'll tell you a lot about those guys, and a lot about Lenny. Maybe it'll tell you something about me, too.

This was 1988. Twenty years since their heyday. Fifteen since his arrest and all that came after it.

In the meantime, my mother and I had found new ways to live. Not better, just different. We'd left the city behind and wandered off into the alternate country that was America, a place where people didn't know what they didn't know, where nobody even asked what we'd done or why. We saw Lenny sometimes, when we had to. Like visiting an invalid. More duty than joy. The Queen made the arrangements and, in her lofty way, made sure we kept to them.

The reunion in Miami lasted barely a day and a few hours into the night. An afternoon of posing for photos and munching on *maduros* in a too-blue Cuban restaurant with ornate iron bars on the windows—chosen for both its symbolic resonance and its carefully maintained "authenticity." Then more photos at dusk as they walked along the beach. And afterward, an evening reception in their honor at the Bleau Bar of the Fontainebleau Hotel, the very spot some of them, Lenny included, had effectively shut down with a bushel of stink bombs during the 1969 OPEC convention, and also the place where Lenny and Sy had built trenches out of US mailbags filled with sand, forcing the delegates to literally walk through a war zone to and from the 1972 Republican National Convention.

Everyone had evolved. Well, everyone but Lenny. Sy, Ray Garrett, Jimbo Jackson, Bobby Seale, a bunch more. The circumstances of their lives had changed dramatically. Sy's aspirations to become the vitamin king had been actualized in an empire of steel and glass stores. Garrett's work in the West Village had transformed him into a different, altogether more fabulous agent for change; at the club he owned, it was always Halloween. One guy had moved to Japan to worship the wind. Another one had become a forum speaker for EST. Tom Hayden, who hadn't bothered to show up, was a California State assemblyman now. He sent a note: *The work we did in the late 60s marked an important turning point in the history of our country. It will stand as an example to future generations of what can be accomplished when the public comes together to demand change and stand up for what's right. I regret that my schedule won't let me get away.*

It wasn't that they'd grown cynical. More that they were satisfied with what they'd become. Though they'd moved on to other less conspicuous lives and were no longer as famous as they'd once been, some gravity in their step, some power emanating off their being, led people on the street to wonder who they were. They'd faced down the beast and come through with the core of their selves more or less unbroken.

Not so with the great Lenny Snyder. He'd cut a deal in '82 and reemerged from the Underground to the blinding sun of Ronald Reagan's new morning, but his eyes had never adjusted. The only thing he knew how to do was to keep on keeping on. Fighting for social justice, as they called it now, chaining himself to nuclear power plants and draping himself in the Sandinista flag. But he no longer made sense to himself, and this country no longer made sense to him. The fault lines had shifted and he didn't know where he was anymore.

What I mean is, he'd forgotten how to laugh.

He barely made it through the day, fumbling to connect with these former comrades, so bizarre, so alien—to him, so compromised. Unlike them, he'd embraced this reunion with a fervor completely lacking in irony, talking for weeks about when-I-see-those-guys this and when-the-band's-back-together that. And he'd dressed the part: a tie-dye starbursting across his chest, a wooden peace symbol hanging from a thong around his neck. He looked like the past and it was blatantly obvious, right from the get, that he'd misjudged the moment. Even after he covered up with the worn-out corduroy sports coat he'd brought along, his deluded yearnings remained wrapped around him like the flag shirt of a deposed regime.

Their attitude was, well, that's Lenny for you.

And the conversations he'd been rehearsing in his head, everyone reminiscing about the cause and boosting themselves up, reminding one another of things they'd forgotten, pining together for things that would never be—these never materialized. Instead there'd been talk of stock tips. Discussions of the expansions people were making on their houses in Marin, in Cape May, Silver Lake and Sun Valley. Talk of second and third and, in one case, fourth wives. Talk of everything money could buy.

By the time they arrived at the Fontainebleau, he'd withdrawn nearly completely. Silent. Glum. Lingering on the fringe of the festivities. Gazing at the neon zigzags mounted on the walls, shrinking under the synthetic music and synthetic magic, not quite confused, but profoundly disappointed by the crisp lighting, both inside and out, that turned the hotel into an illuminated jewel, a setting for the new movie America had conjured in which money was no object and the heroes all wore power ties.

No one seemed to notice how far he'd retreated. Or, if they had, they didn't seem to care. They were an aging Rat Pack, and I'm not saying they'd abandoned their ideals, but they were comfortable with the thought that if someone had to lose, at least it hadn't been them.

Bobby Seale, who'd been primping under a chef's hat branded with a cartoon image of himself all day, spent the evening trailing after the photographer and his weedy sidekick—the writer, I guess—poking them to remember to plug his barbeque sauce. Ray Garrett, decked out in a skinny rainbow-print tie and a jacket tailored out of trash bags, kept up a running monologue about the significant aesthetic differences between the Bleau Bar and his joint in New York, parsing their meaning—and cultural relevancy—to anyone who got sucked into his orbit.

Sy and Imamu Sefu—who under his original name, Carlton Krane, had been "minister of culture" for an organization called the RBP—goofed on the theme of *Miami Vice*. They cast themselves in the starring roles: a short, Jewish Crockett, going wide around the middle; a dramatically balding Tubbs, his slick suit accented with an African-print pocket handkerchief.

As waitresses in miniskirts and tuxedo shirts glided by, flaunting one-bite empanadas and yucca fritters, Sy and Sefu struck casual poses, leaning alert and cool against the bar, and tried to pull them into the game.

"What can you tell me about the notorious Carlos Estevez?" Sy'd ask. "Nothing? Really? Or are you scared to say?"

And as the waitress stared at them in confusion, Sefu would pick up the thread. "Did he threaten you? He threaten your mami in Havana? If you help us, we can help you."

Sometimes the girls would laugh and duck away, politely but effectively, sometimes they'd just wait for Sefu and Sy to let them go. "All right, fine," Sy might say. "Gimme one of those rice puffs— what is that, tuna tartare? I'll take two. You know what? I'll take three. Thanks, babe. Be good."

On and on like that. The two of them entertaining themselves. Content. Free at last, free at last from the versions of themselves they'd outgrown years ago.

"Hey, Lenny, you want in?" Sy called at one point, holding a grilled shrimp up by its sugarcane skewer. "If Lenny's your real name. You sure you're not the notorious Carlos Estevez? I bet you've got a cigarette boat waiting for you offshore, packed to the gills with contraband."

"Shit, you're right," said Sefu. "He's the spitting image of that cagey motherfucker. Quick! To the Lamborghinis! If we chase him at high speed through town for an hour, he'll lead us straight to the cocaine!" He started crooning. "I can feel it coming in the air, tonight. Oh, Lord."

Lenny blinked at them, his eyes tired. Sunken. Dark-ringed. A mark that would never leave him.

Sefu sang on. "If you told me you were drowning, I would not lend a hand . . ."

Lenny couldn't have been five feet from them, but the distance might as well have been five miles. He'd wandered off the path. Or maybe they had. Either way, he'd never catch up.

"It's a joke, Lenny," Sy told him. The two of them had never lost the ability to see through each other. "Hey—"

But Lenny had turned away, shuffling toward the door, not hearing.

It was my job to follow him.

Out in the damp air, with the dark ocean off to one side, far beyond the pale blue lights of the hotel that washed over everything, even us, we meandered through the palm trees and empty cabanas on the pool deck. I watched him like you would a rheumy dog—the one that might have rabies, the one that limps forlornly along in the weeds. I refused to get too close. I was twenty. Old enough to have begun piecing his life together, but not old enough to fully comprehend it. Not old enough to forgive him for it.

"Still with the coke bust," he muttered at one point, knowing I was there but not looking at me. "Like they weren't coked up too. Like the whole world hadn't been coked up back then."

The Queen already had him on suicide watch by this time and she'd sent me along with instructions not to let him out of my sight. She hadn't said I had to talk to him. So I didn't.

He seemed oddly thankful for my silence, thankful to be allowed to wander with me beside him, heading nowhere ever so slowly. Taking in the distance between where he was and the place he understood. The place he cared about. The place where he understood the rhythms because they were his own. The buzz in the air before a fight went down. The way everything grew quiet and the wind stopped blowing just before the streets erupted. And the people. The addicts and crazies so deep in their own dreams that they didn't notice everyone else staring. Folks who couldn't tell the difference between their inner dramas and the reality outside their doors. The squatters and extremists and the lost souls. The actors and painters and puppeteers who'd let their dreams of glory be replaced by a misfit community willing to applaud their every failed endeavor. Those wandering others nobody wanted. The renegades and desperados who played out their turf wars on the flip side of society's coin. The Lower East Side. This place America had abandoned. This ghetto into which the hard-luck had been segregated to fend for themselves—first the freemen and freed slaves, then the Germans, the Irish, the Jews, Poles, Ukrainians. And then the Puerto Ricans and hippie scum like him. He'd imagined what they could get up to while no one was watching. Anything they wanted—such was the irony of poverty. They could upend the paradigm. Not next year, but right now. Bring Jerusalem, that city shining on the hill, into being right here in the place where they were. And he'd tried, oh, he'd tried to lead the people forward, and for a while, he thought he'd succeeded. A shabby freedom began to thrive in the shit-strewn streets of the Lower East Side, growing like mushrooms after a hard rain. And why couldn't its spores cover the whole nation? But then . . . but then . . . but then . . .

At the lip of the swimming pool, he stood and watched the ribbons of light twist and shift in the water. Wondering what would become of him? And what would become of *them*—all those down-and-outers nobody cared about saving anymore?

I know this now. At the time, I was just bitter. Resentful that I'd agreed to be his babysitter, angry that yet again he was the one who got to be self-involved and even angrier that in his presence I couldn't help but get caught up in his despair.

I've thought about this a lot. There's no question he sold cocaine to those cops. The real question has always been why. And depending on the answer, what does that imply about his heart? Was he a good person? Had he ever been a good person?

These were questions I wasn't equipped to answer.

He was my father.

"It's like the whole thing was a game to you," I said.

"No," he said. "No, it wasn't a game."

And he shuffled off to gaze at the balconies of the impossibly expensive hotel suites above our heads.

Later, on the plane, on our way back to New York, I asked him, "Why'd you hate Phil so much?"

"Who?"

"Phil. Phil Ochs."

"I didn't hate him."

"Something must've gone down between you two."

He said nothing, just gazed at me, his face narrowing like he was warding me off.

"You threw him down a flight of stairs," I said.

He mumbled something I couldn't catch.

"What?" I said.

Those eyes. Dark. Crushed. Like somehow I'd hurt him.

It would've been kinder of me to let it go, but I knew I wouldn't get the chance to ask about this again. "Tell me. It never made sense."

"He was embarrassing," Lenny said. He broke away from me. Listing off somewhere. His head sinking toward the half-empty Bloody Mary glass on his tray.

"Lenny?"

Snapping back, he downed the rest of the drink. "He actually believed the revolution was coming. Like the whole world was gonna sprout sunshine and roses and nobody'd ever have to take another shit." He was angry, but not at me. "The guy had no escape plan."

He glanced at me, furtive, like he thought I might hit him and I knew this was as much as I'd ever get out of him.

"Did *you*?" I said.

The ghost of his old self flickered for an instant before melting away into the blank apathy that would kill him two and a half years later.

For a while, half an hour or more, we sat there in our own private thoughts, as comfortable as we'd ever been with each other.

Then he plopped his hand over mine and came back to me. "You remember that day we went to the zoo?"

I hadn't. But then I did. Every detail.

Springtime. A day or two before he went underground.

I'd put on my favorite T-shirt—Lucky Charms, which I'd got in the mail by collecting the proof of purchases and sending them off to the address on the back of the box. We'd made it down the stairs and before we were even out the front door of the building I knew I'd misjudged the weather, confused the crisp sunlight out the window for warmth. The door had been broken since I could remember, the pneumatic pump that was supposed to ease its movements hanging loose on its mount and slapping against the plaster wall every time anybody opened it. You'd touch it with one finger and it would fly open. But on this day, Zoo Day, the door resisted. Lenny braced it with his foot so it wouldn't slam back on me.

Then, out on the stoop, he slid his sunglasses onto his face and raised his arms like he was gathering the day between them. He gulped down air. Morning light flashed off the windows across the street. Fallen blooms raced and twirled along the pavement like they were going somewhere important.

"You smell that, kid?" he said. "Life."

I rubbed at the goose bumps on my arms. "I'm cold," I said.

He appraised me, my sneakers, my jeans, my little green T-shirt. "You're not cold," he said.

"But I am. I need my windbreaker."

"You don't look cold."

I pointed at my arm. "Goose bumps mean you're cold."

"Tough it out. It's good for you."

I pointed at his arm. "You've got goose bumps too."

"Nah, that's just my skin. It's always like that." I couldn't see his eyes through his shades, but I knew he was making fun of me. Busting my chops, as he would've said. He shoved the door open again like he was daring me to chicken out. This time it slammed into the wall like it always did and bounced back, but he caught it and held it still for me and said, "Fine. You want it? Go get it. It's a free country."

I just stood there and stared at the ornate doors of the church across the street.

"Kid?"

"Why can't you do it?"

"Kid. Really." He got down on one knee and perched the glasses on his forehead, above the ridge of his colossal eyebrows. "What're you gonna do? You want that jacket or not?" Some people on the street were wearing jackets. Others were not. "Fuck the jacket," he said. "It's early. We'll get there, the sun'll come up, you'll get hot. And I'll end up carrying it around for you all day. You dig? Fuck the jacket. That shit'll just weigh you down."

I nodded, unconvinced.

"Fuck the jacket," he said again. "Say it with me." He nudged me in the chest. "Come on, kid. Say it with me. Fuck the jacket."

"Fuck the jacket."

"Yeah!" He used his fists for emphasis. "Fuck the jacket!"

We chanted it together: "Fuck the jacket! Fuck the jacket!" We made it our mantra, shouting it as we marched toward Astor Place. "Fuck the jacket! Fuck the jacket! Fuck the jacket! Fuck the jacket!"

And seeing I'd calmed down, he said, "Check this out, another cool thing," and he flicked my nipple with his middle finger, giving me a stinger. It was like he'd built me up just to knock me down again.

"Oh, come on," he said. "That didn't hurt."

What to say? What to do? Sometimes, the shifts between his jokes and his cruelty overwhelmed me. I'd feel myself filling with murky confusion, my breakers overloaded, surging with conflicted, incompatible emotions.

He bopped along. Spinning through pedestrians, pivoting around the women walking by, checking them out, making a spectacle. It was like a street dance. Visual jazz. The cock of the walk in the city. He exuded a horny joy that said I'm no threat to you—unless you want me to be.

And I straggled after him, rubbing my scrawny arms.

Uptown, I was still so cold that we jogged to the park. I remember thinking the sidewalk was a different color than it should be. On the Lower East Side it was a splotchy, beaten gray, like dirty dishwater congealed on a hard surface. But up here it glistened white on white. There wasn't even any gum blackened into it. The one place left in the entire city that hadn't given in to the entropy of the times.

We got to the zoo, and turns out, it was closed. No explanation, no posted hours, just closed. The spear-tipped gates shut up tight.

"See, kid," said Lenny, "this is how they do it. First they close the zoos, then they close the libraries. Before you know it, they've put their chains on your brain."

I peered through the bars. Beyond the shuttered ticket booths there were steps leading to a circular plaza with a ring in the middle, like a circus ring, but encircled by a moat of concrete, half-filled with mucusy green water. A craggy hill of platforms rose from the center. There should've been penguins there, or seals, or polar bears. Animals that could put on an act. I could see the skids and furrows in the platforms where they'd slid down the concrete, but the animals themselves were missing.

"What happened to them?" I asked Lenny.

"Shot for crimes against the state," he said. "If you know where to look, you can find pigs with machine guns patrolling the shadows. You see 'em?"

I went up on the rubberized toes of my Keds and peered around. Images of hunchbacked pigs swam through my mind, hairy and pink, waddling around the zoo's cobblestone pathways on their hind legs, draped in blue shirts, badges pinned to their chests. Not real pigs. Not porcine creatures. But the ones I'd been trained to loathe and never ever, under no circumstances, fear. The ones who'd spit on you to look at you and who'd haunted my days since I could remember. They carried tommy guns. Their torsos were so heavy that they walked all herky-jerky and each step threatened to topple them over, which just made them angrier, meaner. Their tiny black eyes, when they looked at you, glowed with red death.

Lenny clutched his hair—still disorientingly short—with both fists. "Hey, kid, don't get sad, get mad," he said. "There's still hope. Come on. Follow me." Crouched like a burglar, he slid behind the shrubs lining the wall and skulked forward.

I wiped my nose and squeezed in behind him. Toughed out the branches poking and scraping me every time I pushed past another bulge of stone. The ground had this spongy, like, permanent dampness. A mulchy mix of shredded wood and black Manhattan dirt.

Roots sometimes curled up and surprised us. We pressed on foot by foot, Lenny moving in front of me, leading, a role model I could trail, imitate and trust, until he stopped abruptly and stood up tall, listening, tipping his head around a corner. And watching him, not the obstacles in front of me, I caught my shirt on a thorn and felt it rip.

"Lenny!" I held the tear out for him to see and the wind pricked at the newly exposed patch of skin on my belly.

"Never mind that," he said. "We've got work to do."

"But—"

"Kid!" he barked. "It's a shirt." But he knelt down in front of me—for the second time that day—and went through the motions of examining it. "Gives it character," he said. "Okay?"

And as he watched me reconcile with this, something happened. His face. I'll never forget it. The cynicism. The tricksy menacing rage. All the dark violent edges. It vanished. And in its place there was just joy. A wild, uncontainable joy. Beaming up at me. A maniacal happiness at being on this adventure he'd concocted for us.

He said to me, all dramatic, whispering, "Here's the plan, Stan. Just around this corner there's another gate. It's not like the one back there. It's just a little wooden jobby. They use it to bring the trucks in and whatever. We just have to get up enough speed and momentum and we can take it. You up for this? We're gonna storm the fucking barricades."

Took me half a second to make up my mind.

We darted out from behind the shrubs, whooping and hollering like Comanche warriors, Lenny waving me this way and that, up a hill, around a tree, on loop-de-loops through the park until we were on the muddy road leading to the gate, thirty, forty feet away. We reared back and kicked as fast as we could, splashing through the puddles pooled in the ruts where the wheels of trucks had dug deep. I'd never run so fast. It was like my legs were spinning on their own and I just had to keep up with them. And when we were close, we braced our shoulders and aimed and leapt and slammed ourselves against the rotting wooden slats. We heard a crack. The latch had broken.

We were in.

We wandered around the zoo after that, buying imaginary pop-corn and sno-cones from the shuttered vendors' booths, peering into the empty cages and discussing what the animals that weren't there might be doing.

"Look, he's pacing," I'd say. "He must be hungry."

"Throw him some popcorn."

And I'd throw my imaginary popcorn inside for the imaginary leopard.

Or Lenny would ask, "Do you think it's smart to put those chickens in with the foxes? Whose idea was that?"

"Fucking bullshit," I'd say.

And we'd both laugh.

"Wait, there's a peacock in there too. Peacocks are vicious, kid. Mean as hell. He'll protect the chickens. He'll peck that fox's eyes out."

"Hey, let's go see the pandas."

"Let's see the snakes."

"Let's go find the motherfucking jackalope!"

We went on like that, cage by cage. Whimsical. Playful. Kicking around for two, maybe three hours. We didn't see a single other person the whole time. And eventually I got bored, like kids do.

"I'm hungry," I said.

"Eat your popcorn."

"No, really. I'm hungry."

"You're not hungry, kid. You've been eating all morning. Here, you want a hot dog?" He twirled his hand over his head and pulled down yet another imaginary hunk of food.

"That's not real, though."

"What's *real*? What does real mean?" he said. "Is this real?" He shook the pen we were walking past. "Is this sidewalk real? The sky? That fucking tree? Am I real, Freedom? Are you?"

"I'm not having fun anymore," I said.

As we'd wandered around, Lenny had been scooping up pebbles. Little ones, gravel-sized. Bouncing them in his hands. Shooting them back and forth between his palms. He hadn't been conscious of what he was doing. Just another way to burn through his nervous energy. Since they were there, and why not, he zinged one at me.

"Stop it," I said.

He lobbed another one.

"It's not funny."

"I'm not trying to be funny."

"Just stop it."

The next pebble bounced off my forehead.

"You almost hit my eye."

"So it's still funny," he said. "If you still have your eye. 'Cause it's all fun and games till somebody loses one. Remember, kid?"

He tossed another one, this time explicitly aiming it at my face.

"Can't you just stop throwing things at me, please," I said.

"Sure," he said. And then, of course, he did it again.

"And can we, maybe, go home?"

I was shaking. Shivering. Even colder than before. I had a dreadful sense that I was going to lose it and the tears were going to start falling down my cheeks and Lenny'd be so pissed that he'd throw larger rocks at me, harder. Or maybe he'd just flake out and ditch me there. My hands found my arms. Covering up. For protection. For warmth. A little bit of both.

He noticed. I know he did. He—how do I put this? It was like he changed shape. Actually, physically morphed. Shoulders collapsing. Hard edges melting. Realizing all at once that he'd gone too far.

"Fuck it," he said.

He tossed another pebble in my direction, but halfheartedly, like he was saving face. The rest fell through his fingers as he backed away from me and slumped down on the concrete ledge behind him. Shaking his head.

Sad. A pure, simple sadness.

He'd be leaving the next day—or the day after. He was looking at a future in which he might never see me again. And this trip, this visit to this abandoned zoo—it was as much for him as it was for me. So we'd have something to cling to when we missed each other.

I know this now. Even then I'd felt the pressure of its importance.

Edging toward him, grasping for something like courage, I said, "What about our mission? We still have to free the animals."

For a second, he watched to see if I was kidding. Then, slowly, the smirk broke across his face. "All right, kid. Sure. Let's go free the animals."

We did the loop again and again. That zoo's not that big. We'd been walking in circles for hours by then. And as we made our way around and around, Lenny started hopping. He skipped. He cracked his knuckles and did one of his famous cartwheels. Psyching himself up. Returning to form. He did some karate kicks.

"Who we gonna free, kid?"

I didn't know. We'd placed so many animals in so many cages— often in the same cage on successive go-rounds—that I couldn't keep them straight or even remember which ones were where.

"What animals are weakest?" I asked.

"Well." He contemplated the contributing factors. "The mice are the *smallest,* but I don't know that that makes them weakest. They're shrewd little fuckers. You ever try to trap a mouse with your bare hands? Damn near impossible. And they're basically just rats—which you gotta love, right? Rats are tough motherfuckers. One, they've got strength in numbers. Two, they're pests in the best of ways. Vicious. Diseased. They're creative destruction incarnate. When the plague comes, they'll show you what 'all men are equal' really means. They'll inherit the world. You ever hear of the super rat? He can leap thirteen feet from a standing position. His bones have mutated—they're soft, like cartilage—so when he falls out a window or off the top of a building, he bounces like a rubber ball, no broken bones, no punctured organs. Just a bounce, and he's good to go, racing off to the next dumpster. So rats are out, and by extension mice are too."

"There's the insects," I said. "They're even smaller."

"Exactamundo. Beetles, stick bugs, mosquitoes, dragonflies, water bugs, grasshoppers, crickets, cockroaches—can't forget cockroaches! Bees and wasps in all their variety, leaf bugs—you know them? They're green. Shaped like holly. Plus, the millions of butterflies and moths that populate the Earth. And *ants*! All those fucking ants! You get the picture? Strength in numbers again. Times a billion."

This went on for I don't know how long. Propping an animal up, knocking it down, going through the whole menagerie, boom, boom, boom, fish, frog, newt, deer, fucking marmoset.

Finally, as we circled around the plaza again and passed the sculpted hill of slides and ledges, I cracked it. "Penguins!" I said.

Lenny's head bobbed—processing, processing. He pulled at the air like he was trying to grab my meaning. "Tell me more," he said.

"Penguins. They can't fly. They can barely walk. I mean, what do they do? They're just lumpy black-and-white beanbags, really, bopping and sliding around on the ice."

"You're on to something, kid," he said. "But where do they keep the penguins in this motherfucking hole?"

"Right there!" I pointed.

Pounding his forehead with the butt of his hand, he said, "Of course. I'm fucking blind."

We were each pretending for the other, yet somehow, together, we'd conjured up something true. I felt it. A rustling in my brain like gusting leaves. Something about the difference between who we are and who we seem to be. About how the bad—or the problematic—the annoying, destructive, hurtful, negligent parts of a man exist simultaneously with the good. How sometimes these barbed parts of a person *are* the good. They're inseparable from the good, so entwined that the one can't exist without the other, two versions of the same vision, a difference in point of view. These weren't thoughts a six-year-old could manage, and I couldn't have articulated them like this, but I felt them flickering just beyond my comprehension.

What I mean is I saw him, that day at the zoo, as someone separate from my own needs.

"You see that trapdoor?" he said, pointing at a padlocked slab of black plywood hidden on one of the platforms. "They must be jailed up in there."

He ran off to rummage in the trash bags piled up in one corner of the plaza, kicking and rolling them over each other so he could see what was beneath them. Then, not finding what he was looking for there, he poked around the plaza, peering through the chicken-wired windows of the buildings to study the dark spaces locked away inside. Scheming. He waved me along behind him and we wandered down a little path that led around the back of one of the buildings. We found a shed back there, a cramped little room barely bigger than its waxy green parks-and-rec door. No windows, but somehow, Lenny had a sense. He brushed me back and knelt down to study the rusty iron lock.

His overstuffed wallet open in his palm, he coaxed a thin vinyl sheath out of the inner sleeve. A glasses repair kit. Seconds later, he'd jimmied the lock open and slipped into the shed. When he came back out he had a crowbar in his hand.

"Freedom?" he said, meaning me.

"Yes!"

He thrust the crowbar out in front of himself like a sword. "To the penguins! For freedom!" he said, this time meaning the spirit in the air.

Snickering, giggling, delirious, we raced back to the plaza and hopped the moat and scrambled up to the door of the penguins' jail. Lenny wedged the crowbar's spiked end beneath the tab of metal fastened under the padlock. He planted a boot on the lip of the platform and yanked.

"Hey kid, be a champ. Get in here and give me a hand."

Standing behind me, he showed me where to hold my hands on the crowbar, placed his own over them and readjusted the bar.

"You ready?"

"What if we get caught?" I said. I was thinking of the pigs and their billy clubs.

"You've been arrested before, kid. It's part of the fun. There are good laws and bad laws and it's okay to break the bad ones. Think of how betrayed these penguins'll feel if we don't save them. Sometimes, when the cause is great enough, you have to sacrifice yourself. It's a moral imperative."

"I don't know what that means," I said.

"It means let's smash some shit up and free the fucking penguins!"

One flex of his muscles and the screws holding the metal tab in place pulled free from the wood.

"You did it, kid!"

He flipped the door open, and we peered into the stairwell and the black void beyond it.

"Check it out," he said, a hand cupping his ear. They're clapping for us. They're shouting, 'Spartacus, Spartacus, Spartacus!' And look! Here they come!"

And we watched as the penguins hopped up the lip of the platform and slid down the side, hundreds, maybe thousands of them, waddling to freedom. And though they were invisible, though they didn't exist, they seemed, right then, as real as anything could possibly be. They huddled together, a great mob of them, brushing past our knees, moving as one toward the zoo's main exit, which was, of course, also padlocked shut. They bottled up in front of it, bobbing up and down, waiting.

"All right, kid. Our work here isn't done yet," Lenny said. Raising the crowbar over his head with both hands, he strode forward to free them. "Kid? I can't do this without you."

And again guiding me, letting me feel like I was the one doing the job, he slipped the crowbar into the loops of chain bunched around the gate and cranked it like a propeller, twisting the chain around and around until it buckled and froze. And then with one more crank, a great exertion of force that I could feel vibrating through my own arms, he popped it.

He unraveled the slack from around the iron bars and flipped the gate's flimsy lock with his pick. Didn't take but a minute.

"Set them free," he said.

And I did. I swung the gate open on its creaky hinges and the penguins flooded past us. Not just penguins. Leopards and chickens and foxes and peacocks and pandas and snakes. Elephants and tigers and badgers and grizzlies and white-tailed deer and flamingos and platypuses and elk and moose. Squirrels and chipmunks. Voles and moles. Meerkats. Tarantulas and salamanders and geckos and Gila monsters. Otters, mink, rabbits, bobcats, hippos, lemurs and rhinoceroses. Emus and giraffes, hundreds of giraffes. Hummingbirds and woodpeckers and birds of paradise and turkeys and Canadian geese and robins and chickadees and sparrow after sparrow after sparrow after sparrow. Donkeys and wallabies and wildebeests and ferrets and baboons and gorillas. Monkeys of all sorts and sizes—rhesus, howler, capuchin, spider. The horses. The mules. The water buffalo. Koalas and kangaroos. Even domestics: dogs and cats and goats and sheep and steers and animals I didn't know the names of. Animals the world hasn't seen before or since. Jackalope, of course, but many, many more. Animals that could be recognized only by their sounds. The *kra-kraw. The chit-chit-chitter.* The *whee-ee-eeze humpf.* The *chupaboom* and the *gwooaah.* Huffers and hailers and mouth-breathers. Stompers and shufflers and galumphers. And, bringing up the rear, the mice and the rats and the cockroaches, the skeeters, beetles and termites, a great mass of bugs, tumbling over and over itself like one giant vibrating organism. Then the turtles, slow-poking along, skittish. And finally, like trail cars, marking the end, the pigs—not the ones who patrolled the streets, but those other, most intelligent of creatures.

We watched them all go, watched them swarm down Fifth Avenue and march into the traffic that couldn't be bothered to notice they were there.

"Come on, kid," Lenny said.

And we chased after them. Joined their ranks. We ran through the city with them, wild and free, the two of us, Lenny—my father—and me. And at some point, I realized I wasn't cold and I wasn't hungry and I didn't give a fuck anymore that my favorite shirt was torn.

"You remember that?" he asked again that night as we flew back to New York from Miami.

I told him I did. I said, "I remember all of it."

For a while he stared at me, studying my face, searching for something there, some sign that the things that had mattered to him would matter to me too. That he'd made a difference. That hope wasn't lost.

"Yeah," he said. Turning away, he pressed his forehead to the window and gazed out at the clouds piled below us like neon-blue pillows lit up in the moonlight. "Good times."

I could sense him retreating to one of his dark places. If there was a future, he couldn't find it. And so he went silent. He shut me out.

Not another word for the rest of the flight.

Maybe . . .

I guess what I'm saying is I've fought my fights.

You go ahead and change the world if you want. Me, I'm skeptical. I've done my time. I've opted out.

A person's got to live.

You dig?

ACKNOWLEDGMENTS

Revolutionaries would not exist in the form it does now without the help of a great many people. I am indebted to each of them and grateful for the kindnesses they have shown me.

Gary Fisketjon chose to take another chance on me, and he, along with his assistant Genevieve Nierman and the many other folks at Knopf, have shown yet again why they're the best in the business. I thank them, along with Richard Abate, for ensuring that this book found its way into the world.

My early readers included Andrew Altschul, Edward Gauvin, Matthew Goodman, Gordon Haber, Mike Heppner, Nicola Keegan, Binnie Kirshenbaum, Adam Langer and Jeremy Mullem. Each of them provided important perspectives that contributed to helping me focus the work. Hanan Elstein, who read the book in manuscript more than once, was particularly insightful. And Joseph Michaels, who masterfully scrutinized every single word, sentence, paragraph, chapter, etc., refused to let me get away with anything less than the best that I could do (I'll say of him what he once said of me: "Somebody give this man a job!").

Ben Clague, Em Pacheco and David Bradley likely destroyed their eyesight deciphering my microscopic handwriting as they transcribed the raw material of this book into a typewritten electronic form that I could then manipulate and edit. Without them this work would have forever remained nothing more than the lunatic scrawl of a madman.

Throughout the years of drafting and redrafting, Ruth Adams

and the good people at Art Omi consistently provided me with a quiet, encouraging space in which I could disappear entirely into the work. On the basis of nothing more than a whisper in his ear from Brenda Lozano, Cesar Cervantes Tezcucano offered me a transformative monthlong stay in Luis Barragán's magnificent Casa Pedregal in Mexico City. And Todd Lanier Lester allowed me to join, ever so briefly, the brave community of Lanchonete, a coalition of artists and activists roaming like radical nomads around São Paolo. Each of these people and organizations supported me, both materially and spiritually, and reminded me why the work I was doing mattered.

In less tangible but possibly more crucial ways, DW Gibson— my partner in crime for some fifteen years now—as well as Eva Fortes, Uche Nduka, Rien Kuntari and everyone else who's passed through Kristiania, joining the argument, struggling and dreaming and fighting off futility, bolstered me when I didn't know how to bolster myself.

Alicia Maria Meier found value in my work when I had lost all confidence and helped me rebuild my belief in the possible. I'm humbled by her faith in me and my writing and astonished by the ferocity with which she pushed me to stick to my principles. Long may you run.

For no discernable reason, Lee Bob Black has continuously taken it upon himself to do things for me and my career that I would never think to do myself. He claims it's fun, but it seems to me more like hard labor. I don't deserve it.

Finally, there is one person who has sustained me beyond all possible measure: my wife, Elizabeth Grefrath, whose wisdom and compassion know no bounds.

Oh, and of course, I am grateful to Abbie Hoffman—provocation, inspiration—for having ever existed. We need your spirit in the world, now more than ever.

A NOTE ABOUT THE AUTHOR

Joshua Furst is the author of *Short People* and *The Sabotage Café,* as well as several plays that have been produced in New York, where for a number of years he worked in the downtown theater scene. A graduate of the Iowa Writers' Workshop, he is the recipient of a Michener Fellowship, the *Chicago Tribune*'s Nelson Algren Award, and fellowships from the MacDowell Colony and Art Omi. He lives in New York City and teaches at Columbia University.

A NOTE ON THE TYPE

The text of this book was set in Sabon, a typeface designed by Jan Tschichold (1902–1974). Based loosely on the original designs by Claude Garamond (c. 1480–1561), Sabon is unique in that it was explicitly designed for hotmetal composition on both the Monotype and Linotype machines as well as for filmsetting. Designed in 1966 in Frankfurt, Sabon was named for the famous Lyons punch cutter Jacques Sabon, who is thought to have brought some of Garamond's matrices to Frankfurt.

Typeset by North Market Street Graphics, Lancaster, Pennsylvania

Printed and bound by LSC Communications, Harrisonburg, Virginia

Designed by Maggie Hinders